OXFORD WORLD'S CLASSICS

A LOVE STORY

ÉMILE ZOLA was born in Paris in 1840, the son of a Venetian engineer and his French wife. He grew up in Aix-en-Provence where he made friends with Paul Cézanne. After an undistinguished school career and a brief period of dire poverty in Paris, Zola joined the newly founded publishing firm of Hachette which he left in 1866 to live by his pen. He had already published a novel and his first collection of short stories. Other novels and stories followed until in 1871 Zola published the first volume of his Rougon-Macquart series with the subtitle *Histoire naturelle et sociale d'une famille sous le Second Empire*, in which he sets out to illustrate the influence of heredity and environment on a wide range of characters and milieus. However, it was not until 1877 that his novel *L'Assommoir*, a study of alcoholism in the working classes, brought him wealth and fame. The last of the Rougon-Macquart series appeared in 1893 and his subsequent writing was far less successful, although he achieved fame of a different sort in his vigorous and influential intervention in the Dreyfus case. His marriage in 1870 had remained childless but his extremely happy liaison in later life with Jeanne Rozerot, initially one of his domestic servants, gave him a son and a daughter. He died in 1902.

HELEN CONSTANTINE has published four volumes of translated stories, *Paris Tales*, *French Tales*, *Paris Metro Tales*, and *Paris Street Tales*, with OUP. Her translations also include Gautier's *Mademoiselle de Maupin*, Laclos's *Dangerous Liaisons*, Balzac's *The Wild Ass's Skin*, Zola's *The Conquest of Plassans*, and Flaubert's *Sentimental Education*.

BRIAN NELSON is Professor Emeritus (French Studies and Translation Studies) at Monash University, Melbourne, and a Fellow of the Australian Academy of the Humanities. His publications include *The Cambridge Introduction to French Literature*, *The Cambridge Companion to Zola*, *Zola and the Bourgeoisie*, and translations of Zola's *Earth* (with Julie Rose), *The Fortune of the Rougons*, *The Belly of Paris*, *The Kill*, *Pot Luck*, and *The Ladies' Paradise*. He was awarded the New South Wales Premier's Prize for Translation in 2015.

OXFORD WORLD'S CLASSICS

*For over 100 years Oxford World's Classics have brought
readers closer to the world's great literature. Now with over 700
titles—from the 4,000-year-old myths of Mesopotamia to the
twentieth century's greatest novels—the series makes available
lesser-known as well as celebrated writing.*

*The pocket-sized hardbacks of the early years contained
introductions by Virginia Woolf, T. S. Eliot, Graham Greene,
and other literary figures which enriched the experience of reading.
Today the series is recognized for its fine scholarship and
reliability in texts that span world literature, drama and poetry,
religion, philosophy and politics. Each edition includes perceptive
commentary and essential background information to meet the
changing needs of readers.*

OXFORD WORLD'S CLASSICS

ÉMILE ZOLA

A Love Story

Translated by
HELEN CONSTANTINE

With an Introduction and Notes by
BRIAN NELSON

OXFORD
UNIVERSITY PRESS

OXFORD

Great Clarendon Street, Oxford, OX2 6DP,
United Kingdom

Oxford University Press is a department of the University of Oxford.
It furthers the University's objective of excellence in research, scholarship,
and education by publishing worldwide. Oxford is a registered trade mark of
Oxford University Press in the UK and in certain other countries

Translation © Helen Constantine 2017
Editorial material © Brian Nelson 2017

The moral rights of the authors have been asserted

First published as an Oxford World's Classics paperback 2017

Impression: 10

All rights reserved. No part of this publication may be reproduced, stored in
a retrieval system, or transmitted, in any form or by any means, without the
prior permission in writing of Oxford University Press, or as expressly permitted
by law, by licence or under terms agreed with the appropriate reprographics
rights organization. Enquiries concerning reproduction outside the scope of the
above should be sent to the Rights Department, Oxford University Press, at the
address above

You must not circulate this work in any other form
and you must impose this same condition on any acquirer

Published in the United States of America by Oxford University Press
198 Madison Avenue, New York, NY 10016, United States of America

British Library Cataloguing in Publication Data
Data available

Library of Congress Control Number: 2017935261

ISBN 978-0-19-872864-1

Printed and bound in Great Britain by Clays Ltd, Elcograf S.p.A.

CONTENTS

A LOVE STORY

INTRODUCTION

Readers who do not wish to learn details of the plot will prefer to read the Introduction as an Afterword

THE main achievement of Émile Zola (1840–1902) as a writer was *Les Rougon-Macquart* (1871–93), a twenty-volume novel cycle in which the fortunes of a family are followed over several decades. The various family members spread throughout all levels of society, and through their lives Zola examines methodically the social, sexual, and moral landscape of the late nineteenth century, creating an epic sense of social transformation. The Rougons represent the hunt for wealth and position, their members rising to commanding positions in the worlds of government and finance; the Macquarts, the illegitimate branch, are the submerged proletariat, with the exception of Lisa Macquart (*The Belly of Paris*/*Le Ventre de Paris*, 1873); the Mourets, descended from the Macquart line, are the bourgeois tradesmen and provincial bourgeoisie. Zola is the quintessential novelist of modernity, understood as a time of tumultuous change. The motor of change was the rapid growth of capitalism, with all that that entailed in terms of the transformation of the city, new forms of social practice and economic organization, and heightened political pressures. Zola was fascinated by change, and specifically by the emergence of a new mass society.

Converted from a youthful romantic idealism to realism in art and literature, Zola began to promote a 'scientific' view of literature inspired by the aims and methods of experimental medicine. He called this new form of realism 'Naturalism'. The subtitle of the Rougon-Macquart cycle, 'A Natural and Social History of a Family under the Second Empire', suggests his interconnected aims: to use fiction as a vehicle for a great social chronicle; to demonstrate a number of 'scientific' notions about the ways in which human behaviour is determined by heredity and environment; and to exploit the symbolic possibilities of a family with tainted blood to represent a diseased society—the corrupt yet dynamic France of the Second Empire (1852–70), the regime established on the basis of a *coup d'état* by Louis-Napoleon Bonaparte on 2 December 1851 (treated in *The Fortune of the Rougons*, the first volume of the Rougon-Macquart cycle) and which would last until its collapse in 1870 in the face of military defeat by the Prussians at the Battle of Sedan (described in *La Débâcle*, the penultimate novel of the cycle). The 'truth' for which Zola aimed could only be attained, he argued, through meticulous documentation and research. The work of the novelist represented a form of practical sociology, complementing the work of the scientist; their common hope was to improve the world by promoting greater understanding of the laws that determine the material conditions of life.

Zola's commitment to the value of truth in art is above all a moral commitment; and his concern with integrity of representation meant a commitment to the idea that the writer must play a social role: to represent the sorts of things—industrialization, the growth of the city, the birth of consumer culture, the workings of the financial system, the misdeeds of government, crime, poverty, prostitution—that affect people in their daily lives. And he wrote about these things not simply forensically, as a would-be scientist, but ironically and satirically. Naturalist fiction represents a major assault on bourgeois morality and institutions. It takes an unmitigated delight—while also seeing the process as a serious duty—in revealing the vices, follies, and corruption behind the respectable facade. The last line of *The Belly of Paris* is: 'Respectable people... What bastards!' Zola opened the novel up to entirely new areas of representation. The Naturalist emphasis on integrity of representation entailed a new explicitness in the depiction of sexuality and the body; and in his sexual themes he ironically subverts the notion that the social supremacy of the bourgeoisie is a natural rather than a cultural phenomenon. The more searchingly he investigated the theme of middle-class adultery, the more he threatened to uncover the fragility and arbitrariness of the whole bourgeois social order. His new vision of the body is matched by his new vision of the working class, combining carnivalesque images with serious analysis of its sociopolitical condition. In *L'Assommoir* (1877) he describes the misery of the working-class slums behind the public splendour of the Second Empire, while in *Germinal* (1885) he shows how the power of mass working-class movements had become a radically new, and frightening, element in human history. Zola never stopped being a danger to the established order. Representing the most liberal, reforming side of the bourgeoisie, he was consciously, and increasingly, a public writer. It was entirely appropriate that, in 1898, he crowned his literary career with a political act, a frontal attack on state power and its abuse: 'J'accuse...!', his famous open letter to the President of the Republic in defence of Alfred Dreyfus, the Jewish army officer falsely accused of treason.

Zola's 'scientific' representation of society corresponds to a writing method informed by systematic research and fieldwork. While preparing *Germinal*, for example, Zola went down a mine in northern France, and observed the labour and living conditions of the miners and their families; for *La Bête humaine* (1890), he arranged to travel on the footplate of a locomotive, engaged in lengthy correspondence with railway employees, and read several technical works on the railways. The texture of his novels is infused with an intense concern with concrete detail, and the detailed planning notes he assembled for each novel represent a remarkable stock of documentary information about French society in the 1870s and 1880s. But documentary detail, though it helps to create ethnographically rich evocations of particular milieux and modes of life, is not an end in itself. The observed reality of the world is the foundation for a poetic vision. In his narrative practice, Zola combines brilliantly the particular and the general, the everyday and the fantastic. The interaction between people and their environments is evoked in his celebrated physical descriptions. These descriptions are not, however, mechanical products of his aesthetic credo; rather, they express the very meaning, and ideological tendencies, of his narratives. For example, the lengthy descriptions of the luxurious physical decor of bourgeois existence—houses, interiors, social gatherings—in *The Kill* (*La Curée*, 1872) are marked syntactically by the eclipse of human subjects by abstract nouns and things, expressing a vision of a society which, organized under the aegis of the commodity, turns people into objects. Similarly, the descriptions of the sales in *The Ladies' Paradise* (*Au Bonheur des Dames*, 1883), with their cascading images and rising pitch, suggest loss of control, the female shoppers' quasi-sexual abandonment to consumer dreams, at the same time mirroring the perpetual expansion that defines the economic principles of consumerism. Emblematic features of contemporary life—the market, the machine, the tenement building, the mine, the apartment house, the department store, the stock exchange, the city itself—are used as giant symbols of urban and industrial modernity. Through the play of imagery and metaphor Zola magnifies the material world, giving it a hyperbolic, hallucinatory quality.

After reading *Nana* (1880), Flaubert wrote enthusiastically to Zola that Nana 'turns into a myth without ceasing to be real'—thus identifying an important feature of Zola's work: the mythic resonance of his writing. The pithead in *Germinal*, for example, is a modern figuration of the Minotaur, a monstrous beast that breathes, devours, digests, and regurgitates. Heredity not only serves as a general structuring device, but also has great dramatic force, allowing Zola to give a mythical dimension to his representation of the human condition. Reality is transfigured into a theatre of archetypal forces; and it is the mythopoeic dimension of Zola's work that helps to make him one of the great figures of the European novel. Heredity and environment pursue his characters as relentlessly as the forces of fate in an ancient tragedy. His use of myth is inseparable, moreover, from his vision of history, and is essentially Darwinian (a complete translation of Darwin's *Origin of Species*, first published in 1859, appeared in French in 1865). His conception of society is shaped by a biological model informed by the struggle between the life instinct and the death instinct: an endless cycle of life–death–life. This vision reflects an ambivalence characteristic of modernity itself. Despite his faith in science, Zola's vision is marked by the anxiety that accompanied industrialization. The demons of modernity are figured in images of catastrophe: the collapsing pithead in *Germinal*, the runaway locomotive in *La Bête humaine* (1890), the stock market crash in *Money* (*L'Argent*, 1891). A myth of catastrophe is opposed by a myth of hope, degeneration by regeneration. At the end of *Earth* (*La Terre*, 1887), Zola's novel of peasant life and its savagery, the protagonist, Jean Macquart, reflects, as he walks away from the peasant village, that even the crimes and violence perpetrated by human beings may play their part in the evolutionary process, humanity shrinking to relative insignificance, like so many tiny insects, within the great scheme of Nature. The novel closes as it opens, with the image of men sowing seeds: an image of eternal renewal.

A Love Story

A Love Story (*Une page d'amour*, 1878) is the eighth novel in the Rougon-Macquart cycle. The central character is Hélène Grandjean, a widow (of eighteen months) who lives in the closed world of bourgeois Passy, a Paris suburb, with her daughter Jeanne who is 11 at the start of the novel. Hélène is the daughter of Ursule Mouret (née Macquart), the illegitimate daughter of Aunt Dide, who features prominently in the first novel of the Rougon-Macquart cycle, *The Fortune of the Rougons*. The common ancestor of both the Rougon and Macquart families, Dide is the origin of the 'hereditary lesion' that afflicts them. Hélène is unaffected by this inheritance, whereas Jeanne—sickly, nervous, clinging—is firmly placed in the lineage of mental instability that marks the family heredity.

Hélène and Jeanne have only ventured into Paris proper three times. From the window of their apartment, they can see the entire city, which takes on a dreamlike, foreign, romantic, yet inaccessible, character for them. On the night the novel opens, Jeanne has a violent seizure. A neighbour, Dr Henri Deberle, comes to attend her, and his ministrations save her. A few days later, Hélène goes to thank Deberle, and befriends his wife Juliette and her social circle, including Malignon, a handsome, wealthy womanizer. Hélène's only friends, with whom she dines each week, are former friends of her husband: Abbé Jouve, the officiating priest at the local church, and his worthy but dull half-brother Rambaud, a middle-aged oil and produce merchant. The priest asks Hélène to visit one of his invalid parishioners, Mother Fétu. While Hélène is in the old woman's squalid little attic room, Deberle pays a professional visit. They begin to see each other there regularly, and they are increasingly attracted to each other. Meanwhile, the priest urges Hélène to remarry, and relays to her his brother's offer to wed her. This offer dismays Hélène ('the idea that he loved her made her freeze', p. 70), and she asks for time to consider it. Juliette organizes a children's fancy-dress ball, at which Deberle confesses to Hélène that he loves her. She leaves the party in a state of turmoil. On contemplating her life, she realizes that she has never really been in love; though she respected her late husband, she felt no love or passion for him. She finds, however, that she is falling in love with Deberle. Their relationship remains awkward. Hélène immerses herself in religious devotion. Jeanne has another seizure. Her illness lasts three weeks, during which she is attended by Hélène and Deberle alone, drawing them ever closer together. The doctor saves Jeanne a second time, by using leeches. Hélène herself now declares her love for the doctor. However, as Jeanne recuperates, she witnesses the closeness of her mother and Deberle and is consumed by jealousy. The symptoms of her illness return whenever the doctor is present, until at last Hélène forbids his visits. Hélène realizes, meanwhile, that Malignon has been pursuing Juliette and the two are planning an assignation. She learns from Mother Fétu that Malignon has rented a little apartment in her building, and she assumes it is intended as a love nest for him and Juliette. She goes out to look at the rooms. Jeanne is distressed to be left alone. Mother Fétu thinks Hélène is arranging for the doctor and herself to meet. The next day, Hélène tries unsuccessfully to warn Juliette not to keep her rendezvous with Malignon, scheduled for that afternoon. She slips through the Deberles' letter box an anonymous note for Henri with the address and time of the assignation. That afternoon, she decides to go to the apartment and avert the rendezvous, telling Jeanne she cannot go with her. Hélène is met by Mother Fétu, who, feeling she is playing the part of Hélène's procuress, lets her into the apartment. Hélène succeeds in averting the rendezvous, but just as the prospective lovers have departed, Deberle arrives. He thinks Hélène has arranged for them to be alone together. Hélène gives in to her feelings, and they make passionate love at last. Meanwhile, Jeanne, left alone, makes herself sick by hanging her arms out of her bedroom window in the rain. She feels betrayed, and believes her mother does not care for her anymore, especially after witnessing her mother and Deberle exchange silent, knowing glances while planning a joint family excursion to Italy. She falls seriously ill, and dies. Hélène, grief-stricken and feeling that her own actions are the direct cause of her daughter's death, ends the relationship with Deberle. Two years go by. In the last chapter, a postscript, we see Hélène standing in the snow-covered cemetery above Passy; we learn that she has married Rambaud and that the two are about to return to Marseilles, where they now live. Her life has resumed where it had left off when the novel opens, 'in stern tranquillity and proud respectability' (p. 264).

A Love Story gives only glimpses of Zola's most characteristic and powerful gifts as a novelist. Its muted tone and style reflect the writer's aim to produce a relatively inoffensive work after the provocative hyperrealism of *L'Assommoir*. The silent streets of bourgeois Passy contrast with the proletarian clamour of the Rue de la Goutte d'Or. However, while deliberately eliminating a satirical tone and suggesting an innocuous surface, Zola conveys a sharp critique of bourgeois values. The novel deals with bourgeois adultery and the moral laxity beneath respectable appearances (from that perspective, it is a kind of genteel prelude to the savagely satirical *Pot Luck*). But the novel is primarily interesting as a psychological study. It stands out in Zola's fiction for its intense focus on the protagonist and her shifting emotional states. Its basic theme, Zola stated in his planning notes, is sexual passion—its birth, development, effects, consequences, and death.

Paris, Symbolism, and a Dream World

An outstanding feature of *A Love Story* is the series of panoramic descriptions of Paris, in varying seasons and conditions of light, that close each of the five parts of the novel. These descriptions are a literary equivalent of the cityscapes the Impressionists were producing at the time Zola was writing his novel; and they call to mind the celebrated series of paintings by certain Impressionists, notably Monet's versions of the Gare Saint-Lazare and of Rouen Cathedral, and Pissarro's repeated reworkings of such Parisian vistas as the Pont-Neuf and the Boulevard Montmartre.[1] Zola himself claimed that he not only championed the Impressionists but also translated them into literature. One painting in particular is powerfully present in *A Love Story*, for it is so clearly connected with the novel's themes and effects. It is the painting used to illustrate the cover of this volume: Berthe Morisot's *On the Balcony* (1872). In this painting, a woman dressed in black (mourning black?) and a little girl look out over a vast panorama of Paris, from the elevated vantage-point of a balcony on the Rue Franklin, a quiet street in Passy (where the Morisot family actually resided).

Zola's extended descriptions of Paris in *A Love Story* are far from being self-contained virtuoso exercises in style. The appearance of the city changes so as to reflect Hélène's (and later, Jeanne's) emotional states: sunrise, and the awakening of love; Paris ablaze with light as Hélène's passion kindles; Paris in a stormy deluge at passion's

---

[1] The interaction between writers and painters in nineteenth-century France was very strong. For a discussion of the important question of the relations between Zola and the painters of his time, see Robert Lethbridge, 'Zola and Contemporary Painting', in Brian Nelson (ed.), *The Cambridge Companion to Émile Zola* (Cambridge: Cambridge University Press, 2007), 67–85. See also William J. Berg, *The Visual Novel: Émile Zola and the Art of His Times* (University Park, Pa.: Pennsylvania State University Press, 1992) and Anita Brookner, 'Zola', in *The Genius of the Future: Studies in French Art Criticism* (London and New York: Phaidon, 1971), 91–117.

consummation; Paris in the snow, as Hélène looks forward to a cold
and indifferent future. Moreover, the descriptions of Paris are inte-
grally related to Zola's use of space and symbolism throughout his
novel. The symbolic decor of *A Love Story* reflects the conflicts within
Hélène, both conscious and unconscious. Images of open space and
immensity are contrasted with images of enclosure and isolation:
'Her solitude opened out on to this immense vista' (p. 22). Spatial
claustration is opposed to liberation. This opposition is articulated
round the space of the apartment and the linking image of the window. The window motif marks the dividing line between constraint
and constriction on the one hand, excitement and potential release on
the other. The closing chapters of the first three parts all begin with
Hélène's gesture of opening wide the window. Indeed, what better
symbol of the central drama than Jeanne's replacement of her mother
at the window? In Part Five the alienation between Jeanne and Hélène
is embodied in the image of Jeanne at the window looking down at her
mother in the garden; a little later, Jeanne stays by the fire while
Hélène goes out every day; and when Jeanne is about to die, Dr Bodin
opens the window as she tries once more to look out over Paris.

   The calm and order of Hélène's existence before her feelings are
disturbed by the doctor are intimately associated with her apartment:
'She liked this huge, peaceful room with its homely luxury' (p. 21).
When she returns after her 'fall', she seems to need to revisit all the
rooms of the apartment, returning as if to a refuge: 'All the furniture
was in its place; she was glad to see it again' (p. 215). But this refuge
has been furnished by Rambaud, and it reflects his stolid bourgeois
nature. The room gives reassurance, but its association with Rambaud
suggests claustrophobia. Hélène's insulation from life is identified
with the apartment, as temptation is identified with descent: 'It was as
if they had been halted on the threshold of a world whose eternal
spectacle lay in front of them and they refused to enter' (p. 50). The
image of Hélène on the threshold of an unknown world, suspended
between temptation and seclusion, emphasizes the attraction of Paris.
With its dark, indistinct shapes, the city becomes a metaphor of sensuality, inviting but dangerous and disturbing: 'Paris often made
them anxious when she sent them her warm and troubling vapours'
(p. 50). The city is persistently evoked in images of liquidity and ever-
changing light. The variety and mobility of the visual scene set off the
intimacy and immobility of Hélène's apartment. The solidity of the

furnishings emphasizes the sense of fixity, which is opposed to the later, pervasive moods of floating and suspension that characterize Hélène's dreamlike states, and also to the images of dissolution and erosion associated with the development of her feelings. Images of height and depth set off her unexciting past life, evoked as a quiet walk along a straight path. Open space and images of promise are juxtaposed with the dark, damp house of her childhood, with memories of the emotional aridity of her past: the monotony of childhood followed by twelve years of marriage to a man she never loved. Rambaud and Abbé Jouve are associated with Hélène's past through their previous acquaintance with her husband. Zola thus builds up a coherent pattern of connotations: apartment–reclusion–ignorance–Rambaud–past–claustrophobia as opposed to Paris–open space–immensity–the unknown–temptation–descent–knowledge–release.

The second scene of contemplation by the window, precipitated by the doctor's declaration of love, adds a new element to the equation: Deberle. Hélène's reactions to her bedroom, supported by the returning image of the past, mark the progress of her passion:

BACK up there in the gentle, cloistered atmosphere of her room, Hélène felt as if she couldn't breathe. She was astonished to find it so calm, so shut away, so soporific beneath its blue velvet furnishings, when she was bringing to it the breathless fire of this passion that so agitated her. Was this really her room, this solitary, dead place that she found so stifling? She flung open a window and leaned out in the direction of Paris. (p. 94)

The tensions between passion and constraint, agitation and calm, merge into violent revolt as the dullness of Paris after the rain is changed into a resplendent vision dominated by images of gold and fire, and Hélène's fear gives way to delicious self-abandonment: 'It was a fatal passion, she had to admit, and Hélène was helpless to defend herself against it' (p. 98). The wish to escape from the confines of the apartment becomes a desire for a deep, almost transcendent, passion which would be concentrated into a single moment: 'she was begging for the fall, she wanted it to be immediate and profound. Her revolt boiled down to this one imperious desire. Oh, to disappear in an embrace, to live in one minute all that she had not lived up till now!' (p. 99).

Hélène's apartment is opposed to the places in which her love is excited—places that are foreign and unfamiliar, liberating from everyday attachments and associations. The scene of the first indirect meetings between Hélène and Henri is Mother Fétu's attic room, in which stiff deference gives way to deep sympathy:

> in his drawing room she would have displayed the wary reserve natural to her. But here they were far away from the world, sharing the only chair, almost cheerful about this wretchedness and ugliness which brought them together in mutual compassion. By the end of the week they knew each other as though they had lived side by side for years. In their common kindness towards her, Mother Fétu's hovel was filled with light. (p. 29)

Hélène's 'fall' takes place in Malignon's secret bachelor apartment, which is close to Mother Fétu's hovel: 'This room was unknown to her, the objects in it meant nothing to her' (p. 205). And in her later confession to Abbé Jouve, Hélène recognizes that 'she would never have given in to that man if Jeanne had been with her. She had been obliged to go and meet him in that secret room' (p. 241).

The idea of a secret place in which supreme happiness will be achieved gives rise to moments of intense daydreaming. During Jeanne's second convalescence, Hélène's growing resentment of her daughter's jealousy is matched by a vision of wish-fulfilment: 'some vague dream where she imagined herself walking with Henri into an unfamiliar, idyllic world' (p. 137). The revelation of bourgeois morality at the Deberles' reception (Part Four, Chapter 1) marks a similar release of fantasy. Accompanied by the tinkling of the piano, 'she was lulled into a dream: Henri had rid himself of Juliette and she, Hélène, was with him as his wife in far-off countries with unknown tongues' (p. 168). Hélène's torment as to the whereabouts of the rendezvous between Juliette and Malignon merges into the feverish near-fantasy of half-sleep as she imagines a 'secret little room' (p. 172) in a cheap hotel, then 'a delightful apartment with thick hangings, flowers, huge bright fires burning in every hearth' (p. 172); and suddenly the dream-image of Juliette and Malignon is replaced by that of Henri and herself, 'in the depths of this cosy hideaway where the sounds of the world outside could not reach them' (p. 172). Whereas the returning image of the past marks important stages of feeling, dream-moments often project us into an imagined future. Dream, constantly punctuating the narrative and closely linked to spatial imagery, lies at the heart of the novel, expressing unconscious feelings and translating the tensions on which the novel is built. Hélène is often immersed in reveries, in which recurring words and images evoke undercurrents of desire:

In her heart she felt indignation, pride and anger, as well as a *secret*, undeniable desire (p. 96)

Her will failed, unspeakable thoughts were doing their *secret* work in her (p. 183)

This *vertiginous* lifting and dropping delighted her (p. 40)

. . . she felt *giddy*, her mind reeled (p. 265) (my italics)

Vertigo is associated with falling, the sexual connotations of which are clear.

Pressures of feeling reach a climax in Part Four, with its sustained mood of somnambulism. Much of Parts Four and Five conveys a strongly dreamlike impression: the sense of detachment from external reality, the lack of a sense of time and space, the dramatic intensity of particular sensations and images. Part Four, Chapter 2, which leads up to Hélène's 'fall', epitomizes the movement and texture of the novel, for it offers a striking synthesis of its dominant imagery and atmosphere. The ambivalence of Hélène's feelings, a mixture of fascination and disgust, is crystallized in the opposition of images— between the claustrophobic associations of her apartment and the mysterious attraction of Malignon's 'rose-coloured room' (p. 175) in Mother Fétu's tumbledown house—which are held in tension by her mood of reverie. Her frustration wells up by the window: 'It was that room that was making her ill. She loathed it now, cross at having spent two years in it' (p. 177). The images of squalor associated with the 'rose-coloured room', and the emphasis on the muddy weather, reflect a vision of Hélène's imminent 'fall' as a nauseous obscenity, a descent into the 'id'. The room is surrounded by ugliness and poverty: the stairs oozing with damp, the dirty yellow doors on every floor. Hélène's descent down the Passage des Eaux, contrasting with her enjoyment of its shaded seclusion at the time of her first visits to Mother Fétu (now transformed into a kind of Goyaesque procuress), is portrayed as a slow act of self-abasement. The sense of falling or being sucked up ('The passage opened up below her like a black chasm. She couldn't see the bottom', p. 179) is associated with feelings of guilt. Freud writes that in dreams women 'almost always accept the symbolic use of falling as a way of describing a surrender to an erotic temptation'.[2] Hélène hesitates as she holds the handrail to support herself. The shadows, the walls that seem to close in, and the giant shapes of contorted branches, are menacing omens. With the imminence of her 'fall', the black mud becomes a surging torrent.

The 'fall' scene itself occupies several pages. There is a superimpression of significant details in which different threads of the novel are gathered up in a play of associations. When Hélène is left alone in the 'rose-coloured room' with Henri, the image of an abyss, the emphasis on slow slipping and falling, sapped strength and inevitability, recall the descent of the Passage des Eaux: 'It was like an abyss into which she herself was sliding' (p. 202). Hélène yields to Henri in dreamlike acquiescence: 'She forgot everything, she yielded to a superior force. It seemed to her natural and inevitable' (p. 202). The resonances of sensation evoke dreamlike memories of childhood. The interpenetration of silence and memory, the blending of past and present, converge in a sense of oblivion, an ineffable, self-contained moment in which the external world, time, and space recede, suggesting both sensuous liberation (the memory of the summer day with the windows open and the chaffinch flying into the room) and harmonious identity with the unconscious. Simultaneous associations of death and 'the delicious annihilation of her whole being' (p. 203) are evoked by Hélène's memory of a similar winter evening of her childhood when she had nearly died in a small, airless room, also before a large fire. The intensity of the dream-atmosphere is marked by a hallucinatory feeling of detachment from reality.

They were far from the world, a thousand leagues away from the earth. And this forgetfulness of the bonds that attached them to beings and things was so absolute they seemed to have been born there at that moment and would die there in a little while when they took each other into their arms. (p. 204)

The scene ends on a strikingly deflatory note: 'When Hélène came back in her bare feet to fetch her slippers from in front of the dying embers, it occurred to her that never had they loved one another less than they had that day' (p. 205). This statement, together with the introduction of the motif of death, leads us into Jeanne's attitudes.

---

[2] Sigmund Freud, *The Interpretation of Dreams*, ed. and trans. James Strachey (New York: Avon Books, 1967), 430.

There is a modification of perspective as the child assumes a more dominant role in the narrative.

Jeanne

Part Four, Chapter 5, in which Jeanne contemplates Paris from the window while her mother is with Henri, might be analysed as a dream, for it is a dream-landscape that we see, highly sexual in its symbolism. The projection of Jeanne's feelings on to the scene offers, as Jean Borie points out, the most coherently anthropomorphic of the novel's window-scenes.[3] Borie also makes the pertinent observation, following Freud, that a dream-landscape is most often a representation of the sexual organs.[4] The female sexual connotations of the landscape are plain: the focal centre of the city is the Seine, with Paris seen as an immense valley. The violence of a storm as it sweeps across the city matches the phallic significance of the Panthéon, in which Jeanne momentarily imagines her mother to be: 'that was the building she found most astonishing, enormous as it was and sticking up in the air like the city's plume' (p. 210). She tries to identify what is hidden and forbidden: 'She had a vague feeling that her mother was somewhere where children are not allowed to go' (p. 209). Then, resuming the leitmotiv of Part Four, Chapter 2, Hélène is identified with the mud of the city. The scene Jeanne witnesses, and dies of witnessing, is the primal scene, presented as a scene of 'cloacal copulation':[5]

what was that very black monument? And that street in which there was something big running? And all that district she was afraid of, because for certain there were fights going on there. She could not make it out clearly. But truth to tell, there was something moving there, it was very ugly, little girls ought not to look . . . Paris the unknown, with its smoke, its constant rumbling, its powerful life, was breathing out an odour of poverty, putrefaction, and crime which made her young head spin, as if she was leaning over one of those pestilential wells, which exhale their invisible mud . . . Then, at a loss, she remained there, afraid and ashamed, and she couldn't rid herself of the idea that her mother was there among these sordid things, exactly where, she couldn't tell, over there in the distance. (pp. 210–11)

---

[3] Jean Borie, *Zola et les mythes, ou de la nausée au salut* (Paris: Seuil, 1971), 214.
[4] This is argued by Freud in *The Interpretation of Dreams*, 391 ff.
[5] Borie, *Zola et les mythes*, 215.

The sexual nature of the knowledge she and her mother had wished to have while resisting it, and which now causes Jeanne such torment, is clear. The sexual implications of the convulsion that shakes the city, the sharp pain Jeanne experiences simultaneously with Hélène's 'fall', and the transformation of the city into a river of mud, make evident the suggestion of metaphorically lost virginity ('Just now, something in her had been broken, that was certain', p. 213) and clinch the cumulative associations between sexuality—shame—nemesis. Jeanne's lost innocence seems to cry out under the constantly falling rain: 'she lamented for something that could never be mended' (p. 213). The vision translated through her—through her body—is of a sexuality that is unwanted:

Then, half-fainting, she uttered a stifled cry: 'Maman, Maman!' without it being possible to detect if she was crying to her mother for help or if she was accusing her of sending her those ills which were causing her such agony. (p. 211)

As Susan Harrow remarks, if Jeanne blames her mother for her agony, it is as the woman she is afraid to become. 'Acutely aware of her sexually maturing body, she views the doctor, her mother's lover, as her seducer, and his cure as a form of sexual violation.'[6] The description of Jeanne on her sickbed, close to death, gives a clear indication of the psychosomatic nature, and essential significance, of her illness:

as soon as Henri's fingers touched her, a sort of jolt went through her body... She saw her nakedness, she sobbed in shame, rapidly drawing the sheet up round her. In her agony she seemed to have aged ten years all at once, and, near to death, her twelve years were enough to understand that this man should not touch either her, or her mother through her. (p. 239)

'Her willed death', Harrow comments, 'preserves Jeanne from the transition to womanhood and provides an escape from desire: her mother's and her own. In the death of Jeanne, the mother and her lover are separated [and] the child is freed from her own trial of desire . . . [D]aughter and mother merge in a double death, one real and literal, the other psychic and symbolic'.[7]

[6] Susan Harrow, 'The Matter with Jeanne: Narrative and the Nervous Body in Zola's *Une page d'amour*', in Anna Gural-Migdal (ed.), *L'Écriture du féminin chez Zola et dans l'écriture naturaliste* (Bern: Peter Lang, 2003), 249.

[7] Harrow, 'The Matter with Jeanne', 249–50.

Love Stories

The novel contains several love stories, not just that of Hélène and Deberle. The passion of Hélène and Deberle is contrasted with the novel's other illicit affair, between Juliette and Malignon, and with the more down-to-earth and honest relationship of Rosalie and Zéphyrin, as well as the genuine affection between Rambaud and Jeanne.

Sharp relief is given to the ideological framework of the novel by the fact that Hélène is presented as a person of great moral virtue. Her strict provincial morality is shocked by 'the cheerful, insouciant adultery' (p. 168) of the Parisian bourgeoisie which she discovers at the house of Juliette Deberle. Juliette is more than an incidental figure. She serves a narrative, moral, and ideological purpose. The seriousness of Hélène contrasts with the shallowness of Juliette, who leads a life of frivolous socializing. Hélène has a conventional sense of bourgeois values, but the world of bourgeois rituals—Trouville, the latest fashion, a new boulevard play, society gossip—is foreign to her. Her sobriety contrasts with the world of superficial and ephemeral appearances associated with Juliette: the theatre, fancy-dress balls, amateur theatricals, the emphasis on transient and factitious decorative styles such as *japonaiserie*. When Hélène arrives at Juliette's house with the intention of preventing her from keeping the rendezvous with Malignon, she finds her rehearsing Musset's *Un caprice*. When she visits Juliette the day after the rendezvous, she finds her 'pale and with reddened eyes like a tragedy queen' (p. 225). Juliette's life is defined by social convention and fashionable taste. Hélène's struggle to suppress her passion, understood in the original sense of 'suffering', is contrasted with the socially inspired curiosity that, along with ennui, impels Juliette to contemplate adultery. Similarly, Hélène's feelings of guilt and remorse are contrasted with Juliette's superficial shame at having almost failed to keep up appearances, and with her equally superficial easy social acceptance of Malignon afterwards. Looking back on her relationship with Deberle, two years later, Hélène has the impression that she is contemplating, and passing judgement on, 'a stranger, whose conduct she despised and found shocking. What a time of peculiar folly, what an abominable evil act, like a blinding thunderclap!' (p. 263). The narrative is marked by a number of moralizing narratorial intrusions: 'This *self-abasement* satisfied a need in her and she was relishing it' (p. 224); 'she was experiencing the *pusillanimous* happiness of telling herself that nothing was out of bounds' (p. 232) (my italics). The term 'fall', which is frequently used (initially in Hélène's symbolic fall from the swing at the feet of Henri), implies condemnation.

The caricatural figures of the maid Rosalie and her rustic soldier-lover Zéphyrin may initially appear out of place in the novel. But, like Juliette, they serve a structural purpose in relation to the protagonists, Hélène and Jeanne. Hélène's indulgence towards the pair, after Zéphyrin's first appearance, reflects the unconscious softening of her feelings: 'Seeing the two of them, she had felt her heart melt, as it had once before, making her forget to be strict... Their love had a calm certainty about it' (p. 63). After her 'fall', Hélène's nervous excitement is soothed into a kind of complacent oblivion as she watches Rosalie and Zéphyrin eating together in the kitchen. The sensuous delight of the food, the heat, and the childlike happiness of the two young people, evoke in Hélène a feeling of complicity as she becomes absorbed into their world: 'She felt cocooned in their warmth for one another... The distance between them all seemed not so great, she no longer knew which was herself and which the others, where she was or what she was doing there' (p. 224). For Jeanne, Rosalie and Zéphyrin represent a kind of vitality, and an innocent, happy sensuality, which she herself can never know. During her convalescence in the Deberles' garden, she watches them in fascination, and says: 'I was thinking I'd like to live till I'm very old...' (p. 145). Later, on her deathbed, she contemplates them once more, but this time it is as if to say farewell.

Hélène reflects, at the end of the novel, that she never really knew Henri, that he remains a kind of ghostly stranger; and she reflects, too, that the city also remains a mystery. She has returned, as Naomi Schor notes,[8] to her earlier state of willed ignorance: 'she became calm again, without desire, without curiosity, continuing slowly forward on the dead straight path' (p. 264). The retribution wrought upon her for her brief affair and for her transgression upon her sacred role as mother is great. Not only is she deprived of her motherhood (a point given extra emphasis by the birth of the Deberles' second

[8] Naomi Schor, *Breaking the Chain: Women, Theory, and French Realist Fiction* (New York: Columbia University Press, 1985), 38.

child, who, it is noted, resembles Jeanne and was conceived at the time of Jeanne's death), she is also deprived, by the same token, of her sexuality. It is clear that Hélène's second marriage, to Rambaud, will be as passionless as the first. On her wedding night, Rambaud, like her first husband, had kissed her bare feet, 'like those of a statue turning into marble again' (p. 263). As Henri Mitterand remarks,[9] one does not need to be intimately acquainted with Freudian psychology to see Rambaud's fishing-rods (which Hélène has forgotten, moreover) as ironic virility-substitutes;[10] and the reference to the need to be sure that the large trunk is firmly closed (echoing the closing of Jeanne's coffin) may similarly be read in terms of the closure, the ultimate repression, of erotic desire. In the words of Naomi Schor, who argues that the vision of love, marriage, and motherhood developed in *A Love Story* is fundamentally one of patriarchal containment: in Zola's works not only is a woman's place in the home, but 'mothers are forbidden to experience sexual bliss'.[11] We leave Hélène standing, as if petrified, in a frozen landscape.

---

[9] Henri Mitterand, *Zola*, ii. *L'Homme de Germinal, 1871–1893* (Paris: Fayard, 2001), 413.

[10] In Freudian psychology foot fetishism is widely viewed as an act of sexual displacement, a substitutional act aimed at avoiding contact with the genitals.

[11] Schor, *Breaking the Chain*, 47.

TRANSLATOR'S NOTE

WHEN I was asked to translate the eighth in Zola's Rougon-Macquart series of twenty novels my first problem was the title: *Une page d'amour*. It has been variously rendered as 'A Page of Love', 'A Love Episode', 'Hélène', and 'A Love Affair', but feeling that none of these would do—this is not just about an adulterous relationship as implied in the title 'A Love Affair'—I decided on 'A Love Story'. It's one of the lesser-known novels of Zola, to English readers at least, and not only an exploration of love between the characters Hélène and Henri, Juliette and Malignon, Rosalie and Zéphyrin, Jeanne and Hélène, Monsieur Rambaud and Jeanne, and finally Monsieur Rambaud and Hélène, but also, and perhaps almost as important, Zola and the city of Paris itself. His abiding passion for Paris shines throughout its pages and so I felt that 'A Love Story' was a more appropriate way of translating the title.

The novel was serialized first between December and April 1878 before being published by Charpentier in April 1878. Of the relatively few English translations, the Vizetelly versions of 1887 and 1895, the latter with ninety-four delicate engravings, stand out. Two more translations appeared in the twentieth century, C. C. Starkweather's in 1910 and Jean Stewart's in 1957. The book was adapted as a film in 1980 and 1995.

I hope this new translation will fill a gap in the narrative for the many fans of Zola's extraordinary cycle of novels and attract new readers to his masterly storytelling.

Thank you to all those friends and colleagues I have consulted at various times while I have been working on the translation, to Brian Nelson, Perrine Chambon, Arnaud Baignot, Jennie Feldman, Mauro and Anne Pinheiro and the translators at the CITL in Arles; to Judith Luna, my former editor, for her continued encouragement and Luciana O'Flaherty, my present editor at OUP. And a special thanks, as ever, to my husband David, for reading it with his usual care and enthusiasm, and making his always immensely invaluable suggestions.

H.C.

SELECT BIBLIOGRAPHY

A Love Story (*Une page d'amour*) was serialized in the newspaper *Le Bien public* from 11 December 1877 to 4 April 1878. It was published in volume form by the Librairie Charpentier in April 1878. It is included in volume ii of Henri Mitterand's superb scholarly edition of Les Rougon-Macquart in the 'Bibliothèque de la Pléiade', 5 vols. (Paris: Gallimard, 1960–7), and in volume viii of the Nouveau Monde edition of the *Œuvres complètes*, 21 vols. (Paris, 2002–10). Paperback editions exist in the following popular collections: Folio, ed. Henri Mitterand (Paris, 1989); Les Classiques de Poche, ed. Pierre Marotte (Paris, 1975); GF-Flammarion, introduction by Colette Becker (Paris, 1993).

Biographies of Zola in English

Brown, Frederick, *Zola: A Life* (New York: Farrar, Straus, Giroux, 1995; London: Macmillan, 1996).

Hemmings, F. W. J., *The Life and Times of Émile Zola* (London: Elek, 1977).

Studies of Zola and Naturalism in English

Baguley, David, *Naturalist Fiction: The Entropic Vision* (Cambridge: Cambridge University Press, 1990).

Baguley, David (ed.), *Critical Essays on Emile Zola* (Boston: G. K. Hall, 1986).

Harrow, Susan, *Zola, The Body Modern: Pressures and Prospects of Representation* (Oxford: Legenda, 2010).

Hemmings, F. W. J., *Émile Zola* (2nd edn., Oxford: Clarendon Press, 1966).

Lethbridge, R., and Keefe, T. (eds.), *Zola and the Craft of Fiction* (Leicester: Leicester University Press, 1990).

Nelson, Brian (ed.), *The Cambridge Companion to Zola* (Cambridge: Cambridge University Press, 2007), esp. ch. 4: Hannah Thompson, 'Questions of Sexuality and Gender', 53–66.

Nelson, Brian, *Zola and the Bourgeoisie: A Study of Themes and Techniques in* Les Rougon-Macquart (London: Macmillan, 1983), esp. '*Une Page d'amour*: The Ambiguities of Passion', 96–128.

Walker, Philip, *Zola* (London: Routledge & Kegan Paul, 1985).

Wilson, Angus, *Émile Zola: An Introductory Study of His Novels* (1953; London: Secker & Warburg, 1964).

Works in English on or concerning A Love Story

Bishop, Danielle Kent, 'Zola's Women: A Chink in the Armour: A Study of *Une page d'amour* and *L'Œuvre*', in Anna Gural-Migdal (ed.), *L'Écriture du féminin chez Zola et dans l'écriture naturaliste* (Bern: Peter Lang, 2003), 121–43.

Harrow, Susan, 'The Matter with Jeanne: Narrative and the Nervous Body in Zola's *Une page d'amour*', in Anna Gural-Migdal (ed.), *L'Écriture du féminin chez Zola et dans l'écriture naturaliste* (Bern: Peter Lang, 2003), 237–50.

Overton, Bill, *Fictions of Female Adultery, 1684–1890: Theories and Circumtexts* (Houndmills: Palgrave Macmillan, 2002), ch. 7: 'After *Madame Bovary*: Female Adultery in Zola', 154–86.

Richards, Sylvie L. F., 'The Mother–Daughter Relationship in Émile Zola's *Une page d'amour*', *Excavatio*, 2 (1993), 93–102.

Schor, Naomi, *Breaking the Chain: Women, Theory, and French Realist Fiction* (New York: Columbia University Press, 1985), ch. 2: 'Smiles of the Sphinx: Zola and the Riddle of Femininity', 29–47.

Schor, Naomi, 'Mother's Day: Zola's Women', *Diacritics*, 5 (Winter 1975), 11–17.

Further Reading in Oxford World's Classics

Zola, Émile, *L'Assommoir*, trans. Margaret Mauldon, ed. Robert Lethbridge.

Zola, Émile, *The Belly of Paris*, trans. Brian Nelson.

Zola, Émile, *La Bête humaine*, trans. Roger Pearson.

Zola, Émile, *The Conquest of Plassans*, trans. Helen Constantine, ed. Patrick McGuinness.

Zola, Émile, *Earth*, trans. Brian Nelson and Julie Rose.

Zola, Émile, *The Fortune of the Rougons*, trans. Brian Nelson.

Zola, Émile, *Germinal*, trans. Peter Collier, ed. Robert Lethbridge.

Zola, Émile, *The Kill*, trans. Brian Nelson.

Zola, Émile, *The Ladies' Paradise*, trans. Brian Nelson.

Zola, Émile, *The Masterpiece*, trans. Thomas Walton, rev. Roger Pearson.

Zola, Émile, *Money*, trans. Valerie Minogue.

Zola, Émile, *Nana*, trans. Douglas Parmée.

Zola, Émile, *Pot Luck*, trans. Brian Nelson.

Zola, Émile, *The Sin of Abbé Mouret*, trans. Valerie Minogue.

Zola, Émile, *Thérèse Raquin*, trans. Andrew Rothwell.

A CHRONOLOGY OF ÉMILE ZOLA

1840 (2 April) Born in Paris, the only child of Francesco Zola (b. 1795), an Italian engineer, and Émilie, née Aubert (b. 1819), the daughter of a glazier. The naturalist novelist was later proud that 'zolla' in Italian means 'clod of earth'

1843 Family moves to Aix-en-Provence

1847 (27 March) Death of father from pneumonia following a chill caught while supervising work on his scheme to supply Aix-en-Provence with drinking water

1852–8 Boarder at the Collège Bourbon at Aix. Friendship with Baptistin Baille and Paul Cézanne. Zola, not Cézanne, wins the school prize for drawing

1858 (February) Leaves Aix to settle in Paris with his mother (who had preceded him in December). Offered a place and bursary at the Lycée Saint-Louis. (November) Falls ill with 'brain fever' (typhoid) and convalescence is slow

1859 Fails his *baccalauréat* twice

1860 (Spring) Is found employment as a copy-clerk but abandons it after two months, preferring to eke out an existence as an impecunious writer in the Latin Quarter of Paris

1861 Cézanne follows Zola to Paris, where he meets Camille Pissarro, fails the entrance examination to the École des Beaux-Arts, and returns to Aix in September

1862 (February) Taken on by Hachette, the well-known publishing house, at first in the dispatch office and subsequently as head of the publicity department. (31 October) Naturalized as a French citizen. Cézanne returns to Paris and stays with Zola

1863 (31 January) First literary article published. (1 May) Manet's *Déjeuner sur l'herbe* exhibited at the Salon des Refusés, which Zola visits with Cézanne

1864 (October) *Tales for Ninon*

1865 *Claude's Confession*. A *succès de scandale* thanks to its bedroom scenes. Meets future wife Alexandrine-Gabrielle Meley (b. 1839), the illegitimate daughter of teenage parents who soon separated; Alexandrine's mother died in September 1849

1866 Resigns his position at Hachette (salary: 200 francs a month) and becomes a literary critic on the recently launched daily *L'Événement* (salary: 500 francs a month). Self-styled 'humble disciple' of Hippolyte Taine. Writes a series of provocative articles condemning the official Salon Selection Committee, expressing reservations about Courbet, and praising Manet and Monet. Begins to frequent the Café Guerbois in the Batignolles quarter of Paris, the meeting-place of the future Impressionists. Antoine Guillemet takes Zola to meet Manet. Summer months spent with Cézanne at Bennecourt on the Seine. (15 November) *L'Événement* suppressed by the authorities

1867 (November) *Thérèse Raquin*

1868 (April) Preface to second edition of *Thérèse Raquin*. (May) Manet's portrait of Zola exhibited at the Salon. (December) *Madeleine Férat*. Begins to plan for the Rougon-Macquart series of novels

1868–70 Working as journalist for a number of different newspapers

1870 (31 May) Marries Alexandrine in a registry office. (September) Moves temporarily to Marseilles because of the Franco-Prussian War

1871 Political reporter for *La Cloche* (in Paris) and *Le Sémaphore de Marseille*. (March) Returns to Paris. (October) Publishes *The Fortune of the Rougons*, the first of the twenty novels making up the Rougon-Macquart series

1872 *The Kill*

1873 (April) *The Belly of Paris*

1874 (May) *The Conquest of Plassans*. First independent Impressionist exhibition. (November) *Further Tales for Ninon*

1875 Begins to contribute articles to the Russian newspaper *Vestnik Evropy* (*European Herald*). (April) *The Sin of Abbé Mouret*

1876 (February) *His Excellency Eugène Rougon*. Second Impressionist exhibition

1877 (February) *L'Assommoir*

1878 Buys a house at Médan on the Seine, 40 kilometres west of Paris. (June) *A Page of Love*

1880 (March) *Nana*. (May) *Les Soirées de Médan* (an anthology of short stories by Zola and some of his naturalist 'disciples', including Maupassant). (8 May) Death of Flaubert. (September) First of a series of articles for *Le Figaro*. (17 October) Death of his mother. (December) *The Experimental Novel*

1882 (April) *Pot Luck* (*Pot-Bouille*). (3 September) Death of Turgenev

1883 (13 February) Death of Wagner. (March) *The Ladies' Paradise* (*Au Bonheur des Dames*). (30 April) Death of Manet

1884 (March) *La Joie de vivre*. Preface to catalogue of Manet exhibition

1885 (March) *Germinal*. (12 May) Begins writing *The Masterpiece* (*L'Œuvre*). (22 May) Death of Victor Hugo. (23 December) First instalment of *The Masterpiece* appears in *Le Gil Blas*

1886 (27 March) Final instalment of *The Masterpiece*, which is published in book form in April

1887 (18 August) Denounced as an onanistic pornographer in the *Manifesto of the Five* in *Le Figaro*. (November) *Earth*

1888 (October) *The Dream*. Jeanne Rozerot becomes his mistress

1889 (20 September) Birth of Denise, daughter of Zola and Jeanne

1890 (March) *The Beast in Man*

1891 (March) *Money*. (April) Elected President of the Société des Gens de Lettres. (25 September) Birth of Jacques, son of Zola and Jeanne

1892 (June) *La Débâcle*

1893 (July) *Doctor Pascal*, the last of the Rougon-Macquart novels. Fêted on visit to London

1894 (August) *Lourdes*, the first novel of the trilogy *Three Cities*. (22 December) Dreyfus found guilty by a court martial

1896 (May) *Rome*

1898 (13 January) 'J'accuse', his article in defence of Dreyfus, published in *L'Aurore*. (21 February) Found guilty of libelling the Minister of War and given the maximum sentence of one year's imprisonment and a fine of 3,000 francs. Appeal for retrial granted on a technicality. (March) *Paris*. (23 May) Retrial delayed. (18 July) Leaves for England instead of attending court

1899 (4 June) Returns to France. (October) *Fecundity*, the first of his *Four Gospels*

1901 (May) *Toil*, the second 'Gospel'

1902 (29 September) Dies of fumes from his bedroom fire, the chimney having been capped either by accident or anti-Dreyfusard design. Wife survives. (5 October) Public funeral

1903 (March) *Truth*, the third 'Gospel', published posthumously. *Justice* was to be the fourth

1908 (4 June) Remains transferred to the Panthéon

A LOVE STORY

A LOVE STORY

PART ONE

CHAPTER 1

THE night light in the blue-tinged glass on the mantelshelf burned behind a book, which cast a shadow across half the bedroom. The quiet glow spreading over the bedside table and the chaise longue, bathed the wide folds of the velvet curtains, and flooded the mirror on the rosewood cupboard between the two windows with azure. The harmonious tones of this homely room, the blue of the curtains, the furniture and the carpet acquired a softness, like clouds, at this time of the evening. And opposite the windows, in the shadow, the bed, also draped in velvet, was a dark shape, brightened only by the whiteness of the sheets. Hélène, a mother and a widow, her arms serenely crossed, was breathing lightly.

The clock struck one into the silence. The sounds from the streets round about had died away. Up there on the heights of the Trocadéro all you could hear of Paris was a distant hum. Hélène's breathing was so soft and gentle, her chaste bosom scarcely moved. In a deep, peaceful slumber, her neat head to one side, chestnut hair securely fastened, she looked to have fallen asleep while listening to something. On the other side, the wide-open door to the adjoining room cast a dark shadow on the wall.

But there was not a sound to be heard. It struck the half-hour. The pendulum on the clock seemed to move more slowly in the overwhelming feeling of sleepiness that engulfed the entire bedroom. The night light, the furniture, a woman's needlework lying on the little table by the snuffed-out lamp, all seemed to be sleeping. Even in her sleep, Hélène retained her grave, benign expression.

When two o'clock struck, the peace was disturbed; a sigh could be heard in the darkness of the adjoining room. It was followed by a rustle of sheets before all fell silent again. Then came a more laboured breathing. Hélène had not moved. But suddenly she sat up. She had just been woken by the confused babble of a child in pain. She put her hands to her forehead, still half asleep, when a muffled cry startled her from her bed.

'Jeanne, Jeanne! What's the matter?' she asked. 'Answer me!'

And as her daughter did not answer she rushed to fetch the night light, saying under her breath:

'My God, she wasn't well, I shouldn't have gone to bed.'

She went quickly into the adjoining room that was heavy with silence. The night light, drowning in oil, was just a flickering flame throwing a single circle of light on to the ceiling. Leaning over the iron bedstead, at first Hélène could make out nothing. Then, in the blue glow, in the middle of the cast-off sheets she saw Jeanne, rigid and with her head thrown back, the muscles in her neck stiff and hard. Her poor, beloved face was distorted in a seizure, her eyes were open, she was staring at the tops of the curtains.

'My God, my God!' Hélène cried. 'My God, she's dying.'

And putting the night light down with trembling hands, she felt her daughter all over. She could not find the pulse. Her heart seemed to have stopped. Her small arms and legs were splayed out violently. At that point Hélène lost her head and panicked:

'My child is dying!' she stammered. 'Help me! My child! My child!'

She came back into her bedroom, stumbling around, falling over objects, not knowing where she was going. Then she returned to the other room and threw herself in front of the bed again, still calling for help. She took Jeanne in her arms, kissed her hair, feeling her all over with her hands, pleading with her to say something. One word, just one word. Where did it hurt? Did she want some of the medicine she had given her the other day? Would fresh air bring her round? And she tried over and over again to get her to say something.

'Speak to me, Jeanne, please, speak to me!'

Oh God... not knowing what to do! Just like that, suddenly in the night. No light, even. Her thoughts became confused. She chattered on to her daughter, asking questions and answering for her. Was the pain in her stomach? No, it was in her throat. Nothing serious. One must stay calm. And she made an effort to retain all her own common sense. But her stomach turned over when she felt her daughter stiff in her arms. She looked at her convulsing, not breathing. She tried to be sensible, to resist her need to shout. Then suddenly in spite of herself, she cried out.

She crossed the dining room and kitchen and called:

'Rosalie, Rosalie! Quick, get a doctor! My daughter's dying!'

There was an answering cry from the servant, who slept in a small room behind the kitchen. Hélène ran back. She paced to and fro in her nightgown, not seeming to feel the cold of the icy February night.* This servant would let her daughter die! But scarcely a minute had passed. She returned to the kitchen, went into the bedroom again. She flung on a skirt, threw a shawl roughly over her shoulders. She knocked over the furniture, and the room, where such peace had reigned a short while ago, was now filled with the violence of her desperation. Then, still in her slippers and leaving the doors open, she ran down the three flights of stairs, with the notion of fetching a doctor herself.

The concierge pulled the cord and Hélène found herself outside, her ears buzzing and her head spinning. She ran down the Rue Vineuse,* rang Doctor Bodin's bell; he had treated Jeanne before. After what seemed an eternity, a servant came to say that Doctor Bodin was attending a woman having a baby. Hélène remained stupefied on the pavement. She did not know any other doctor in Passy. For a moment she paced up and down, looking at the houses. An icy little wind was blowing. Still in her slippers, she walked across the sprinkling of snow which had fallen the night before. And constantly before her eyes was the vision of her daughter, accompanied by the anguished thought that she was letting her die by not finding a doctor straight away. Then, as she retraced her steps up the Rue Vineuse, she tugged at a bell pull. She would ask someone, perhaps they could give her an address. She rang again, they took their time coming to open the door. The wind flattened her thin petticoat against her legs and loosened the strands of her hair.

Finally a servant came and said that Doctor Deberle was in bed. She had rung at a doctor's house, so Heaven had not abandoned her after all! Then she insisted on entering, saying over and over:

'My child is dying! My child! Tell him to come.'

It was a well-furnished town house. She went upstairs, arguing with the servant, countering all objections with the words that her child was dying. When she reached the landing, she agreed to wait; but as soon as she heard the doctor getting up in the adjoining room, she went and spoke to him through the door.

'Come as soon as you can, Doctor, I beg you... My child is dying!'

When the doctor appeared in his waistcoat, without a tie, she urged him to be quick and would not let him finish getting dressed. He had recognized her. She lived in the house next door and was his tenant. So when he took a short cut through the garden with her and passed through the communicating gate between the two houses, she suddenly remembered.

'Of course,' she said softly, 'you are a doctor and I knew that... I'm taking leave of my senses, as you see... Let's be quick.'

On the stairs, she ushered him ahead of her. Had he been the Almighty, she could not have brought him into her home with more reverence. Upstairs Rosalie had stayed by Jeanne, and had lit the lamp placed on the small table. As soon as the doctor went in, he took this lamp and shone it directly on the child, who was still painfully stiff, except that her head had slipped down and her face was twitching rapidly. For a minute he remained tight-lipped, and did not speak. Hélène looked anxiously at him. When he saw this imploring look from her mother, he murmured:

'It's not serious... But you mustn't leave her here. She needs air.'

Hélène hoisted her on to her shoulders. She could have kissed the doctor's hands for his reassuring words and waves of relief coursed through her. But scarcely had she placed Jeanne in her big bed when the little girl's body shook with violent convulsions. The doctor had taken off the lampshade, a white light illuminated the room. He went over and opened the window a little, ordered Rosalie to pull the bed away from the curtains. Hélène, again overwhelmed with anxiety, stammered:

'She's dying, Doctor! Look at her, look at her! I can't recognize her!'

He did not answer, but keenly studied the progress of the attack.

'Go into the recess and hold her hands so that she doesn't scratch herself... There, gently, be careful not to hurt her. Don't worry, the crisis must take its course.'

And both, leaning over the bed, held Jeanne, whose limbs were slackening in a series of abrupt shocks. The doctor had buttoned up his waistcoat to cover his bare neck. Hélène had remained wrapped in the shawl she had thrown around her shoulders. But Jeanne, flailing around her, tugged at a corner of the shawl and undid the top of the waistcoat. They were unaware of it. Neither was conscious of the other.

The attack was nearly over. The little girl, exhausted, seemed to collapse. Despite the doctor's reassurance to her mother about the outcome of the crisis, he still looked thoughtful. He continued to study the sick child and finally asked Hélène some questions as he stood by her bed.

'How old is she?'

'Eleven and a half, Monsieur.'

There was a silence. He nodded, leaned down to raise Jeanne's closed eyelids and look inside. Then he continued his questioning, without looking directly at Hélène.

'Did she have convulsions when she was small?'

'Yes, Doctor, but they subsided when she was about six... She's very delicate. I've noticed that she has been unwell these last few days.'

'Do you know of any nervous illnesses in the family?'

'I don't know... My mother died of a chest infection.'

She hesitated, overcome with shame, not wanting to admit to having had a relative locked up in an asylum.* Her whole family had a tragic history.

'Careful,' said the doctor rapidly. 'She's having another attack.'

Jeanne had just opened her eyes. Bewildered, she looked about her for a moment, without uttering a word. Then her eyes started to stare, she threw herself backwards, her limbs tensed and stiffened. She was very flushed. Suddenly she went white, livid, and began to convulse.

'Keep hold of her,' the doctor directed. 'Take her other hand.'

He hurried to the side table, on which he had put a little array of medicaments. He came back with a bottle, which he held to her nose. But it was like a whiplash, Jeanne shook so hard she jerked out of her mother's hands.

'No, no, not ether!' her mother cried, when she smelled the bottle. 'Ether drives her mad.'

The two of them could scarcely hold her. Her contractions were violent, her body raised up on her heels and on her neck, as if bent double. Then she fell back, she ranged from one side of the bed to the other. Her fists were tight shut, her thumbs turned in towards her palms; from time to time she opened them and spread out her fingers, attempting to seize things in thin air and twist them. Her fingers found her mother's shawl and clung on to it. But the most upsetting thing for her mother was, as she said, that she couldn't recognize her daughter any more. Her sweet little angelic face was utterly changed, her eyes, a bluish pearly colour, were sunk in their sockets.

'Do something, I beg you, Doctor,' she whispered. 'I haven't the strength any more...' She had just remembered that the daughter of one of her neighbours in Marseilles had died of asphyxiation in a similar crisis. Perhaps the doctor was withholding the truth, to spare her? Jeanne's breathing was sporadic and halting so that the mother thought every breath she felt on her face might be her last. Then in despair, and overwhelmed by pity and terror, she wept. Her tears fell on the innocent naked body of the little girl, who had thrown back the covers.

Meanwhile the doctor's long supple fingers were applying light pressure to the base of her neck. The intensity of the attack was lessening. Jeanne's movements grew slower and then she remained inert. She had fallen back into the centre of the bed, her body taut and her arms spread wide, her head propped up by the pillow, lolling on to her chest. She looked like an infant Christ. Hélène bent down and gave her a long kiss on her forehead.

'Is it over?' she asked in a small voice. 'Do you think there will be another attack?'

He made an evasive gesture. Then replied:

'Well, further attacks will be less violent anyway.'

He asked Rosalie for a glass and a jug. He half-filled the glass, took two new flasks, counted out the drops and, with Hélène's help, raising the child's head, inserted a spoonful of this potion in between her clenched teeth. The white flame of the lamp rose high, lighting the untidy room, in which some of the furniture had been knocked over. The clothes Hélène had thrown down on the back of a chair when she went to bed had slipped on to the floor and lay on the rug. Having trodden on a bodice, the doctor picked it up so that it shouldn't get under his feet again. The scent of verbena wafted up from the unmade bed and from these few underclothes. All the intimate possessions of this woman were on shocking display. The doctor himself went to fetch the basin, soaked a towel, and applied it to Jeanne's temples.

'You'll catch cold, Madame,' Rosalie said, shivering. 'Perhaps we should shut the window... It's very chilly.'

'No, no,' Hélène cried. 'Leave the window open... That's right, Doctor, isn't it?'

A little breeze came through, lifting the curtains. She was unaware of it, yet the shawl had completely fallen off her shoulders, uncovering part of her bosom. At the back of her head, her chignon had worked loose and disordered strands of hair were hanging down to her hips. Her bare arms had freed themselves in order to move more quickly and she forgot everything in the total devotion to caring for her child. Beside her, the doctor was quite unaware of his open waist-coat, or his collar that Jeanne had just torn off.

'Lift her up a little,' he said. 'No, not that way... Give me your hand.'

He took her hand and placed it himself under the head of the little girl, whom he was trying to induce to take another spoonful of the medicine. Then he got her to come over next to him. He was using her as an assistant and she obeyed him religiously, seeing that her daughter appeared to be more calm.

'Come here... You put her head on your shoulder while I listen to her chest.'

Hélène did what he ordered. Then he bent over her to place his ear on Jeanne's chest. He touched her bare shoulder lightly with his cheek, and as he listened to the child's heart he might also have heard the mother's beating. When he stood up again their breaths mingled.

'Nothing wrong there,' he said quietly, much to Hélène's relief. 'Put her back to bed, we won't torment her any more.'

But a fresh attack occurred. It was much less serious. Jeanne mumbled a few halting words. Two more spasms one after the other came and went. The child had fallen into a state of prostration, and that seemed to make the doctor anxious once more. He had laid her down with her head raised high, the covers pulled up under her chin, and for almost an hour he stayed watching her, appearing to be waiting for the regular sound of her breathing. From the other side of the bed, Hélène also waited, not moving.

Gradually a deep peace stole over Jeanne's face. The lamp lit her with its soft yellow light. Her face returned to its lovely oval shape, slightly elongated, as graceful and fine as a young fawn's. You could imagine the dark expression of her closed eyes under their wide, blue, translucent lids. The breath came lightly from her small nose, her rather wide mouth wore a vague smile. And so she slept, her hair, black as ink, spread out like a cloth around her.

'It's over this time,' the doctor said in a low voice. And he turned to put away his bottles, getting ready to leave. Hélène went over to him.

'Oh, Doctor,' she begged, 'don't leave me. Wait a few minutes. If she were to have another attack... You are the one who has saved her.'

He indicated that now there was nothing to worry about. But he stayed, wanting to reassure her. She had sent Rosalie back to bed.

Soon daylight came, a soft grey light on the snow that whitened the roofs. The doctor went over and closed the window. And the two of them exchanged a few whispered words, in the deep silence.

'It's not serious, I assure you,' he was saying. 'Only at her age you have to be very careful... Make sure that she's leading a regular life, is happy, and doesn't get upset.'

After a moment it was Hélène's turn to say:

'She's so delicate, so nervous... I don't always have any influence on her. She gets joyful or sad over the most trivial things, it worries me, they are so intense... She loves me with a jealous passion; it makes her weep when I kiss another child.'

He nodded, repeating:

'Yes, yes. Delicate, nervous, jealous... It's Doctor Bodin who looks after her, isn't it? I'll talk to him about her. We'll put her on a course of intense treatment. She is at a stage in her life which will determine her health when she's a woman.'

When she saw he was so trustworthy, Hélène had a surge of gratitude:

'Oh, Monsieur, thank you so much for all the trouble you have taken!'

Then, having raised her voice, she went and leaned over the bed, afraid she had woken Jeanne. The child was asleep, flushed pink, a vague smile on her lips. In the bedroom, now restored to calm, there was a feeling of languor. It was as though a quiet, comfortable lassitude had returned to the curtains, the furniture, the scattered clothes. Everything seemed to relax, as if swallowed up by the light of dawn coming in through the two windows.

Once again Hélène was standing by the bed. The doctor was on the other side. And between them was Jeanne, slumbering, breathing lightly.

'Her father was often ill,' Hélène went on quietly, returning to his question. 'I have always been in good health.'

The doctor, who had not yet looked at her at all, raised his eyes and could not help smiling, she seemed to him so strong and healthy. She smiled back, a happy, quiet smile. She enjoyed her good health.

Meanwhile his eyes remained on her. He had never seen a woman with such a regular, beautiful face. She was Junoesque, tall, magnificent, with golden lights in her chestnut hair. When she slowly turned her head, her profile took on the gravity of a statue. Her grey eyes and white teeth lit up her entire face. She had a round chin, a little pronounced, which gave her a look of common sense and determination. But what surprised the doctor was her superb figure. The shawl had slipped down again, her shoulders were uncovered, her arms were bare. A thick plait, the colour of burnished gold, hung down her shoulder and disappeared between her breasts. And in her half-undone petticoat, with her hair untidy and disarranged, she yet retained her stateliness, a decent, honest dignity, chaste beneath this male gaze, which was beginning to disturb him greatly.

For a moment she studied him too. Doctor Deberle was a man of thirty-five, with a longish, clean-shaven face, an intelligent expression and thin lips. As she looked at him she, in her turn, noticed his neck was bare. And they remained there face to face with little Jeanne asleep between them. But this space, which had been immense a little while ago, seemed to have got smaller. The child's breath was too light. Then Hélène slowly pulled up her shawl and wrapped it around her, while the doctor buttoned up the collar of his waistcoat.

'Maman, Maman,' stammered the child in her sleep.

She was waking. When she opened her eyes she saw the doctor and was worried.

'Who is that? Who is that?' she asked.

But her mother gave her a kiss.

'Go to sleep, darling, you were a bit poorly... He's a friend.'

The child seemed surprised. She remembered nothing. Sleep came over her again and she dozed off, murmuring fondly:

'Oh, I'm so sleepy!... Goodnight, Mother dear... If he's your friend, he'll be mine too.'

The doctor had cleared away his array of medicines. He quietly said goodbye and left. Hélène listened to the child's breathing for a moment. Then she sat on the edge of the bed, gazing at nothing, lost in her thoughts. The lamp, left burning, paled in the light of day.

CHAPTER 2

NEXT day Hélène thought it would be polite to go and thank Doctor Deberle. The hasty manner in which she had forced him to come with her, the good turn he had done her in spending that whole night at Jeanne's bedside, embarrassed her when she thought about it—it seemed to her beyond the call of duty for a doctor. However, she hesitated for a couple of days, reluctant to go, for reasons she could not quite articulate. While in this state of indecision, she was busy thinking about the doctor; one morning she saw him and hid, like a child. She was cross with herself afterwards for being so timid. Her calm, forthright character was at variance with this emotion that had entered her life. So she decided she would go and thank the doctor that very day.

Her little daughter's crisis had taken place in the night of Tuesday to Wednesday, and it was now Saturday. Jeanne had completely recovered. Doctor Bodin, much concerned, had hurried over to visit, and spoken of Doctor Deberle with the reverence a poor old local doctor has for a young, well-off colleague who has already made a name for himself. But he let people know, with a sly smile, that his money came from his father, Monsieur Deberle, a man venerated by the whole of Passy. The son had simply had the trouble of inheriting one and a half million francs and a superb clientele. A clever boy, though, Doctor Bodin was quick to add, with whom he would be honoured to consult on the subject of the precious health of his young friend Jeanne.

Towards three o'clock, Hélène and her daughter went down and had gone only a few steps along the Rue Vineuse before they were ringing the bell at the big house next door. Both were still in deep mourning. A uniformed servant in a white tie opened the door. Hélène recognized the wide hall hung with oriental door-curtains; but now she could see a multitude of flowers to right and left blooming in the jardinières. The valet ushered them into a small sitting room with dark green hangings and furniture, and stood waiting. Hélène gave her name.

'Madame Grandjean.'

The servant opened the door to an extraordinarily bright yellow and black salon, before withdrawing and repeating:

'Madame Grandjean.'

Hélène, in the doorway, shrank back a moment. She had just caught sight of a young lady at the other end of the room, sitting by the fire with her wide skirts taking up the whole of a narrow sofa. Opposite her, an elderly person, still wearing her hat and shawl, was visiting.

'I'm sorry,' Hélène faltered, 'I was hoping to see Doctor Deberle.'

And she caught hold of her daughter's hand, having ushered her into the room in front of her. She was surprised and embarrassed to have intruded on this lady in this fashion. Why had she not asked for the doctor? She knew he was married.

Madame Deberle was just finishing an anecdote in a rapid and rather shrill voice:

'Oh, she's marvellous, just marvellous!... She dies so realistically!... Look, she clutches at her breast like this, throws her head back, and turns green... I swear you have to go and see it, Mademoiselle Aurélie.'

She rose then and came over to the door with a loud rustling of skirts, and said with a charmingly courteous manner:

'Do come in, Madame... My husband isn't at home... But you are most welcome, most welcome... And this must be the beautiful young lady who was so poorly the other night... Do come and sit down a moment.'

Hélène was obliged to sit in an armchair, while Jeanne perched shyly on the edge of a seat. Madame Deberle had sunk once more on to her small sofa, adding with a pretty laugh:

'It's my *day*. Yes, I have people round on Saturdays... Pierre introduces them. The week before last he brought along a colonel who had gout.'

'You are mad, Juliette!' murmured Mademoiselle Aurélie, the stiff elderly lady, an old and indigent friend, who had known her from the cradle.

There was a short silence. Hélène looked around at the richly furnished salon, the curtains and the black and gold seats that shone bright as stars. Flowers bloomed on the mantelpiece, the piano, the tables, and the daylight from the garden came in through the windows, through which you could see the leafless trees and the bare earth. It was very warm, the stove giving out an even heat and in the hearth one single log burning away to ashes. Then, with another glance, Hélène realized that the flame-coloured salon was a decor that had been chosen with taste.

Madame Deberle had jet-black hair and a skin as white as milk. She was small, dimpled, relaxed, and graceful. In all this gold, under her heavy dark coiffure, her pale complexion was lit by a rosy blush. Hélène thought her really lovely.

'Convulsions are terrible,' drawled Madame Deberle. 'My little boy Lucien had them, but it was when he was a baby... You must have been so worried, Madame! Well, the dear child seems quite well again now.'

And she in her turn looked at Hélène, surprised and delighted by her beauty. She had never seen a woman of such regal splendour, her black mourning draping her tall, grave figure. Her admiration was expressed in an involuntary smile, while she exchanged glances with Mademoiselle Aurélie. The two women studied her with such open admiration that Hélène also smiled.

Then Madame Deberle lay back comfortably on her sofa and, taking the fan which hung from her sash, asked:

'You didn't go to the premiere at the Vaudeville* yesterday, Madame?'

'I never go to the theatre,' Hélène replied.

'Oh, young Noëmi was wonderful, just wonderful! Her death is so realistic! She clutches at her bodice like this, throws back her head, turns quite green... The effect is remarkable.'

For a minute or two she discussed the actress's performance—approvingly, moreover. Then she went on to the other things happening in Paris, a painting exhibition where she had seen some amazing canvases, a silly novel that was receiving a great deal of publicity, some risqué affair which she hinted at to Mademoiselle Aurélie. And she passed from one subject to the next, tirelessly, rapidly, reliving it, in her element. Hélène, a stranger to this world, simply listened and now and then uttered a word or made a brief remark.

The door opened and the valet announced:

'Madame de Chermettes... Madame Tissot...'

Two very smartly-dressed ladies came in. Madame Deberle went forward eagerly. And the train of her much-ornamented black silk dress was so long that she had to sweep it out of the way with her heel every time she turned round. For a short time there was a rapid chattering of shrill voices.

'How lovely to see you! It's been so long...'

'We've come about this lottery, you know.'

'Yes, of course, of course.'

'Oh, we mustn't stay. We have twenty more houses to do.'

'Oh no, you can't go yet.'

And the two ladies perched on the edge of a sofa. Then the shrill voices piped up again, at an even higher pitch.

'Well, what did you think of the Vaudeville?'

'Oh, superb!'

'You know how she unfastens her hair and lets it down. That creates the whole effect.'

'They say she takes something to make herself turn green.'

'No no, the movements are carefully worked out... But they had to be planned beforehand.'

'Marvellous!'

The two ladies had risen. They vanished. The salon resumed its cosy tranquillity. On the mantelpiece hyacinths exhaled their penetrating perfume. A quarrelsome flock of sparrows could be heard for a moment fighting as they landed on the lawn. Before she took a seat, Madame Deberle went over and pulled down the embroidered tulle blind on a window opposite. And she took up her place again in the now softer gold of the salon.

'I do beg your pardon,' she said. 'We are being invaded.'

And she went on comfortably chatting to Hélène in the most affectionate tones. She appeared to know something of her background, no doubt through the servants' talking in the house, which belonged to her. With some boldness but also with tact, she spoke sympathetically of Hélène's husband and of his terrible death in a hotel in the Rue de Richelieu, the Hôtel du Var.

'And you had just arrived, hadn't you? You hadn't been to Paris before... It must be dreadful to be in mourning amongst strangers the day after a long journey, when you don't yet know your way around.' Hélène nodded slowly. Yes, she had spent many terrible hours then. The illness which was to carry her husband off had declared itself suddenly the day after their arrival, just when they were about to go out. She wasn't familiar with a single street, she didn't even know which *quartier* she was in; and for a week she had stayed shut up with the dying man, listening to Paris rumbling beneath her window, feeling alone, abandoned, lost, in the depths of her solitude. The thought of that great bare room full of medicine bottles where the trunks were not even unpacked still made her shudder.

'They say your husband was almost twice your age?' Madame Deberle asked with an air of deep interest, while Mademoiselle Aurélie pricked up her ears so as not to miss anything.

'No no,' Hélène answered. 'He was scarcely six years older than me.'

And she went so far as to tell the history of her marriage in a few sentences: how her husband had fallen deeply in love with her when she was living with her father, Mouret, the hatmaker,* in the Rue des Petites-Maries in Marseilles; how the Grandjeans, a rich family of

refiners exasperated by the poverty of his young lady, had been very
much opposed to the marriage; and how they had married in haste,
without telling anyone, after the banns were read, and had lived on
very little until the day when a dying uncle had left them about ten
thousand francs. It was then that Grandjean, who nurtured a hatred
for Marseilles, had decided they would come and live in Paris.

'So how old were you when you got married?' Madame Deberle
enquired.

'Seventeen.'

'You must have been so beautiful.'

The conversation lapsed. Hélène had apparently not heard her.

'Madame Manguelin,' announced the valet.

A young woman appeared, discreet and embarrassed. It was one of
her protégées who had come to thank her for something she had done.
She stayed only a few minutes and curtseyed as she left.

Then Madame Deberle took up the conversation again, speaking
of Abbé Jouve, whom both knew. He was a humble priest of Notre-
Dame-de-Grâce in the parish of Passy, but his charitable works made
him the most beloved and respected in the area.

'Oh, the sweetest man!' she murmured with a look of devotion.

'He was very good to us,' said Hélène. 'My husband used to know
him in Marseilles... As soon as he knew about my misfortune he took
charge of everything. He's the one who found us lodgings in Passy.'

'Does he not have a brother?' enquired Juliette.

'Yes, his mother remarried.'

'Monsieur Rambaud also knew my husband. He set up shop in the
Rue de Rambuteau specializing in oils and products from the South
of France, and is making a lot of money, I believe.'

Then she added gaily:

'The abbé and his brother are my only admirers!'

Jeanne, getting bored sitting on the edge of her chair, was eyeing
her mother with impatience. Her delicate face, which resembled
a young fawn's, showed signs of distress, as though she did not want
to hear the things that were being talked about. And at times she
seemed to be breathing in the heavy, suffocating scents of the salon,
throwing sidelong glances at the furniture, mistrustful, as though
warned of hidden dangers by her extreme sensitivity. Then she
brought her gaze back to her mother with a tyrannical adoration.

Madame Deberle could see the young girl was ill at ease.

'Here's a little girl who is bored with being sensible like a grown-up... Look, there are some picture books on that little table.'

Jeanne went to pick up an album; but her eyes, above the book, kept lighting on her mother, pleading with her. Hélène, won over by the welcome she was receiving, did not move. She was naturally calm and would willingly sit for hours. But when the valet announced three ladies, one after the other—Madame Berthier, Madame de Guiraud, and Madame Levasseur—she thought she should take her leave. But Madame Deberle cried:

'Do stay, I must introduce my son to you.'

The circle around the hearth grew wider. All these ladies talked at once. There was one who said she was 'all in'. And she told them how, for the last five days, she had not gone to bed until four in the morning. Another was complaining bitterly about her nurses. You couldn't get one who was trustworthy. Then the conversation turned to dressmakers. Madame Deberle was of the opinion that a woman couldn't dress one satisfactorily; you needed a man. Meanwhile two women were whispering between themselves, and as there was a break in the conversation, you could hear three or four words. They all began to laugh and fan themselves in a languid fashion.

'Monsieur Malignon,' announced the servant.

A tall young man arrived, dressed very correctly. He was greeted with cries. Madame Deberle, without getting up, held out her hand, saying:

'Well, what do you think of yesterday's Vaudeville?'

'Terrible!' he cried.

'What do you mean!... She was marvellous. When she clutched at her dress and threw back her head...'

'Oh, don't! Such realism is disgusting.'

A discussion ensued. There were many kinds of realism. But the young man would have none of them.

'None whatsoever, do you understand?' he said, raising his voice. 'None! Art is degraded by realism.'

They'd see some choice things in the theatre before long! Why shouldn't Noëmi push things to the limits? And he made a gesture that scandalized all the ladies. They were horrified. But when Madame Deberle had said her piece about the prodigious effect produced by the actress and Madame Levasseur had told everyone that a woman had swooned on the balcony, they all agreed it was a great success. At this, the conversation came to an abrupt halt.

The young man, in an armchair, reclined among the spreading skirts. He seemed to be very much at home in the doctor's house. He had idly picked a flower out of the jardinière and was chewing it. Madame Deberle asked him:

'Have you read the novel...?'

Without letting her finish he replied in a superior tone:

'I only read two novels a year.'

As for the exhibition at the Arts Circle, it really wasn't worth going out of your way to see it. Then, when all the subjects of the day had been exhausted, he came and leaned over Juliette's small sofa and exchanged a few hushed words with her, while the rest of the ladies chattered brightly among themselves.

'Oh my goodness, he's gone!' cried Madame Berthier, turning round. 'I came across him an hour ago at Madame Robinot's.'

'Yes, and he visits Madame Lecomte too,' said Madame Deberle. 'He's the busiest man in Paris.'

And addressing herself to Hélène, who had witnessed the exchange, she continued:

'He's a very distinguished young man, a favourite of ours... He's involved in stockbroking—moreover, he's very wealthy and knows everybody's affairs.'

The ladies left.

'Goodbye, dear Madame, I hope we shall see you on Wednesday.'

'Yes, that's right, till Wednesday.'

'Tell me, shall we see you at that soirée? You never know who might be there. I shall go if you do.'

'Well yes, I'll go, I promise. Give Monsieur de Guiraud my kind regards.'

When Madame Deberle came back she found Hélène standing in the middle of the salon. Jeanne was flattened against her mother, holding her hand, her fingers tugging her little by little in the direction of the door.

'Ah, yes,' said the mistress of the house.

She rang for the servant.

'Pierre, tell Mademoiselle Smithson to bring Lucien here.'

And in the short interval they were waiting, the door opened again unceremoniously, without anyone being announced. A lovely girl of sixteen came in, followed by a small elderly man with puffy cheeks.

'Hello, Sister,' said the girl, kissing Madame Deberle.

'Hello, Pauline... Hello, Father...,' she replied.

Mademoiselle Aurélie, who had not budged from the chimney corner, got up to greet Monsieur Letellier. He kept a big shop that sold silks on the Boulevard des Capucines. Since the death of his wife, he took his younger daughter everywhere in his efforts to find her a rich husband.

'Were you at the Vaudeville yesterday?' Pauline asked.

'It was amazing!' Juliette repeated mechanically, standing in front of a mirror, in the process of capturing a rebellious curl.

Pauline pouted like a spoiled child.

'It's so annoying to be a girl, you can't go to anything!... I went as far as the door with Papa at midnight to see how the play had been received.'

'Yes,' said her father. 'We met Malignon. He said it was very good.'

'What!' Juliette cried. 'He was here a little while ago, he said he thought it was dreadful... You never know where you are with him.'

'Did you have many visitors?' Pauline asked, leaping abruptly to another subject.

'Oh, all those ladies, it was quite mad! They stayed and stayed. I'm exhausted.'

Then, thinking she was forgetting to make formal introductions, she broke off:

'My father and sister... Madame Grandjean...'

And they had just begun a conversation about children and their bumps that mothers get so anxious about, when Miss Smithson, an English governess, came in holding a little boy by the hand. Madame Deberle said a few rapid words to her in English, reprimanding her for keeping them waiting.

'Oh, here's my little Lucien!' cried Pauline, kneeling down to the child, with a loud rustle of skirts.

'Let him alone,' Juliette said. 'Come here, Lucien. Come and say hello to this young lady.'

The little boy came forward, shyly. He was at most seven years old, sturdy and short, dressed up like a little doll. When he saw that everyone was smiling at him, he stopped and, wide-eyed, studied Jeanne.

'Go on,' his mother murmured.

He glanced at her, took another step forward. He displayed that heaviness that boys have, his shoulders hunched, his lips thick and sulky, his eyebrows suspicious and slightly frowning. He must have been intimidated by Jeanne because she looked serious, pale, and was dressed in black from head to toe.

'You be nice to him as well, dear,' said Hélène, seeing her daughter stiffen.

The little girl had not let go her mother's wrist, and her fingers stroked her skin between the sleeve and the glove. Her head bowed, she waited for Lucien with the worried expression of a nervous girl unused to society, ready to escape at any physical contact. However, when her mother gave her a gentle push she took a step forward too.

'You must kiss him, Mademoiselle,' Madame Deberle said with a laugh. 'Ladies always have to make the first move with him. Oh, the silly little boy!'

'Kiss him, Jeanne!' said Hélène.

The child raised her eyes to look at her mother. Then, as though won over by his dull expression, and suddenly sympathetic to his patent embarrassment, she gave him a charming smile. Her face suddenly lit up with deep emotion.

'Of course, Maman,' she murmured.

And taking hold of Lucien by the shoulders, almost lifting him up, she planted a firm kiss on both cheeks. He was happy to kiss her after that.

'Well done!' cried everybody present.

Hélène said her goodbyes and made for the door, accompanied by Madame Deberle.

'Please give my sincerest thanks to the doctor, Madame... He saved me from my worst fears the other night.'

'So is Henri not here?' Monsieur Letellier broke in.

'No, he'll be back late,' replied Juliette.

And seeing Mademoiselle Aurélie get up to leave with Madame Grandjean, she added:

'But you must stay and dine with us, of course.'

The old spinster, who expected this invitation each Saturday, decided to take off her shawl and hat. It was hot and stuffy in the salon. Monsieur Letellier had just opened a window, and remained standing in front of it, very taken by a lilac which was already in bloom. Pauline was playing a game of chase with Lucien, in amongst the chairs and armchairs, which were in disarray after the visits.

On the threshold, Madame Deberle held out her hand to Hélène, in a frank, friendly gesture.

'If I may...', she said. 'My husband spoke to me about you, I felt drawn towards you. Your bad luck, your being on your own... In short, I am very happy to have made your acquaintance and I hope we shall get to know one another better.'

'I promise, and I am grateful to you,' answered Hélène, deeply touched by this impulsive display of affection from a woman who had struck her before as somewhat scatterbrained.

They did not let go their hands but smiled at each other. Juliette warmly declared the reason for her sudden friendliness:

'You are so beautiful, everyone is bound to love you!'

Hélène laughed happily, for her beauty did not trouble her. She called to Jeanne who was absorbed in watching Lucien and Pauline playing. But Madame Deberle kept the little girl a moment longer, saying:

'You are good friends from now on, say goodbye.'

And the two children blew one another a kiss.

CHAPTER 3

EVERY Tuesday Hélène had Monsieur Rambaud and Abbé Jouve to dinner. They were the ones who, when she had just been widowed, had insisted on making regular visits and, with a friendly informality, sitting at her supper table at least once a week, to draw her out of her solitude. After that, these Tuesday dinners had become a regular institution. The guests met, as though performing a duty, at the precise stroke of seven, always with the same warmth and contentment.

That Tuesday Hélène was sitting by the window, working on some sewing, making the most of the last rays of the setting sun, as she waited for her guests. She spent her days there in sweet tranquillity. Noise scarcely reached her up there, on the hill . She liked this huge, peaceful room with its homely luxury, its rosewood and its blue velvet. During those first few weeks when her friends had furnished it, without consulting her, she had not been especially pleased by this excess of comfort, in which Monsieur Rambaud—to the great admiration of the abbé, who had declined to intervene—had indulged his own ideas of art and luxury to the maximum. But she had come round to liking her surroundings very much, feeling them to be solid and simple, like herself. The heavy curtains, the dark, comfortable furniture, gave her added peace of mind. The only recreation she took during those long hours of work was to cast her eyes on the vast horizon, the great city with its turbulent sea of roofs spreading out before her. Her solitude opened out on to this immense vista.

'Maman, it's too dark to see,' said Jeanne, seated on a low chair beside her.

And she dropped her work, looking out at Paris as it slowly descended into darkness. She was generally a quiet child. Her mother had to get cross in order to make her go out. On the strict orders of Doctor Bodin, she took her for a walk in the Bois de Boulogne two hours each day. And that was their only outing; they had not ventured out into Paris three times in the last eighteen months. It was in the big blue room that the little girl seemed happiest. Hélène had been forced to give up teaching her music. A barrel organ playing in the quiet neighbourhood made her shake and tears would come into her eyes. She helped her mother sew layettes for Abbé Jouve's poor. When Rosalie came in with the lamp, night had fallen. She seemed to be in a rush and a fluster over her cooking. The Tuesday dinner was the one excitement in the household's week.

'Are the gentlemen not coming this evening, Madame?' she asked.

Hélène looked at the clock.

'It's a quarter to seven, they'll be here soon.'

Rosalie was a gift from Abbé Jouve. He had taken her on at the Gare d'Orléans the day she arrived, so she wasn't familiar with any locality in Paris. She had been sent by a former colleague from the seminary, a priest from a village in the Beauce. She was short and plump, with a round face beneath her narrow bonnet; she had coarse black hair, a snub nose, and a red mouth. And she was excellent at preparing little dishes, for she had grown up in the presbytery with her godmother, the priest's servant.

'Ah, there's Monsieur Rambaud!' she said, going to open the door before he had a chance to ring.

Monsieur Rambaud appeared, tall and gaunt, with a face like a country lawyer's. He was forty-five, already going grey. But his wide blue eyes, naive and gentle as a child's, still had a wondering look.

'And here is Monsieur l'Abbé, so we are all here!' Rosalie said, opening the door again.

While Monsieur Rambaud shook Hélène's hand and sat down quietly, smiling like a man quite at home, Jeanne had thrown herself on the abbé.

'Hullo, dear Abbé!' she said. 'I've been very poorly.'

'Very poorly, my little one!'

The two men expressed concern, especially the abbé, a shrunken little man with a large head, dressed without any regard to his appearance, and whose half-closed eyes grew large and filled with tenderness. Jeanne relinquished one of his hands and offered the other to Monsieur Rambaud. Both men held them and bestowed anxious looks upon her. Hélène had to tell the tale of the crisis. The priest almost got cross because she had not let him know about it before. And they plied her with questions: was it over now, at least? Had nothing more befallen the little girl? Her mother smiled.

'You care for her more than I do, you'll frighten me,' she said. 'No, there were no repercussions, just a few aches and pains, and a heaviness in her head. But we are going to wage war against that.'

'Madame is served,' announced the maid.

The dining room was furnished with a mahogany table, sideboard, and eight chairs. Rosalie went over and closed the red rep curtains. A very simple pendant lamp of white porcelain in a copper ring hung above the tablecloth, the neat row of plates, and steaming soup. Every Tuesday the dinner generated the same conversations. But that day they naturally chatted about Doctor Deberle. Abbé Jouve praised him to the skies although the doctor wasn't at all religious. He spoke of him as a man of good character, with a warm heart, an excellent father and husband, in short, an example to us all. As to Madame Deberle, she was a very fine woman, if a little effervescent, a trait which resulted from her slightly unconventional education in Paris. In a word, they were a charming couple. This made Hélène happy. She had judged them to be so, and the abbé's words encouraged her to continue the friendship which she had at first found a little intimidating.

'You don't go out enough,' declared the priest.

'That's true,' Monsieur Rambaud affirmed.

Hélène smiled at them quietly, as much as to say that they were all she needed and she was chary of meeting new people. But ten o'clock chimed, the priest and his brother picked up their hats. Jeanne had just fallen asleep in an armchair in the bedroom. They bent over her a moment, nodded with an air of satisfaction at seeing her so peacefully asleep. Then they tiptoed out, and in the hall, lowering their voices, they said:

'Till Tuesday.'

'I nearly forgot,' whispered the priest who had come back up the two steps. 'Old Mother Fétu is poorly. You ought to go and see her.'

'I'll go tomorrow,' Hélène replied.

The priest often sent her to visit his poor parishioners. They had all sorts of quiet conversations together about their concerns, which they did not need to spell out to one another and never mentioned to anyone else. Next day Hélène went out alone. She avoided taking Jeanne with her, since the child had not stopped trembling for two whole days after returning from a charitable visit to an old man with paralysis. Once outside she went along the Rue Vineuse, took the Rue Raynouard and down into the Passage des Eaux, a curious, narrow flight of steps squeezed in between neighbouring gardens, a steep little passageway leading down to the river from the heights of Passy. At the bottom of this hill, in a dilapidated house lived old Mother Fétu, in an attic room lit by a small dormer window, where a wretched bed, a rickety table, and a chair with the stuffing coming out occupied the entire space.

'Oh, dear lady, dear lady...' she began to groan when she saw Hélène.

Old Mother Fétu was in bed. Her roundness belied her poverty; her face was swollen and puffy, and she pulled up the ragged sheet covering her with numb fingers. She had little beady eyes, a whining voice, a strident humility that manifested itself in an outpouring of words.

'Oh, thank you, dear lady! Oh, my life, how I suffer! It's just like hounds eating away at my side... Oh yes, I've got a beast in my belly. Look, right there. Not on the outside, the pain's inside... Oh, it's been like that for two days. Oh my Lord, can a body bear so much... Oh, thank you, good lady, you haven't forgotten us poor people. You'll get your reward, oh, you will.'

Hélène sat down. Then, seeing a pot of herb tea steaming on the table, she filled a cup beside it and held it out to the sick woman. By the pot there was a packet of sugar, two oranges, other sweetmeats.

'Someone has been to see you?' she enquired.

'Yes, a lady. But she didn't know... I don't need all that stuff. Oh, if only I had a bit of meat! The neighbour could put a stew on... Oh, there, it hurts more. You'd think a hound was biting me, I tell you. Oh, if I had a drop of soup.'

And despite writhing with the pain, she eyed Hélène sharply as she

put her hands in her pocket. When she saw her put a ten-franc coin
on the table, the effort of sitting up brought forth more groans. She
struggled to put her hand out and the coin disappeared, while she
said over and over again:

'Oh my Lord, another attack's coming on. I can't be enduring it
much longer. God will make it up to you, dear lady, I'll tell Him to
make it up to you. I've got shooting pains through my whole body...
Monsieur l'Abbé promised me you'd come. You're the only one who
knows what to do. I'm going to buy a bit of meat. Now it's going down
into my legs. Help me, help me, I can't bear it!'

She tried to turn over. Hélène took off her gloves, caught hold of
her as gently as she could and laid her down again. As she was still
bent over her, the door opened and she was so surprised to see Doctor
Deberle come in that she blushed. So he too had visits he didn't tell
people about!

'It's the doctor,' muttered the old woman. 'You are so good to me,
God bless you all!'

The doctor had quietly acknowledged Hélène. Since his arrival old
Mother Fétu's groans had not been so loud. The only sound she made
was a continual little whistling, like a child in pain. She had seen that
the good lady and the doctor knew each other, and she kept her eyes
constantly fixed on them, the myriad lines on her face working silently
as she looked from one to the other. The doctor asked her a few questions, tapped her right side. Then, turning to Hélène, who had just sat
down again, he murmured:

'It's ulcerative colitis. She'll be on her feet again in a few days.'

And, tearing out a page from his notebook on which he had written
a few lines, he said to old Mother Fétu:

'Here you are, send someone with it to the pharmacist in the Rue
de Passy, and take a spoonful of the medicine he gives you every two
hours.'

At that point the old woman again started to invoke the Almighty's
blessing. Hélène remained in her seat. The doctor seemed to pause
a moment to look at her, and their eyes met. Then he said goodbye
and was the first to leave, discreetly. He had scarcely got to the floor
below when Mother Fétu began groaning again.

'Oh, what a lovely doctor! Let's hope his remedy cures me! I should
have crushed a tallow candle with some dandelions, that gets rid
of the water in your body. Oh, you know a good doctor there, sure

enough! Perhaps you've known him a good while? Oh my lord, I'm thirsty! My blood's on fire... He's married, isn't he? He deserves to have a good wife and beautiful children. Well anyhow, it's good to see nice folks who know one another.'

Hélène stood up to give her a drink.

'Well, goodbye, Mother Fétu,' she said. 'I'll see you tomorrow.'

'That's right... How kind you are... If only I had some decent linen! Look at my chemise, it's coming to bits. I'm lying on a dungheap... No matter, the good Lord will make it up to you.'

The next day when Hélène arrived at Mother Fétu's, Doctor Deberle was there. He was sitting on a chair, writing out a prescription while the garrulous old woman gabbled away in her weepy fashion.

'Now it feels like a lead weight, Doctor. I must have lead in my side. It weighs a ton, I can't turn over.'

But when she saw Hélène she couldn't stop.

'Oh, here's the dear lady... I was just telling this good man, she'll be coming, she'll be coming even if the sky falls down... A real saint, an angel from paradise, and lovely, so lovely you'd go down on your knees in the street when she went by... My dear lady, it's no better. Now I've got a lead weight here... Yes, I've been telling him all the things you do for me, the emperor himself couldn't do more. Oh, you'd have to be really full of wickedness not to love you, full of wickedness.'

While these words spilled out, her head turned this way and that on the bolster. Her small eyes were half-closed, the doctor was smiling at Hélène, who was very embarrassed.

'Mother Fétu,' she said, 'I was just bringing you a little linen.'

'Thank you, thank you, the dear Lord will make it up to you. Just like this dear man here, he does us poor folk more good than all the rest whose job it is to look after us. He's been tending me for four months, with medicine, broth, and wine. You don't find many rich people like him, who treat everybody so civil. Another of God's angels... Oh my, it's like a ton of bricks in my belly.'

Now the doctor appeared embarrassed too. He got up to offer his chair to Hélène. But although she had come with the intention of spending a quarter of an hour with her, she refused, saying:

'Thank you, Doctor, but I'm in a great hurry.'

In the meantime Mother Fétu, her head still turning from side to side, had stretched her arm out and the parcel of linen had disappeared under the bedclothes.

Then she continued:

'Oh, you would make a fine pair for sure. I say that not to cause offence, because it's true. You're as good as gold, both of you. Kind folk understand one another. Give me a hand to turn me over! Yes, they understand one another.'

'Goodbye, Mother Fétu,' said Hélène, giving up her seat to the doctor. 'I don't think I'll be coming tomorrow.'

But she did go down again next day. The old woman was dozing. As soon as she woke and recognized her dark figure seated on the chair, she cried:

'He came. But I don't know what he made me take, I'm as stiff as a board... Oh yes, we had a little chat about you. He asked me all kinds of things, if you were always sad, if you always looked like that. Such a nice man!'

She had started to speak more slowly, as if waiting to see what effect her words would have on Hélène, in the coaxing, anxious manner of poor people who want to be obliging. She must have thought she could detect the 'good lady' frowning, for her large puffy face, eagerly held up to her, suddenly fell. She started gabbling again:

'I sleep all the time. Perhaps I've been poisoned. There's a woman in the Rue de l'Annonciation was murdered by a pharmacist who mixed up his medicines.'

That day Hélène stayed almost half an hour at Mother Fétu's, listening to her chatter about Normandy where she had been born, and where they had such good milk to drink. After a silence she asked in a casual tone:

'Have you known the doctor long?'

The old woman lying on her back raised her eyelids a fraction and closed them again.

'To be sure!' she replied, almost in a whisper. 'His father tended me before '48 and he used to come with him.'

'They tell me his father was a saintly man.'

'Yes, yes. A little bit unbalanced. The son is even better, you know. When he touches you, you'd think he had velvet hands.'

There was another silence.

'I advise you to do everything he suggests,' Hélène continued. 'He is very clever, he saved my daughter.'

'Quite right!' cried Mother Fétu, brightening up. 'You can trust him, he resuscitated a little boy who was nearly gone. Oh, he's one in

a million, I'll say it again and again. I've struck lucky, I've landed up
with the cream of good people. And so I thank the good Lord every
evening. I shan't forget either of you, you know. You are both in my
prayers. May the good Lord keep you and grant you all you wish! May
he shower his riches upon you! May he keep you a place in paradise!'

She had sat up and with her hands together seemed to be beseech-
ing Heaven with extraordinary fervour. Hélène let her carry on like
that for some time, and a smile even played upon her lips. The garrulous humility of the old woman in the end lulled and soothed her.
When she left, she promised her a hat and dress for when she was on
her feet again.

All week Hélène looked after Mother Fétu. The visits to her every
afternoon became a habit. She had grown especially fond of the
Passage des Eaux. The steep street pleased her, its freshness and its
silence, the invariably clean cobbles washed on rainy days by a stream
running down from the heights. When she arrived at the top she had
a strange feeling as she looked down at the steeply sloping alley that
was most often deserted, since only a few people living in the streets
around knew it was there. Then she ventured down through an arch
under a house on the Rue Raynouard, and made her way gingerly
down the seven wide steps, alongside the bed of a pebbly watercourse
that took up half the narrow passage. The garden walls to left and
right bulged, eaten away by the grey damp. Branches of trees hung
over, leaves dripped, ivy draped them in a thick cloak; and all this
greenery, through which only small patches of sky were visible, created a very soft, subtle greenish light. Halfway down the hill she
stopped to draw breath, observing the street lamp hanging there, listening to the laughter in the gardens behind gates she had never seen
open. Occasionally an old woman climbed up, with the help of the
shiny black iron railing fixed to the right-hand wall; a lady leaned on
her sunshade as though it were a walking stick, or a group of boys
clattered down, clacking their boots. But almost always she was on
her own and these secret steps, shaded like a sunken lane in the woods,
held a great attraction for her. At the bottom she raised her eyes. The
sight of the steep slope she had just climbed down made her feel
a little fearful.

At Mother Fétu's her clothes still retained the freshness and peace-
fulness of the Passage des Eaux. This miserable, distressing hovel no
longer offended her. She behaved as though she were in her own

house, opening the round window to freshen the air, moving the table when it was in the way. The bareness of this attic room, the white-washed walls, the rickety furniture, took her back to the simple life she had sometimes dreamed of as a girl. But what she enjoyed most was the feeling it gave her being there; her caring role, the constant complaining of the old lady, everything she saw and felt around her filled her with immense compassion. Before long she looked forward with obvious impatience to Doctor Deberle's visit. She questioned him about Mother Fétu's health, then they chatted for a moment about other things, standing close, looking at each other. An intimacy was growing between them. They were surprised to discover they had similar tastes. They often understood one another without a word passing their lips, their hearts suddenly full of the same overflowing charity. And nothing was sweeter to Hélène than this sympathy which bound them in these unusual circumstances; she was happy to accept it, melting with compassion. She had been afraid of the doctor at first; in his drawing room she would have displayed the wary reserve natural to her. But here they were far away from the world, sharing the only chair, almost cheerful about this wretchedness and ugliness which brought them together in mutual compassion. By the end of the week they knew each other as though they had lived side by side for years. In their common kindness towards her, Mother Fétu's hovel was filled with light.

The old woman was getting better, but it was slow. The doctor was surprised and scolded her for cosseting herself when she told him that now her legs were heavy as lead. She was still on her back groaning, rolling her head from side to side, and she closed her eyes, as though to give the couple their freedom. One day she actually seemed to have fallen asleep, but under her lids those small black eyes peeped out at them from the corners. The time came when she had to get up. The next day Hélène brought her the promised dress and hat. When the doctor came she suddenly cried:

'Oh my word! The neighbour asked me to keep an eye on her stew!'

She went out and pulled the door to behind her, leaving them alone. First they carried on with their conversation, without noticing they were shut in. The doctor pressed Hélène to come down and spend the afternoon occasionally in his garden in the Rue Vineuse.

'My wife', he said, 'must return your visit, and she will renew my invitation... It would do your daughter a lot of good.'

'That would be lovely, but you don't have to issue a formal invitation,' she laughed. 'Only I'm afraid of intruding... Well, we'll see.'

They went on chatting. Then the doctor expressed surprise.

'Where on earth has she gone? She went out to see to that stew a quarter of an hour ago.'

Hélène saw then that the door was shut. It didn't bother her at first. She chatted about Madame Deberle, praising her warmly to her husband. But as the doctor was constantly looking in the direction of the door, after a while she grew embarrassed.

'How very odd that she has not come back,' she echoed.

Their conversation faltered. At a loss what to do, Hélène opened the window, and when she turned round they avoided looking at each other. Children's laughter came in through the window which framed the blue moon high up in the sky. They were really on their own, hidden from all eyes, with only this hole in the wall staring at them. In the distance the children's voices faded. A quivering silence reigned. Nobody would have come to look for them in this forgotten attic. Their embarrassment increased. Hélène then, dissatisfied with herself, stared at the doctor.

'I am very busy with my rounds,' he said immediately. 'Since she hasn't come back, I'll go.'

And he left. Hélène sat down again. Mother Fétu instantly came back, prattling.

'Oh, I could hardly drag myself there and back, I had a bit of a turn... Has that lovely man gone then? Of course there are no amenities here. You two are angels from heaven to spend your time with a poor woman like me. But God will reward you. It's gone to my feet today. I had to sit down on the stairs. And I didn't know, because you weren't making any noise... Well anyway, I'd like some chairs. If only I had an armchair! My mattress is really bad. I'm ashamed when you come to see me. The whole house is yours, I'd risk my immortal soul for you two. The good Lord knows that, I tell Him often enough. O God, let the good gentleman and the good lady have all they desire. In the name of the Father, Son, and Holy Ghost, Amen.'

Hélène listened to her and felt a peculiar unease. Mother Fétu's swollen face worried her. And she had never felt such discomfort in the narrow room. She saw how poor and squalid it was, she couldn't bear the lack of air, the degrading wretchedness. She hastened to take her leave, offended by Mother Fétu's blessings called after her.

Another upsetting thing awaited her in the Passage des Eaux. In the middle of this passage on the right going down there is a kind of quarry in the wall, some abandoned well, sealed off by iron railings. For the last two days she had heard the mewing of a cat at the bottom of this hole. As she went up the mewing began again, but so desperate it was obviously dying. The thought that the poor animal, thrown into that old well, was slowly dying of hunger, suddenly broke Hélène's heart. She walked faster, thinking that she would not risk going up those steps for a long time, in case she heard this deathly mewing.

And it happened to be a Tuesday. In the evening at seven, as Hélène was finishing a little vest, the usual two rings on the doorbell sounded and Rosalie opened the door, saying:

'Monsieur l'Abbé has arrived first today. Oh, here's Monsieur Rambaud.'

Dinner was a jolly affair, Jeanne was feeling ever better and the two brothers, who spoiled her, managed to get her to eat a little salad, which she loved, though Doctor Bodin had strictly forbidden it. Then when they moved into the other room, the child, emboldened, hung on her mother's neck and murmured:

'Please, please, Maman, take me with you tomorrow to see the old woman.'

But the priest and Monsieur Rambaud immediately scolded her. They couldn't take her to visit poor folk because she didn't behave properly. Last time she'd gone she had fainted twice, and for three days even when she was asleep her eyes had swollen up and they'd been watering.

'Oh please,' she repeated, 'I shan't cry, I promise.'

Then her mother kissed her, saying:

'There's no point, darling. The old woman is better... I shan't go out any more, I'll stay with you all day.'

CHAPTER 4

THE following week, when Madame Deberle returned Madame Grandjean's visit, she showered affection upon her. And in the doorway as she was leaving:

'You know you promised... The first fine day you come down to our garden and bring Jeanne with you. Doctor's orders.'

Hélène smiled.

'Yes, yes, I promise. You can count on it.'

And on a bright February afternoon, three days later, she did go down there with her daughter. The concierge opened the communicating gate for them. They found Madame Deberle with her sister Pauline at the end of the garden in a sort of glasshouse which had been transformed into a Japanese conservatory, both of them empty-handed, having put down, and forgotten, their embroidery on a little table.

'Oh, how nice of you!' Juliette said. 'Do come over here. Pauline, push that table away. As you see, it is still a little cool when you are sitting down, and from this conservatory we can keep a careful eye on the children. Go off and play, children. And mind you don't fall.'

The wide bay of the conservatory was open and the sliding glass doors were closed at each side, so the garden was extended on the same level, as though outside the entrance to a tent. It was a typically bourgeois garden, with a lawn in the middle, and two circular flower beds on each side. It was closed off from the Rue Vineuse simply by a railing, but such a thick curtain of greenery had grown up it that no one could possibly see through from the street. Ivy, clematis, and woodbine twined around one another and over the gate, and behind and above this first wall of greenery rose another of lilac and laburnum. Even in winter the evergreen ivy leaves and the interlacing of branches were enough to hide the garden from public gaze. But its most charming feature was at the bottom, where mature trees, superb elms, obscured the dark wall of a five-storey house. They gave you the illusion, among these oppressive neighbouring buildings, of being in the corner of a park, seeming to increase disproportionately the size of this little Parisian garden that was swept clean as a drawing room. Between two elms hung a swing, its seat green with damp.

Hélène looked out, leaning forward for a better view.

'Oh, it's nothing special,' said Madame Deberle in a casual tone of voice. 'But trees are so rare in Paris. We are very lucky to have half a dozen ourselves.'

'Oh, but you are very well situated,' murmured Hélène. 'It's lovely.'

That day the sun in the pastel sky was sending forth a powdery golden dust. The rays streamed steadily through the leafless branches. The trees were reddening, you could see the tiny violet buds softening the grey of the bark. And on the lawn, along the paths, there were clear specks of light on the grass and gravel, drowning, melting in a slight mist just above the ground. There were no flowers, it was just the bright sun on the bare earth that foretold the coming of spring.

'It's still rather depressing at the moment,' went on Madame Deberle. 'But in June you'll see we are really sheltered. The trees prevent the people next door spying on us and we are completely on our own...'

But she broke off to cry:

'Lucien, please don't touch the fountain!'

The little boy, who was showing Jeanne round the garden, had just led her to a fountain, under the steps, and there he had turned on the tap, sticking out the ends of his little boots to wet them. He loved that game. With a grave look on her face, Jeanne watched him getting his feet wet.

'Wait,' said Pauline, getting up. 'I'll go down and make him behave.'

'No no, you are worse than him. The other day you'd have thought you had both taken a bath. It's odd that a big girl like you can't sit down for two minutes.' And, turning her head:

'Lucien, do you hear? Turn that tap off straight away!'

The child was frightened and tried to do what he was told. But he turned it on even more, the water gushed out with a force and a noise which made him panic. He stepped back, splashed from head to foot.

'Turn that tap off straight away!' repeated his mother, going red in the face.

Then Jeanne, who until then had not said anything, went very cautiously over to the fountain, while Lucien burst out sobbing, confronted by this furious gush of water which scared him and which he didn't know how to stop. She put her skirt between her legs, stretched out her bare arms so as not to wet her sleeves and turned off the tap, without being splashed at all. Abruptly the deluge stopped. Lucien, suddenly respectful, choked back his tears and looked at the girl in wide-eyed astonishment.

'Really, that boy makes me so angry,' Madame Deberle went on, now very pale again and stretching out on her chair as though completely exhausted.

Hélène thought it might be prudent to intervene.

'Jeanne,' she said, 'take his hand and play going for a walk.'

Jeanne took Lucien's hand and the solemn pair started off down the paths at a leisurely pace. She was much taller than him, his arm had to reach up to hers; but this noble game, which consisted of taking ceremonial turns around the lawn, seemed to absorb them both and bestow great importance on their persons. Jeanne cast vague glances around her, like a real lady. Lucien could not help stealing a glance at his companion from time to time. They did not speak to each other.

'They are so funny,' murmured Madame Deberle, who was smiling again now and relaxed. 'I must say your Jeanne is a most delightful little girl. She does what she's told, she's so well behaved.'

'Yes, when she's at other people's houses,' Hélène agreed. 'She's dreadful at times. But she worships me, so she tries to be good so that I shan't get cross.'

The ladies chatted about children. Girls were more advanced than boys. But you couldn't judge Lucien from that silly behaviour; in another year when he had sorted himself out a little, he would be a fine boy. And without any noticeable transition, they began to talk about a woman who lived in a little house opposite where some really strange things were going on...

Madame Deberle stopped talking, to say to her sister:

'Pauline, go into the garden a moment.'

The young woman went meekly outside and stood under the trees. She was used to being sent out every time something cropped up in the conversation that was too vulgar and could not be discussed in her presence.

'I was at the window yesterday,' said Juliette, 'and that woman was clearly visible. She doesn't even draw the curtains! So immoral! A child might see.'

She was whispering, and looked scandalized, but a thin smile played around the corners of her mouth. Then, raising her voice, she shouted:

'You can come back now, Pauline.'

Beneath the trees Pauline looked up in the air with a show of indifference, waiting for her sister to finish. She came back into the conservatory and sat down again while Juliette carried on talking to Hélène:

'Have *you* never noticed anything, Madame?'

'No,' Hélène replied. 'My windows don't look out on to the house.'

Although there had been a gap in the conversation as far as the young woman was concerned, she listened with her pale, virginal expression, as though she had understood.

'Oh!' she said, looking out through the door, up in the air again. 'There are lots of nests in those trees!'

Madame Deberle meanwhile had resumed her embroidery, for the appearance of doing something. Every minute she sewed another two stitches. Hélène, who could not remain idle, asked if it would be all right to bring her needlework with her another time. And feeling slightly at a loose end, she turned to study the Japanese pavilion.* The walls and ceiling were hung with gold brocade, with flights of cranes, butterflies and gaudy flowers, landscapes where blue boats sailed on yellow rivers. There were hardwood seats and jardinières. On the floor were finely knotted mats, a whole host of trinkets, small bronzes, small vases, strange gaudily-coloured knick-knacks. At the back, a huge *magot* in Meissen porcelain with legs folded, naked, and with a protruding belly, laughed hysterically and nodded his head like a mad thing at the slightest touch.

'He's so ugly, isn't he?' cried Pauline, who had followed Hélène's eyes. 'Do you realize that all you bought is rubbish? That handsome Malignon calls your Japanese things "the penny bazaar"... By the way, I saw Malignon. He was with a lady, well, a lady from the Variétés*— that little Florence.'

'Whereabouts, so that I can tease him!' asked Juliette quickly.

'On the boulevard. Isn't he supposed to come today?'

But no one answered her. The ladies were concerned about their children, who had vanished. Where could they be? And as they called, two shrill voices were heard.

'We're here!'

And indeed there they were, in the middle of the lawn sitting in the grass half-concealed by a spindleberry.

'What on earth are you doing?'

'We've arrived at the inn!' cried Lucien. 'We are resting in our bedroom.'

They glanced at the children, in much amusement. Jeanne was happy to take part in this game. She was picking off the grass all around her, no doubt to prepare lunch. The travellers' luggage was represented by a piece of wood they had picked up in a flower bed. Now they were having a conversation. Jeanne was entering into it, confidently asserting that they were in Switzerland and they were going to visit the glaciers, which seemed to perplex Lucien.

'Ah, there he is!' Pauline said suddenly.

Madame Deberle turned and saw Malignon coming down the steps. She hardly allowed him time to greet everyone and sit down.

'Well, that was nice of you, I must say! Telling everybody I have only rubbish in my house!'

'Ah yes,' he replied calmly, 'this little room. Definitely full of rubbish. You haven't one thing worth looking at.'

She was very offended.

'What about the *magot*?'

'No no, all that's very bourgeois. You've no taste. But you wouldn't let me take charge of the decorations.'

At that she cut him off, flushed and really angry with him.

'Ha, you can talk about taste! You were seen with a lady...'

'What lady?' he asked, surprised at the harshness of this attack.

'A fine choice, I congratulate you, my dear Malignon. A girl the whole of Paris...'

But she stopped at the sight of Pauline. She had forgotten she was there.

'Pauline,' she said, 'go out into the garden for a moment.'

'Oh no, I'm tired of doing that all the time!' declared the young woman in revolt. 'I'm always having to go out.'

'Go into the garden,' Juliette repeated more sternly.

The young woman went reluctantly. Then she turned round to add:

'But at least be quick about it.'

As soon as she had gone Madame Deberle renewed her attack on Malignon. How could a young man like him parade around in public with this Florence? She was at least forty, ugly as sin, and every man in the stalls was more than familiar with her at the premieres.

'Have you finished?' shouted Pauline, who was walking sulkily around under the trees. 'I'm so bored.'

But Malignon protested. He didn't know this Florence; he'd never spoken one word to her. He had probably been seen with a lady, sometimes he escorted the wife of one of his friends. Anyway, who was it who saw him? You had to have proof, witnesses.

'Pauline,' Madame Deberle asked abruptly, raising her voice, 'didn't you meet him when he was with Florence?'

'Yes, yes,' the girl replied, 'on the boulevard, opposite Bignon's.'*

Then Madame Deberle, triumphant at Malignon's embarrassed smile, cried:

'You can come back now, Pauline. We've finished.'

Malignon had a box for the following day in the Folies-Dramatiques.* He gallantly offered it to Madame Deberle, without seeming to bear her a grudge; in any case they were always squabbling. Pauline wanted to know if she could go and see the play that was on; and when Malignon laughed and shook his head, she said it was very silly and that authors ought to write plays suitable for young women. She was only allowed to see *La Dame blanche** and the classics.

Meanwhile the ladies were not supervising the children. Suddenly Lucien started screaming.

'What did you do to him, Jeanne?' Hélène asked.

'Nothing, Maman,' the little girl replied. 'He just threw himself on the ground.'

What had happened was that the children had just left for the aforementioned glaciers. As Jeanne was pretending they had reached the mountains, they were both taking very big strides to get over the rocks. But Lucien, panting with the exercise, lost his footing and tumbled headlong into the middle of a flower bed. Once on the ground, the extremely cross little boy had burst into tears of rage.

'Pick him up,' Hélène shouted again.

'He doesn't want to be picked up, Maman. He's rolling around on the ground.'

And Jeanne went away, as though she was put out and annoyed to see the little boy behaving so badly. He couldn't play properly, he'd be sure to make her dirty. She pouted like a duchess risking her reputation. Then Madame Deberle, losing patience with Lucien's screaming, asked her sister to pick him up and make him be quiet. Pauline was only too delighted. She ran and lay down on the ground next to the little boy and rolled around with him for a moment. He fought, and didn't want her to pick him up, but she got up and caught hold of him under his arms, and in order to calm him down, said:

'Be quiet, you noisy child! We're going to go and have a swing.'

Lucien stopped immediately, Jeanne's serious expression changed, and her face lit up in delight. All three ran to the swing. But it was Pauline who sat down on the seat.

'Give me a push,' she said to the children.

They pushed her with all the strength their small hands could muster. But she was heavy, they could scarcely move her.

'Come on, push!' she repeated. 'Oh, the silly little things, they can't do it.'

In the conservatory Madame Deberle had just shivered a little. Despite the bright sunlight she was finding it rather cool and she asked Malignon to hand her a white cashmere wrap that was hanging on a window-catch. Malignon got up and placed the wrap around her shoulders. Both were chatting about things which did not interest Hélène. So she went into the garden, worried and afraid that Pauline, without meaning to, might knock the children over. She left Juliette and Malignon discussing a particular fashion in hats they favoured.

As soon as Jeanne saw her mother she went over, coaxingly. Pleading was written all over her.

'Oh, Maman,' she murmured. 'Oh, Maman...'

'No, no,' Hélène replied, who knew very well what she meant. 'You know you are not allowed to.'

Jeanne adored swinging. She felt as if she were changing into a bird, she said. The wind blowing past her face, the sudden take-off, the continuous to and fro, rhythmical as the beat of a wing, delighted her, she felt she was floating off into the clouds. She believed she was rising into heaven; only it always ended badly. On one occasion they had found her clutching on to the rope, in a faint, her eyes staring, full of terror of the void. Another time she had fallen, stiff like a swallow hit by lead shot.

'Oh, Maman,' she begged, 'just a little, a very little.'

To have a little peace, her mother finally sat her on the swing. The child was radiant, her face saintly, her bare wrists trembling a little in delight. And as Hélène was pushing her very gently, she murmured:

'Harder, harder!'

But Hélène did not listen to her. She did not let go the rope. And she herself grew more animated, pink-cheeked, vibrant with every push she gave to the seat of the swing. Her habitual seriousness melted into a kind of complicity with her daughter.

'That's enough,' she declared, lifting Jeanne off.

'Go on, Maman, you have a swing,' the child pleaded, her arms still around her neck.

She loved to see her mother fly away, as she said, taking even more pleasure in watching her than in swinging herself. But the latter asked her with a laugh, who would push her? When she had a swing, it was in earnest. She rose higher than the treetops. Just at that moment Monsieur Rambaud appeared, brought through by the concierge. He had made the acquaintance of Madame Deberle at Hélène's and, not finding Hélène at home, had thought it was in order for him to come and look for her. Madame Deberle was very hospitable, touched by his neighbourliness. Then she plunged again into lively conversation with Malignon.

'Our friend will push you, he'll push you!' shouted Jeanne, jumping up and down next to her mother.

'Be quiet! We're not at home,' said Hélène, assuming a strict expression.

'Goodness me,' said Monsieur Rambaud, 'I'm only too happy to oblige, if you like. When one is in the country...'

Hélène allowed herself to be tempted. As a girl she had swung for hours, and the memory of these distant days filled her with nostalgia. Pauline, who had been sitting on the edge of the lawn with Lucien, intervened, with the airy look of an emancipated young woman.

'Yes, go on, the gentleman will push you... And afterwards he'll push me, won't you, Monsieur?'

That decided Hélène. Her youthfulness burst forth with a charming naivety from under that cool, beautiful exterior. She was simple and gay as a schoolgirl. And above all she wasn't prudish; but, with a laugh, she said she didn't want to show her legs, and asked for some string, to tie her skirts above her ankles. Then standing on the swing, her arms spread wide and hanging on to the ropes, she shouted gaily:

'Come on then, Monsieur Rambaud... Gently at first!'

Monsieur Rambaud hung his hat on a branch. His wide, pleasant face lit up with a fatherly smile. He made certain the ropes were strong, looked at the trees, and decided to give her a light push. Hélène had just cast off her widow's weeds for the first time. She wore a grey dress, decorated with mauve bows. And sitting straight, she started off slowly, skimming the ground, as though rocked in a cradle.

'Faster!' she said.

Then, his arms at full length, Monsieur Rambaud seized the swing as it came back, pushed on it harder. Hélène rose into the air, each time increasing her height. But she still retained her steady rhythm. She looked correct still, rather serious, eyes shining bright in her fine, quiet face, her nostrils alone distended, as if to drink in the wind. Not a fold in her skirts was out of place. One of the plaits in her chignon was coming undone.

'Faster, faster!'

A sudden push carried her up. She rose up to the sun, higher and higher. The displaced air blew over the garden; and she was moving at such a speed you could no longer see her very clearly. She was surely smiling now, her face was pink, her eyes were like shooting stars. The plait had come undone and tapped against her neck. Despite the string holding them together, her skirts billowed out and revealed her white ankles. And you felt she was in her true element, breathing and living in the air as though that were her home.

'Faster, faster!'

Monsieur Rambaud, red-faced and perspiring, pushed as hard as he could. There was a little cry. Hélène was swinging still higher.

'Oh, Maman! Oh, Maman!' Jeanne shouted, in ecstasy.

She had sat down on the lawn looking at her mother with her small hands clasped to her chest as though she had herself drunk in all the air that was blowing. She gasped, instinctively following the long oscillations of the swing with the rhythm of her shoulders. And she was shouting:

'Harder, harder!'

Her mother was going higher still. At the top her feet touched the branches of the trees.

'Harder, harder, oh Maman, harder!'

But Hélène was right up in the sky. The trees were bending and cracking as though beneath gusts of wind. All you could see were her skirts whirling round, making a noise as though in a storm. When she came down, her arms spread out, breast thrust forward, she lowered her head a little, paused for a second; then she was sent aloft and came down again, head thrown back, fleeing and swooning, her eyelids closed. This vertiginous lifting and dropping delighted her. Up there she was going to meet the sun, the white February sun, pouring down like golden dust. Her chestnut hair shone with amber lights; and you would have thought she was quite aflame, as her bows of purple silk, like fire flowers, glowed upon her light dress. Around her spring came to life, the violet-coloured buds showed their fine lacquer tones against the blue of the sky.

Then Jeanne put her hands together. Her mother seemed to her a kind of saint with a golden halo rising into paradise.* And she continued to stammer 'Oh, Maman! Oh, Maman!...' in a husky voice.

Meanwhile Madame Deberle and Malignon, becoming interested, had moved nearer the trees. Malignon said he thought the lady very brave. Madame Deberle said, looking alarmed:

'I'm sure I'd feel sick.'

Hélène heard, for she answered from the middle of the branches:

'Oh, I'm all right! Go on, Monsieur Rambaud.' And her voice was indeed as calm as ever. She seemed not to care about the two men who were present. Probably they didn't count for her. Her plait had unravelled; the string must have loosened and her petticoats flapped around like flags. The swing was going up again, but suddenly she shouted:

'Stop, Monsieur Rambaud, stop!'

Doctor Deberle had just appeared on the steps. He came over and kissed his wife fondly, lifted Lucien up and planted a kiss on his forehead. Then he smiled at Hélène.

'Stop, stop!' she repeated.

'But why?' he asked. 'Am I disturbing you?'

She did not answer. She had grown solemn. The swing which had been pushed as far as it could go did not stop. It kept making long, regular swaying motions which still carried Hélène high in the air. And the doctor, surprised and delighted, looked at her admiringly, at her superb figure, tall, strong and pure as a Greek statue, swinging gently like that in the spring sunshine. But she seemed put out. Suddenly she jumped off.

Everyone shouted, 'Wait, wait!'

Hélène uttered a muffled cry. She fell on to the gravel path and couldn't get up.

'Oh no, how foolish!' said the doctor, going very pale.

They all crowded round her. Jeanne was wailing so loudly that Monsieur Rambaud, almost fainting himself, had to pick her up. Meanwhile the doctor was firing rapid questions at Hélène.

'It's your right leg that took the weight, isn't it? Can you stand?'

And as she remained confused, not saying anything, he asked her again:

'Are you in pain?'

'My knee aches a little here,' she said, with some difficulty.

Then he sent his wife to get his medicine chest and some bandages.

'We'll have a look,' he said. 'I don't expect it's serious.'

He knelt on the gravel. Hélène let him do what he wanted. But when he touched her she got up with an effort and gathered her dress around her legs.

'No no,' she said softly.

'But,' he said, 'we must have a look...'

She trembled a little and murmured:

'I don't want... it's nothing.'

He looked at her, at first astonished. Her neck had flushed red. For an instant their eyes met and each seemed to read the depths of the other's soul. Then, troubled himself, he got up slowly and remained by her side but did not ask again to examine her.

Hélène made a sign to Monsieur Rambaud to come over. She said to him in a low voice:

'Go and get Doctor Bodin and tell him what has happened to me.'

Ten minutes later when Doctor Bodin arrived, she got to her feet with a superhuman effort, and leaning on him and on Monsieur Rambaud, went back to her house. Jeanne followed, sobbing.

'You must come back,' Doctor Deberle said to his colleague, 'and tell us if she is all right.'

In the garden they were in animated conversation. Malignon was exclaiming that women needed their heads seeing to. Why on earth did the lady think it a good idea to jump off the swing? Pauline, very put out by this adventure, which deprived her of what she enjoyed doing, thought it was foolhardy to swing so hard. The doctor did not speak, seemed anxious.

'Nothing serious,' said Doctor Bodin, on his return. 'A straightforward sprain, that's all... But she will have to lie on the chaise longue for at least two weeks.'

Monsieur Deberle gave Malignon a friendly tap on the shoulder. He urged his wife to go in, because it was definitely too cold. And gathering up Lucien, he carried him indoors himself, covering him with kisses.

CHAPTER 5

Both windows in the room were open wide and below the house, which was built high up on the hillside, there in a deep chasm lay the immense plain that stretched to Paris. Ten o'clock chimed, the beautiful February morning had the softness and fragrance of spring.

Lying on her chaise longue with her knee still bandaged, Hélène was reading in front of the window. She was no longer in pain, but for the last week she had been trapped there, not even able to do her usual needlework. Not knowing how to occupy herself, she, who never read anything, had opened a book lying on the little table. It was the one she used every evening to hide the lamp, the only one she had taken out in eighteen months from the little bookcase stocked with suitable books by Monsieur Rambaud. Usually novels seemed to her fanciful and childish. This one, *Ivanhoe** by Walter Scott, she had at first found boring. Then she had begun to feel an unusual curiosity. She was getting to the end, sometimes moved, overcome with lassitude, and she let the book fall from her hands for quite some minutes, with her eyes fixed on the vast horizon.

That morning, Paris woke with an indolent smile. A haze, which travelled up the valley of the Seine, engulfed the two banks. The milky-white cloud brightened as the sun gradually rose higher. Beneath this floating muslin veil of pale blue, the city was invisible. In the dips the thick cloud darkened and took on a bluish tint, but over large expanses it was transparent, extremely fine, a golden dust through which you could just make out where the streets cut through; and higher up, grey shapes of domes and towers, still wrapped in shreds of mist, poking up through the fog. From time to time clouds of yellow haze detached themselves like the wings of a giant bird, and melted into the air, which seemed to drink them up. And above all this immensity, above this cloud which had descended and lay sleeping over Paris, there unfurled a deep vault of purest sky, of a washed-out blue that was almost white. The sun rose, its rays soft and powdery, and the pale light, nebulous as childhood, turned into showers, filling the space with its lukewarm frisson. It was a celebration, a sovereign peace, and a tender, infinite delight, while the city, shot through with golden arrows, lethargic and still full of sleep, had not yet made up its mind to reveal itself from under its gown of lace.

For a week Hélène had enjoyed this vast spectacle of Paris before her. She never tired of it. It was unfathomable and changing as the sea, innocent in the morning and passionate at night, reflecting the joy and the sadness of the heavens. A flash of sunlight and it unfurled in waves of gold, a cloud darkened it and raised storms. It was always different: there were times when it was an orangey flat calm; gusts of wind which from one hour to the next turned everything leaden; clear, bright weather making the top of each roof shine; downpours which drowned the heavens and the earth, blotting out the horizon in a chaotic, total collapse. In all this, Hélène savoured all the melancholy and all the hope of the open sea. She even fancied she could feel the strong gusts of wind in her face, the tang of the ocean; and everything that lay between her, including the constant rumbling of the city, gave her the illusion of an incoming tide, beating against the cliffs.

The book slipped from her hands. She dreamed, gazing into the distance. When she dropped it like that, it was because she needed to pause in her reading, take stock and wait awhile. She took pleasure in not satisfying her curiosity immediately. The story filled her with sensations that overwhelmed her. Paris did indeed that morning reflect the joys and the vague troubles of her heart. There was great charm in that: not to know, to half-guess, to abandon herself to a slow initiation, with the inexplicable feeling that she was starting to live her life all over again.

How these novels lied! And how right she was never to read them! They were fables good for empty-headed folk, who drifted vaguely through life. And yet she was fascinated, could not keep her mind off Ivanhoe, so passionately loved by two women, Rebecca, the beautiful Jewess, and the noble Lady Rowena. She thought she would have loved like the latter, with pride and a patient serenity. Love, love! And that word that she did not utter aloud but that came unbidden into her mind, astonished her and brought a smile to her lips. In the distance pale flakes were floating over Paris, like a flock of swans borne along by the wind. Thick blankets of mist moved across; one moment the Left Bank appeared, trembling and shrouded like a fairy city seen in a dream and then the haze disintegrated and the city was engulfed as by a flood. Now the haziness, distributed equally over all the *quartiers*, seemed to float around a beautiful lake of smooth white water. But a thicker grey streak was curling its way up the course of the Seine. Shadows seemed to propel rosy sailing boats over these calm white waters and the young woman followed them with a thoughtful eye. Love! Love! And she smiled at her fleeting fancy.

Meanwhile Hélène had taken up her book again. She was reading the episode about the attack on the castle, where Rebecca looks after the injured Ivanhoe and tells him about the battle which she can see from her window. She felt she was in a beautiful fiction, walking around in it as though in an ideal garden, with golden fruit, from which she was drinking in all illusions. Then at the end of the scene when Rebecca, wrapped in her veil, pours out her feelings to the sleeping knight, Hélène let the book drop once more, her heart so full, she could not carry on.

Goodness, could it all be true? And, leaning back in her chaise longue, stiff with having to remain constantly in one position, she contemplated Paris, drowned, mysterious Paris, in the pale sunlight. Hélène's own life, brought back by the pages of the novel, rose up before her. She had a vision of herself as a young girl in Marseilles at home with her father, Mouret, the hatmaker. The Rue des Petites-Maries was dark and the house with its vat of boiling water for hat-making gave off a stale, damp odour, even when the weather was fine. She had a vision of her mother too, always ill, kissing her silently with her pale lips. As a child, she had never seen a ray of sunlight in her bedroom. Around her they all earned a living by the sweat of their brow. And that was all. Until she was married, nothing happened to disturb the monotony of those days. Then one morning as she was coming back from the market with her mother she bumped into the Grandjean boy with his basket full of vegetables. Charles had turned and followed them. That was the whole story of her love life. For three months he had been there the whole time, humble and awkward, not daring to talk to her. She was sixteen, rather proud of this lover, who she knew was from a wealthy family. But she thought him ugly, she often made fun of him, and her nights in the darkness of the big damp house were undisturbed. Then they were married. This marriage was still surprising to her. Charles adored her, went on his knees to kiss her naked feet at night when she went to bed. She smiled, full of amicable feelings towards him, reproaching him for being a real child. Then her unexciting life had begun again. For twelve years nothing she could recall had come to upset it. She was very calm and contented, with no fleshly or emotional desires, mired as she was in the daily worries of a lowly domesticity. Charles still kissed her marble-white feet, and she was indulgent towards him and mothered him. Nothing more than that. And then suddenly there was the room in the Hôtel du Var, her dead husband, her widow's weeds draped over the chair. She had wept, as she had wept that winter evening when her mother died. Afterwards the days had gone on much the same as before. For the last two months with her daughter she had felt very happy, very serene again. God! Was that all there was to life? And what did this book mean, when it talked about the great passions which light up one's whole life?

On the horizon, long ripples travelled across the sleeping lake. Then all of a sudden it seemed to break in two; fissures appeared and there was a great crack from end to end that presaged a catastrophe. The sun, higher now, in the triumphant glory of its beams, attacked the fog, and was victorious. Gradually the great lake seemed to dry up as if the plain had been invisibly drained by some wasteweir. The mist, which had been so thick a moment ago, was thinning out and becoming transparent, taking on the bright colours of a rainbow. The whole of the Left Bank was a soft blue, gradually darkening to violet in the background near the Jardin des Plantes. On the Right Bank, the Tuileries were a pale pink, like flesh-coloured material, while in the direction of Montmartre it was like embers, carmine flaming into gold; then a very long way off, the working suburbs went a darker brick shade, fading gradually into the bluish grey of slate. The quivering, elusive city remained indistinct, like submarine depths just visible through clear water, with their terrifying forests of tall weed, their scary swarms of creatures, half-perceived monsters. Meanwhile the mists, like water, continued to ebb away. All that remained were scraps of delicate muslin; and one by one, the muslin scraps vanished, the image of the city took shape and woke from its dream.

Love, love! Why did this word come to mind again, with all its sweetness, while she was watching the fog disperse? Had she not loved her husband, whom she looked after like a child? But she suddenly had a piercing memory of her father found hanged after his wife's death, at the back of a wardrobe where her dresses still hung. He died there, stiffening, his face buried in a skirt, wrapped in those clothes which still gave off a slight scent of the woman he adored. Then, in her reverie, she broke off abruptly: she thought about domestic details, about the monthly accounts she had gone through that very morning with Rosalie, and she felt extremely proud of her good housekeeping. She had lived a dignified life for more than thirty years in an absolute firmness of purpose. Right behaviour was all that mattered to her. When her mind turned to her past life she did not consider she had been weak, not for a moment; she saw herself travelling steadily along a smooth, straight path. The days might come or go, she would walk quietly on, without stumbling on the way. And that made her stern, angry, and scornful towards those fictitious lives led astray by the affections of the heart. Hers was the only true life, lived in such tranquillity. But over Paris all that was left was a thin mist, one single shred of quivering gauze about to fly away; and a sudden warmth came over her. Love, love! Everything, even her pride in her principled behaviour brought her back to this tender word. Her reverie grew so light, she was no longer thinking about anything, but, with tears in her eyes, was suffused in the springtime.

Meanwhile Hélène was about to start reading her book again, when Paris slowly appeared; not a breath of wind, it was like an evocation. The last scrap of gauze detached itself, rose, and vanished into the air. And the city stretched out, shadowless under the all-conquering sun. Hélène sat with her chin in her hands contemplating this colossal awakening.

One endless valley of heaped-up buildings. On the vanishing line of hills, you could make out piles of roofs; while in the distance, behind the dips in the landscape, in countryside no longer visible, you could sense the overflow of houses. It was like the open sea, with its mysterious never-ending waves. Paris was unfolding, as vast as the sky. On this radiant morning the city, yellow in the sunlight, looked like a field of ripe corn; and the huge picture had simplicity, being of two colours only, the pale blue of the air and the golden reflection on the roofs. These waves of spring sunshine lent an innocent grace to everything. The light was so pure, you could clearly see the smallest details. Paris, a fathomless chaos of stone, shone like crystal. But now and then there was a breath of wind in this brilliant and motionless serenity. And then you could see *quartiers* whose lines softened and flickered as though you were looking at them through some invisible flame.

At first Hélène was fascinated by the wide expanse of land beneath her window, the slope of the Trocadéro and the diminishing banks. She had to lean out to get a view of the barren rectangle of the Champ-de-Mars, cut off at the back by the dark block of the École Militaire. Below it on the huge square and on the paths each side of the Seine, she could make out pedestrians, a milling crowd of black spots swarming like ants. A spark was emitted from a yellow omnibus. Trucks and cabs crossed the bridge, small as children's playthings, with fragile horses that looked like clockwork toys. And along the grassy banks, in amongst other people walking, a maid in a white apron made a bright spot against the green. Hélène raised her eyes, but the crowd was breaking up and vanishing, even the cabs were turning into grains of sand. The only thing that remained was the gigantic carcass of a city, seeming empty and deserted, existing only in the unseen bustle that animated it. There in the foreground, on the left, red roofs glowed, the tall chimneys of the Military Depot* smoked slowly, while on the other side of the river, between the esplanade and the Champ-de-Mars, a clump of tall elms formed a corner of a park, and you could clearly see the branches, the rounded tops, with tips already greening. Between them the Seine widened and reigned supreme, encased by its grey banks, where the unloaded barrels, the steam-powered cranes, and rows of tip-trucks were like the setting for some seaport. Hélène's eyes returned time and again to this splendid stretch of water where the boats sailed along like ink-coloured birds. She could not resist tracing and retracing the superb length of the river. It was like a length of silver braid dividing Paris in two. That morning the water flowed with sunshine, there was no brighter light on the horizon. And the eyes of the young woman first lit on the Pont des Invalides, then the Pont de la Concorde, then the Pont Royal; the bridges carried on, seeming to become closer to one another, one superimposed upon another, creating strange viaducts on several levels, pierced with a variety of differently shaped arches; while the river, in between these delicate constructions, revealed patches of her blue gown, tapering away before petering out altogether. She raised her eyes again. Over there in the crazy jumble of houses the river divided. The bridges on either side of the Cité were like threads stretched from one bank to the other. The towers of Notre-Dame, all golden, rose up like milestones on the horizon, and beyond them the river, the buildings, the clumps of trees, were nothing more than clouds of sundust. Dazzled, she looked away from this triumphal heart of Paris blazing forth in all its glory. On the Right Bank through the trees on the Champs-Élysées, the Palais de l'Industrie with its great glass walls looked like pure snow. Further down, behind the flattened roof of the Madeleine, was the huge bulk of the Opéra,* resembling a tombstone; and there were other buildings, cupolas and towers, the Vendôme column, Saint-Vincent-de-Paul, the Tour Saint-Jacques; nearer still were the ungainly blocks of the new wings in the Louvre and the Tuileries, half buried in a forest of chestnut trees. On the Left Bank the Dôme des Invalides streamed with gold; beyond, the two uneven towers of Saint-Sulpice grew paler in the light; and still further back to the right of the new spires of Sainte-Clotilde, the bluish Panthéon, sitting squarely on the hill, towered over the city, raising its fine colonnade to the sky, motionless in the air, with the silky hue of a captured balloon.

Now Hélène, glancing idly around, could encompass the whole of Paris. Valleys were discernible as the flowing of rooftops. The Butte des Moulins emerged from a seething tide of old slates, while the Grands Boulevards ran down like a river, swallowing up a flurry of houses, so that not even their tiles were visible. At that hour of the morning the slant of the sun did not light up the facades facing the Trocadéro. No window shone. Only the glass on the roofs cast a glow, like bright sparks of mica, in the brick red of the surrounding potteries. The houses were still grey, a grey warmed by reflections; but shafts of light pierced the *quartiers*, long, straight streets leading away from Hélène, cutting through the shadows with their rays of sunshine. Only on the left the Butte Montmartre and the hills of Père-Lachaise made bumps on the unbroken curve of the immense flat horizon. The details that were so clear in the foreground, the denticulation of innumerable chimneys, the small black hachures of a thousand windows, were blotted out, flecked with yellow and blue, jumbled up in the pell-mell of the endless city whose invisible faubourgs seemed to be pebbled shores, extending and drowning, drowning in a violet haze beneath the vast and vibrant brightness spreading across the sky.

With great seriousness, Hélène was contemplating all this when Jeanne came in, very excited.

'Maman, Maman, look!'

The little girl was holding a large bunch of yellow wallflowers. And she told her delightedly that she had watched out for Rosalie coming back with the shopping, so that she could look into her basket. She loved rummaging around in her basket.

'Look, Maman! These were in the bottom... Smell them, how nice they smell!'

The beige flowers with their purplish stripes gave off a penetrating odour that scented the whole room. Then Hélène, in a passionate gesture, pulled Jeanne to her breast, and the bunch of wallflowers dropped to her knees. Love, love! Yes, she surely loved her little girl. Was that not enough, this great love which had filled her life until now? Such quiet, tender love ought to suffice, it would last for ever, no weariness would destroy it. And she hugged her daughter more, as though to ward off those thoughts which threatened to separate them. Jeanne meanwhile abandoned herself to this windfall of kisses. There were tears in her eyes, she snuggled affectionately against her mother's shoulder, and nuzzled against her with her delicate neck. Then she put an arm around her waist, and remained in that position, very meekly, her cheek on her mother's breast. Between them, the wall-flowers exhaled their perfume.

For a long time they didn't speak. Jeanne, without moving, finally asked in a low voice:

'Maman, do you see that pink dome over there by the river... What is it?'

It was the dome of the Institute. Hélène looked and for a moment seemed to ponder. Then, gently, she said:

'I don't know, darling.'

The little girl was satisfied with this answer, they fell silent again. But she soon had another question:

'And over there, nearby, those lovely trees?'—pointing to part of the Tuileries gardens.

'Those lovely trees?' said her mother softly. 'On the left?... I don't know, darling.'

'Oh,' said Jeanne.

Then after a thoughtful pause, she added, frowning:

'We don't know anything.'

That was right, they knew nothing about Paris. For the last eighteen months they had looked at it at all times of the day, and yet could not recognize one stone of it. They had gone into the city on just three occasions, but had returned home, heads aching from the effort, and had not managed to find anything in the chaotic jumble of the *quartiers*.

But Jeanne would sometimes insist.

'Oh, please tell me!' she begged. 'Those windows that are all white?... It's so big, surely you must know.'

She pointed to the Palais de l'Industrie. Hélène hesitated.

'It's a station. No, I think it's a theatre...'

She smiled. She kissed Jeanne's hair and made her usual reply:

'I don't know, darling.'

Then they went on looking at Paris, no longer trying to work out what everything was. It was very peaceful, having the city there and being ignorant of it, an infinity, unknown to them. It was as if they had been halted on the threshold of a world whose eternal spectacle lay in front of them and they refused to enter. Paris often made them anxious when she sent them her warm and troubling vapours. But that morning she was gay and innocent as a child, in her mystery wafting across to them there was nothing but gentleness.

Hélène took up her book again while Jeanne snuggled up close and continued to gaze. In the bright still sky there was not a breath of wind. The smoke from the Military Depot went straight up in wisps which rose high in the sky and disappeared. And along the tops of the houses, ripples passed over the city, throbbing with life, pulsating with all the life contained within it. The shrill voice of the streets took on a relaxed and happy note in the sunshine. But a noise attracted Jeanne's attention. It was a flight of white pigeons, which had set off from some neighbouring loft and were crossing in front of the window. They filled the horizon, the fluttering snow of their wings obscured the immensity that was Paris.

Looking up again, gazing into space, Hélène was in deep thought. She was the Lady Rowena, a noble soul, deeply and silently in love. This spring morning, this great, beloved city, these first scented wallflowers on her knees, were little by little melting her heart.

PART TWO

CHAPTER 1

ONE morning, Hélène was busy tidying her little bookcase, where for the last few days she had left the books in disarray, when Jeanne came in, jumping up and down and clapping her hands.

'Maman,' she cried, 'a soldier! A soldier!'

'A soldier? What do you mean, a soldier?' the young woman asked.

But the little girl was in one of her gay, exuberant moods; she jumped up and down even more, repeating: 'A soldier! A soldier!' without further explanation. Then, as she had left the door of her room open, Hélène got up and was astonished to catch sight of a little soldier in the hallway. Rosalie had gone out; Jeanne must have been playing on the landing despite it being strictly forbidden by her mother.

'What do you want, my friend?' asked Hélène.

The little soldier, very uneasy at the appearance of such a beautiful lady in her white lace dressing gown, scuffed his foot on the wooden floor, bowed, and blurted out:

'I'm sorry, excuse me...'

And he could think of nothing more to say, but retreated, still shuffling, to the wall. Unable to find any more words and seeing that the lady, who couldn't repress a smile, was waiting, he rummaged energetically in his right-hand pocket and took out a blue handkerchief, a knife, and a hunk of bread. He examined each object and shoved them back again. Then he tried the other pocket. In it was a bit of rope, two rusty nails, pictures wrapped in half a newspaper. He stuffed it all back again and tapped his legs with an anxious expression. And stuttered, terrified:

'I'm sorry, excuse me.'

But all of a sudden he placed one finger to his nose and burst out laughing. What a fool he was! Now he remembered. He undid two buttons on his greatcoat, and felt around in his chest, pushing his arm in as far as the elbow. Finally he got out a letter, and gave it a violent shake as if to get rid of the dust, before handing it over to Hélène.

'A letter for me, are you sure?' she asked.

On the envelope was, indeed, her name and address in large unformed letters, with downstrokes that fell on top of one another like a row of dominoes. And as soon as she had managed to understand, halting at each line by the extraordinary turns of phrase and spelling, she smiled again. It was a letter from Rosalie's aunt, who was sending Zéphyrin to her. He had been conscripted 'in spite of the two Masses said for him by Monsieur le Curé'. So, given that Zéphyrin was in love with Rosalie, she begged Madame to allow the children to see each other on Sundays. This request was made over three pages, in the same terms, but more and more muddled, with a constant effort to express something which she wasn't managing to articulate. But then, before signing, the aunt had seemed suddenly to hit on what she was trying to say, and had written: 'Monsieur le Curé says it's all right', and splattering ink all over it as she pressed down hard with her pen.

Hélène slowly folded the letter. While she was puzzling out what it could mean she had looked up two or three times to glance at the soldier. He was still standing against the wall and his lips were moving, he seemed to be emphasizing each phrase with a little movement of his chin. No doubt he knew the letter by heart.

'So you are Zéphyrin Lacour?' she said.

He began to laugh, then wagged his head.

'Come in, my friend, don't stay out there.'

He decided to follow her in, but when Hélène sat down he remained standing by the door. She had not been able to have a good look at him in the dark hall. He must have been exactly Rosalie's height. A centimetre less and he would have not been in the army. Clean-shaven, and with his red hair cropped very short, he had a very round freckled face, with two piercing eyes thin as gimlet holes. His new greatcoat, too big for him, made him look even rounder. And his legs akimbo in his red trousers, and swinging his *képi* with the wide peak in front of him, he was a funny and pathetic sight with his small, round face, and still the peasant beneath his army uniform. Hélène wanted to question him and find out some things about him.

'Did you leave the Beauce a week ago?'

'Yes, Madame.'

'And now you are in Paris. Are you not unhappy about that?'

'No, Madame.'

He was emboldened, looking around the room, greatly impressed by the blue velvet furnishings.

'Rosalie isn't here,' Hélène went on, 'but she won't be long. Her aunt tells me you are her good friend.'

The little soldier didn't answer. He bowed his head, laughing uncomfortably, and started scuffing the rug again with his foot.

'So you are going to marry her when you finish in the army?' continued the young woman.

'Of course,' he said, blushing red, 'of course, I swear.'

And won over by the kindly attitude of this lady, turning his *képi* round and round between his fingers, he decided to tell her everything.

'Oh, I've known her a long time. When we were kids we went scrumping together. We got the stick a lot; that's the truth. The Lacours and the Pichons lived next door to each other in the same street, you see. So Rosalie and I were brought up practically eating off the same plate... Then all her family died. Her Aunt Marguerite fed her, but my word, she was already as strong as an ox...'

He stopped, feeling that he was getting excited, and he asked in a hesitant voice:

'But maybe she's told you all that?'

'Yes, but tell me again,' replied Hélène, amused by him.

'Well then,' he went on, 'she was pretty strong, though no bigger than a sparrow; but she could do the business, you ought to have seen her! One day she slapped someone of my acquaintance, oh, indeed she did! Slap me she did! My arm was black and blue for a week. Yes, that's how it was. Everybody in the neighbourhood had us married. We were hardly ten years old when we were going together, and we still are, Madame, we still are...'

He put one hand on his heart, spreading out his fingers. But Hélène had become very grave again. The idea of letting a soldier into her household bothered her. Monsieur le Curé might well allow it, but she found it a little risky. In the country you are very free, lovers do as they please. She allowed her fears to show. When Zéphyrin had understood, he thought he would die laughing. But he held back, out of respect.

'Oh Madame, oh Madame, I can see you don't know what she's like. She's given me many a slap! Goodness, we lads like a laugh, don't we? I used to pinch her bottom sometimes. Then she turns round and "whack!" straight on the snout! Her aunt used to say to her: "Listen, my girl, don't let yourself be tickled, it's unlucky." The curé got involved too and perhaps that's why we are still friends... We were supposed to get married after the drawing of the lots. Then, what do you know! Things didn't go too well. Rosalie said she would go into service in Paris to earn enough for her dowry while she waited for me. So that's the long and short of it!'

He stood on one leg, then the other, passing his *képi* from right hand to left. But as Hélène didn't say anything he thought she doubted his good faith. That wounded him. He cried fervently:

'Mebbe you think I'll cheat on her? I told you I've sworn to be true! I shall marry her, you see, as sure as eggs is eggs. And I'm ready to put my name to that. Yes, if you like I'll sign a paper.' His passion roused him. He walked around the room, looking for a pen and some ink. Hélène did her utmost to calm him down. He said again:

'I'd rather sign a paper. Wouldn't that be enough? You'll trust me after that.'

But at that moment Jeanne, who had again vanished, came dancing back, clapping her hands.

'Rosalie! Rosalie, Rosalie!' she sang, in a catchy little tune she had invented.

And through the open door you could indeed hear the maid puffing as she climbed the stairs, laden with her basket. Zéphyrin withdrew into a corner; he laughed silently, a smile spread from ear to ear and his gimlet eyes glowed with a peasant's mischievousness. Without further ado Rosalie came straight into the room as she was in the habit of doing, to show her mistress what she had bought that morning.

'Madame,' she said, 'I've bought some cauliflowers. Look, two for eighteen sous, not dear!'

She half-opened her basket when, looking up, she caught sight of Zéphyrin there chuckling. Flabbergasted, she was rooted to the spot. Two or three seconds elapsed before she recognized him beneath his uniform. Her round eyes widened, her little fat face paled, and her coarse black hair shook to and fro.

'Oh,' was all she could say.

And, in her surprise, she let go her basket. The provisions fell to the floor, the cauliflowers, onions and apples. Jeanne uttered a cry of delight and threw herself down in the middle of the room, scrambling after the apples, even under the armchairs and the wardrobe with the mirror. Meanwhile Rosalie, still in a state of shock, did not move, but said over and over again:

'What, you! What are you doing here? Tell me, what are you doing here?'

She turned to Hélène and asked:

'So was it you that let him in?'

Zéphyrin did not speak, but made do with a wink and a mischievous smile. Then Rosalie's eyes filled with tears of love and to show how happy she was to see him again, all she could do was make fun of him.

'Oh, go on with you,' she said. 'What a sight you look in that get-up! I might have passed you by in the street and not even said "God bless you!" Just look at you! You look as if you're wearing your sentry box. And they've given your head a real good shave, you look like the sacristan's poodle. How ugly you are, God, you are a sight!'

Zéphyrin, vexed, decided to open his mouth.

'It's not my fault, don't blame me. You wouldn't look any better if they sent you to the regiment.'

They had quite forgotten where they were, the room, Hélène, and Jeanne, who was still picking up apples. The maid stood in front of the little soldier, hands clasped on her apron.

'So is everything going all right back home?' she asked.

'Yes, except the Guignards' cow's full of water, the quack came and told them she was full of water.'

'If she's full of water, there's no hope for her. Apart from that, is everything all right?'

'Oh yes, the beadle's broken his arm, Old Canivet's dead. Monsieur le Curé's lost his purse, there were thirty sous in it, when he was coming back from Grandval. Otherwise everything's good.'

Then they stopped. They looked at one another with shining eyes, and their mouths puckered into an affectionate smile. That must have been their manner of embracing, for they hadn't even shaken hands. But Rosalie suddenly came out of her daze and was upset to see her vegetables on the floor. What a mess! He made her do some fine things to be sure! Madame should have let him wait on the stairs. As she scolded him she bent down and put the apples, onions, cauliflowers into the bottom of her basket, much to Jeanne's dismay, who did not want anyone to help her. And as Rosalie was returning to her kitchen without a backward glance at Zéphyrin, Hélène, won over by the quiet strength of the pair of lovers, kept her back to say:

'Listen, Rosalie. Your aunt asked me to let this young man come and see you on Sundays... He can come in the afternoon and you must try not to let your work suffer too much.'

Rosalie stopped and simply turned her head. She was really very pleased but still looked put out.

'Oh, Madame, he'll be bound to get under my feet!' she cried.

And over her shoulder she threw a glance at Zéphyrin and again made an affectionate face at him. The little soldier remained motionless for a moment, his half-open mouth suppressing a laugh. Then he backed out of the door, saying his thank-yous and placing his *képi* over his heart. The door had shut, but he was still taking his leave as he reached the landing.

'Is that Rosalie's brother?' asked Jeanne.

Hélène was very embarrassed by the question. She was sorry she had just given her consent to this, in that impulse of generosity, which had surprised herself. She reflected for a second or two and replied:

'No, it's her cousin.'

'Oh,' said the little girl solemnly.

Rosalie's kitchen looked out on to the garden of Doctor Deberle, full in the sun. In the summer the branches of the elms came in through the very wide window. It was the sunniest room in the apartment, extremely light and bright, so bright indeed that Rosalie had had to put up a blue cotton curtain, which she drew in the afternoons. All she complained about was the size of this kitchen, which was long and narrow, the oven on the right, a table and a sideboard on the left. But she had arranged the utensils and furniture so skilfully that she had made room near the window for some free space where she worked in the evenings. Keeping the saucepans, kettles, and plates in tip-top condition was a matter of pride for her. So when the sun appeared, the walls glittered splendidly, the copper pans threw out gold sparks, the round iron pans shone like dazzling silver moons, while the blue and white china tiles on the stove lent a paler note to this blaze of light.

The following Saturday in the course of the evening, Hélène heard such a noise that she decided to see what was going on.

'What is it?' she asked. 'Are you having a fight with the furniture?'

'I'm washing the floor, Madame,' Rosalie replied, dishevelled and perspiring, crouching on the tiles and scrubbing as hard as her small arms could manage.

It was finished, she was mopping. She had never cleaned her kitchen so thoroughly. A newly-wed could have slept there, everything was white, as for a wedding. The table and sideboard looked as if they had been planed down, she had worn out her fingers to such an extent. And the saucepans and pots arranged in their proper order of size were a sight to see, each one on its nail, even the frying pan and the grill pan shining without a spot of black on them. Hélène remained there for a moment, not speaking. Then she smiled and withdrew.

Thereafter, every Saturday, Rosalie did the same amount of cleaning, four hours spent in dust and water. On Sundays she wanted to show Zéphyrin how cleanly she was. That was her 'at home' day. She would have been ashamed to see a spider's web. When everything was shining she was in a good mood and began to sing. At three o'clock she was still washing her hands, and putting on a bonnet with ribbons. Then, pulling the cotton curtain halfway down so that the light was like that of a boudoir, in the middle of her tidy kitchen beautifully scented with thyme and laurel, she waited for Zéphyrin to arrive.

Zéphyrin arrived at precisely half-past three. He had been walking up and down the street until the half-hour chimed on the clocks all around. Rosalie listened to the sound of his shoes clumping up the stairs, and opened the door when he paused on the landing. She had forbidden him to touch the bell-pull. Each time the same words were exchanged:

'Is that you?'

'Yes, it's me.'

And they stayed there, their noses touching, eyes sparkling and mouths pursed. Then Zéphyrin followed Rosalie in, but she stopped him before she had taken off his shako and his sword. She didn't want them in her kitchen, she hid the sword and the shako at the back of a cupboard. Then she sat her lover down near the window in the place she had prepared and did not let him move.

'Behave yourself, you can watch me prepare Madame's dinner, if you like.'

But he almost never arrived empty-handed. Usually he had spent the morning with his comrades in the woods of Meudon, trailing around on interminable walks, drinking in the fresh air at his leisure, vaguely nostalgic for home. To keep his hands busy, he cut sticks, sharpened them, decorated them as he walked along with all kinds of curlicues; and he would slow down even more, stop near the fortifications, his shako tipped back, his eyes fixed on his knife carving the wood. Then, as he couldn't bring himself to throw his sticks away, he brought them to Rosalie in the afternoon, who took them off him, protesting a little, because it made the kitchen dirty. The truth was that she made a collection of them. Under her bed she had a bundle, of different lengths and designs.

One day he arrived with a nest full of eggs that he had put in the bottom of his shako under his handkerchief. He said an omelette made of birds' eggs was really delicious. Rosalie threw the disgusting things away but kept the nest, which went to join the sticks. In any case his pockets were always full to bursting. He took out strange things from them, translucent pebbles, found on the banks of the Seine, old iron objects, wild berries which were drying, unidentifiable bits and pieces that the rag and bone men didn't want. Above all he liked pictures. Along the road he collected wrapping papers of chocolate or soap on which there were negroes and palm trees, belly dancers or bunches of roses. Old tins with blonde and rapturous ladies on the lids, polished engravings and silver paper from apple sugar jettisoned in the fairs round about were among his precious finds and made him swell with happiness. All this booty disappeared into his pockets. He wrapped the best pieces in a sheet of newspaper. And on Sundays whenever Rosalie had a minute to spare between a sauce and a roast, he showed her these pictures. She could have them if she liked. But since the paper wrapped around them wasn't always clean, he cut out the pictures, which he greatly enjoyed doing. Rosalie got annoyed, shreds of paper fluttered up into her dishes, and the peasant cunning he employed, the lengths he went to to get hold of her scissors had to be seen to be believed. Sometimes she gave them to him impatiently, to be rid of him.

Meanwhile a roux sauce was bubbling in a pan, Rosalie was watching the sauce, wielding a wooden spoon, while Zéphyrin, his shoulders looking wider because of the red epaulettes, bent over and cut out his pictures. He was so closely shaven, you could see his bare head. And his yellow collar gaped at the back, revealing his sunburnt neck. For an entire quarter of an hour neither would speak. When Zéphyrin raised his head, he watched Rosalie with the deepest interest as she took some flour, chopped up parsley and seasoned the dish with salt and pepper. Then he would utter the odd word.

'Hmm! Smells good!'

The cook, in the middle of her cooking, did not deign to answer immediately. After a long silence she said:

'It has to simmer, you see.'

And their conversations went no further than that. They did not even talk any more about where they came from. When they were reminded of something, they only had to say one word to understand each other, and laughed inwardly for the rest of the afternoon. That was enough for them. By the time Rosalie showed Zéphyrin the door, they had enjoyed each other's company enormously.

'Right, time you went. I am going to serve up Madame's dinner.'

She gave him back his shako and his sword, pushed him away and served Madame, her flushed cheeks betraying her pleasure, while he, swinging his arms, went back to the barracks with his nostrils still tingling with the sweet scents of thyme and bay.

For the first few times Hélène thought she should keep an eye on them. She sometimes arrived without warning to give her orders. But she always found Zéphyrin in his place between the table and the window near the clay water tank which obliged him to keep his legs tucked under him. As soon as Madame appeared, he got up as if he were presenting arms and remained standing. If Madame spoke to him he answered with only respectful greetings and mutterings. Little by little Hélène was reassured, noticing that she was never in their way and that in the patience of their love they were never perturbed.

Rosalie seemed at that time a lot sharper than Zéphyrin. She had already spent some months in Paris, so was becoming more savvy, although she only knew three streets, the Rue de Passy, the Rue Franklin, and the Rue Vineuse. He, in his regiment, was still a bumpkin. She insisted to Madame that they were 'coarsening' him; for where he came from, of course, he'd been smarter than that. It was the fault of the uniform, she claimed. All the boys who ended up as soldiers became stupid as could be. It was true, Zéphyrin, his head turned by this new existence, had the round eyes and the gawkiness of a goose. Beneath his epaulettes he was still stolid like a countryman, the barracks had not yet taught him the fine phrases or the swaggering manner of the Parisian infantryman. Oh, Madame need not worry! He was not a man to lark about.

So Rosalie was maternal towards him. She lectured Zéphyrin while roasting meat on the spit, gave him good advice about the terrible dangers he must avoid. And he obeyed, giving a vigorous nod to each piece of advice. Every Sunday he had to swear to her he had been to Mass and had said his prayers dutifully morning and night. She exhorted him to be cleanly, brushed his coat when he left, sewed a button tighter on his jacket, and looked him over from top to toe, to see that nothing was out of place. She worried about his health as well and suggested remedies for all sorts of maladies. Zéphyrin, grateful for all her little kindnesses, offered to fill her water tank. For quite some time she refused, fearing he might spill the water. But one day he brought up the two pails without letting so much as a drop fall on the stairs; and from then on, he it was who filled it on Sundays. He did other jobs for her, all the heavy ones, and would go and get butter from the grocer's if she had forgotten to buy any. Eventually he even helped with the cooking. First he peeled the vegetables. Later she allowed him to cut them up. After six weeks he did not make the sauces, but he watched over them, wooden spoon in hand. Rosalie had made him her assistant and sometimes burst out laughing to see him in his red trousers and yellow collar in action in front of the stove, a tea towel over his arm like a kitchen boy.

One Sunday, Hélène came into the kitchen. Her slippers muffled the sound of her steps, she stayed outside the door without either the maid or the soldier hearing her. In his corner, Zéphyrin was at the table in front of a steaming bowl of soup. Rosalie, who had her back to the door, was cutting long pieces of bread to dip in the soup.

'Come on, eat up, my dear!' she said. 'You do too much walking, that's why you are empty. Here, have you got enough? Do you want some more?'

And she brooded over him, with an expression of loving concern. He was bent squarely over his bowl, swallowing a piece of bread with every mouthful. His yellow-freckled face was reddening in the steam that bathed it. He muttered:

'Well, this is good stuff, sure enough! Whatever do you put in it?'

'Wait a minute,' she went on, 'if you like leeks...'

But as she turned round she caught sight of Madame. She uttered a little cry. Both were turned to stone. Then Rosalie started to apologize and the words came flooding out.

'It's my share, Madame. Oh, believe you me... I wouldn't have had a second helping, it's God's truth! I told him: "If you want my share of the soup I'll give it you." Well, say something, you, you know quite well that's what happened...'

And worried by the silence of her mistress, thinking her cross, she went on in a broken voice:

'He was dying of hunger, Madame. He stole a raw carrot from me... They don't feed them properly! And imagine, Madame, he walked such a long way up the river, I don't know where. You would have said yourself: "Rosalie, give him some soup."'

Then Hélène, looking at the little soldier, there with his mouth full, not daring to swallow, could not be stern with him. She answered gently:

'Well, my dear, when he's hungry you must let him stay for dinner, that's all. I give you permission.'

Seeing the two of them, she had felt her heart melt, as it had once before, making her forget to be strict. They were so happy in this kitchen! The cotton curtain, half-pulled down, let in the setting sun. On the back wall the copper pans were blazing, lighting up the darkening room with rosy reflections. And there in that golden shadow, their two small round faces were visible, quiet and clear as moons. Their love had a calm certainty about it, it was entirely in keeping with the order and beauty of the kitchen utensils. The good smells from the stove made them relax, their appetites were sharpened and their hearts nourished.

'Tell me, Maman,' said Jeanne that evening, after pondering the matter at some length. 'Rosalie's cousin doesn't ever kiss her, why is that?'

'And why should they kiss each other?' Hélène replied. 'They'll kiss on their wedding day.'

CHAPTER 2

AFTER the soup that Tuesday Hélène looked up and remarked:

'It's pouring down, can you hear? My dear friends, you'll be soaked this evening.'

'Oh, it's just a drop or two,' said the abbé quietly. His old soutane was already damp on the shoulders.

'I've got a good little way to go,' said Monsieur Rambaud, 'but I'll walk back all the same. I enjoy that and besides I have an umbrella.'

Jeanne was thoughtful, and was solemnly contemplating her last spoonful of vermicelli. Then she said slowly:

'Rosalie was saying you wouldn't come because of the bad weather...
Maman said you would... You are really nice, you always do come.'

Around the table everyone smiled. Hélène nodded affectionately in
the direction of the two brothers. Outside the thudding rain did not
cease and sudden gusts of wind rattled the blinds. Winter seemed to
be back. Rosalie had carefully drawn the red rep curtain. Amidst the
battering of the strong winds, there was a delightful atmosphere of
loving intimacy in the little dining room, all its doors tight shut, and
lit by the tranquil beam of the white pendant light. On the mahogany
sideboard the china reflected its quiet glow. And in this peaceful
ambience the four talked in a leisurely fashion around a table where
all was just as it should be, and waited for the maid to put in an
appearance.

'Oh, you were waiting for me! Never mind!' said Rosalie, unceremoniously, coming in with a dish. 'It's grilled fillets of sole for Monsieur
Rambaud, and they don't need cooking till the last minute.'

Monsieur Rambaud pretended to love his food, to amuse Jeanne
and to please Rosalie, who was very proud of her talents as a cook. He
turned to her, saying:

'Tell me, what have you got for us today? You always bring us treats
when I'm no longer hungry.'

'Oh,' she replied. 'There are three dishes, as usual; no more, no
less. After the sole fillets, you are going to have lamb and brussel
sprouts... that's all, I swear.'

But Monsieur Rambaud was looking at Jeanne out of the corner of
his eyes. The little girl enjoyed that, stifling her merriment behind
her hands, shaking her head as much as to say that the maid was fib-
bing. Then he clicked his tongue doubtfully and Rosalie pretended to
get cross.

'You don't believe me,' she said, 'because Mademoiselle is laughing... Well, you can rely upon it, if you don't eat your fill, you'll see if
you don't have to have something else to eat when you go back home.'

When the maid had gone, Jeanne, in fits of laughter, was itching to
say something.

'You do love your food,' she began; 'I went into the kitchen...'
But she broke off.

'Oh no, we mustn't tell him, must we, Maman? It's nothing, nothing at all. I was only laughing to catch you out.'

This scene was replayed every Tuesday with always the same success.

Hélène was touched by the good humour with which Monsieur Rambaud lent himself to this game, for she was well aware that he had once lived, with Provençal frugality, on anchovies and a dozen olives a day. As for Abbé Jouve, he was never aware of what he was eating. They often even teased him about this and his absent-mindedness. Jeanne watched him with glowing eyes. When they had been served, she said to the priest:

'The whiting's delicious!'

'Delicious, my pet,' he murmured. 'Oh yes, it's whiting. I thought it was turbot.'

And as everyone was laughing, he naively asked why Rosalie, who had just come in, seemed very hurt. Well, where she came from, the priest knew his food. He could tell how old a chicken was, to the nearest week, just by carving it. He didn't need to go into the kitchen to know in advance what was for dinner, he could smell what it was going to be. Goodness, if she had been in the service of a priest like Monsieur l'Abbé she wouldn't even know now how to cook an omelette. And the priest apologized in an embarrassed way as if the absolute lack of any appreciation of good food was a fault he was desperate to correct. But in reality he had a lot of other things on his mind.

'This is a joint of lamb,' declared Rosalie, putting the lamb on the table.

Everyone started to laugh again, Abbé Jouve was the first. He thrust out his large head, winking his little eyes.

'Yes that's definitely a leg of lamb,' he said. 'I think I should have known that.'

In fact that day the abbé was more distracted than usual. He ate quickly with the haste of someone who doesn't care what is placed in front of him, and who eats standing up when he's at home. Then he waited for the others, absorbed in his own thoughts, just smiling in reply to what was said. Every minute he threw a glance of both encouragement and anxiety at his brother. Monsieur Rambaud did not seem to be his usual calm self either; his anxiety expressed itself in the need to talk and to fidget on his chair, which was not natural to a man normally so thoughtful. After the brussel sprouts, there was a silence, as Rosalie was slow in bringing the dessert. Outside, torrents of rain, even louder now, were beating at the house. In the dining room they found the air rather stuffy. Then Hélène realized that the atmosphere had changed, that there was something between the two brothers they were not saying. She looked at them in some concern and finally said:

'Goodness me, what dreadful rain!... Is it bothering you? You both seem to be rather troubled about something?'

But they said no, they hastened to reassure her. And as Rosalie arrived carrying a huge dish, Monsieur Rambaud cried, to hide his feelings:

'What did I tell you! Another treat!'

The treat that day was a vanilla cream, one of the cook's specialities. The wide smile with which she put it on the table, without a word, was something to be seen. Jeanne clapped her hands, saying over and over:

'I knew it, I knew it! I saw the eggs in the kitchen.'

'But I'm not hungry any more!' said Monsieur Rambaud, desperately. 'I can't possibly eat any.'

Then Rosalie's face fell, and she was full of repressed resentment. But she simply said, in a dignified voice:

'What! A cream I made for you! Well, just try to stop yourself eating any! Yes, just you try!'

He resigned himself, and took a large helping of the cream. The abbé remained distracted. He rolled up his napkin, got up before the dessert was over, as he often did. He walked around for a moment, his head on one side. Then, when Hélène in her turn left the table, he threw Monsieur Rambaud a meaningful glance and took the young woman into the bedroom. Behind them, through the door which had been left open, the measured tone of their voices could be heard almost immediately, without the words being audible.

'Hurry up!' said Jeanne to Monsieur Rambaud, who seemed quite unable to finish his biscuit. 'I want to show you what I've been doing.'

He was in no hurry to do so; but when Rosalie started to clear the table, he had to get up.

'Wait a moment, wait,' he murmured when the little girl wanted to make him come into the bedroom.

And he kept away from the door, embarrassed and uneasy. Then as the abbé raised his voice, he felt so weak that he had to sit down once more at the empty table. He took a newspaper out of his pocket.

'I'll make you a little cart,' he offered.

Jeanne immediately stopped talking about going into the bedroom. Monsieur Rambaud astonished her with his skill in making all sorts of things to play with out of his newspaper. He made paper hens, boats, hats, carts, cages. But today his fingers shook as they twisted the paper and he had difficulty folding the small corners. At the least noise from the room next door he bent his head. Meanwhile Jeanne, very absorbed, leaned over the table next to him.

'Afterwards you can make a little bird to harness to the cart,' she said.

At the back of the bedroom, Abbé Jouve remained standing in the pale shadow cast by the lampshade. Hélène sat in her usual seat again, by the little table, and, as she did not stand on ceremony on a Tuesday amongst friends, she was doing her needlework. Her small white hands sewing a child's bonnet were the only things to be seen in the circle of bright light.

'Is Jeanne not a worry to you at all any more?' asked the abbé.

She shook her head before she spoke.

'Doctor Deberle seems quite confident now,' she said. 'But the poor little thing is still very highly strung. Yesterday I found her half unconscious on a chair.'

'She doesn't take enough exercise,' the priest said. 'You don't get out enough, you don't have a very normal life.'

He stopped and there was silence. He had no doubt found the opportunity he was looking for to broach the subject. But just as he was going to speak, he contained himself. He took a chair, sat down at Hélène's side and said:

'Listen, my child, I've been wanting to have a serious talk with you for some time... The life you are living is not good. Such a cloistered existence at your age is not recommended and this renunciation is as bad for your daughter as it is for you... There are many, many dangers; it's dangerous for your health and for other things besides.'

Hélène looked up at him in surprise.

'What are you trying to say, my friend?' she asked.

'Heaven knows I am not a man of the world,' the priest continued, rather embarrassed, 'but I know that a woman is very vulnerable when she is left without anyone to look after her... I mean that you are very much on your own and this degree of solitude is not healthy, believe you me. The day will come when you will suffer because of it.'

'But I'm not complaining, I think I'm very well off as I am!' she cried, with some feeling.

The old priest shook his large head gently.

'That's all well and good. And I understand that you feel perfectly contented. Only one never knows where it will lead, this slippery slope of solitude and reverie. Oh, I know you, I know you are incapable of wrongdoing... But sooner or later you might lose that sense of peace and quiet. And one morning it will be too late, the void in your life will be filled by feelings that are painful and that you cannot speak of.'

In the shadows Hélène's face had turned pink. Could the abbé read her secret thoughts? Was he aware then of the feelings which had been growing in her, this agitation in her heart which filled her life and which she herself had not wanted to question until now? Her needlework fell on to her lap. She became rather limp, she was expecting a kind of complicity from this man of the cloth, which would allow her finally to confess it aloud and define those vague things that she was shutting away in the back of her mind. Since he knew everything, he could ask her questions and she would try to answer them.

'I put myself in your hands, my friend,' she murmured. 'You know I've always listened to you.'

The priest was quiet for a moment, then slowly and solemnly he said: 'You must marry again, my child.'

She was dumbstruck, her arms had fallen to her side, she was flabbergasted by this piece of advice. She was expecting something different, she didn't follow him. But the priest carried on, giving her reasons why she should make up her mind to remarry.

'Remember you are still young... You can't stay in this backwater of Paris any longer, hardly daring to go out, not knowing anything of life. You must return to living in society, or you may bitterly regret your isolation later on. You don't realize how this reclusive behaviour gradually affects you, but your friends see how pale you are and worry about you.'

He stopped at every phrase, hoping she would interrupt him and discuss his proposition. But she remained very cold, as though frozen in disbelief.

'Of course you have a child,' he went on, 'so it's always a delicate matter... But remember that in the interests of Jeanne herself, a man would be a real support... Oh, I know you would have to find a perfectly good man, who would be a proper father to her.'

She did not allow him to finish. She answered him tersely and with unusual revulsion and rebellion.

'No no, I don't want that. How can you give me such advice, my friend? Never, do you hear, never!'

Her heart rose in her mouth, she frightened herself by the vehemence of her refusal. The priest's proposition had just touched that hidden place inside her which she shied away from knowing. And by the way it hurt, she at last realized the extent of her suffering. She felt the fearful modesty of a woman whose last item of clothing is being torn away.

Then beneath the clear and smiling gaze of the old priest, she struggled to defend herself.

'But I don't want to! I'm not in love with anyone!'

Yet as he continued to look at her, she thought he could read the lie written all over her face. She reddened and stammered:

'But just think, I only came out of mourning two weeks ago... no, it's not possible...'

'My child,' said the priest, 'I have thought for a long time before speaking out. I think your happiness lies there. Calm yourself. You will never be forced to do anything against your will.'

The conversation came to an end. Hélène tried to swallow the flood of protests which rose to her lips. She took up her work again, sewed a stitch or two, her head bowed. And in the midst of the silence the fluting tones of Jeanne could be heard from the dining room:

'You don't harness a little bird to a cab, you harness a horse. Don't you know how to make a horse?'

'Oh no, horses are too difficult,' said Monsieur Rambaud. 'But if you like, I'll teach you how to make carts.'

The game always ended that way. Jeanne, concentrating hard, watched her friend fold the paper into lots of little squares. Then she tried to make one herself. But she got it wrong, stamped her foot. Yet she already knew how to make boats and hats.

'It's like this,' Monsieur Rambaud said patiently, 'you fold down the four corners like that and then you turn it over...'

For a minute or two, cocking his ear, he must have heard something of what was being said in the room next door; and his poor hands shook even more, he was so tongue-tied he swallowed half his words.

Hélène, who could not compose herself, resumed the conversation.

'But who would I get married to?' she asked the priest suddenly, putting her sewing back on the little table. 'You have someone in mind, do you?'

Abbé Jouve had risen to his feet and was walking slowly around the room. He nodded his head, but carried on walking.

'Well, tell me who you are thinking of,' she said. For one moment he stood in front of her, then shrugged slightly:

'What's the point, if you are set against it?'

'It doesn't matter, I want to know,' she said. 'How am I to decide if I don't know?'

He did not answer immediately, but stood there looking straight at her. He gave a rather sad smile. It was almost in a whisper that he said finally:

'What, you can't guess?'

No she couldn't. She thought hard, in puzzlement. Then he simply gestured. He nodded in the direction of the dining room.

'Him!' she exclaimed, struggling to keep her voice down.

And she grew very solemn. She no longer protested with such violence. On her face there was only surprise and sorrow. For a long time she remained with her eyes cast down, reflecting. No, she would surely never have guessed. And yet she couldn't find any objection to it. Monsieur Rambaud was the only man in whose hand she would have faithfully placed her own, without a qualm. She knew how kind he was, she did not find his bourgeois heaviness laughable. But despite all her affection for him, the idea that he loved her made her freeze.

Meanwhile the abbé had started walking up and down the room again, and as he passed in front of the door to the dining room, he called to Hélène softly.

'Come over here and see.'

She got up and went to look.

In the end Monsieur Rambaud had seated Jeanne on his own chair. He had been leaning against the table and now was kneeling down in front of the little girl, one arm around her waist. On the table was the cart harnessed to the little paper hen, then some boats, boxes, bishops' mitres.

'So do you love me then?' he asked. 'Tell me you love me.'

'Yes, of course I do, you know I do.'

He hesitated, trembling as though he were about to make a declaration of love.

'And if I asked if I could stay here with you always, what would you say?'

'Oh, I'd be very happy. We'd play together, wouldn't we? It would be fun.'

'Always, do you understand? I'd always be here.' Jeanne had picked up a boat and was shaping it into a gendarme's helmet. She said quietly:

'Only Maman would have to say it was all right.'

At this reply all his worries seemed to return. His fate was being decided.

'Of course,' he said. 'But if Maman said it was all right, you wouldn't say no, would you?'

Jeanne, who was finishing her gendarme's cap, was full of glee and started singing a little song she made up:

'I'd say yes, yes, yes... Look at my pretty cap!'

Monsieur Rambaud, moved to tears, kneeled up and put his arms around her and she threw her arms around his neck. He had charged his brother with asking Hélène's consent and now he was trying to obtain Jeanne's.

'As you see,' said the priest, 'the child wants him to.'

Hélène remained grave. She no longer disputed it. The abbé had started to plead on his behalf again and was emphasizing Monsieur Rambaud's qualities. Was he not a ready-made father for Jeanne? She knew him well, she would not be leaving anything to chance if she entrusted herself to him. Then, as she was still silent, the abbé added with feeling and great dignity that, though he was responsible for this proposal, it was not of his brother's happiness but of hers that he was thinking.

'I believe you, I know how much you care for me,' said Hélène quickly. 'Wait, I will give your brother an answer and you shall be there too.'

Ten o'clock struck. Monsieur Rambaud came into the bedroom.

She went to meet him, her hand stretched out, saying:

'Thank you for your offer, my friend. I am very grateful to you. You did right to speak out.'

She looked at him calmly and kept his large hand in her own. He did not dare to raise his eyes, in his trembling state.

'The only thing is, I ask you to let me think about it,' she went on. 'I may need a lot of time.'

'Oh, as long as you like, six months, a year, even more,' he stammered, relieved, happy not to be shown the door straight away.

Then she smiled faintly.

'But of course we shall remain friends. You will come as you have always done, only you must promise to wait until I bring up the subject again. Is that all right?'

He had withdrawn his hand, looked around feverishly for his hat, agreed to everything, with a constant nodding of his head. Then just when he was about to leave he found his tongue again.

'Listen,' he said, 'you know now that I am there for you, don't you? Well, you may be certain that I always will be, come what may. That's what the abbé should have made clear... In ten years, if it's your wish, you will only have to give me a sign. I shall do whatever you ask.'

And it was he who took Hélène's hand one last time and squeezed it so hard that it hurt. On the stairs, the two brothers turned round in the usual way and said:

'See you on Tuesday.'

'Yes, till Tuesday,' Hélène answered.

When she went back into her room, she was depressed by the sound of another downpour beating against the blinds. My goodness, this rain went on and on, her poor friends would get soaked! She opened the window and glanced out into the street. Sudden gusts of wind were blowing against the gas lamps. And among the pale puddles and the hatching of the gleaming raindrops she caught sight of the round form of the disappearing Monsieur Rambaud as he waltzed off happily into the night, not seeming to notice the deluge.

Jeanne, however, had grown very serious since hearing something of what her good friend had said at the end. She had just taken off her little boots and was sitting in her nightdress on the edge of her bed, deep in thought. When her mother came in to kiss her goodnight that was how she found her.

'Goodnight Jeanne. Give me a kiss.'

Then, as the child did not apparently hear, Hélène crouched down beside her and put her arms round her waist. And she questioned her in a low voice.

'Would you like it if he came to live with us?'

Jeanne apparently was not surprised by the question. No doubt she was mulling it over in her head. Slowly she nodded.

'But you know,' said her mother, 'he would be there all the time, by night, by day, when we eat, everywhere.'

The little girl's bright eyes clouded over gradually. She put her cheek against her mother's shoulder, kissed her neck, and then whispering in her ear, said, trembling:

'Maman, would he kiss you?'

A flush crept up Hélène's face. At first she couldn't think how to answer this childish question. Finally she whispered:

'He would be like your father, darling.'

Then Jeanne's little arms stiffened and without warning she burst out in a wild sobbing. She stammered:

'Oh no, no, I don't want him to come any more. Oh, Maman, I beg you, tell him I don't, I don't...'

And she was choking, she threw herself on her mother's breast, and covered her with tears and kisses. Hélène tried to calm her, saying again and again that they would sort things out. But Jeanne wanted a decisive answer straight away.

'Oh, say no, Maman, say no... It would kill me, you can see it would. Never—say you never would!'

'Well, all right, I promise. Be a good girl now and get into bed.'

For a few minutes longer the silent, passionate child hugged her tightly, as though she couldn't let her go, and was guarding her against people who wanted to take her away from her. At last Hélène managed to get her into bed, but she had to sit there for some of the night. In her sleep she was racked by shaking and every half-hour she opened her eyes to make certain Hélène was there, and then fell asleep again with her mouth still pressed to her mother's hand.

CHAPTER 3

It was a wonderful month. The garden grew green in the April sun, a soft green as light and fine as lace. The unruly stems of the clematis pushed their thin shoots up the iron fence, while from the honey-suckle wafted a delicate, almost sugary scent. At the two sides of the lawn, which was cared for and well trimmed, red geraniums and white stocks were flowering in tubs. And at the bottom in the clump of elms, between the neighbouring buildings which pressed against it on either side, there hung a green canopy of branches, whose tiny leaves fluttered at the merest breath of wind.

For more than three weeks the sky remained blue and cloudless. It was as if the miracle of spring was celebrating the new lease of life, the blossoming, that Hélène was feeling in her heart. Each afternoon she went down into the garden with Jeanne. She had her own place by the first elm tree on the right. Her chair was waiting. And the day after she sat there she could see the bits of cotton that she had dropped the previous day.

'Please treat this as your home,' said Madame Deberle each evening, having become obsessed by her for the last six months. 'Goodbye till tomorrow. Try to come earlier, won't you?'

And Hélène did indeed feel at home there. She had got used to this verdant spot, and, like a child, she looked forward to when it would be time to visit. What she found especially attractive about this bourgeois family's garden was the cleanliness and tidiness of the lawn and the flower beds. No stray weed spoiled the symmetry of the greenery. The paths, raked every morning, were soft as carpet underfoot. She lived there in a state of calm repose, not suffering from the rising sap. There was nothing to trouble her in these corbeils which had been so carefully designed, in the cloaks of ivy whose yellow leaves were removed one by one by the gardener. In the secure shadow of the elms, in this hidden bower, perfumed with a note of musk whenever Madame Deberle was present, she could imagine herself in a salon; but the mere sight of the sky when she looked up, reminded her she was in the fresh air, and she took great breaths of it into her lungs.

The two of them often spent the afternoon there without seeing a soul. Jeanne and Lucien played around them. There were long interludes when it was quiet. Then Madame Deberle, who could not stand periods of contemplation, chatted for hours, contenting herself with the silent approval of Hélène, and at the slightest nod from her would continue her chatter more energetically than ever. She told endless stories about the ladies of her acquaintance, plans for parties next winter, chattering like a magpie about current events, and all the chaotic tittle-tattle that collided in that pretty little head of hers. It was mixed with abrupt outbursts of affection towards the children, and passionate words extolling the delights of friendship. Hélène let her catch hold of her hands. She didn't always listen, but living as she was in a tenderly emotional state, she showed she was very touched by Juliette's affection and said she was immensely kind, a real angel.

At other times there were visits. These were a delight to Madame Deberle. Since Easter she had finished having her 'Saturdays' as was right and proper at this time of the year. But she was fearful of solitude, and thrilled when people came to call on her informally in her garden. Her chief preoccupation on those occasions was the choosing of the seaside resort where she would spend the month of August.

With each visitor she began the same discussion again. She explained that her husband would not go with her to the seaside; then she questioned everyone, could not decide. It wasn't for her sake, it was for Lucien's. When the handsome Malignon arrived, he straddled a rustic chair. He hated the country. You had to be mad to leave Paris on the pretext of going to catch cold on the edge of the ocean. Yet he discussed beaches. They were all unhealthy, and he declared that apart from Trouville there were absolutely none anywhere near clean. Each day Hélène heard the same discussion without growing tired of it, even contented with the monotony of her days, which soothed her and sent her to sleep with one thought in mind. At the end of the month, Madame Deberle still did not know where she was going.

One evening as Hélène was leaving, Juliette said:

'I have to go out tomorrow, but don't let that prevent you from coming down. Wait there for me, I shan't be late.'

Hélène accepted. She spent a delightful afternoon alone in the garden. Above her head she could hear nothing but the sparrows' wings fluttering in the trees. All the charm of this sunny little spot entered into her. And from that day, her happiest afternoons were those when her friend left her on her own.

Relations between her and the Deberles grew steadily stronger. She dined with them, was invited at the last minute, as a close friend, to eat with them. When she was sitting late under the elms and Pierre came out on to the steps saying dinner was ready, Juliette begged her to stay and sometimes she agreed. These were family meals, enlivened by the noise of the children. Doctor Deberle and Hélène appeared to be good friends of a reasonable, rather cool, disposition, who liked one another. So Juliette often cried:

'Oh, you'd get on very well together... But it exasperates me that you are so quiet!'

Every afternoon the doctor came back from his visits at about six o'clock. He would find the women in the garden and sit down next to them. At first Hélène had said she would leave straight away, to let husband and wife be together. But Juliette had become so cross at her sudden departure that now she stayed. She found herself included in the domestic life of this family, which always seemed so united. When the doctor arrived, his wife, with the same friendly gesture, always offered her cheek to be kissed, and he kissed it. Then as Lucien seized hold of his legs, he helped him climb up and took him on his lap, chatting the while. The child closed his mouth with his little hands, pulled his hair in the middle of a sentence, behaved so badly that in the end he put him down and told him to go and play with Jeanne. And Hélène smiled at their games, looking up from her sewing for a moment in order to quietly encompass the father, mother, and little boy. The husband's kiss caused her not the slightest embarrassment, and she found Lucien's mischievous ways endearing. You would have supposed she was basking in their serene domesticity.

Meanwhile the sun was setting, yellowing the highest branches. Peace descended from the pale sky. Juliette, who loved to ask questions, even of people she did not know at all well, bombarded her husband with enquiries, often not waiting to hear his answers.

'Where did you go? What have you been doing?'

Then he would tell her about the visits he'd made, somebody he'd met, give her some information about a fabric or piece of furniture seen in a shop window. And often, as he talked, his eyes met Hélène's. Neither turned away. They looked straight at one another, serious for a moment, as though they were able to read each other's hearts. Then they smiled, eyelids slightly closed. The nervous gaiety of Juliette, which she masked with a studied languorousness, did not let them chat for long, for the young woman interrupted all conversation. Yet they did exchange some words, slow banalities which seemed to take on a deeper meaning, reaching beyond the sound of their own voices. Every time they uttered a word they gave a little nod of approval as if all their thoughts were shared. It was an absolute understanding, intimate, issuing from the depths of their being, growing stronger even in the silences. Sometimes Juliette ceased her prattling, slightly ashamed of always talking so much.

'You are not enjoying yourself, are you?' she said. 'We are speaking about things you are not at all interested in.'

'No, don't pay any attention to me,' Hélène answered brightly. 'I am never bored... It makes me happy to listen and not talk.'

She was not lying. It was during those long silences that she most enjoyed being there. Head bowed over her needlework, looking up from time to time to exchange those long glances with the doctor that connected them to each other, she was happy to be enfolded in the privacy of her own emotions. She now admitted to herself that there was a secret feeling between them, something very precious that was all the sweeter because no one in the world shared it with them. But she kept her secret with composure and without shame, for no bad feelings troubled her. How lovely he was with his wife and his child! She loved him even more when he tossed Lucien up in the air and kissed Juliette on the cheek. Ever since she had seen him in his home surroundings their friendship had grown. Now she was one of the family, she didn't think they would ever be apart. And inwardly she called him Henri, quite naturally through hearing Juliette call him that. Her lips would form the word 'Monsieur' but her whole being echoed 'Henri'.

One day the doctor found Hélène under the elm trees. Juliette went out almost every afternoon.

'Oh, is my wife not here?' he asked.

'No, she has abandoned me,' she laughed. 'But you have come back earlier, you know.'

The children were playing at the other end of the garden. He sat down beside her. Their closeness did not bother them at all. For more than an hour they chatted about a multitude of things, without for a moment wishing to allude to the loving feeling which filled their hearts. What was the point of talking about that? Did they not already know what they would have said to each other? All that was necessary to their pleasure was to be together, to agree on everything, to enjoy their carefree reclusion in that very place where he kissed his wife every evening in her presence. That day he teased her about her industriousness.

'Do you know,' he said, 'I don't even know what colour your eyes are, you keep them on your needle the whole time.'

She lifted her head and gazed at him as she usually did, right in the eyes.

'Are you teasing me by any chance?' she asked softly.

But he went on:

'Oh, they are grey, grey with a fleck of blue. Is that right?'

That was all they dared say, but these words, the first that came to mind, were infused with infinite sweetness. Often after that day he found her on her own in the twilight. In spite of themselves, all unawares, their familiarity grew. Their voices changed and contained tender inflexions which they did not have when in company. And yet, when Juliette arrived with her feverish chatter after shopping in Paris, they were not embarrassed by her, they were able to continue the conversation they had begun without having to worry or move their seats further apart. It seemed that this beautiful spring, the garden where the lilacs were in bloom, made the first delights of their passion last longer.

Towards the end of the month Madame Deberle was all agog with a great plan. She had suddenly conceived the idea of having a children's party. The season was well advanced but this idea obsessed her so much, she straight away threw herself into preparing for it with her usual frenzy. She wanted to put on something quite out of the ordinary. It should be a fancy-dress ball. Then that was all she talked about, at home, in other people's houses, everywhere. In the garden there were endless conversations. Malignon found the plan a bit 'silly' but he deigned to take an interest and promised to bring along a singer of comic songs whom he knew. One afternoon when everybody was down under the trees, Juliette was pondering the all-important question of Lucien's and Jeanne's costumes.

'I can't decide,' she said. 'I thought perhaps a Pierrot in white satin.'

'Oh, everyone does that,' said Malignon. 'You'll have at least a dozen Pierrots at your ball... Wait, we must think of something more original.'

And he began to think hard, sucking the knob on his cane. Pauline, arriving, cried:

'I want to go as a soubrette...'

'You!' said Madame Deberle, taken aback. 'But you're not going to dress up! Do you think you are a child, you silly? You will do me the pleasure of wearing a white frock.'

'Well, I should have enjoyed that,' said Pauline, who, in spite of being eighteen and having womanly curves, loved to romp around with very small children.

Hélène meanwhile was doing her needlework at the foot of a tree, looking up now and then to smile at the doctor and Monsieur Rambaud who were standing in front of her, chatting.

Monsieur Rambaud had ended up becoming very friendly with the Deberles.

'And what about Jeanne,' enquired the doctor. 'What will you dress her as?'

But his question was interrupted by an exclamation from Malignon: 'I've got it!... A Louis XV marquis!'

And he twirled his cane, with a look of triumph. Then as nobody present seemed to get excited by the idea he looked very surprised.

'What? Don't you understand? Lucien is entertaining his little guests, isn't he? Well, so you position him at the door to the drawing room dressed as a marquis with a large bouquet of roses beside him and he bows to the ladies.'

'But we shall have dozens of marquises,' Juliette objected.

'What difference does that make?' said Malignon calmly. The more marquises, the funnier it will be. I tell you it's a wonderful idea... The master of the house has to be dressed as a marquis, otherwise your ball will be a disaster.'

He seemed so convinced, that before long Juliette got very enthusiastic about the idea too. It was true that dressed as the Marquis de Pompadour in white satin, with little sprigs of flowers, he would be charming.

'And what about Jeanne?' the doctor asked again.

The little girl had come over and was leaning affectionately on her mother's shoulder, as she was so fond of doing. As Hélène was about to say something, she murmured:

'Oh Maman, you know what you promised?'

'What?' asked those around her.

So, while her daughter threw her a pleading look, Hélène replied with a smile:

'Jeanne doesn't want to tell what she will wear.'

'That's right!' cried the little girl. 'When you tell people what you are going to wear, you don't create an effect at all.'

This coquettish remark made them all laugh for a moment. Monsieur Rambaud started to joke with her. Jeanne had been sulky with him for some time and the poor man, desperate, not knowing how to get back in his little friend's good graces, had begun to tease her, to bring her round to liking him again. He said several times, looking at her:

'I shall tell, I shall tell...'

The little girl had gone very pale. Her sweet little worried face grew hard and angry, her brow was furrowed and her chin tensed and protruding.

'You are not to say anything,' she stammered. And wildly, as he still looked as though he was going to tell everyone, she flung herself at him, shouting:

'Be quiet, I tell you, be quiet! I tell you!'

Hélène had not had time to intervene and stop her burst of temper, one of those blind outbursts that shook the little girl so violently. She admonished her:

'Jeanne, be careful, or I shall have to smack you.'

But Jeanne wasn't listening. Trembling all over, stumbling, choking, she repeated: 'I tell you, I tell you!' in a voice that was more and more hoarse and broken; and with clenched hands she took hold of Monsieur Rambaud's arm and was twisting it with extraordinary strength. Hélène threatened her in vain. Then, unable to control her with sternness, and very distressed by this public display, she made do with murmuring softly:

'Jeanne, you are making me very sad.'

The child immediately let go and turned round. And when she saw her mother's unhappy face with her eyes full of unshed tears, she burst out crying and threw her arms round her neck, stammering:

'No, Maman, no, Maman...'

She placed her hands over her mother's face to stop her crying. Her mother slowly put her from her. Then, broken-hearted, not knowing what she was doing, the little girl dropped on to a seat a few steps away and cried all the more. Lucien, to whom she was always being held up as an example, looked at her, surprised and in a way pleased. And as Hélène was folding up her needlework and apologizing for such a scene, Juliette said that for heaven's sake, children ought to be forgiven everything; the little girl was after all very good-natured and the poor little love was so upset that she had already been punished more than enough. She called her over to embrace her, but Jeanne, refusing to be forgiven, remained on her bench convulsed with tears.

Meanwhile Monsieur Rambaud and the doctor had gone over to her. The former leaned down and asked in his kind, concerned voice:

'Come, darling, why are you so cross? What have I done?'

'You wanted to take Maman away from me,' said the child, spreading out her hands and showing him her desolated face.

The doctor, who was listening, began to laugh. Monsieur Rambaud did not understand at first.

'What are you saying?'

'Yes, yes, the Tuesday before last... You know very well, you got down on your knees and asked me what I would say if you lived in our house.'

The doctor's smile faded. His pale lips trembled slightly. But a blush had spread over Monsieur Rambaud's cheeks, and he stammered, in a low voice:

'But you said we would always play together.'

'Yes, but I didn't realize,' the little girl went on violently. 'I don't want to, do you hear? Don't ever speak of it again, and we can be friends.'

Hélène, standing up with her needlework in her bag, had heard these last words.

'Come on, Jeanne, let's go,' she said. 'You don't want to annoy people by crying.'

She said goodbye, pushing the little girl in front of her. The doctor, very pale, was staring at her. Monsieur Rambaud was in a state of consternation. As for Madame Deberle and Pauline, with the help of Malignon, they had caught hold of Lucien and were turning him round between them, having an animated discussion about how his Marquis de Pompadour costume would look on his little shoulders.

The next day Hélène was by herself under the elm trees. Madame Deberle, rushing here and there with her preparations, had taken Lucien and Jeanne with her. When the doctor got home, earlier than usual, he went quickly down the steps, but did not sit down, he walked round the young woman, pulling bits of bark off the trees. She glanced at him for a second, unnerved by his agitated behaviour.

'The weather is worsening,' she said, embarrassed by the silence. 'It's almost cold this afternoon.'

'It's only April,' he murmured, making an effort to keep his voice level.

He seemed to want to go. But he came over and asked her abruptly:

'So are you getting married?'

This brutal question took her by surprise and made her drop her needlework. She went very white. In a superb effort of will she managed to keep her unruffled countenance, looking at him with wide eyes. She didn't answer and he pleaded with her:

'Oh, tell me, just tell me, are you getting married?'

'Yes, perhaps,' she finally answered in icy tones. 'What is it to you?'

He threw up his hands and shouted:

'But that's impossible!'

'Why?' she responded, her eyes fixed on him.

Then, beneath that gaze that choked back the words on the tip of his tongue, he was forced to stop talking. He remained there a moment longer, putting his hands to his head. Then, as he was filled with emotion and afraid he might do something violent, he went away, while she pretended to take up her needlework again, unconcerned.

But the charm of these precious afternoons had been broken. He tried in vain next day to be affectionate and respectful, but Hélène looked uncomfortable as soon as she was alone with him. There was no longer that pleasant informality, that carefree trust which let them be together without worrying, just enjoying the pure delight of each other's company. Despite the care he took not to frighten her, he would look at her sometimes, and a sudden shudder would go through him, his face reddening. She too had lost her lovely repose. She trembled all over, languished, her hands were weak and idle. All sorts of angry feelings and desires seemed to have been aroused in them.

Hélène got to the point of not wanting Jeanne to be away from her. The doctor found she was there between them all the time, watching them with her big, limpid eyes. But the thing that Hélène simply could not bear was feeling embarrassed now in Madame Deberle's company. When she came back, her hair flying in the wind, and called her 'my dear', telling her about her errands, she no longer listened with her usual cheerful calm. A storm was beginning to rage in the depths of her being, feelings she did not want to analyse. Shame and resentment played a part in it. But then her honest nature was dismayed. She held out her hand to Juliette but could not repress a physical shiver when she touched the warm hands of her friend. Meanwhile the weather had worsened. Heavy showers forced the ladies to take refuge in the Japanese pavilion. The garden, beautifully clean and tidy, had become a lake, and you did not dare walk on the paths for fear of bringing the dirt in on the soles of your shoes. When a ray of light shone through between two clouds, the sodden greenery dried its leaves, the lilacs had pearls hanging on each of their little florets. Under the elms large raindrops fell.

'So it's on Saturday,' Madame Deberle said one day. 'Oh, my dear, I'm exhausted. Aren't you? Be there at two, Jeanne will open the ball with Lucien.'

And, delighted with the preparations for her ball, she gushingly embraced the two children. Then, laughing, she put both arms round Hélène and planted two big kisses on her cheeks.

'That's my reward,' she went on gaily. 'Well, I've deserved it, I've been rushing around enough! You'll see what a success it'll be.'

Hélène remained unmoved, while the doctor observed them over the blond head of Lucien, who had his arms around his neck.

CHAPTER 4

PIERRE was standing in the hall of the big house, in a suit and white tie, opening the door every time a cab drew up. A breath of damp air wafted in, a yellow reflection of the rainy afternoon lit up the narrow hall filled with portières and pot plants. It was two o'clock and the light was fading, as though it were a gloomy winter's day.

But as soon as the valet pushed open the door of the first drawing room, the guests were greeted by a dazzling light. They had closed the blinds and pulled the curtains carefully across, not a glimmer filtered in from the murky sky, and the lamps placed on the furniture, the candles burning in the chandeliers, and the crystal wall-lights illumined what resembled a chapel of rest. Beyond the small drawing room, whose pale green curtains somewhat tempered the dazzle of the lights, the resplendent large black and gold salon was decorated as it was for the ball that Madame Deberle gave every year during the month of January.

In the meantime, children were beginning to arrive, while Pauline was very busy organizing lines of chairs in the drawing room in front of the dining-room door, which had been removed and replaced with a red curtain.

'Papa,' she cried, 'give me a hand! We shan't ever finish!'

Monsieur Letellier who, arms clasped behind his back, was examining the chandelier, hurried over to help. Pauline carried some chairs herself. She had done what her sister asked and put on a white frock. Except that her blouse fell open in a square shape, showing her bosom.

'There,' she said, 'that's it. They can come now. But whatever is Juliette thinking of? She has been an age dressing Lucien.'

At that very moment, Madame Deberle brought along the little marquis. All the people present exclaimed. Oh, what a little love! How sweet he was in his white satin costume, with flowers in his buttonholes, his wide gold-embroidered waistcoat, and his cerise silk culottes! His chin and his delicate hands were swamped with lace. A toy sword with a large pink bow tapped against his leg.

'Come on, do the honours,' said his mother leading him into the first room.

He had been practising for a week. So he adopted a casual stance on his little legs, threw his powdered head back a little, put his three-cornered hat under his left arm. And as each guest arrived he bowed, offered them his arm, greeted them, and went back again. People laughed to see him, he was so solemn, with a hint of cheekiness about him. In this manner he conducted Marguerite Tissot in, a little girl of five, wearing a charming milkmaid's costume, her milk-can hanging from her belt; he led in the two little Berthier girls, Blanche and Sophie, one of whom was dressed as Folly and the other as a soubrette; he even dared to escort Valentine de Chermette, a big girl of fourteen whom her mother always dressed as a Spanish lady, and he was so slight she seemed to be carrying him. But he was dreadfully embarrassed when confronted by the Levasseur family composed of five young ladies who arrived in order of height, the youngest aged scarcely two, the eldest, ten. All five, dressed as Little Red Riding Hood, had fur hoods and bright red satin cloaks edged in black velvet, with wide lace aprons on top. He made a brave decision, threw down his hat, took the two biggest on his right and left arms and made his entry into the salon, followed by the other three. Everyone found it very hilarious, but the little man didn't lose his aplomb in the least.

All this time Madame Deberle was telling her sister off in a corner.

'I don't believe it! Showing your bosom like that!'

'Huh, what difference does it make? Papa didn't say anything,' Pauline answered calmly. 'If you like, I'll wear some flowers.'

She picked a little sprig of flowers from a jardinière and shoved them down between her breasts. But the ladies, mothers in all their finery, were surrounding Madame Deberle and complimenting her already on her ball. As Lucien was passing, his mother adjusted a curl in his powdered hair and he stood on tiptoe to ask:

'What about Jeanne?'

'She'll be coming soon, darling... Be careful you don't fall over. Hurry, there's the little Guiraud girl. Ah, she's dressed up as a lady from Alsace.'

The salon was filling up. The rows of chairs opposite the red curtain were almost all occupied, and there was an increasing din of children's voices. Groups of boys were arriving. There were already three Harlequins, four Mister Punches, one Figaro, Tyroleans, Scotsmen.

The little Berthier boy was a page. The little Guiraud boy, a toddler of two and a half, was wearing his Pierrot's costume in such a droll fashion that everyone picked him up to give him a kiss as he went past.

'Oh, here's Jeanne,' Madame Deberle said suddenly. 'How adorable!'

There was a general murmur, heads turned and there were little cries. Jeanne had stopped on the threshold of the first drawing room, while her mother, still in the hallway, was taking off her coat. The child was wearing a Japanese costume of splendid originality. The dress, embroidered with flowers and exotic birds, reached down and covered her small feet, while below her wide belt, the spaces between the panels revealed a petticoat of greenish silk, shot through with yellow. Nothing was so delightfully strange as her fine face under the high chignon fastened with long hairpins, her chin and her narrow, bright doe's eyes, which gave her the air of a true daughter of Yeddo,* walking along in a perfume of benzoin and tea rose. And she stood there, hesitating, with the sickly languor of a flower longing for her native land.

But behind her came Hélène. Both of them, passing abruptly from the pale light of the street into the dazzle of the candles, were blinking as though blinded, but still smiling. The sudden rush of warmth, this predominantly violet-scented salon, they found rather stifling, and their cool cheeks flushed pink. Each guest who arrived wore the same surprised, hesitant expression.

'Well, Lucien?' said Madame Deberle.

The little boy had not seen Jeanne. He rushed forward, took her arm, forgetting to make his bow. And both were so delicate, so exquisite, the little marquis with his sprigged costume and the Japanese girl with her purple embroidered gown, you might have thought they were two Meissen statuettes, finely painted and gilded, suddenly come to life.

'I've been waiting for you, you know,' faltered Lucien. 'I feel silly giving you my arm. Let's stay together.'

And he sat down with her on the first row of chairs. He completely forgot his duties as host.

'I was really worried,' said Juliette to Hélène. 'I thought Jeanne might be poorly.'

Hélène apologized. Children took forever to get ready. She was still standing with a group of ladies in a corner of the drawing room, when she sensed the doctor approaching from behind. In fact he had just come in, pulling back the red curtain which he had ducked back under again to give a final order. But suddenly he stopped. He too divined the young woman's presence, although she had not turned round. Dressed in black grenadine silk, she had never looked so regally beautiful. And the breath of fresh air that she brought, seeming to emanate from her shoulders and her arms, naked under the gauzy material, made him tremble.

'Henri hasn't noticed we are here,' Pauline said with a laugh. 'Why, hello Henri!'

At that he went in to greet the ladies. Mademoiselle Aurélie, who was present, kept him back a moment in order to point out a nephew of hers whom she had brought along. The doctor remained there, to be affable. Hélène, saying nothing, held out her black-gloved hand to him, but he did not dare shake it too warmly.

'So you're there, are you?' cried Madame Deberle, reappearing. 'I've been looking for you everywhere... It's almost three, we can start.'

'Of course,' he said. 'Right away.'

At that moment the drawing room was full. The mothers and fathers were laying their outdoor cloaks around the walls, making a dark border round the room lit by the dazzlingly bright chandelier. The ladies, pulling up their chairs, formed little separate groups; the men, standing against the walls, were crammed in the space in between, while at the door of the adjacent drawing room the more numerous frock coats were piling up one on top of the other. The spotlight fell on the noisy little world which was animating the centre of the huge room. There were nearly a hundred children all jostling together in their gay multicoloured costumes, bright with their blues and pinks. There was an expanse of fair heads, of every shade, from a fine ash blonde to a reddish gold, with *réveils** of bows and flowers, a harvest of corn-coloured hair rippling with laughter, as though in a breeze. Occasionally in this tangle of ribbons and lace, silks and velvet, you would see a face: a pink nose, two blue eyes, a smiling or pouting mouth, looking lost. Some did not come up over the height of a boot, and were hidden between big boys of ten, their mothers looking for them all over the place but unable to find them. Embarrassed boys looked gauche, next to little girls who were making their skirts billow out. Others were already showing off, elbowing the girls next to them whom they didn't know and laughing in their faces. But the little girls were still the queens, groups of three or four friends swung back and forth on their chairs as if they would break them, talking so loudly that nobody could hear a word they were saying. All eyes were on the red curtain.

'Your attention please!' called the doctor, tapping three times on the dining-room door.

The red curtain slowly opened and in the doorway appeared a puppet theatre. There was silence. Suddenly Mister Punch leapt out from the wings, with such a fierce squeak, that the little Guiraud boy responded with one of those cries which are equally scared and fascinated. It was one of those terrifying set scenes where Punch, having beaten the Sergeant, kills the Policeman and, with cruel delight, tramples over all laws human and divine. With each blow of the stick that cut open the wooden heads, the pitiless spectators howled with laughter; and the blades thrust into chests, the duels where the adversaries bashed one another's heads as if they were empty gourds, the massacred limbs and arms of the pulped characters caused the shouts of laughter from all sides to helplessly redouble in volume. Best of all was when Punch sawed the Policeman's neck in half on the edge of the stage; the operation caused such a degree of hilarity that the rows of spectators all pushed and fell one on top of another. A little girl of four, white and pink, clutched her tiny hands to her heart in ecstasy, she loved it so much. Others applauded, while, on a lower note, the boys chuckled open-mouthed, in accompaniment to the girls' fluting tones.

'They are so enjoying it!' said the doctor quietly.

He had come to sit near Hélène. She was enjoying it as much as the children. And, sitting behind her, he was intoxicated by the scent of her hair. At one blow of the stick, louder than the rest, she turned round and said to him:

'It really is very funny!'

But the excited children were now completely involved in the action. They answered the actors back. A little girl who must have been familiar with the play, explained what was going to happen. 'In a little while he's going to beat his wife to death... Now they are going to hang him...' The smallest Levasseur, the two-year-old, suddenly shouted:

'Maman, are they going to put him on dry bread?'

Then everyone exclaimed and made loud remarks. Meanwhile Hélène was searching amongst the children.

'I can't see Jeanne,' she said. 'Is she enjoying it?'

Then the doctor leaned over and his head was next to hers.

'Look, over there,' he murmured, 'between that Harlequin and that girl from Normandy, you can see the pins on her chignon... She is laughing out loud.'

And he remained in that position, feeling on his cheek the warmth of Hélène's face. Until that moment no declaration had passed their lips; this silence left them in that state of intimacy disturbed by nothing more than a vague unease for a while. But in the midst of all this laughter and at the sight of all these children, Hélène was becoming a child herself again and she let her defences drop, while Henri's breath warmed the back of her neck. The sound of the blows made her shudder and her bosom rose; she turned to him, eyes shining:

'How silly!' she said, each time it happened. 'How hard they hit!'

Trembling, he replied:

'Oh, their heads are solid enough!'

That was the best he could manage. They were both reduced to childish remarks. Punch's scarcely exemplary life made them relax. Then when the play reached its conclusion, when the Devil appeared and there was a final fight and everybody's throat was cut, Hélène leaned back on her chair and crushed Henri's hand placed there; while the little ones in the front row, shouting and clapping, made the chairs crack in their enthusiasm.

The red curtain had fallen again. Then in the midst of the din Pauline announced the arrival of Malignon, in her usual way:

'Oh, here's our handsome Malignon.'

He arrived out of breath, pushing his way through the chairs.

'What a silly idea to close all the doors!' he shouted, surprised and hesitant. You'd think someone had died in the house.'

And, turning to Madame Deberle, who had gone over to him:

'Congratulations! You've had me running all over the place! I've been looking for Perdiguet all morning, you know, my singer. So, since I couldn't get hold of him, I've brought you the Great Morizot.'

The Great Morizot was an amateur who entertained drawing-room society with his conjuring. They gave him a little table and he performed his best tricks but didn't manage to gain the interest of the audience in the slightest. The poor little things had become very quiet. Toddlers were falling asleep sucking their thumbs. The older ones were turning round, smiling at their parents, who were yawning behind their hands. So it was a relief to all when the Great Morizot decided to take his table away.

'He's very good!' whispered Malignon, close to Madame Deberle's neck.

But the red curtain opened again and a magic spectacle brought all the children to their feet.

Under the bright light of the main lamp and two candelabra with ten stems, the dining room with its long table was laid and decorated as for a grand dinner. Fifty places were set. In the middle and at both ends in low baskets, there bloomed flowering branches, separated by tall compotiers* on which were 'surprises' piled high, with gold and coloured glitter paper. Then came tiered cakes, pyramids of glacé fruits, piles of sandwiches, and below them numerous plates full of sweetmeats and pastries all in symmetrical order; babas, cream cakes, brioches alternating with biscuits, *croquignoles*,* petits fours with almonds. Jellies wobbled in crystal glasses. Creams filled the large china bowls. And on the bottles of champagne, which were hand-high, befitting the size of the guests, the silver caps sparkled all around the table. You would have thought it was one of those gigantic tea parties such as children must have in their dreams, a tea party served with all the ceremony of an adult dinner, the fairyland equivalent of the parents' table onto which had been poured a cornucopia from patisseries and toyshops.

'Come on, let's escort the ladies!' said Madame Deberle, smiling at the children's delight.

But the little procession was unable to get organized. Lucien had triumphantly taken Jeanne's arm and was marching at the head. The others pushed and shoved a little in his wake. The mothers had to come and put them in order. And they remained there, especially behind the little ones, whom they were watching, fearing accidents. The guests at first seemed shy; they looked, not daring to touch all these goodies, somewhat troubled by this reversal of the normal order of things, children sitting at table and parents standing. Finally the oldest ones grew braver and held out their hands. Then when the mothers got involved, cutting the tiers of cakes, serving those around them, the tea party came to life and was soon very noisy. The beautiful symmetry of the table was hit as though by a gust of wind. Everything was passed round at the same time, between the stretched-out hands which emptied the dishes as they went by. The two little Berthiers,

Blanche and Sophie, laughed when they looked at their plates on which there was a bit of everything, jam, cream, cakes, fruit. The five Levasseur girls monopolized a section of delicacies, while Valentine, proud of being fourteen, behaved like a sensible grown-up and looked after her neighbours. In the meantime Lucien, to show how chivalrous he was, uncorked a bottle of champagne and did it so clumsily that he almost upset the contents over his cerise silk trousers. It was quite a business.

'Please leave the bottles alone!' cried Pauline. 'I'm the one who uncorks the champagne.'

She was in a frenzy of activity. She was enjoying herself. As soon as a servant arrived, she snatched the jug of chocolate away from him and took a real delight in filling the cups, with a waiter's promptness. Then she passed round the ices and glasses of fruit squash, abandoned it all to go and fill up the plate of a little girl who had been forgotten, and then, leaving her, fired questions at all of them.

'What would you like, dear? Would you like a roll? Wait a minute, love, I'll pass you the oranges. Eat up, sillies, you can play afterwards!'

Madame Deberle, calmer than her, kept saying they ought to leave them alone and they would get on perfectly well. At one end of the room, Hélène and a few ladies were laughing at the sight of the table. All those little pink mouths with their brilliant white teeth were champing away. And nothing was funnier than these well-brought-up children who from time to time forgot their manners to indulge in behaviour more typical of young savages. They clasped their glasses with both hands to drink up the dregs, got it all over their faces, stained their costumes. The din increased. They pillaged the last plates. Even Jeanne was dancing on her chair when she heard a quadrille in the salon; and as her mother came over, telling her off for eating too much, she said:

'Oh, Maman, I feel so good today!'

But the music had caused other children to get off their chairs. Gradually they left the table and soon nobody remained but a plump baby right in the middle. He appeared not to care a jot about the piano. A napkin round his neck, his chin on the tablecloth, he was so small, he opened his big eyes and thrust his mouth forward each time his mother gave him a spoonful of chocolate. The cup was nearly empty, and he let them wipe his mouth, but he was still taking great gulps and opening his eyes wide.

'You're doing well, old chap!' Malignon said contemplating him thoughtfully.

It was then that they had the distribution of 'surprises'. When the children left the table they took with them one of the large gold packages and were in a hurry to tear open the wrapping. And they took out toys, wigs made out of tissue paper, birds and butterflies. But the greatest delight was the firecrackers. Each 'surprise' contained a cracker which the boys were brave enough to pull, delighted with the noise, while the girls closed their eyes, and had several goes. For a moment all you could hear was these dry pistol-cracks. And it was while this hubbub was going on that the children went back into the drawing room where the piano continued to play figures of a quadrille.

'I could fancy a brioche,' muttered Mademoiselle Aurélie, as she sat down.

Then, around the table which was now free, though still very cluttered after the enormous dessert, the ladies sat down. There were about ten who had prudently waited before starting to eat. As they couldn't get hold of anyone to serve them, it was Malignon who offered. He emptied the jug of chocolate, held up the bottles to see what was left, and even managed to produce some ices. But, gallant as he was, he still kept referring to the bizarre idea they'd had of closing the blinds.

'It's exactly like being in a cellar!' he repeated.

Hélène had stayed standing, talking to Madame Deberle. The latter was going back into the drawing room, and she was preparing to follow her when she felt a gentle touch. The doctor was there smiling behind her and it seemed he did not intend to leave.

'Are you not having anything to eat?' he enquired.

And behind this banal question lay such an intense plea that she felt very troubled. She understood his real meaning perfectly. She was gradually becoming more and more excited by all this gaiety round about her. All these children jumping and shouting gave her a headache. Her cheeks pink and her eyes bright, she at first refused.

'No thank you. Nothing.'

Then, as he insisted, she was instantly anxious, and wanted to get rid of him:

'Well, a cup of tea, then.'

He rushed to get her a cup. His hands were shaking as he gave it to her. And while she drank, he drew nearer, his lips swollen and trembling with the declaration which rose from the depths of his being. Then she withdrew, held out her empty cup and escaped while he put it on a dresser, leaving him alone in the dining room with Mademoiselle Aurélie, who was slowly chewing her food and inspecting the plates in a meticulous fashion.

The pianoforte was being played very loud at the back of the drawing room. And from one end to the other the excited dancers were funny and charming. A circle had formed around the quadrille in which Jeanne and Lucien were dancing. The little marquis was muddling up his steps somewhat. He only got it right when he had to take Jeanne by the waist; then he caught hold of her and whirled her round. Jeanne was poised in a ladylike manner, cross when he creased her dress; then, carried away with the pleasure of the dance, it was her turn to seize hold of him and lift him off the ground. And these two Meissen statues, the white brocade satin suit with flowers on and the dress embroidered with flowers and strange birds, took on the grace and strangeness of an ornament on a shelf. When the quadrille finished, Hélène called to Jeanne to tie her dress.

'It's his fault, Maman,' the little girl complained. 'He keeps brushing against me, I can't bear it.'

Around the drawing room the parents were smiling. When the piano began again all the children leaped into action once more. But they were apprehensive when they saw people looking at them. They became solemn and took care not to gallop around, so as to seem well behaved. Some of them could dance; most, not knowing the movements, shuffled around where they were, their arms and legs getting in their way. But Pauline intervened.

'I'd better dance with them. What chumps they are!'

She dived into the middle of the quadrille and took two by the hand, one on the left, one on the right, and whipped up the dancing so much that the floorboards cracked. All you could hear was the thundering of little feet with their heels thudding out of time, while the piano alone continued to play to the beat. A few more adults joined in. Seeing some little girls were shy and did not dare to dance, Madame Deberle and Hélène guided them into the thick of it. They led the figures, pushed their partners around, and formed the circles. And the mothers passed them their youngest offspring to be jumped about for a minute or two, holding them by both hands. Then the dance was at its best. The dancers gave themselves up to it joyfully, laughing and pushing, like a school boarding-house suddenly overcome by mad gaiety when the teacher is not there. And nothing was jollier than this carnival of children, these little men and women in their small world mingling the fashions of every race, fantasies of fiction and theatre. The costumes lent the freshness of childhood to their pink mouths, blue eyes and gentle faces. You would have thought it was the gala of some fairy tale, with cherubs dressed up for Prince Charming's wedding feast.

'It's so stuffy,' said Malignon. 'I'm going to get some air.'

He went out, flinging wide the drawing-room door. The daylight of the street entered then in a pallid flash and cast a sort of sadness over the brilliance of the lamps and candles. And every quarter of an hour, Malignon slammed the door.

But the piano played on. The little Guiraud girl, with a black Alsatian butterfly on her blonde hair, was dancing on the arm of a Harlequin twice as big as her. A Scotsman was whirling Marguerite Tissot around so fast that she lost her milkmaid's boot on the way. The two Berthiers, Blanche and Sophie, inseparable, were jumping up and down together, the Soubrette on the arm of Folly, whose bells were jangling. And your eyes could not avoid lighting on one or other of the Levasseur girls; there seemed to be scores of Little Red Riding Hoods. Everywhere there were hoods and red satin dresses edged in black velvet. Meanwhile, to have more space to dance in, the older boys and girls had taken refuge at the back of the other drawing room. Valentine de Chermette, enveloped in her Spanish mantilla, was showing great prowess with her young partner, who had come in a suit. Suddenly there was laughter, people called to one another to come and look. Behind a door in a corner the little Guiraud boy, the two-year-old Pierrot, and a little girl of the same age dressed as a peasant, had their arms round one another, holding on very tight in case they fell, and were moving round surreptitiously all by themselves, cheek to cheek.

'I'm exhausted,' said Hélène, coming to lean against the dining-room door.

She was fanning herself, red in the face from jumping about. Her breasts rose and fell beneath the transparent grenadine of her blouse. And she sensed again Henri breathing at her shoulder, always there. Then she realized he was about to say something, but she no longer had the strength to avoid his declaration. He moved forward and said very softly into her hair:

'I love you! Oh, I love you!'

It was as though a tongue of flame burned her from head to toe. Oh God! He had spoken. She would no longer be able to feign the sweet peace of ignorance. She hid her blushes behind her fan. The stamping of the children, carried away by the last quadrilles, had grown louder. Silvery laughter sounded, birdlike voices made little cries of pleasure. A freshness emanated from this circle of innocents, let loose to gallop around like so many little devils.

'I love you, oh I love you!' Henri said again.

She shivered, could not listen any more. Her head whirling, she took refuge in the dining room. But that room was empty. Monsieur Letellier was peacefully asleep on his own on a chair. Henri followed her. He went so far as to catch hold of her wrists, risking a scandal, with a face so ravaged by passion that she trembled. He kept on repeating:

'I love you, I love you...'

'Leave me,' she murmured feebly, 'leave me, you are mad...'

And the ball was going on next door, a wild scurrying of tiny feet! You could hear the little bells of Blanche Berthier accompanying the softer notes of the piano. Madame Deberle and Pauline were clapping in time. It was a polka. Hélène saw Jeanne and Lucien go by smiling, with their hands round each other's waists.

Then, with a sudden movement she jerked away, and escaped into the next room, a pantry where there was broad daylight. This sudden clarity blinded her. She was panicky, she was not in a fit state to return to the salon with the passion that must surely be visible on her face. And, crossing the garden, with the noise of the dancers still in her ears as she left, she went back up to her own apartment to recover.

CHAPTER 5

BACK up there in the gentle, cloistered atmosphere of her room, Hélène felt as if she couldn't breathe. She was astonished to find it so calm, so shut away, so soporific beneath its blue velvet furnishings, when she was bringing to it the breathless fire of this passion that so agitated her. Was this really her room, this solitary, dead place that she found so stifling? She flung open a window and leaned out in the direction of Paris.

The rain had stopped, the clouds were dispersing like a monstrous flock of sheep, their unruly line disappearing out to the misty horizon. A gap of blue had opened up above the city, and was slowly widening. But Hélène, her elbows trembling on the sill, and still trying to catch her breath after rushing upstairs, saw nothing, heard only the pulsating of her heart in her breast, that rose and fell. She breathed in deeply, it seemed to her that the huge valley, with its river, its two million lives, its gigantic heart, its distant hills, would not have air enough to restore to her the regularity and peace of her breathing.

For a few minutes she remained there, distraught, utterly transfixed by this crisis. Confused thoughts and feelings coursed through her, their murmur preventing her from listening to herself and making sense of it all. Her ears were buzzing, her eyes saw large bright spots travelling slowly across her field of vision. She was surprised when she looked at her gloved hands and remembered she had forgotten to sew a button on to the left one again. Then she said aloud, repeating several times in a voice that grew ever softer:

'I love you... I love you... Oh God, I love you.'

And instinctively she put her head in her clasped hands, pressing on her closed lids as though to increase the blackness into which she was sinking. She was seized by a wish to annihilate herself, to not see any more, to be alone in the shadowy depths. Her breathing grew quieter. Paris blew a strong breath of wind into her face. She felt the city's presence, not wanting to look at it, and yet panic-stricken at the idea of leaving the window, and not having beneath her this place whose endlessness she found so reassuring.

Before long she forgot everything. She relived the scene of his declaration, despite herself. Against a black, inky background, Henri appeared particularly vividly, so alive that she could make out the small nervous trembling of his lips. He was coming closer, he was leaning over her. Then, she was pulling herself wildly away. And yet she was feeling her shoulders burn, hearing a voice that whispered: 'I love you... I love you...' Then, when in one supreme effort she banished this vision, it re-formed a little further off, and gradually grew bigger; and there was Henri again following her into the dining room with those same words: 'I love you... I love you', their repetition like the continuous pealing of a bell. All she could hear were those words vibrating through her limbs. They pierced her breasts. But she wanted to reflect, she attempted once more to escape from the image of Henri. He had declared himself, she would never be able to look him in the face again. With a man's brutality he had just spoiled their love. And she remembered the days when he had been in love with her without being cruel enough to tell her so, those times spent at the bottom of the garden in the serenity of the coming spring. Oh God! Now he had spoken! This thought insisted, became so large, so heavy that a lightning bolt that destroyed Paris in front of her eyes would not have seemed of equal importance. In her heart she felt indignation, pride and anger, as well as a secret, undeniable desire that rose from her loins and intoxicated her. He had spoken, and was speaking still, again and again he appeared before her, saying 'I love you... I love you...', those ardent words which bore away with them the whole of her past life as a wife and mother.

And yet, in remembering this, she was nevertheless aware of the vast spaces stretching out below, beyond this darkness in which she was blinding herself. There was a loud voice, and the waves of life rose higher and engulfed her. The sounds, the smells, the light itself beat against her face despite her clenched, nervous hands. From time to time a sudden glow seemed to pass through her closed eyelids. And in this light she thought she could see monuments, spires, and domes rising up in the diffused light of her dream.

Then she spread out her hands, opened her eyes and was dazzled. The sky emptied, Henri had disappeared.

All you could see in the far distance was a bank of clouds which were heaping up a landslip of chalky boulders. Now in the pure, intense blue sky, puffs of cotton wool were sailing by at a leisurely pace, like flotillas of little boats billowing out in the wind. To the north, over Montmartre, a web of exquisite pale silk stretched over a section of the sky, like a fishing net on a calm sea. But as the sun went down over the hills of Meudon, invisible to Hélène, the last of the downpour must still have been obscuring the sun, for Paris, under the brightness, was still dark and damp, beneath the steam of the drying roofs. It was a city of unvarying tone, a bluish slate grey stained black by the trees, yet very distinct with its sharp edges and thousands of windows. The Seine had the dull sheen of an old silver ingot. On both sides the monuments looked as if they had been spattered with soot; the Tour Saint-Jacques stood like a piece of old junk from a museum eaten away by rust, while the silhouette of the Panthéon towered above its shrouded *quartier* like a gigantic catafalque. Only the gilded Dôme des Invalides retained its glowing flames; and you might have thought they were lamps lit up in the middle of the day, dreamy and melancholic among the crepuscular gloom draped over the city. Outlines were missing. Paris, veiled in a cloud, was a smudge on the horizon, like a colossal but delicate charcoal drawing in the limpid sky.

As she looked out at this bleak city Hélène reflected that she did not know Henri very well. She felt stronger now that his image no longer pursued her. Her rebelliousness drove her to reject this obsession which in the space of a few weeks had filled her life with this man. No, she did not know him. She was ignorant of everything, his actions, his thoughts; she would not even have been able to say whether or not he was very intelligent. Perhaps he was deficient in matters of the heart even more than in the head. And she exhausted all the suppositions, her heart swelling with the animosity she found at the bottom of them all, always coming up against her lack of knowledge, that wall that separated her from Henri, and which prevented her from knowing him. She knew nothing, she would never know anything. In her imagination he was always brutal, whispering passionate words which excited her, causing her the only trouble which, until then, had disturbed the happy equilibrium of her life. Where had he come from, that he had made her so sad? Suddenly she thought that six weeks ago she had not existed for him, and that idea was unbearable. Oh God! Not to mean anything to one another, to pass by without seeing one another, not meeting at all perhaps! She put her hands together in despair, her eyes wet with tears.

Hélène gazed at the towers of Notre-Dame, in the far distance. A ray of light, in the gap between two clouds, gilded them. Her head was heavy, as if it were too full of the tumult of conflicting ideas inside it. She was suffering, she would have liked her mind to be on Paris, to recover her serenity in her usual quiet contemplation of its sea of roofs. How many times at that hour had the secret nature of the city in the calm of a beautiful evening lulled her in a tender reverie! Meanwhile, before her eyes Paris was brightening in the bursts of sunshine. After the first ray of light had fallen on Notre-Dame, other rays followed and struck the city. As it went down, the sun caused breaks in the clouds. Then the *quartiers* spread out in variegations of shade and light. At one minute all the Left Bank was a leaden grey, while circles of light streaked along the Right Bank, unrolling next to the river like the pelt of some gigantic beast. Then the shapes shifted and moved at the whim of the wind that carried away the wisps of cloud. Against the gold hue of the roofs, blankets of darkness all travelling in the same direction, slid by softly and silently. There were enormous ones, sailing majestically across like an admiral's ship, surrounded by smaller ones which moved in symmetry like a squadron in battle order. An immensely long shadow opening like the mouth of a reptile obscured Paris for a moment and seemed to be trying to devour it. And when that one had vanished, diminished now to the size of a worm on the distant horizon, a ray of light, whose shafts sprang out like rain from the fissure in the cloud, fell into the empty chasm that it left. You could see its golden dust trickle like fine sand, grow into a vast cone, and pour down in torrents on the Champs-Élysées, dancing and splashing with light. This sparkling shower lasted a long time, like the constant firing of a rocket.

It was a fatal passion, she had to admit, and Hélène was helpless to defend herself against it. She felt at the end of her strength in the struggle with her heart. Henri could take her, she would surrender. Then she felt a boundless happiness in the fact that she was not fighting it any more. Why should she go on refusing him? Had she not waited long enough? The memory of her past life filled her with scorn and anger. How had she been able to go on living in that state of indifference she was once so proud of? She saw herself as a young girl again, in Marseilles, Rue des Petites-Maries, in that street where she had always been shivering with cold. She saw herself as a married woman, cold as ice in front of that overgrown child who kissed her bare feet, and as housewife, immersing herself in domestic concerns, by way of escape. She saw herself at every stage of her life, walking steadily along the same path, her peace and quiet undisturbed by any passion; but now this regularity, this slumbering of love in her life, exasperated her. To think that she had considered herself happy, proceeding in that lack of all feeling for thirty years, having nothing to fill the void in her heart but the pride of being a respectable woman! Oh, how hypocritical this inflexibility, those scruples of respectability, which confined her within the fruitless pleasures of a nunnery! No, she had had enough, she wanted to live! And she turned in angry contempt against her reason. Her reason! In truth she pitied it, this reason, which in a life that had already lasted quite some while, had not given her anything like the joy she had experienced for the last hour. She had denied she would fall, she had flattered herself foolishly, thinking she would be able to reach the end without even stumbling.

Well, now today she was begging for the fall, she wanted it to be immediate and profound. Her revolt boiled down to this one imperious desire. Oh, to disappear in an embrace, to live in one minute all that she had not lived up till now!

Yet deep down a great sorrow was making her weep. It felt tight inside, a sensation of black nothingness. Then she argued her case. Was she not free? Loving Henri, she wasn't being unfaithful to anyone, she could do what she wanted with his affections. So wasn't it excusable because of all this? What had her life been like these last two years? She realized that everything had conspired to render her more docile and ready for passion, her widowhood, her total freedom, her solitude. Passion must have been smouldering in her during those long evenings she spent with her two old friends, the priest and his brother, those simple men whose calm serenity soothed her. It smouldered when she sequestered herself so thoroughly from the world, as Paris rumbled away on the horizon; it smouldered each time she leaned on the windowsill, in a trance, such as she was unaware of in the old days, and which was gradually making her so weak. And she remembered something, that bright spring morning when the city was white and clear as if in a crystal, a Paris fair and fresh as a child, which she had so lazily contemplated as she stretched out on her chaise longue, her book fallen into her lap. That morning, love was awakening; it was no more than a thrill she couldn't put a name to and against which she considered herself very strong. Today she was sitting in the same place, but passion was triumphant and devouring her, while before her eyes, in the setting sun the city caught fire. It seemed to her that it had only taken one day, that this was the evening of the same day, the crimson evening after the bright morning, and she felt that all those flames were burning in her heart.

But the sky had changed. The radiant sun, going down over the hills of Meudon, had just chased the last clouds away. A glory* flamed across the blue sky. On the far horizon, the landslip of chalk rocks that blocked distant Charenton and Choisy-le-Roi was heaped now with carmine blocks edged with bright lacquer; the flotilla of little clouds sailing slowly through the blue sky over Paris was covered now with veils of crimson; while the fine web, the net of white silk stretched over Montmartre, unexpectedly appeared to be made of gold braid, its neat stitches about to catch the rising stars. And beneath this flaming arch spread out the golden city, with its big dark stripes. Down below on the vast square and along the avenues the cabs and omnibuses passed one another in the middle of an orange cloud, amongst the crowd of pedestrians, whose ant-like blackness was lessened and lit up by drops of light. Students from the seminary in a line of soutanes, moving rapidly in serried ranks along the Quai de Billy, made a flash of yellow ochre in the diffuse brightness. Then the cabs and the pedestrians vanished, far away you could only guess at a line of carriages, with gleaming lamps, on some bridge or other. On the left the tall chimneys of the Military Depot, pink and straight, loosed thick swirls of pale smoke of a delicate fleshy hue; while on the other side of the river the beautiful elms along the Quai d'Orsay formed a dark clump, with gaps where the sun pierced through. Between the banks of the Seine, threaded by glancing rays of sunshine, little waves danced together in blue, yellow, and green before they broke apart in a scattering of many colours. But as you looked back up the river this agglomeration of colour, like an oriental seascape, assumed a single gold hue that became ever more dazzling. And there on the horizon it might have been an ingot taken out of some invisible crucible, getting gradually bigger with a mixture of bright colours as it cooled. On this shining river the staggered bridges with their slender, tapering curves cast rods of grey before disappearing in a burning pile of houses, over which the twin towers of Notre-Dame shone red like torches. To right and left the monuments were on fire. The glass of the Palais de l'Industrie in the middle of the trees on the Champs-Élysées was a bed of smouldering embers; a little further off behind the crushed roof of the Madeleine, the immense form of the Opéra looked like a block of copper; and the other buildings, the cupolas and towers, the Vendôme column, Saint-Vincent-de-Paul, and nearer, the wings of the new Louvre and Tuileries were crowned with flames, raising gigantic pyres at every intersection of the streets. The Dôme des Invalides was ablaze, and so bright you would think it was going to collapse at any moment, covering the *quartier* with sparks from its wooden frame.

Beyond the irregular towers of Saint-Sulpice, the Panthéon stood out on the skyline with a subdued glow like a royal palace of fire about to be burnt to cinders. Then the whole of Paris was lit up at the pyres of monuments as the sun went down. Flickers of light gleamed on the tops of roofs, while black smoke slumbered down below in the dips. All the façades which faced towards the Trocadéro were reddening, their glass sending out showers of sparks, which rose from the city as though some bellows were ceaselessly firing up that colossal forge.

Fountains of light, constantly renewing themselves, escaped from the neighbouring *quartiers* in the hollows of the dark, burnt streets. Even on the far plain, from beyond the rusty embers that buried the ruined faubourgs, which were still hot, the odd rocket, shooting up from some suddenly reignited fire, blazed.

Soon it was a furnace. Paris burned. The sky had grown more crimson, the clouds bled over the huge red and gold city.

Hélène, immersed in these flames and giving herself up to the passion which was devouring her, was watching Paris blaze when a little hand on her shoulder made her start. It was Jeanne.

'Maman, Maman!'

And when she turned round:

'Oh, that's good!... Couldn't you hear me? I called you ten times.'

The little girl, still in her Japanese lady costume, had shining eyes and cheeks that were all flushed with pleasure. She did not allow her mother time to reply.

'You left me all alone... We looked everywhere for you afterwards, you know. If it hadn't been for Pauline who came with me to the foot of the stairs I would not have dared cross the street.'

And with a sweet little gesture she put her face to her mother's lips and asked immediately:

'Do you love me?'

Hélène kissed her on the lips, but as though thinking of something else. She was surprised, seemed impatient that she had come home so soon. Was it really an hour since she had escaped from the ball? And in answer to the child's worried questions, she said that she had indeed felt a little unwell. The fresh air did her good. She needed a bit of peace and quiet.

'Oh, don't worry, I'm really tired,' said Jeanne quietly. 'I'll stay here and be a good girl. But Mother, I may talk, mayn't I?'

She snuggled up to Hélène, pressing against her, pleased that she wasn't having to take off her costume straight away. Her dress embroidered in crimson, her greenish silk petticoat, pleased her enormously. And she nodded her fine head to hear her chignon tapping against the pendants of the long pins that were in it. Then a flood of words came rushing from her lips. Despite looking a bit foolish and out of her depth, she had observed, heard, and remembered everything. Now she was compensating for having been so well behaved, so tight-lipped and apparently unconcerned.

'Do you know, Maman, it was an old man with a grey beard who was pulling Punch's strings. I could see clearly when the curtain went up... The little Guiraud boy was crying. He's so silly, isn't he! So they told him that the policeman would come and put water in his soup and they had to take him away he was screaming so much... It was like at tea-time, Marguerite got her milkmaid costume all spotted with jam. Her mother wiped her, shouting: "Oh, what a dirty girl!" Marguerite had got some in her hair even. I didn't say anything but it was really funny to see them grab the cakes. They are not polite are they, Mother?'

She broke off for a few seconds, absorbed by remembering something; then she asked thoughtfully:

'Maman, by the way, did you have any of those cakes that were yellow and had white cream inside? Oh, they were so delicious! I kept the plate near me the whole time.'

Hélène was not listening to this childish babble. But Jeanne was talking to ease her head which was too full. She started again with an extraordinary wealth of detail about the ball. The least little action took on an enormous importance.

'Didn't you notice, at the beginning, that my belt came undone? A lady I didn't know put a pin in it for me. I said to her: "Thank you, Madame." Then when Lucien was dancing, he pricked himself. He asked me: "What have you got on your front that pricked me?" I didn't know, I answered that I didn't have anything. It was Pauline who came and fixed the pin... But you wouldn't believe it, Maman! Everyone was pushing and shoving and a stupid great boy banged into Sophie's bottom and she nearly fell over. The Levasseur girls were jumping up and down. You just don't dance like that, do you? But the best bit was the last, you weren't there, you don't know what it was like. We all linked arms and danced in a circle, we were dying of laughter. There were grown men dancing round too. It's true, cross my heart! Don't you believe what I'm saying, Mother?'

In the end Hélène's silence made her cross. She pressed against her harder and shook her hand. Then, seeing she was only managing to extract the odd word, she gradually fell silent herself, slipping into a daze at the thought of this ball that so preoccupied her young heart. Then both of them, mother and daughter, said nothing more, looking out at the blaze that was Paris. It was as unknowable as ever, lit up like that by blood-red clouds, just like some city of legend expiating its passion beneath a rain of fire.

'Did you dance in a round?' Hélène suddenly asked, coming to with a start.

'Yes, yes,' murmured Jeanne. It was her turn to be rapt.

'What about the doctor? Did he dance?'

'Yes, of course, he went round with me... He lifted me up and kept asking me: "Where is your Maman? Where is your Maman?" Then he kissed me.'

Hélène was unaware that she was smiling. She laughed at these signs of his affection. Why did she need to know Henri? It seemed to her sweeter not to know, never to know, but just accept him as the man she had so long been waiting for. Why be surprised or worried? He had crossed her path at the right moment in her life. That was good. Her open nature accepted it all. She felt a sense of calm at the thought that she loved and was loved in return. And she promised herself she would have the courage not to spoil her happiness.

But night was coming, a cold wind was blowing. Jeanne, lost in her own thoughts, shivered. She put her head on her mother's breast; and, as if the question had been part of her deepest contemplations, she murmured again:

'Do you love me?'

Then Hélène, still smiling, took her head in both hands and seemed to study her face a moment. Then she let her lips linger a long time above a little pink mark on her mouth. She could tell that it was there that Henri had kissed the little girl.

The dark line of hills in Meudon was already cutting across the moonlike disc of the sun. Over Paris the glancing rays had now lengthened. The shadow of the Dôme des Invalides, immeasurably increased, was drowning all of the Quartier Saint-Germain, while the Opéra, the Tour Saint-Jacques, the columns and the spires, were black strips on the Right Bank. The lines of the façades, the dips of the streets, the raised islands of roofs were burning with less intensity. In the darkened windows the bright little sparks were dying, as if the houses had become embers. Distant bells tolled, a clamour, and then all was quiet. And the sky, wider as evening approached, spread its crimson cloth veined with gold and mauve in an arc round the burning city. Suddenly there was another terrifying incandescence, Paris made one last flamboyant gesture, which lit up even the farthest faubourgs. Then grey ash seemed to fall, and the *quartiers* remained, insubstantial and black, like burnt-out coals.

PART THREE

CHAPTER 1

ONE morning in May, Rosalie came rushing out of her kitchen still holding a dishcloth in her hand. And speaking as if she were a member of the family:

'Oh, Madame, come quickly... Monsieur l'Abbé's down in the doctor's garden digging around in the earth!'

Hélène did not move. But Jeanne had already run to the window to have a look.

When she came back she cried:

'Rosalie's so silly! He isn't digging around in the earth at all. He's with the gardener who's putting plants into a little cart... Madame Deberle is cutting all her roses...'

'It must be for the church,' said Hélène quietly, very busy with her tapestry.

A few minutes later there was a ring on the doorbell and Abbé Jouve appeared. He had come to tell them not to expect him the following Tuesday. His evenings were all taken up with the celebrations for the Month of Mary. The curé had made him responsible for decorating the church. It would be superb. All the ladies were giving him flowers. He was expecting two palm trees four metres high to put on the right and left of the altar.

'Oh, Maman... Maman...', murmured Jeanne, who was listening, entranced.

'Well, my friend, that's all right,' said Hélène, smiling, 'since you can't come to us, we'll come and pay you a visit... You have quite turned Jeanne's head with all your talk of flowers.'

She was scarcely religious at all, and never even went to Mass, on the pretext of the poor health of her daughter, who always came out of churches shivering. The old priest avoided speaking about religion to her. He would simply say, with good-natured tolerance, that beautiful souls achieve their own salvation by their wise behaviour and their good deeds. One day God would certainly lay His hand upon them.

All Jeanne could think about till the following evening was the Month of Mary. She questioned her mother, dreamed of the church filled with white roses, thousands of candles, heavenly voices, and sweet scents. And she wanted to sit near the altar so that she could see the Virgin's lacy dress, a dress which was worth a fortune according to the priest. But Hélène calmed her down by threatening not to take her if she made herself ill beforehand.

After dinner in the evening they finally left. The nights were still fresh. As they reached the Rue de l'Annonciation where the church of Notre-Dame-de-Grâce was, the child was shivering.

'The church is heated,' her mother said. 'We'll sit near a vent.'

She pushed open the padded door, which fell back with a soft thud, and they were enveloped by warmth, a bright light dazzled them, and hymns rang out. The service had begun. Seeing the central nave already full, Hélène tried to go down one of the side aisles. But she had the most dreadful difficulty getting near the altar. She was holding Jeanne's hand and patiently moving forward; but then she gave up and took the first two free seats which came along. A pillar hid half the choir.

'I can't see anything, Maman,' the little girl whispered sadly. 'We are in very bad seats.'

Hélène made her be quiet. Then the child began to sulk. All she could see in front of her was an old lady's enormous back. When her mother turned her head, she saw she was standing on her chair.

'Get down!' she admonished in a whisper. 'You're impossible.'

But Jeanne would not.

'Listen Maman, that's Madame Deberle. She's over there waving to us.'

The young woman was very cross and showed her annoyance. She gave the little girl, who was still refusing to sit down, a shake. For the last three days since the ball, she had avoided going back to the doctor's, giving as her excuse that she was extremely busy.

'Maman,' Jeanne went on with a childish obstinacy, 'she's looking at you, she's saying hello.'

So Hélène was obliged to turn her head and acknowledge her. The two women exchanged a nod. Madame Deberle in a silk dress covered with stripes, embroidered with white lace, occupied the central nave, right near the choir, very smart and very much in evidence. She had brought her sister Pauline, who began to gesticulate wildly. The hymns continued, the congregation's voice spread through a descending scale while the high-pitched notes of the children could occasionally be heard above the long-drawn-out cadence of the canticle.

'You see, they're telling you to come over!' Jeanne said again triumphantly.

'It's not necessary, we're very well here.'

'Oh, Maman, let's go and join them... They have two chairs.'

'No, get down, sit on your chair.'

But as these ladies insisted smilingly, without troubling in the least about the little scandal they had caused—quite the opposite, they were pleased to see people turning round to look at them—Hélène had to give in. She gave the delighted Jeanne a little push, tried to make a way through, her hands trembling with suppressed anger. It was not an easy job. The pious singers did not want be disturbed and, still in full throttle, looked at them in much annoyance. For five whole minutes in the midst of the storm of voices, roaring louder than ever, she tried to get through. When she couldn't move forward, Jeanne squeezed closer to her mother, looking at all those cavernous mouths. Finally they reached the space left free in front of the choir, and had only a few steps to go.

'Over here,' whispered Madame Deberle, 'the abbé said you were coming, I've kept you two chairs.'

Hélène thanked her and, to cut the conversation short, immediately started to rustle the leaves in her missal. But Juliette behaved exactly as she did in polite society. She was as charming and chatty there as she was in her drawing room, very much at ease. So she leaned over, and carried on chatting:

'We don't see you any more. I was intending to come and visit tomorrow. You haven't been poorly, have you?'

'Thank you, no I haven't. I've had so much to do...'

'Listen, you must come and dine with us tomorrow. Just us, nobody else.'

'It's very nice of you, we'll see.'

And she seemed to draw away and follow the hymn, determined not to reply. Pauline had put Jeanne next to her to let her share the heating vent, and she was slowly getting warmer and warmer, in the blissful happiness of someone who usually feels the cold. In the warm rising air, both sat up on their seats, full of curiosity, studying everything, the low ceiling divided by wooden panels, the pillars with their capitals connected by the full arches from which lamps were hanging, the carved oak pulpit, and over the mass of heads moving in rhythm to the strains of the hymn, they could see right into the dark corners of the side aisles which led to the hidden chapels, gleaming with gold, to the baptistry closed by a grill near the main door. But they constantly returned to the splendour of the chancel painted in bright colours, sparkling with gold. A lighted crystal lamp hung there from the high arch. Gigantic candelabra strung together tiers of candles which pierced the shadowy depths of the church in a shower of symmetrical stars, illuminating the high altar like an enormous bouquet of greenery and flowers. Above it in a harvest of roses a Virgin dressed in satin and lace, crowned with pearls, held Jesus clothed in a long robe, in her arms.

'Now are you warm?' asked Pauline. 'This is really nice.'

But Jeanne was in ecstasy contemplating the Virgin in the midst of all the flowers. She shivered. She was afraid she might not be good any longer and she lowered her eyes, staring hard at the black and white tiles on the floor, to stop herself bursting into tears. The thin voices of the choirboys wafted gently through her hair.

Meanwhile Hélène, her eyes on her missal, drew away each time she felt Juliette brush against her with her lace. She was not at all prepared for this encounter. In spite of the vow she had made to herself to love Henri in a holy way without ever belonging to him, she felt uneasy to think she was betraying this gay, confident woman sitting beside her. One thought preoccupied her. She would not go to the dinner. And she wondered how she might gradually break off relations that affronted that loyalty. But the droning voices of the cantors a few steps away from her prevented her from thinking clearly. Unable to formulate a thought, she gave herself up to the rhythms of the canticle, enjoying a spiritual well-being which she had never experienced in a church until that moment.

'Have you heard about Madame de Chermette?' asked Juliette, again indulging her burning desire to talk.

'No, I know nothing about her.'

'Well, just imagine... You've seen her daughter, who is so tall for fifteen? They are thinking about marrying her next year, and to the little dark-haired boy you always see clinging to his mother. Everybody's talking about it.'

'Oh,' said Hélène, who wasn't listening.

Madame Deberle provided more details. But suddenly the hymn

ended, the organ ground to a halt. Then she stopped talking, surprised by her loud voice in the silence which had fallen. A priest had just appeared in the pulpit. There was a thrill of expectation. Then he started to speak. No indeed, Hélène wouldn't attend this dinner. Her eyes fixed on the priest, she imagined the first meeting with Henri she had been dreading so much for the last three days. She had visions of him pale with anger, telling her off for shutting herself away in her house. And she feared she would not be able to show enough self-composure. Deep in her thoughts, she did not see the priest; she caught only a few phrases, a booming voice from somewhere above her saying:

'It was an ineffable moment when the Virgin Mary, bowing her head, replied: "Behold the handmaid of the Lord..." '

Oh, she would be brave, all her common sense had returned. She would enjoy being loved, but she would never admit her love, for that would be certainly at the cost of her peace of mind. And she would love him from the bottom of her heart, without ever admitting it, contenting herself with a word from Henri, with the occasional glance exchanged when chance brought them together! It was a dream that filled her with thoughts of eternity. She felt the church around her to be friendly and pleasing. The priest intoned:

'The angel departed. Mary was lost in the contemplation of the divine mystery working within her, flooding her with light and love.'

'He speaks very well,' Madame Deberle whispered, leaning over to her. 'And he's so young—scarcely thirty, wouldn't you say?'

Madame Deberle was moved. She approved of religion as an emotion that was in good taste. Giving flowers to the church, having to do with priests, people who were polite, discreet and smelled nice, dressing up to go to church, where, as she liked to think, she extended the protection of her class to the God of the poor. All this made her especially happy; and the more so because her husband was not a practising Christian and so her devotions had acquired the taste of forbidden fruit. Hélène looked at her and replied only with a nod. Both faces were ecstatic and smiling. There was a loud scraping of chairs and blowing of handkerchiefs, the priest had just left the pulpit with this last exhortation:

'O pious Christian souls, go and may your love be increased. God gave himself to you, your hearts are full of His presence, your souls are overflowing with His grace!'

The organ promptly thundered in response. There followed the litanies of the Virgin with their passionate appeals of love. From the shadows of the hidden chapels in the side aisles came a distant faint chanting, as though the earth was answering the angelic voices of the choirboys. A breath of air wafted over the heads of the congregation, lengthening the tall flames of the candles, while the Holy Mother, with her bouquet of roses in the midst of the flowers, bruising as they exhaled the last of their scent, looked as if she had bowed her head to smile at her Jesus.

Suddenly Hélène turned, with an instinctive concern.

'You are not ill, are you, Jeanne?' she enquired.

The child was very pale, her eyes damp, as if carried away by the torrent of love in the litanies, gazing at the altar, seeing the roses multiply and fall like rain. She whispered:

'Oh no, Maman... I'm happy, really happy.'

Then she asked:

'But where's my friend?'

She meant the abbé. Pauline spied him. He was in one of the choirstalls. But she had to lift Jeanne up to see.

'Oh, I can see him. He's looking at us, he's winking at us.'

According to Jeanne he 'winked' at them when he was concealing his laughter. Hélène exchanged a friendly nod with him. For her it was like an assurance of peace, a conclusive reason to be calm, which made her fond of the church and lulled her into a happy and tolerant state of mind. Censers were being waved in front of the altar, smoke wafted up; and there was a benediction, a monstrance like a sun, slowly raised and waved above the foreheads that were bent to the floor. Hélène was bowed low, in a beatific numbness when she heard Madame Deberle say:

'It's over, let's go.'

There was a scraping of chairs and tread of feet beneath the vault. Pauline took Jeanne's hand. Walking in front with the child, she questioned her.

'You've never been to the theatre before?'

'No, is it better than this?'

The little girl, sighing with an excess of passion, poked her chin out as much as to say that nothing could be more beautiful. But Pauline did not answer. She had just stopped stock-still in front of a priest, who was passing, dressed in his surplice; and scarcely had he gone by than she said aloud:

'Oh, how handsome he is!' with such conviction that two members of the congregation turned round and stared at her.

In the meantime Hélène had risen. She was shuffling along next to Juliette in the middle of the crowd which was working its way forward. Weak and weary, and with her whole being suffused with love, she no longer felt troubled by the proximity of Juliette. At one moment their bare wrists touched and they smiled at one another. They could hardly breathe. Hélène tried to make Juliette go first, to protect her. All their previous intimacy seemed to have returned.

'It's agreed, then?' Madame Deberle asked. 'We'll expect you tomorrow night.'

Hélène no longer had the strength to say no. She would think about it when they were out in the street. Finally they left, among the last to do so. Pauline and Jeanne were waiting for them on the opposite side of the road. But a whining voice brought them up short.

'Oh my dear lady, what good fortune! Such a long time since I saw you last!'

It was Mother Fétu. She was begging outside the church door. Blocking Hélène's way, as though she had been lying in wait for her, she went on:

'Oh, I've been very poorly, it's always there in my belly, you know... Now it's like hammer blows... And nothing I can do about it. I didn't dare ask you to tell him... God bless you!'

Hélène had just slipped a coin into her hand, promising to keep her in mind.

'Gracious!' said Madame Deberle still standing under the porch, 'someone's chatting to Pauline and Jeanne... Oh, look, it's Henri!'

'Yes, yes,' Mother Fétu went on, looking slyly from one lady to the other. 'It's the kind doctor. I watched him all the time during the service. He stood on the pavement waiting for you, I'll be bound. And what a saintly man! I say it because it's the truth, in front of God, who hears us... Oh, I know you, Madame. You've got a husband there who deserves to be happy... May Heaven fulfil your desires, and all blessings be upon you! In the name of the Father, Son, and Holy Ghost, Amen!'

And in the thousand wrinkles on her face, which was lined like an old apple, her little eyes kept darting around, worried and mischievous, going from Juliette to Hélène without it being certain which of the two she was addressing when she spoke of the kind doctor. She kept up her continual babbling, shreds of whining phrases interspersed with pious exclamations.

Hélène was surprised and touched by Henri's reserve. He hardly dared raised his eyes to look at her. When his wife teased him about his opinions which prevented him entering a church, he said simply that he had come to meet the ladies and smoke his cigar. And Hélène realized that he had wanted to see her again to show her how wrong she was to fear some new offensiveness on his part. No doubt he had sworn, as she had, to be sensible. She did not study him to see if he really meant what he said, since it saddened her to see him unhappy. So, as she left the Deberles in the Rue Vineuse, she said cheerily:

'All right, I'll come, tomorrow at seven.'

Then relations became closer than ever, a wonderful sort of life began. For Hélène it was as if Henri had never given in to that moment of folly. This was what she had dreamed of; they loved each other but they just would not say it any more, they would be happy just to know it. Delightful hours during which, without speaking of their affection, they continually communicated it to each other by a gesture, an inflexion in the voice, or just silence. Everything revolved around their love. They were constantly bathed in a passion that they carried with them, around them, as though it were the only air they could breathe. And under the cover of their close friendship, they knowingly acted out this comedy of the heart, for they did not allow themselves to shake hands, which imparted a peerless voluptuousness to the simple greeting they exchanged when they met.

Each evening the ladies insisted on going to church. Madame Deberle, enchanted, took pleasure in it again, it was a change from going dancing, going to concerts, to premieres. She adored these new feelings, she was seen constantly in the company of nuns and priests. The basic religious instruction that she had received from boarding school entered her empty head once more, and was translated into little practices which she enjoyed, as if she was remembering her childhood games. Hélène, who had grown up without any religious education, allowed herself to enjoy these practices in the Month of Mary, happy to see the pleasure that Jeanne seemed to be taking in them. They dined earlier, they hustled Rosalie so that they wouldn't arrive late and get a bad seat. Then they called for Juliette on the way. One day they took Lucien, but he behaved so badly that now they left him at home. And as they went into the warm church all glowing with the candles, they experienced a feeling of quietness and peace, which was gradually becoming a necessity for Hélène. When she had had doubts during the day, or a vague anxiety had taken hold of her at the thought of Henri, the church soothed her spirits again in the evening. The psalms rose and overflowed with holy passion. The fresh-cut flowers, heavy with perfume, were overpowering under the vault. She breathed in the first intoxication of spring, the adoration of womanhood elevated to a religion, and she let herself be carried away by this mystery of love and purity as she contemplated Mary, Virgin and mother, crowned with her white roses. She remained kneeling longer and longer every day. She was surprised to find she sometimes had her hands joined. Then after the service, going home was delightful. Henri would be waiting at the church door, the evenings were getting warmer, they went back through the dark silent streets of Passy, exchanging the odd word.

'You are becoming very religious, my dear!' Madame Deberle said with a laugh one evening.

It was true. Hélène had opened her heart wide and embraced the life of devotion. She would never have thought loving would make her feel so good. She returned to the church as to a place of love, where she was allowed to weep, not to think, to lose herself completely in silent adoration. Each evening for an hour she lowered her defences; the flowering of her love, contained within her during the day, was able to rise up in her heart, grow in her prayers, there in front of everyone, in the midst of the religious fervour of the congregation. The stammered prayers, the kneelings, the salutations, these words and vague gestures repeated over and over again lulled her and seemed to her the one true language, always the same passion, translated by the same word or the same sign. She needed to believe it, she was transported up into the love of God.

And it was not only Hélène that Juliette teased, she claimed that Henri himself was turning to the church. Did he not go into the church now to wait for them! An atheist, a pagan, who declared that he had looked for the soul on the end of his scalpel and not found it yet! As soon as she caught sight of him behind the pulpit standing in front of a pillar, Juliette nudged Hélène's elbow.

'Look, he's there already. Do you know, he wouldn't go to confession before we got married... No, his expression is priceless, he is watching us in such a funny way! Just look at him!'

Hélène did not raise her eyes straight away. The service was about to finish, the incense was burning, the joyous notes of the organ rang out. But as her friend wasn't the kind of woman to leave her be, she had to answer her.

'Yes, yes, I can see him,' she mumbled, not turning her head.

She had guessed he was there when she heard the hosanna rise from the whole church. Henri's breathing seemed to wing its way on the words of the hymns to the nape of her neck, and, as she knelt, she felt as though his eyes were behind her lighting up the nave and enveloping them in a golden light. Then she prayed with such fervour that words failed her. He, very serious, had the proper expression of a husband coming to fetch the ladies from the house of God, just as he would have gone to fetch them in the foyer of a theatre. But when they met as the congregation filed slowly out, they both felt as though they were more tightly bound together, united by the flowers and the hymns; and, hearts in their mouths, they avoided speaking to each other.

After a fortnight Madame Deberle grew tired of it. She leaped from one passion to the next, tormented with the need to do what everyone else was doing. So now she was involved in charity sales, climbing sixty different floors in an afternoon to go and beg canvases from well-known painters, and spending her evenings presiding, with a bell, over the meetings of lady patrons. So one Thursday evening Hélène and her daughter were on their own in the church. After the sermon when the cantors were attacking the Magnificat, the young woman felt her heart leap and she turned her head: Henri was there in his usual place. So she stayed with her eyes cast down till the end of the service, waiting for the return home.

'Oh, how nice of you to come!' cried Jeanne on their way out, with her childish familiarity. 'I should have been scared in these dark streets.'

But Henri pretended to be surprised. He assumed he was coming to meet his wife. Hélène allowed her daughter to answer, she was behind them, not speaking. As they all passed through the porch, a voice whined:

'Can you spare... God bless you!'

Each evening Jeanne slipped a ten-sou coin into Mother Fétu's hand. When the latter saw the doctor alone with Hélène, she simply nodded her head understandingly, instead of coming out with her usual torrents of thanks. And once the church was empty, she began to follow them, dragging her feet, mumbling words under her breath. When it was a fine night, instead of going home by way of the Rue de Passy, the ladies sometimes went via the Rue Raynouard, thus lengthening their walk by five or six minutes. That evening Hélène took the Rue Raynouard, wanting darkness and quiet, yielding to the charms of that long and empty street lit at intervals by gaslight, without the shadow of a passer-by falling across her path.

At that hour in this somewhat remote district, Passy was already asleep, breathing quietly like a provincial town. On both sides of the street stood rows of mansions, dark, sleepy boarding-houses for young ladies and dining premises where the kitchens were still lit up. No light from the window of a single shop shone through the darkness. And this solitude was a great delight to Hélène and Henri. He did not dare offer her his arm. Jeanne walked between them in the middle of the road, which was sandy like a path in a park. The houses petered out, clematis and lilacs in flower tumbled over long walls. Gardens stretched between the large houses, through a barred gate you occasionally caught a glimpse of dark green shrubberies, with light green lawns in between the trees. And you could almost make out the tubs full of iris scenting the air. All three walked more slowly in the warmth of this spring night which soaked them with its perfumes. And when Jeanne playing a childish game walked with her face lifted to the sky, she said over and over:

'Oh, Maman, look at all those stars!'

But behind them the footsteps of Mother Fétu seemed to be echoing theirs. She was drawing nearer. You could hear the last words of the Latin phrase 'Ave Maria, gratia plena', repeated time and again with the same mumbling inflection. Mother Fétu was telling her beads as she walked home.

'I've got a coin left, shall I give it to her?' Jeanne asked her mother.

And without waiting for an answer she ran over to the old woman who was about to start her descent down the Passage des Eaux. Mother Fétu, invoking all the saints of paradise, took the coin. But at the same time she caught hold of the child's arm. She kept hold of it, and changing her tone:

'Is the other lady poorly then?'

'No,' answered Jeanne, surprised.

'Oh, may Heaven preserve her! May God shower her with riches,

her and her husband! Don't go, little girl. Let me say an Ave Maria for
your Maman and you will say amen with me... Your Maman will let
you, you can catch them up.'

Meanwhile Hélène and Henri stood nervously there, finding themselves suddenly on their own in the shadow of a line of tall chestnut
trees bordering the road. They took a hesitant step or two. On the
ground the chestnuts had dropped a shower of their delicate blossoms
and they were walking on that pink carpet. Then they stopped, too
choked to go any further.

'Forgive me,' said Henri simply.

'Yes, yes,' Hélène stammered. 'Don't say anything, I beg you.'

But she felt his hand lightly touch hers. She drew back. Fortunately
Jeanne was running back.

'Maman, Maman!' she cried. 'She made me say an Ave so as to
bring you luck.'

And all three turned into the Rue Vineuse while Mother Fétu
climbed down the Passage des Eaux, as she finished telling her rosary.
The month wore on. Madame Deberle put in an appearance at services two or three times. One Sunday—the last—Henri once again
dared to go and wait for Hélène and Jeanne. Their walk home was
delightful. That month had passed in extraordinary sweetness. The
little church seemed to have come to soothe them and make them fit
for this passion. At the outset Hélène had settled down, happy to have
this refuge in religion where she felt she could love someone without
shame; but the secret feelings had been doing their work in her and
when she woke out of her religious torpor she felt as if she was being
invaded, bound by ties which would have torn the flesh off her body
had she attempted to break them. Henri remained respectful. However,
his feverish longing was written all over his face. She feared some
uncontrollable outburst on his part. And she herself was afraid of her
own feelings, shaken as she was by the sudden inrush of passion.

One afternoon, coming back from a walk with Jeanne, she went up
the Rue de l'Annonciation and entered the church. The little girl had
complained of being terribly tired. Until the last day she had been
unwilling to admit that the evening service was tiring her out because
she enjoyed it so very much. But her cheeks were becoming pale as
wax and the doctor advised Hélène to take her for long walks.

'Sit there,' said her mother. 'You can rest. We shall only stay for ten
minutes.'

She seated her next to a pillar. She herself got down on her knees, a few chairs further along. At the back of the nave workmen were taking the nails out of the draperies, shifting pots of flowers, the Month of Mary celebrations having finished the day before. Hélène, her face in her hands, saw nothing and heard nothing, asking herself anxiously if she ought to confess to Abbé Jouve the terrible crisis she was going through. He would give her advice, give her back her lost tranquillity perhaps. But in the depths of her being an unquenchable joy was rising out of her very anguish. She nursed her sickness, trembling at the thought that the priest might cure it. Ten minutes went by, an hour. She was plunged deep into the struggle of her heart.

And when she finally raised her head, eyes wet with tears, she saw Abbé Jouve next to her, looking at her with a sorrowful expression. He was directing the workmen. He had recognized Jeanne and come over.

'What's the matter, child?' he asked Hélène, who had got up with a start and was drying her eyes.

She couldn't think what to answer, fearing to fall once more on her knees and burst out sobbing. He drew nearer and went on quietly:

'I don't want to question you but why not confide in me, as priest and not as friend?'

'Later,' she stammered, 'later, I promise.'

Meanwhile Jeanne had been patiently waiting, passing the time by studying the stained glass, the statues round the great door, the scenes from the Way of the Cross depicted in little bas-reliefs along the side naves. Gradually the cold church had enveloped her like a shroud. And in this lassitude which even prevented her from having any thoughts, a sense of unease came over her from the holy silence of the chapels, the prolonged echo of the least noise in this sacred place where it seemed to her she would die. But most of all she was sad to see them taking away the flowers. As the large bouquets of roses vanished, the altar was revealed, bare and cold. This glacial marble, with no candles, no smoke from the incense, made her blood run cold. One moment later the Virgin dressed in lace teetered, then fell backwards into the arms of two workmen. Jeanne uttered a little cry, flung out her arms and became rigid, twisted by the crisis that had been threatening for some days.

And when Hélène, worried out of her mind, took her home in a cab helped by the distraught abbé, she turned back towards the church porch with tense, trembling hands.

'It's that church! It's that church!' she repeated, with a violence in which there was both regret and blame for the month of the love of God she had experienced there.

CHAPTER 2

BY evening Jeanne was feeling better. She was able to get up. She insisted on doing so, to reassure her mother, and she trailed around in the dining room and sat down in front of her empty plate.

'It's nothing,' she said, forcing a smile. 'You know I am a bit off colour. You eat. You must eat.'

And seeing that her mother saw her turn pale and shiver, and unable to swallow a mouthful, she eventually pretended to be a bit hungry. She promised faithfully she'd have a little fruit jelly. Then Hélène hurried to give her some while the child, still smiling, with a slight nervous tremor, contemplated her with her adoring expression. At dessert she tried to keep her promise. But there were unshed tears in her eyes.

'I can't swallow, you see,' she said in a small voice. 'You mustn't scold me.'

She felt a dreadful weariness annihilating her. Her legs seemed as if they were dead, an iron hand gripping her by the shoulder. But she was being brave, she was stifling the little cries caused by the throbbing ache in her neck. For one moment she forgot herself, her head was too heavy, and she curled up in pain. Her mother, seeing her sweet child so thin and feeble, could not finish the pear she was forcing herself to eat. Sobs choked her. She let her serviette drop, and went over to take Jeanne in her arms.

'My child, my child...', she stammered, heartbroken at the sight of the dining room where she had so often been delighted by the little girl's appetite when she was in good health. Jeanne sat up and tried to smile again.

'Don't torment yourself, it's nothing, I tell you. Now you've finished, you can put me back in bed... I wanted to see you at table, because I know you, you wouldn't have eaten anything otherwise, not the smallest crumb.'

Hélène carried her off. She had pushed her little bed next to hers in her bedroom. When Jeanne lay down, covered up to her chin, she felt a lot better. She complained only of a dull ache at the back of her head. Then she became more emotional, her love for Hélène seemed to have become more intense since her illness. Hélène had to kiss her, swearing that she loved her and promising to kiss her again when she came to bed.

'It doesn't matter if I'm asleep,' said Jeanne. 'I can feel you just the same.'

She closed her eyes and fell asleep. Hélène stayed beside her, watching her as she slumbered. When Rosalie tiptoed in to ask if she could stop work, she nodded at her. Eleven o'clock chimed, Hélène was still there when she thought she had heard a soft tap on the door to the landing. Startled, she took the lamp and went to see who it was.

'Who's there?'

'Me, open the door,' came a muffled voice.

It was Henri. She opened it quickly, no doubt thinking the visit quite natural, that the doctor had got to know about Jeanne's attack, and was hurrying over, although she hadn't called him because she felt a sort of embarrassment at the thought of involving him in the well-being of her daughter.

But Henri did not allow her time to speak. He had followed her into the dining room, trembling, his face flushed.

'I beg you to forgive me,' he stammered, catching hold of her hand. 'It's been three whole days and I just had to see you.'

Hélène had disengaged her hand. He stood there looking at her and went on:

'Don't be afraid, I love you. If you hadn't opened the door I should have stayed outside till you did. Oh, I know it's crazy but I love you, I love you...'

She listened very solemnly and with a stern expression on her face, saying nothing, and to him this was torture. At this reception, all his passion came pouring out in a great flood.

'Oh, why are we playing these terrible games? I am at the end of my strength, my heart is about to burst. I shall do something crazy, worse than I have done this evening. I shall capture you in front of everyone and carry you off...'

An uncontrollable desire made him reach out to her. He had come closer, he was kissing her dress, his feverish hands were all over her. She remained frozen, standing stiff and straight.

'So you haven't heard?' she asked.

And as he had taken hold of her bare wrist beneath the open sleeve of the gown and was covering it with eager kisses, she made an impatient movement.

'Leave me alone! You can see that I'm not even listening to you. I can't think about things like that!'

She calmed down and asked him a second time.

'So you know nothing?... Well, my daughter is ill. I'm happy to see you, you will be able to set my mind at rest.'

Taking the lamp, she led the way; but as she went into the room she turned to say harshly, looking at him straight in the eyes:

'I forbid you to do that again here. Never, never!'

He went in after her, still trembling, not properly understanding what she was telling him. In the bedroom at that time of night surrounded by the linen and the scattered clothes, he again smelled the scent of verbena that had so troubled him that first evening when he had seen Hélène with her hair dishevelled and her shawl slipping down over her shoulders. To find himself there on his knees, to drink in the scent of love wafting in the air, to spend the night adoring her and forget everything in the possession of his dream! His head was bursting, he leaned on the child's little iron bed.

'She's asleep,' said Hélène, in a whisper. 'Look at her.'

He didn't hear, his passion would not be silenced. She leaned forward, he caught sight of her golden nape with its fine curly hair. And he shut his eyes so as to resist the need to kiss that spot.

'Doctor, look, she's burning... Please tell me it's not serious?'

So with the mad desire still beating in his head, he mechanically felt Jeanne's pulse, acceding to the habit of his profession. But the struggle was too great, he stayed stock-still for a moment, apparently unaware he was holding that poor little hand in his own.

'Has she got a high temperature?'

'A high temperature,' he echoed. 'Do you think so?'

The little hand was warming his own. Silence fell again. The doctor in him was awakening. He took her pulse. In his eyes a flame was dying. Slowly his face grew pale, he bent forward over Jeanne and studied her with an anxious expression. And he muttered:

'The attack is very violent, you are right. Oh God, the poor child!'

His desire was dead and his only concern was to be of use to her. He collected himself entirely. He sat down, and was questioning the mother about the events which had preceded this crisis, when the little girl woke up with a moan. She complained of a terrible headache. The pain in the neck and shoulders had become so bad that she couldn't move without sobbing. Hélène kneeling on the other side of the bed encouraged her, smiled at her, her heart breaking to see her suffering like that.

'Is someone there, Maman?' she asked, turning and seeing the doctor.

'A friend, you know who it is.'

The child studied him a moment, thoughtful and as if she wasn't quite sure. Then her face softened.

'Oh yes, I know him. I like him.'

And with a coaxing air:

'You must make me better, Monsieur, mustn't you? So that Maman will be happy. I'll take whatever you give me, I promise.'

The doctor had felt her pulse again and Hélène held her other hand; and between the two of them, she studied them, one after the other, with that little nervous tremor, as though she had never seen them so clearly before. Then, she stirred, in some discomfort. Her little hands tensed and tightened on them both:

'Don't go away; I'm scared... Look after me, stop all those people coming near... I only want you, I only want you two, close to me, oh, close by me, together...'

She was pulling them nearer to each other in sudden jerky movements, repeating:

'Together, together...'

The delirium recurred several times. In the moments of calm, Jeanne sank into a sleep where she appeared not to be breathing, as if she were dead. When, with a start, she came out of these short periods of unconsciousness, she could not hear or see, her eyes were veiled in a white film. For a part of the night, which was particularly bad, the doctor stayed at her bedside. He only went down for a moment to swallow a draught of something himself. Towards morning when he left, Hélène anxiously went with him into the hall.

'Well?' she asked.

'Her condition is very serious,' he replied. 'But please believe I shall do what I can. Count on me. I'll come again this morning at ten.'

Going back into the room, Hélène found Jeanne sitting up, looking around her, as if lost.'

'You left me, you left me!' she cried. 'Oh, I'm scared, I don't want you to leave me by myself.'

Her mother kissed her to console her, but she was still looking around.

'Where is he? Oh, tell him not to go... I want him to be there, I want...'

'He's coming back, my angel,' Hélène repeated, her tears mingling with her daughter's. 'He won't leave us, I swear. He loves us too much... Look, be a good girl and go back to sleep. I'm staying here, waiting for him to come back.'

'Really and truly?' whispered the child, falling deeper and deeper into sleep.

Then terrible days, three weeks of dreadful anguish began. The fever did not abate for a moment. Jeanne was only a little calmer when the doctor was there and she had given him one of her small hands to hold, while her mother held the other. She took refuge in them, she shared out her tyrannical adoration between them as if she had realized under what ardent and loving protection she had placed herself. Her exquisite nervous sensitivity, refined even more by her illness, no doubt alerted her that only a miracle of their love could save her. For hours she looked at them on each side of her bed with eyes that were grave and far-seeing. All human passion, half-perceived and guessed-at, was written in the gaze of this little girl who was drifting towards death. She did not speak, she squeezed their hands tight, begging them not to go away, giving them to understand how restful it was for her to see them there. When after an absence the doctor reappeared, she was ravished with joy, her eyes which had not left the door, lit up. Then, soothed, she fell asleep, reassured at hearing him and her mother moving around her, chatting softly.

The day after the crisis, Doctor Bodin arrived. But Jeanne was in a sulk, and turned her head away, refusing to allow herself to be examined.

'Not him, Maman,' she murmured. 'Not him, please.'

And when he came back the following day, Hélène had to tell him that the child did not want him. So the old doctor did not go into the bedroom again. He came up every two days, asking for news, sometimes chatting with his colleague, Doctor Deberle, who was deferential because of the other's advanced age.

Anyway it was no good seeking to deceive Jeanne. Her senses were refined to a remarkable degree. The abbé and Monsieur Rambaud came each evening, sat down, and spent an hour there in silent despair. One day as the doctor was leaving, Hélène made a sign to Monsieur Rambaud to take his place and hold the little girl's hand, so that she did not realize her friend had left. But after two or three minutes, Jeanne, who was asleep, opened her eyes again and pulled her hand away. And she wept, saying they were playing tricks on her.

'Don't you love me any more, you don't want me any more?' repeated poor Monsieur Rambaud, tears in his eyes.

She looked at him without speaking, she seemed not even to try and recognize him. And the good fellow returned to his place with a heavy heart. After a while he took to coming in silently and slipping into the recess where he remained, half hidden behind a curtain, throughout the evening, numb with sadness, gazing at the sick girl. The abbé was there too, his large face very white on his thin shoulders. He blew his nose noisily in his handkerchief to hide his tears. The danger his little friend was facing upset him to such an extent that he forgot about the poor of his parish.

But try as they might to conceal themselves in a corner of the room, Jeanne sensed their presence. She did not want them there, she tossed and turned uncomfortably even when lulled to sleep by the fever. Her mother leaned over her to hear the words she was uttering.

'Oh, Maman, I feel so poorly! I can't breathe. Tell them to go away now, now!'

As gently as possible, Hélène explained to the two brothers that the little girl wanted to sleep. They understood, and went away with heads bowed. As soon as they had gone, Jeanne breathed more deeply, glanced around the bedroom, then focused again, with infinite sweetness, on her mother and the doctor.

'Hello,' she murmured. 'I'm all right now, stay there.'

For three weeks she clung to them like that. Henri had come twice a day at first, but then spent entire evenings there, giving as much time as he could to be with the child. At the beginning he had feared it might be typhoid fever; but such contradictory symptoms manifested themselves that before long he was very puzzled. He thought this must be one of those chloro-anaemic infections, which are so difficult to diagnose, and whose complications are dreadful at an age when a girl is growing into womanhood. He suspected, one after the other, a lesion in the heart and incipient consumption. He was very concerned by Jeanne's nervous hypersensitivity which he could not assuage, and especially her high fever, which wouldn't go away and refused to be brought down by even the strongest medication. He put all his energy and medical expertise into her treatment, with the thought uppermost in his mind that he was nurturing his own happiness, his own life. He fell into a profound silence, and gravely awaited the outcome. Not once during those three weeks of anxiety did his passion awake. He was no longer affected by Hélène's nearness, and when their eyes met, they were full of the sympathetic sadness of two people who are threatened by a common misfortune.

Yet every minute their hearts melted more and more into one. They both lived with a single thought in mind. As soon as he arrived he could tell from her expression how Jeanne had spent the night, and he did not need to say anything for her to know how he had found the sick girl. In any case, she, with fine maternal courage, had made him swear not to deceive her, but to tell her what he feared. Always on her feet, not having slept three hours together in twenty nights, she demonstrated a superhuman strength and calm, without shedding a tear, overcoming her despair in order to keep her head in this struggle against her child's illness. An immense void had opened up in and around her, into which her world, her feelings every hour, the awareness of her own existence even, had sunk. Nothing existed now. She was only connected with life through this dear child near to death and this man who promised her a miracle. It was him and him alone that she saw, that she heard, his slightest word took on a supreme importance, and she abandoned herself unreservedly, dreaming of being present within him, to give him some of her strength. Silently, inexorably, this possession was coming about. When Jeanne was having an attack, almost every evening, at the times when the fever intensified, they were there silent and alone in the stuffy room. And despite themselves, as though they needed to feel they were two against death, trembling with anxiety and pity, their hands found one another and coupled for some time on the edge of the bed, uniting them, until a little sigh from the child, her calm, regular breathing, told them that the crisis was over. Then, they exchanged a reassuring nod. Once more their love had triumphed. And each time their touch grew more overt, their union was closer. One evening Hélène guessed that Henri was hiding something from her. He had been examining Jeanne for ten minutes without a word. The little girl was complaining that she was terribly thirsty; she was choking and from her throat came a continuous whistling noise. Then she had become very sleepy, her face very red, so heavy she could no longer open her eyelids. And she remained inert, you would have thought she was dead except for the whistling in her throat.

'You think she's very ill, don't you?' asked Hélène curtly.

He replied that no, there was no change. But he was very pale, he sat there, crushed by his inability to do anything. So despite feeling so tense in her whole body, she sank on to a chair on the other side of the bed.

'Tell me everything. You swore you would... Have we lost her?'

And, as he said nothing, she went on violently:

'I'm strong, you know... Am I crying? Am I in despair? Talk to me. I want to know the truth.'

Henri gazed at her. He spoke slowly.

'Well,' he said, 'if within one hour she doesn't come out of this drowsiness, it will be over.'

Hélène did not give so much as a sob. Her cold horror was hair-raising. Her eyes fell on Jeanne, she fell to her knees and took her child in her arms, in a superb gesture of possession, as though to keep her there against her shoulder. For more than a minute she leaned her face next to hers, drinking her in with her eyes, wanting to breathe life, her own life, into her. The halting breath of the sick little girl became shorter.

'Can't we do anything?' she went on, looking up. 'Why are you still standing there? Do something!'

He made a dispirited gesture.

'Do something... I don't know what. Anything at all. There must be something we can do. You are not going to let her die? It's not possible.'

'I'll do all I can,' the doctor answered simply.

He had risen. Then there was in him a supreme struggle. All his confidence and practical decisiveness as a doctor returned. Until that moment he had not dared use violent means, fearing to weaken the little body that was already so feeble. But hesitating no longer, he sent Rosalie to get twelve leeches, and he did not hide from her mother that it was a desperate measure, which might save or kill her child. When the leeches arrived, he saw her weaken a moment.

'Oh God,' she whispered. 'Supposing you kill her...' He had to extract her consent.

'Well, put them on her, but may Heaven be with you!'

She had not let go of Jeanne, she refused to get up, wanting to keep her head there against her shoulder. His face expressionless, he said nothing more, absorbed in the effort of what he was trying to do. First the leeches did not cling on properly. The minutes ticked by, the pitiless, obstinate ticking of the clock in the big room sunk in shadow was the only thing you could hear. Each second dashed another hope. Beneath the circle of yellow light from the lampshade, Jeanne's lovely little naked, suffering body in the middle of the disarrayed sheets looked pale as wax. Hélène dry-eyed, unable to speak, gazed at those small limbs, that looked already dead. To see a drop of her daughter's blood, she would willingly have given all of her own. Finally a drop of red appeared, the leeches were working. One by one they attached themselves. The life of the child was in the balance. Those were terrifying minutes, of poignant emotion. Was that sigh Jeanne gave her last breath? Or was she coming back to life? One moment Hélène, feeling her stiffen, thought she was passing away, and she had an uncontrollable desire to pull off those beasts that were so thirstily sucking her blood. But a greater force held her back; she sat there motionless, with parted lips. The clock continued to tick, the anxious bedroom seemed to be waiting.

The child moved. Her eyelids slowly lifted, then closed again, as though surprised and weary. A slight vibration, like a breath of air, passed over her face. Her lips moved. Hélène eager, tense, leaned over in fierce expectation.

'Maman, Maman,' murmured Jeanne.

Henri came over then to the young woman, saying:

'She is saved.'

'She is saved,' Hélène stammered. And again: 'She is saved.' Suffused with such joy, she sank on to the floor by the side of the bed looking at her daughter, looking at the doctor as if she had lost her mind.

And with a violent movement she rose and threw herself at Henri's neck.

'Oh, I love you,' she cried.

She kissed him, she hugged him. It was her declaration of love, the admission which had been so long delayed, and had at long last burst forth in the crisis of her heart. Mother and lover were one being, in this moment of delight. She offered the burning love of her gratitude.

'I'm crying, look, I can cry now,' she stammered. 'Oh God, how I love you, how happy we shall be!'

She called him 'tu', she sobbed. The fount of her tears, dried up for the last three weeks, poured down her cheeks. She stayed in his arms, embracing and stroking him like a child, carried away by this opening and flowering of her love. Then she fell to her knees again, moving Jeanne against her shoulder to sleep, and from time to time, while her daughter was resting, she raised her moist, passionate eyes to Henri's face.

It was a night of great happiness. The doctor stayed very late. Lying in her bed, with the covers up to her chin, her fine brown head in the middle of the pillow, Jeanne shut her eyes, not asleep but comforted and oblivious. The lamp placed on the little table they had pulled up next to the hearth was only lighting one end of the room, leaving Hélène and Henri in the half-shadow, sitting in their usual places on the two sides of the narrow bed. But the child did not separate them, on the contrary she brought them together, and added an innocence to the first evening of their love. Both savoured the calm after the long days of anguish they had just spent. Finally they found each other, side by side, with their hearts more open than ever; and they realized their love was greater through sharing the terror and joy which had so shaken them. And in all this, the bedroom itself, so warm, so discreet, so charged with the religious silence that surrounds a sickbed, became complicit. From time to time Hélène got up, went on tiptoe to fetch a potion, turn up the lamp, give an order to Rosalie; and the doctor, watching, signalled to her to move quietly. Then when she sat down again they exchanged a smile. They did not say a word, their sole concern was Jeanne, who was like their love itself. But sometimes while they tended her, when they pulled up the coverlet or raised her head, their hands met and forgot everything for a moment in their nearness to one another. It was the only caress, involuntary and furtive, that they allowed themselves.

'I'm not asleep,' whispered Jeanne. 'I know you are there.'

Then they rejoiced to hear her speak. Their hands unlocked, they had no other desire. The child was enough for them, calming their passion.

'Are you all right, darling?' asked Hélène when she saw her stirring.

Jeanne did not answer straight away. She spoke as though in a dream.

'Oh yes... I don't feel... I can hear you, I like to hear you.'

After a moment she made an effort to open her eyes and look at them. Then she gave a beatific smile and shut her eyes again.

The next day when the abbé and Monsieur Rambaud appeared,

Hélène made an involuntary gesture of impatience. They were encroaching on her little zone of happiness. And as they questioned her, worried that they might hear some bad news, she was cruel enough to say that Jeanne was no better. She spoke without thinking, impelled by the selfish need to keep the joy of having saved her for herself and Henri, and to be the only ones who knew that. Why did anyone want to share their happiness? It belonged to them, it would be diminished in her eyes if someone else knew about it. It would have seemed like a stranger intervening, in their love.

The priest went over to the bed.

'Jeanne, it's us, your friends... Don't you know us?'

She nodded gravely. She knew them but did not want to chat. Deep in thought, she looked up at her mother as if she understood. And the two kindly men left, sadder than on other evenings. Three days later Henri allowed the sick girl her first boiled egg. It was quite a business. Jeanne insisted on eating it alone with her mother and the doctor, with the door shut. As Monsieur Rambaud was indeed there, she whispered in her mother's ear, as she was spreading a serviette on the bed to serve as tablecloth:

'Wait till he's gone.'

Then, when he had gone away:

'Now, now... It's nicer when there's no one here.'

Hélène had sat her up, while Henri was putting two pillows behind her back to prop her. And once the serviette was spread out and a plate on her knees, Jeanne waited with an expectant smile.

'I'll crack it for you, shall I?' asked her mother.

'Yes all right, Maman.'

'And I'll cut you three pieces of bread to dip in,' said the doctor.

'Oh, four, I can eat four, you'll see.'

She called the doctor 'tu' now. When he gave her the first piece, she caught hold of his hand and, still holding her mother's, she kissed them both, going from one to the other with the same passionate show of affection.

'Come now, be a good girl,' Hélène said, seeing she was about to start sobbing. 'Eat up your egg, to please us.'

Then Jeanne began to eat, but she was so weak that after the second piece of bread she was very weary. She smiled every time she took a mouthful, saying her teeth couldn't bite properly. Henri encouraged her, Hélène's eyes full of unshed tears. Oh God, she was watching her daughter eat! She kept her eye on the piece of bread, this first egg she ate, and was moved to the depths of her being. The sudden thought of Jeanne, dead and stiff beneath a sheet, made her blood run cold. And she was eating, she was eating so nice and slowly, hesitatingly, like a convalescent!

'You won't scold me, Maman... I'm doing my best, I'm on to my third piece... Are you pleased with me?'

'Yes, very pleased, darling... You can't believe what pleasure you are giving me.'

And in the surfeit of happiness which was choking her, she forgot herself and leaned against Henri's shoulder. Both laughed at the little girl. But she seemed to be more uncomfortable now. She looked at them suspiciously, then her head drooped and she stopped eating. A shadow of mistrust and anger spread over her pale face. She had to be put back to bed.

CHAPTER 3

THE convalescence lasted for months. In August Jeanne was still in bed. She got up for an hour or two towards evening and it tired her dreadfully to walk even as far as the window, where she remained lying back in an armchair, looking at Paris ablaze in the setting sun. Her poor legs refused to carry her. As she said with a faint smile, she did not have as much blood as a little bird, they should wait until she could eat a lot of soup. They cut up raw meat and put it in her broth. She had got to liking that in the end because she wanted to go down and play in the garden.

Those weeks, months, went by, in a dull but pleasant routine and Hélène was not aware of time passing. She no longer went out, she forgot everything when looking after Jeanne. No news from elsewhere reached her. With its view over Paris, that filled the horizon with its smoke and noise, it was a retreat that was more remote and secluded than the holy hermitages of the saints deep in the rocks. Her child was saved, this certainty was enough for her, she spent her days watching for any improvement in her health, happy at any subtle change, a bright glance, a happy wave. Every hour her daughter was growing a little more like her old self, with her lovely eyes and hair that was shiny again. She felt as if she was giving birth to her a second time. The slower the resurrection, the more she appreciated its delights, remembering when she had fed her from her breast long ago, and when she saw her regain her strength, she felt an emotion even more powerful than in those days, when she had measured the two tiny feet in her clasped hands to find out if she would be walking soon.

But she was still worried about something. On several occasions she had noticed a shadow come over Jeanne's face and render it mistrustful and fierce. Why in the midst of gaiety did she suddenly change like that? Was she suffering, was she concealing some recurring pain?

'Tell me, darling, what's the matter? You were laughing just now, and now you are sad. Answer me, do you hurt somewhere?'

But Jeanne turned violently away, burying her face in her pillow.

'I'm all right,' she snapped. 'Please leave me alone.'

And for afternoons at a time she was resentful and obstinate, her face to the wall, falling into some dreadful trough of despair that her stricken mother could not fathom. The doctor was baffled. The attacks always occurred when he was present, and he attributed them to the nervous disposition of the sick girl. Above all they should avoid crossing her, was his advice.

One afternoon, Jeanne was asleep. Henri, who had found her doing very well, had stayed in the bedroom chatting to Hélène, once more busy with her never-ending sewing in front of the window. Ever since the terrible night when in a cry of passion she had declared her love, they had both relaxed, letting themselves enjoy the sweet sensation of loving one another, not caring about tomorrow, forgetful of the world. Near Jeanne's bed in the room which was still charged with the memory of the child's suffering, their chastity protected them from all untoward surprises of the senses. It calmed them to hear her innocent breathing. Yet as the invalid recovered her strength, so too did their love. It grew stronger, they relished the present and did not attempt to think about what they were going to do when Jeanne was on her feet again and their passion could express itself, freely and strongly.

For hours they nourished their love with a few words, spoken from time to time in low voices so as not to wake the little girl. The words might be banal, but they were heartfelt. That day they were both very much in love.

'I promise you she is a lot better,' said the doctor. 'In a fortnight she'll be able to go down in the garden.'

Hélène's needle worked more quickly. She said quietly:

'Just yesterday she was really downhearted again. But this morning she was laughing, she said she would be a very good girl.'

There was a long silence. The child was still sunk in a sleep that cocooned them both in immense peace. When she rested like that, they felt relieved, they felt closer together.

'Have you seen the garden?' Henri asked. 'It's full of flowers at the moment.'

'The daisies have grown, haven't they?' she asked.

'Oh, the tubs are splendid... The clematis has climbed up into the elms. You'd think it was a nest of leaves.'

Silence fell again. Hélène dropping her needlework, smiled at him, and they imagined walking together down long idyllic shady avenues, where the ground was covered in showers of rose petals. When he leaned over her, he drank in the light fragrance of verbena, which emanated from her robe. But a rustle of the bed sheets disturbed them.

'She's waking,' said Hélène, looking up.

Henri had drawn aside. He also threw a glance at the edge of the bed. Jeanne had just clasped the pillow in her little arms; and with her chin tucked into the eiderdown, she now had her face turned entirely in their direction. But her eyelids remained closed; she appeared to fall asleep again, her breathing steady and regular.

'So are you sewing still?' he asked, drawing near to her again.

'I can't sit doing nothing,' she replied. 'It's automatic. It keeps my thoughts under control. For hours I can think of the same thing and not get tired.'

He said no more, but watched her needle pricking the cotton with a little regular click; and it seemed to him that this thread pulled and knotted something of their two lives together. She could go on sewing for hours, while he sat there listening to the clicking of her needle; they never tired of that language, lulled as they were in their love for one another. That was their one desire, days spent like that in this peaceful room, growing in intimacy, while the child slept and they avoided all movement so as not to disturb her sleep. It was a delicious stillness in which they listened to each other's hearts, an infinite sweetness delighting them with a special feeling of love and eternity!

'You are so good, so good,' he whispered on several occasions, finding only that word to express the joy he felt because of her.

She had raised her head again, feeling no embarrassment at being loved so ardently. Henri's face was near her own. They looked at each other for a moment.

'Let me get on with my work,' she said, in no more than a whisper. 'I shall never finish.'

But at that moment an instinctive worry made her turn her head. And she saw Jeanne, her face all white, looking at them with her wide-open eyes black as ink. The child had not moved, her chin in the eiderdown, squeezing the pillow in her small arms. She had just opened her eyes and was watching them.

'Jeanne, what's the matter?' Hélène asked. 'Are you ill? Do you want anything?'

She did not answer, she did not move, did not even close her great staring, flashing eyes. A fierce dark shadow had fallen across her forehead, her cheeks were pale and hollow. Already her wrists were turning over as though she was about to have a convulsion. Hélène jumped to her feet, begging her to say something. But she remained stiff, casting such black glances at her mother that the latter blushed red and stammered:

'Doctor, come and look, what's wrong with her?'

Henri had pulled his chair away from Hélène's. He drew nearer the bed, tried to take hold of one of the little hands that were clutching at the pillow for dear life. Then, as he touched her, Jeanne seemed to get very agitated. With a sudden movement she turned to the wall, crying out:

'Leave me be! You are hurting me!'

She dived under the covers. Vainly for a quarter of an hour both of them tried to soothe her with gentle words. Then as they did not desist, she raised herself, and, her hands clasped, pleaded with them.

'Please, please, let me alone... You are hurting me. Leave me alone.'

Hélène, very upset, went to sit down by the window. But Henri did not take his place again next to her. They had finally realized, Jeanne was jealous. They were at a loss for words. The doctor walked up and down quietly for a minute, then withdrew when he saw the anxious looks her mother was casting at the bed. As soon as he had gone, she returned to her daughter and lifted her up in her arms. And she talked to her for a long time.

'Listen, sweetheart, I'm on my own... Look at me, answer me... You don't have a pain anywhere? So have I hurt you? You must tell me everything... Are you cross with me? What is on your mind?'

But it was useless to question her, no matter how she put it, Jeanne swore there was nothing wrong. Then suddenly she cried out twice:

'You don't love me any more... You don't love me any more...'

And she burst out crying, loud sobs, she entwined her arms around her mother in a convulsive movement, swamping her with desperate kisses. Hélène, her heart bruised, choked by an inexpressible sadness, hugged her close, her tears mingling with Jeanne's and swearing she would never love anyone as much as her.

From that day onwards, Jeanne's jealousy was aroused by a word or a look. While her life had been in danger, an instinct made her accept the tenderness that was surrounding her, saving her. But now she was getting stronger she did not want to share her mother with anyone. So she became resentful towards the doctor, with a bitterness that was growing inside her and that was turning into hatred the more she recovered her health. It simmered away in her obstinate little head, in her mute, suspicious soul. She never consented to explain anything clearly. She herself didn't know. She had a pain *there* when the doctor came too close to her mother; and she placed her two hands on her chest. That was all, it burned her, she was choked with an uncontrollable anger and her face grew pale. She couldn't do anything to prevent it; she thought people were being very unfair to her, she became more stubborn, not replying when they scolded her for being naughty. Hélène was nervous and did not dare make her aware of what was wrong with her, turned her eyes away from the precocious look of this child of twelve blazing with all the passions of a woman.

'Jeanne, you are causing me a lot of pain,' she told her, tears in her eyes, when she saw her in an access of mad fury, which she bottled up, and which was suffocating her.

But these words, which had been so potent before, which sent her weeping into Hélène's arms, no longer had any effect. Her character was altering. Her mood changed ten times a day. Most often she spoke curtly to her mother, giving orders as though speaking to Rosalie, bothering her for the slightest thing, getting impatient, always complaining.

'Give me a cup of herb tea. You are so slow! You'd let me die of thirst.'

Then, when Hélène gave her the cup:

'There's no sugar in it, I don't want any.'

She flounced back on the bed, pushed away the tea again, saying it was too sweet. They didn't want to look after her, they were doing it on purpose. Hélène, who was afraid to enrage her even more, did not reply, looking at her with great tears on her cheeks.

Jeanne reserved her worst anger for when the doctor arrived. As soon as he came in she lay down flat in the bed, slyly hiding her head like those wild animals who do not tolerate the approach of a stranger. Some days she refused to talk, giving him her pulse, allowing herself to be examined, inert with her eyes on the ceiling. Other days she would not even look at him, and she hid her eyes in her hands in such a rage that you would have had to twist her hands to wrench them apart. One evening she said harshly to her mother who was giving her a spoonful of medicine:

'No, it's poisoning me.'

Hélène was transfixed, cut to the quick, fearing to find out what she meant.

'What are you saying, child?' she asked. 'Do you know what you are saying? Medicine never tastes nice. You must take this.'

But Jeanne remained obstinately silent, turning her head so that she didn't swallow the potion. From that day on she was capricious, taking or not taking the medicine according to how she felt at the time. She sniffed at the phials, examined them on the bedside table with suspicion. And when she had refused it once, she recognized it. She would die rather than touch a drop. The kindly Monsieur Rambaud was the only one who could persuade her sometimes. She swamped him with exaggerated tenderness, especially when the doctor was present. And she glanced brightly at her mother, to see if she was suffering at this demonstration of so much affection for someone else.

'Ah, it's you, my friend!' she would cry as soon as he appeared. 'Come and sit here by me... Have you got any oranges?'

She sat up and, laughing out loud, felt in his pockets, where there were always treats for her. Then she kissed him, pretending to passionate love, satisfied and avenged by the torment she thought she could see on her mother's face. Monsieur Rambaud was radiant at having made peace with his little darling. But in the antechamber, Hélène, going to meet him, had just had a rapid word with him. So all of a sudden he pretended to catch sight of the potion on the table.

'Well then, are you taking the syrup?'

Jeanne's face darkened. She said in a small voice:

'No, it's bad, it stinks, I'm not drinking that!'

'What, you are not taking that?' Monsieur Rambaud went on, with a cheery air. 'But I bet it's really nice... Will you let me drink a little?'

And without waiting for permission he poured himself a big spoonful and swallowed it without making a face, affecting a gourmand's delight.

'Oh, exquisite!' he muttered. 'You are quite wrong... Wait... Just a little drop.'

Jeanne, who thought that was funny, did not argue any more. She wanted to taste everything that Monsieur Rambaud tasted, she followed his movements with attention, apparently studying on his face the effects of the drug. And the good fellow swallowed a great deal of medicine in a month. When Hélène thanked him he shrugged.

'Don't thank me! It's delicious!' he said in the end, having convinced himself, and pleased to share the little girl's medicine.

He spent the evenings with her. The abbé for his part came regularly every two or three days. She kept them there for as long as possible, and got cross when they went to fetch their hats. At present she was afraid of being left on her own with her mother and the doctor, she would have liked there always to be visitors so that she could keep them apart. She often called for Rosalie without a reason. When they were alone, her eyes never left them, pursuing them in all the corners of the room. She grew pale as soon as their hands touched. If they happened to whisper to one another, she sat up annoyed, wanting to know what they were saying. She would not even tolerate her mother's dress on the carpet brushing against the doctor's foot. They could not go near one another, look at one another, without her starting to shake. Her aching flesh, her poor little innocent invalid's body was irritated to such a degree that she would suddenly turn her head when she guessed that they had smiled at each other behind her back. She could sense the days when they were more loving to one another; and those days she was more depressed, she suffered just as nervous women do at the approach of a violent storm.

Around Hélène everyone regarded Jeanne as having recovered. She had gradually come round to believing it herself. So she ended up treating these crises like any spoilt child's aches and pains, of no consequence. After the six anguished weeks she had just endured, she felt the need to live her own life again. Her daughter could now do without her care for hours at a time; it was a time of delightful relaxation, rest, and pleasure; for so long she had not known if she had any kind of life at all. She rummaged in her drawers, found forgotten items again, busied herself with all sorts of little jobs in order to resume the happy routine of her daily life. And during this time of renewal, her love increased. Henri was a sort of reward for all that she had gone through. At the back of that bedroom, they were hidden away, and forgot there had ever been an obstacle to their love. Nothing now separated them but the child, shaken to the core by their passion. So in fact it was Jeanne who fomented their desire. Always between them, with her eyes spying on them, she forced them into a constant constraint, a comedy of indifference from which they emerged more tense than ever. For days at a time they were not able to say a word to each other, feeling that she was listening to them, even when she was apparently slumbering. One evening Hélène accompanied Henri to the door. In the hall, silent, overcome, she was about to collapse into his arms when Jeanne, behind the shut door started to shout: 'Maman, Maman!' in a furious voice, as though the doctor's lightly and passionately touching her mother's hair had an immediate effect on her. Hélène beat a hasty retreat, for she had just heard the little girl get out of bed. She found her shivering, exasperatedly rushing out in her nightdress. Jeanne did not want to be left.

From that day on, all they could do was shake hands when they met or took their leave. Madame Deberle had been at the seaside for a month with little Lucien; the doctor, who had plenty of time to spare, did not dare spend more than ten minutes with Hélène. They had given up the lengthy conversations they enjoyed so much in the window recess. When they looked at each other, a flame burned brighter than ever in their eyes.

What tormented them most of all were Jeanne's changes of mood. She burst into tears one morning when the doctor leaned over her. For a whole day her hatred turned into a feverish tenderness; she wanted him to stay next to her bed, she called to her mother a score of times, as if to see them side by side, concerned and with smiling faces. Her delighted mother was already dreaming of a long succession of days like that. But the next day when Henri arrived, the child received him so frostily that her mother, with one look, begged him to leave; the whole night Jeanne had been agitated, enraged with the regret of having been friendly to him. And scenes like that took place time and again. After the exquisite hours the little girl allowed them to have, the moments when she would kiss them passionately, the bad times descended like a whiplash and made them want to belong to one another.

Then a feeling of revolt gradually came over Hélène. Certainly, she would have given up her life for her daughter. But why did the naughty girl torment her to such a degree now she was out of danger? When she indulged in one of these reveries that lulled her into some vague dream where she imagined herself walking with Henri into an unfamiliar, idyllic world, suddenly she could see the image of the rigid little girl; and she felt a continual anguish in her heart and in her belly. She suffered unbearably in this struggle between her motherhood and her love.

One night the doctor came despite Hélène's strictly forbidding him. For a week they had not been able to exchange a word. She refused to let him in, but gently he pushed her into the room as if to reassure her. There both of them thought they were safe. Jeanne was sleeping deeply. They sat down in the usual place, near the window, far from the lamp; and a peaceful darkness enveloped them. They chatted for two hours, their faces drawing closer together to talk very quietly, so quietly that no more than a whisper could be heard in the large sleep-filled room. Sometimes they turned their heads, glancing briefly at Jeanne whose head was on one side with her small clasped hands resting in the middle of the sheet. But in the end they forgot her. Their whispered conversation grew louder. Suddenly Hélène roused herself, disengaged her hands which were burning under Henri's kisses. And she had a cold horror of the abomination they had nearly committed there.

'Maman! Maman!' stammered Jeanne, suddenly agitated as though tormented by some nightmare.

She was struggling to sit up in her bed, her eyes still heavy with sleep.

'Hide, hide away, please,' repeated Hélène, in anguished tones. 'You'll kill her if you stay there.'

Henri disappeared rapidly into the window recess, behind one of the blue velvet curtains. But the child carried on moaning.

'Maman, Maman, oh, it hurts so much!'

'I'm here near you, darling. Where does it hurt?'

'I don't know... It's around there, see, it's burning me.'

She had opened her eyes, her face contracted, and she was holding her two small hands to her chest.

'It attacked me suddenly. I was asleep, wasn't I? I felt as though there was a great fire.'

'Well, it's gone now, you can't feel it any more?'

'Oh yes, I can.'

And she cast a worried look around the room. Now she was completely awake, the frightful shadow fell across her pale face.

'Are you on your own, Maman?'

'Yes, darling!'

She shook her head and went on looking, sniffing the air, with a growing agitation.

'No. I know you aren't. There's someone here... I'm scared, Maman, I'm scared! Oh, you are lying to me, you are not on your own.'

She was about to have a nervous breakdown. She threw herself backwards on the bed, sobbing, hiding under the covers as though to escape from some danger. Hélène, at her wits' end, made Henri leave immediately. He wanted to stay and look after the little girl. But she pushed him out. She came back and took Jeanne in her arms, the child repeating her complaint that summed up her awful pain each time.

'You don't love me any more, you don't love me!'

'Be quiet my angel, don't say that,' cried her mother. 'I love you more than anything else in the world. You'll see if I love you!'

She tended her till morning, resolved to pour out all her love on her, horrified to see her own love have such painful repercussions on this dear creature. Her daughter was living her love. The next day she demanded a consultation. Doctor Bodin came, as if he were just dropping in, and examined the invalid, listened to her chest, joking the while. Then he had a long conversation with Doctor Deberle, who had remained in the room next door. Both were in agreement that her present condition wasn't serious, but they were afraid of complications, they questioned Hélène for a long time, feeling they had before them one of those nervous conditions which run in families and are disconcerting for medical science. Then she told them what they already partly knew, about her grandmother shut away in the asylum in Les Tulettes, some kilometres from Plassans, her mother's sudden death from galloping consumption after a life of derangement and nervous crises. She herself took after her father, whom she resembled, and whose equilibrium she had inherited. Jeanne, on the other hand, was the spitting image of her grandmother; but she was frailer, she would never have her stature or her strong bony build. The two doctors said again that they had to manage it carefully. One could not take too many precautions with these chloro-anaemic infections, which are the breeding ground for so many cruel illnesses.

Henri had listened to old Doctor Bodin with a deference that he had never shown before for a colleague. He consulted him about Jeanne with the expression of a student who is unsure of himself. The truth was that he was very nervous dealing with this child; she eluded his scientific knowledge, he was afraid of killing her and losing her mother. A week went by. Hélène did not let him into the sickroom any more. So, cut to the quick and ill himself, he stopped coming to visit.

Towards the end of the month of August, Jeanne was finally able to get up and walk around the apartment. She laughed in relief. She had not had an attack for a fortnight. Her mother whom she had to herself, always at her side, had been enough to cure her. At first the child was still suspicious, eager for kisses, worried about what she was doing, demanded that she held her hand when she went to sleep, and wanted her to stay there while she slept. Then when she saw that no one else was visiting, that she didn't have to share her, she regained confidence, happy at beginning their old life again, both of them alone, working in front of the window. Every day she became more pink-cheeked. Rosalie said you could watch her blooming.

However, on certain evenings when night fell, Hélène let her emotions show. Ever since her daughter's illness she had remained serious, a little pale, her forehead lined as never before. And when Jeanne saw one of these moments of weariness, one of those desperate, empty moments, she herself felt very unhappy, her heart heavy with a vague remorse. Gently, without saying anything, she put her arms around her neck. Then she whispered:

'Are you happy, Maman?'

Hélène started. She replied hastily:

'Yes of course, my love.'

The child insisted:

'Are you happy, are you happy, are you sure?'

'Sure. Why do you think I'm not?'

Then Jeanne squeezed her tight in her little arms, as though to reward her. She wanted to love her so much, she said, that you could not find a mother so happy in the whole of Paris.

CHAPTER 4

IN August Doctor Deberle's garden was like a verdant leafy well. The branches of the lilac and laburnum intertwined against the railing while the climbers, the ivies, the honeysuckle, the clematis, put out endless shoots in all directions, sliding, tangling, cascading down, growing into the elms at the bottom after running along the walls; and it looked as though an awning were draped there from one tree to the next, the elms rising like great pillars of dense foliage out of a room of greenery. This garden was so small that the least bit of shade covered it. In the centre the midday sun made a single splash of yellow, empha-sizing the shape of the round lawn, with its two large tubs of flowers on either side. By the flight of steps there was a large rose bush, with hundreds of large tea roses in bloom. In the evening when the heat was lessening, their perfume became penetrating, the hot scent of roses heavy under the elms. And nothing was more delightful than this secret place, so fragrant and hidden away from the neighbours, and which made you imagine a virgin forest, while barrel organs played polkas outside in the Rue Vineuse.

'Madame,' Rosalie enquired every day, 'why doesn't Mademoiselle go down into the garden? She would be really comfortable under the trees.'

Rosalie's kitchen was invaded by the branches of one of the young elms. She plucked the leaves off with her hands, she took enormous pleasure in this colossal bouquet, behind which nothing was visible. But Hélène replied:

'She's not strong enough yet, the coolness of the shade might harm her.'

But Rosalie held her ground. When she thought she had a good idea, she did not easily let it go. Madame was wrong to suppose the shade would be bad for her. It was rather that Madame was afraid of imposing; but she was wrong, Mademoiselle would surely not be in anybody's way, for there wasn't a soul there. The gentleman did not go there any more, the lady was supposed to be staying at the seaside until the middle of September. It was indeed true—the concierge had asked Zéphyrin to do some raking in the garden, and for the last two Sundays Zéphyrin and she had spent the afternoon there. Oh, it was so pretty, you wouldn't believe it!

Hélène still refused. Jeanne seemed to have a burning desire to go into the garden, which she had often mentioned when she was ill; but a strange feeling, a sort of embarrassment which caused her to lower her eyes, seemed to prevent her from insisting to her mother that she go. Finally the following Sunday, the maid came in, saying breathlessly:

'Oh, Madame, nobody's there, I swear. There's only me, and Zéphyrin raking... Let her go down. You can't imagine how nice it is. Come down and see, just for a little while.'

And she was so insistent that Hélène gave in. She wrapped Jeanne up in a shawl and told Rosalie to take a big rug. The child, quietly thrilled, with a silent delight that was only visible in her large shining eyes, wanted to go down the stairs unaided to prove how strong she was. Behind her came her mother, hands outstretched ready to support her. Once down, when they stepped into the garden, they both uttered a cry. They did not recognize it, this impenetrable thicket bore so little resemblance to the tidy, bourgeois garden they had seen in the spring.

'I told you so!' Rosalie crowed.

The flower beds had grown out, labyrinth-like, narrowing the paths, and your skirts caught against them as you walked. You would have thought it was the edge of a distant wood beneath the canopy of foliage which cast a green light, sweet and mysterious. Hélène sought the elm tree at whose foot she had sat in April.

'But I don't want to sit there,' she said. 'It's too cold in the shade.'

'Just wait,' said the maid. 'You'll see.'

In a few paces they had walked through the wood. And there in the middle of the greenery, on the grass, they found some sun, a wide, golden light which fell, warm and silent, like in a clearing. When you looked up you could see only branches, delicate as lace, against the blue cloth of the sky. The tea roses of the great rose bush, wilting a little in the heat, were bending sleepily on their stems. In the pots, red and white daisies, of traditional tones, looked like pieces of ancient tapestry.

'You'll see,' repeated Rosalie. 'Leave it to me, I'll see to it.'

She had folded and spread the rug on the edge of a path just where the shade stopped. Then she sat Jeanne down, her shoulders covered by a shawl, telling her to stretch her little legs out. Like that, the child had her head in the shade and her feet in the sun.

'Are you all right, darling?' Hélène asked.

'Oh yes,' she replied. 'I'm not cold. I feel as if I am warming myself by a big fire... Oh, how good it is to breathe the fresh air!' Then

Hélène, who was looking anxiously at the closed shutters of the large house, said she would go back for a moment. And she issued all sorts of injunctions to Rosalie: to be careful of the sun, to let her stay there no more than half an hour, to watch her constantly.

'Don't worry, Maman,' cried the little girl, laughing. 'There are no cabs going past here.'

When she was left alone, she picked up handfuls of gravel, next to her, playing at letting them trickle like rain from one hand to the other. Meanwhile Zéphyrin was raking. Seeing Madame and Mademoiselle, he had been quick to put on his cap again, which he'd hung on a branch; and he stood there, having stopped his raking out of respect. For the whole duration of Jeanne's illness he had come every Sunday; but he slipped into the kitchen so gingerly that Hélène would never have suspected he was there had it not been for Rosalie asking for news on his behalf, adding that he shared in the worries of the household.

He was learning a few manners, she said, he was polishing himself up a treat in Paris. So, leaning on his rake, he nodded at her sympathetically. When she saw that, she smiled.

'I've been very poorly,' she said.

'I know, Mademoiselle,' he replied, putting his hand to his heart.

Then he tried to find something kind to say, a joke to cheer her up. And he added:

'Your health was asleep, you see. Now it's woken up and will start chirping like a cricket!'

Jeanne took another handful of gravel. Then, pleased with himself, and laughing silently with a smile that split his face from ear to ear, he began to rake again, as hard as he could. The rake made a regular, scraping noise on the gravel. After a few minutes Rosalie, who saw the little girl was calm and happy and absorbed in her game, gradually moved away as though drawn by the scratching of the rake. Zéphyrin was on the other side of the lawn, in full sun.

'You are sweating like a pig,' she said to him in a low voice. 'Take off your cap. Mademoiselle won't be offended, go on with you!'

He took off his cap and again hung it on a branch. His red trousers, held at the waist by a strap, came up very high, while his shirt of coarse grey calico tied at the neck by a horsehair collar was so stiff that it stuck out and made him look even rounder. He rolled up his sleeves as he swaggered about, wanting to show off to Rosalie the two scarlet hearts that he'd had tattooed in the regiment with this motto: *For ever.*

'Did you go to Mass this morning?' enquired Rosalie, who put him through the same interrogation each Sunday.

'To Mass, to Mass,' he repeated with a chuckle.

His two red ears stuck out from under his hair which was shaved very short, and his whole round little person gave off an air that was deeply sardonic.

'Of course I went to Mass,' he finally brought out.

'You are telling fibs!' Rosalie shouted at him. 'I can see you are lying, your nose is twitching. Oh, Zéphyrin, you are a lost soul, you haven't any religion now. Be careful!'

His only answer was to make a gallant grab for her waist. But she was scandalized, crying:

'I'll make you put your cap on again if you don't behave yourself. You should be ashamed! Mademoiselle is watching you.'

Then Zéphyrin went on raking harder than ever. In fact Jeanne had looked up. She was rather bored with her game; after the gravel she had picked leaves and pulled out grasses; but she was feeling very lazy, it was more fun not doing anything, looking at the sun that was creeping over her. A little while ago only her legs up to the knees were soaking in this hot bath of sunshine; now it had come up to her waist and was getting hotter, she could feel it caressing her more and more, tickling her agreeably. What she liked most were the round spots of a beautiful golden yellow dancing on her shawl. They looked like little insects. And she threw back her head to see if they would crawl over her face. In the meantime she had clasped her two little hands together in the sunshine. How thin they looked! How transparent! The sun shone right through them, but she thought they were pretty just the same, pink like shells, fine and slim like Jesus' tiny hands. The fresh air, these great trees around her, this heat made her feel rather heady. She thought she must be asleep and yet she could see and hear. It was very good, very pleasant.

'Mademoiselle, supposing you move back a little,' said Rosalie, who had returned. 'You are getting too hot in the sun.'

But Jeanne refused to move. She was fine there. At that moment it was the maid and the little soldier who interested her, she was indulging in one of those fits of curiosity about things that adults hide from children. Slyly she lowered her eyes, wanting to make them think she wasn't looking; but between her long eyelashes she was watching them, while pretending to be dozing.

Rosalie stayed there a few minutes more. She could not resist the noise of the rake. She joined Zéphyrin again, one step at a time, as though she couldn't help herself. She grumbled at him about the new airs he was putting on. But to tell the truth she was fascinated by him, her heart was full of silent admiration. In his long walks with his comrades in the Jardin des Plantes and the Place du Château d'Eau where his barracks were, the little soldier was acquiring the accomplishments and flowery manners of the Parisian infantryman. He was learning the rhetoric, the gallantries, the mannerisms which women find so attractive. Sometimes she couldn't speak for pleasure and swelled with pride when she heard him saying things with a swagger of his shoulders, using words she did not understand. He no longer felt constrained by the uniform: he threw his arms around wildly, so fearlessly it seemed they might drop off; and especially he had a way of wearing his shako on the back of his neck, which revealed his round face, his protruding nose, while his shako gently bobbed up and down on the rolling of his body. Then he conquered his inhibitions, drank a drop or two of brandy, showed off his manhood. He chuckled with innuendo, he definitely knew more about life than she did now. Paris was making him too clever by half. And she stood facing him, delighted and furious at the same time, hesitating between the twin urges to scratch him or allow him to flirt with her.

Meanwhile as he raked, Zéphyrin had turned down another path. He was behind a huge spindleberry bush, glancing sideways at Rosalie, while he seemed to be drawing her gradually nearer, with each movement of his rake. When she was very near he pinched her bottom...

'Don't scream, it's 'cos I love you!' he growled. 'And here's another one!'

He kissed her ear carelessly. Then, as Rosalie in her turn pinched him as hard as she could, he planted another kiss, this time on her nose. She blushed scarlet, deep down very happy, though exasperated that she couldn't slap him because of Mademoiselle.

'I got pricked,' she said coming back to Jeanne, by way of explanation for the little scream.

But the child had seen what happened through the thin branches of the spindleberry. The soldier's red trousers and shirt made a vivid splash of colour amongst the greenery. She raised her eyes slowly to Rosalie, looked at her for a moment as she blushed redder still, her lips damp and her hair awry. Then she lowered her eyelids again, picked up another handful of gravel, but did not have the strength to play. And she remained with her hands in the warm earth, sleepy, the sun beating down on her. Waves of well-being entered her and took her breath away. The trees seemed to her gigantic and powerful, the roses drowned her with their perfume. She was surprised and delighted, as vague thoughts ran through her head.

'Whatever are you thinking about, Mademoiselle?' Rosalie was worried.

'Oh, nothing, I don't know,' said Jeanne. 'Oh yes, I know. I was thinking I'd like to live till I'm very old...'

And she could not explain why she said that. It was just something that came into her head. But in the evening after dinner as she was still dreamy and her mother questioned her, she suddenly asked:

'Maman, do boy and girl cousins get married?'

'Yes, they do,' said Hélène. 'Why do you ask?'

'Nothing, I just wanted to know.'

Hélène was used to these extraordinary questions in any case. The child was so much restored by her hour spent in the garden that she went down whenever it was a sunny day. Hélène's reservations gradually vanished. The house remained shut up, Henri did not appear, she had ended up sitting down next to Jeanne on a piece of the rug. But the following Sunday she was worried when she saw the windows open in the morning.

'Oh, they're just airing up the rooms,' said Rosalie, trying to persuade her to go down. 'I tell you nobody's there!'

That day was hotter still. Showers of golden arrows pierced the leaves. Jeanne, who was beginning to regain her strength, walked for nearly ten minutes leaning on her mother's arm. Then, fatigued, she came back to sit on the rug, making room on it for Hélène. They exchanged smiles, amused to see each other on the ground like that. Zéphyrin, having finished his raking, was helping Rosalie cut bunches of parsley, which was growing wild along the wall at the bottom.

Suddenly a loud noise could be heard in the house. And just as Hélène was thinking of going, Madame Deberle appeared on the steps. She arrived in her travelling costume, talking loudly, very full of arrangements. But when she caught sight of Madame Grandjean and her daughter sitting on the ground at the front of the lawn, she rushed out, overwhelming them with kisses and a profusion of words.

'What, are you there? Oh, how pleased I am to see you! Give me a kiss, Jeanne. You have been really poorly, haven't you, my poor darling? But you are better now, you have some colour in your cheeks. I've thought of you such a lot, my dear! I wrote, did you get my letters? You must have been through some terrible times. Well, it's over now... May I give you a kiss?'

Hélène had got to her feet. She had to let her plant two kisses on her cheeks and to do so in her turn. These kisses made her freeze. She stammered:

'Please excuse us for invading your garden.'

'You are joking!' responded Juliette impetuously. 'You are at home here, aren't you?'

She left them a moment, went up the steps again to shout through the open rooms:

'Pierre, don't forget anything, there are seventeen bags!' But she came back straight away and talked about her journey.

'Oh, it was a delightful holiday. We were in Trouville,* you know. So many people on the beach, what a crush! Oh, we had a lovely time... I had visitors, lots of visitors... Papa came with Pauline for two weeks. All the same it's nice to be back. Oh, I was going to tell you... No, I'll tell you later.'

She bent down to give Jeanne another kiss, then became serious and asked:

'Am I sunburnt?'

'No, I can't see that you are,' replied Hélène, looking at her.

Juliette's eyes were clear and limpid, her hands dimpled, her pretty face agreeable to look at. She never seemed to age. The sea air itself had not made an impact on that serene unconcern. She might have just been returning from a trip to Paris, from a shopping expedition, all aglow with the excitement of making her purchases. And yet she was gushing with affection, and Hélène was all the more embarrassed because she felt she was being stiff and ungracious. Jeanne, sitting on the rug, did not move. All she did was raise her sorrowful, delicate head, her hands clasped together in the sunshine as though she was chilly.

'But wait, you haven't seen Lucien,' cried Juliette. 'You must see him, he's enormous!'

And when the little boy had been brought out to her, the chambermaid having cleaned him up after getting dirty on the journey, she gave him a little push and turned him round to show him off. Lucien, round-faced, sturdy, and all sunburnt from playing on the beach in the sea breezes, looked the picture of health, and as though he had put on weight, although he was grumpy because he had just been washed. He wasn't properly dry, one cheek was still wet, pink with the rubbing of the towel. When he saw Jeanne he stopped in surprise. She looked at him with her poor thin face, white as a sheet, the black tresses falling to her shoulders. Her wide eyes, so sad and beautiful, seemed to occupy the whole of her face. And in spite of the great heat, she trembled a little, while her hands, feeling chilly, constantly reached out as if to a great fire.

'Well, are you not going to give her a kiss?' asked Juliette.

But Lucien seemed nervous. He finally made up his mind and was careful as he put out his lips to keep his distance from the sick girl as much as possible. Then he withdrew quickly. Hélène had tears in her eyes. How healthy this boy was! And her own Jeanne, who was so out of breath when she had walked round the lawn once! Some mothers were very fortunate! Suddenly Juliette understood how cruel she was being. Then she got cross with Lucien.

'You silly little boy!... You don't kiss young ladies like that! My dear, you can't imagine how impossible he was in Trouville.'

She was getting into a muddle. Luckily for her the doctor appeared. She got out of it by exclaiming:

'Oh, there's Henri!'

He wasn't expecting them till evening. But she had caught another train. And she went into long explanations why, without managing to be clear. The doctor listened with a smile.

'Well, you are here,' he said. 'That's the main thing.'

He had just acknowledged Hélène with a silent nod. His eyes for a moment fell on Jeanne, then, embarrassed, he turned aside. The little girl had looked back at him gravely; and unlocking her hands in an instinctive gesture, pulled her mother closer.

'Oh, what a big boy!' the doctor said again, lifting up Lucien, who was kissing him on the cheeks. 'He's shooting up.'

'And what about me, do I get a kiss?' Juliette asked.

She leaned towards him. He did not put Lucien down, he kept him on one arm at the same time as he kissed his wife. All three smiled at each other.

Hélène, very pale, said she must go back. But Jeanne refused. She wanted to see, she gave the Deberles a long stare and then looked back at her mother. When Juliette held out her lips to her husband to be kissed, the child's eyes had brightened.

'He's such a heavy boy,' the doctor went on, putting Lucien down. 'So did you have a good holiday? I saw Malignon yesterday, he told me about his trip over there... Did you let him come home before you then?'

'Oh, he's impossible!' Juliette said, becoming serious and looking embarrassed. 'He annoyed us the whole time.'

'Your father had hopes for Pauline... Did our friend not declare himself?'

'Who, him, Malignon?' she cried in surprise and as if offended.

Then she made a gesture of annoyance.

'Oh, don't go on about him, he's crazy! What a relief to be home!'

And without any apparent transition, she surprised everyone in her charming, birdlike way with an effusive gesture. She pressed against her husband, looking up at him. Indulgent and tender, he held her a moment in his arms, they seemed to have forgotten they were not on their own.

Jeanne did not take her eyes off them. Her pale lips trembled and coloured, she looked like any jealous, vindictive woman... The pain she suffered was so acute that she had to look away. And it was at that moment that she caught sight of Rosalie and Zéphyrin at the bottom of the garden still looking for parsley. No doubt in order to avoid disturbing the others, they had slipped into the denser part of the copse, both crouching down. Zéphyrin had slyly caught hold of one of Rosalie's feet, while she was beating him off. Between two branches, Jeanne could see the little soldier's face, a pleasant, very red moonlike face, creasing in amorous laughter. There was a shove and the little soldier and the maid rolled over behind the greenery. The sun beat down, the trees slept, unmoving in the warm air, not a leaf stirred. From under the elms rose a scent, the rich scent of earth which was never dug. Slowly the last tea roses showered their petals one by one on to the steps. Then Jeanne, her heart full, looked back at her mother, and seeing that she was standing stock-still and silent in front of what was going on there, she gave her a look of terrible anguish, one of those childish looks that you don't dare question.

Meanwhile Madame Deberle had drawn near, saying:

'I hope we shall see you... Since Jeanne is better, she must come down every afternoon.'

Hélène was already searching for an excuse, pretending she did not want to tire her. But Jeanne intervened swiftly:

'No, no, the sun is really nice. We'll come down, Madame. You'll keep my place won't you?'

And as the doctor stayed back, she smiled at him.

'Doctor, tell Maman the fresh air is good for me.'

He came forward and this man who was so used to human pain reddened a little because the child was talking to him so sweetly.

'Of course,' he said softly. 'Fresh air can only make you better more quickly.'

'So you see, Maman dear, we have to,' she said, looking at them cajolingly, but her sobs were choking her.

Pierre had reappeared on the steps. Madame's seventeen bags had all been brought in. Juliette, followed by her husband and Lucien, slipped away declaring that she was horribly dirty and was going to take a bath. When they were alone, Hélène knelt on the rug as if to fix the shawl around Jeanne's neck again. Then in a low voice:

'So aren't you cross with the doctor any more?'

The child shook her head slowly.

'No, Maman.'

Silence fell. Hélène, hands trembling and fumbling, seemed unable to tie the knot in the shawl. Then Jeanne murmured:

'Why does he love other people? I don't want...'

And her dark expression hardened, while her tense little hands stroked her mother's shoulders. The latter was about to exclaim but was afraid of the words that rose to her lips. The sun was going down. They both went upstairs again. Meanwhile Zéphyrin had reappeared with a bunch of parsley which he was trimming, throwing murderous glances at Rosalie the while. The maid, keeping her distance, did not trust him now that no one else was there. And as he pinched her the minute she bent over to roll up the rug, she gave him a punch in the back which made a sound like an empty barrel. That gave him great pleasure. He was still laughing about it as he went back into the kitchen, still trimming his parsley.

From that day Jeanne obstinately insisted on going down into the garden as soon as she heard Madame Deberle's voice. She listened eagerly to Rosalie's gossip about the neighbours, concerned about what was going on there, sometimes slipping away from the bedroom and coming to watch at the kitchen window too. Down in the garden, she settled back in a little armchair that Juliette had had brought out from the drawing room, she seemed to be keeping an eye on the whole family, reserved with Lucien, impatient at his questions and his games, especially when the doctor was there. Then she stretched out as if weary, eyes open, looking. For Hélène these afternoons were very difficult to bear. Yet she went down there, she went down though her whole being revolted against it. Each time Henri came back and planted a kiss on Juliette's head, her heart missed a beat. And if at those moments to hide her distress she pretended to be busy looking after Jeanne, she could see that the child was paler than herself, with her great black eyes and her chin tense with mute anger. Jeanne was going through torture. Those days when her mother, at the end of her tether, was hiding her face in agonies of love, she herself remained so glum and so exhausted that they had to take her upstairs again and put her to bed. She could no longer watch the doctor embrace his wife without her face dropping, but watched him nervously with the angry look of a betrayed mistress.

'I am coughing in the mornings,' she said to him. 'You ought to come and see.'

It started raining. Jeanne wanted the doctor to begin visiting her again. Yet she was in much better health. In order to please her, her mother had been forced to accept an invitation to two or three dinners at the Deberles. The child, whose heart had for so long been broken by her hidden struggle, seemed to calm down when her health was completely restored. She repeated her question:

'Are you happy, Maman?'

'Yes, very happy, darling.'

Then she was radiant. She said they must forgive her for her past behaviour. She talked about it as if she was being attacked, independent of her will, as of a headache that she might suddenly have. Something was growing inside her, and of course she didn't know what. All sorts of conflicting ideas in her head, vague thoughts, bad dreams which she could not tell anyone about. But it was over, she was getting better, it would not return.

CHAPTER 5

NIGHT was falling. From the pale sky where the first stars were shining, a fine ash seemed to be raining down on the city, that slowly but surely was disappearing. Shadows were already massing in the dips while an ink-black line rose from below the horizon, devouring the remains of the day, the hesitant glow that was retreating towards the setting sun. Beneath Passy there remained only a few stretches of roof still visible. Then came the black flood as darkness fell.

'How hot it is tonight!' Hélène said softly, as she sat languidly in front of her window, in the warm breeze blowing across from Paris.

'A good night for the poor,' said the abbé standing behind her. 'We shall have a lovely autumn.'

That Tuesday Jeanne had been drowsy at dessert and her mother had put her to bed when she saw she was rather tired. She was already asleep in her little bed while at the little table Monsieur Rambaud concentrated on mending a toy, a clockwork doll that walked and talked, which he had given her as a present and she had broken. He was extremely good at this kind of thing. Hélène, needing some air and suffering from this last September heatwave, had just opened wide the window, comforted by the great sea of shadow, this black immensity stretching out before her. She had pushed a chair forward to be on her own and was surprised to hear the priest's voice. He gently remarked:

'Did you cover her up properly? The air is still quite cool up here.'

But she needed to be quiet, and made no reply. She was enjoying the delights of the twilight, the final extinguishing of things, the noise slowly abating. A night light was burning on top of the spires and towers. Saint-Augustin's was the first to go out, the Panthéon retained its bluish glow for a moment, the dazzling Dôme des Invalides disappeared like the moon in a rising tide of cloud. It was the ocean, the night, stretching great distances into the darkness, an abyss of blackness where you could imagine whole worlds. A strong, warm gust of wind came from the invisible city. In the roaring, sustained voice, there were still sounds, some faint, some distinct, the sudden rumble of a bus travelling along the banks, the whistle of a train crossing the bridge at the Point-du-Jour. And the Seine, higher after the recent thunderstorms, flowed by, much wider, breathing hard like a living being, longer right at the bottom, in a fold of shadow. A warm smell emanated from the roofs that were still burning; the river, in this slow exhalation of the heat of the day, sent up little breaths of cool air. Paris had vanished and was dreaming in its sleep, like a colossus which allows the night to wrap it round and remains there motionless for a moment with its eyes open. Nothing moved Hélène more than this suspended moment in the life of the city. In the three months she had been confined there next to Jeanne's bed, her only companion in keeping watch over the invalid had been the great city of Paris stretching out to the horizon. In this July and August heatwave the windows were almost continuously open; she couldn't cross the room, move, turn her head, without seeing its eternal picture on display for her. It was there in all weathers sharing her sufferings and her hopes like a friend who called on her regularly. But she still did not know it properly, she had never been so far away from it, or more indifferent to its streets and its inhabitants. Yet it filled her solitude. These few square feet, this sickroom whose door she kept so firmly shut, opened out and received the city through the two windows. She had very often wept to see it when she came over and leaned on the sill to hide her tears from the invalid. Once, the day she had thought she was lost, she had stood there choking and unable to catch her breath for a long time, looking at the smoke from the Military Depot floating up. Often too in the hours of hope she had entrusted the happiness of her heart to the distant faubourgs. There was not one monument that did not recall a sad or happy feeling. Paris lived through her life. But she never loved it so much as when the twilight came, when at the end of the day, it allowed itself a quarter of an hour's peace, forgetfulness and dreaming, before the lighting of the lamps.

'What a lot of stars!' muttered Abbé Jouve. 'Thousands of them shining.'

He had just taken a chair and sat down near her. Then she looked up at the summer sky. The night was studded with golden constellations. A planet, almost on the line of the horizon, was shining like a garnet, while a sparkling cloud of almost invisible stars was scattered across the heavens. The Plough was slowly turning, with its shafts uplifted.

'Look', she said in her turn, 'at that little blue star in the corner of the sky, I see it every evening... But it is going further away every night.'

Now she did not mind the abbé being there. She felt him beside her like another reassuring presence. They exchanged a few words with long silences in between. Twice she asked him about the stars' names; always the view of the sky had tormented her. But he hesitated, he didn't know.

'Can you see that lovely star with such a pure light?' she asked.

'On the left?' he said. 'Near another smaller one, greenish...? There are too many, I've forgotten.'

They were silent, their eyes still raised, dazzled and trembling a little beneath this, as it seemed, ever vaster teeming in the heavens. Beyond the thousands of stars, thousands more appeared, more and more, in the infinite depths of the firmament. It was a continual flowering, an ember fanned into life, of worlds that burned with the quiet brightness of jewels. The Milky Way was already whiter, spreading its starry atoms so innumerable and distant that they were no more than a scarf of light in the round firmament.

'I am frightened,' said Hélène in a very small voice.

And she bowed her head so as not to look any more, bringing her eyes back to the open chasm in which Paris seemed to be swallowed up. Not one gleam of light was yet there, the complete blackness was equally dispersed. A blinding darkness. The long high note had grown sweeter.

'Are you weeping?' the abbé asked, for he had just heard a sob.

'Yes,' Hélène replied, simply.

They could not see each other. She was weeping copiously, her whole body trembling. Meanwhile behind them Jeanne was sleeping the sleep of the innocent while Monsieur Rambaud, absorbed, bent his greying head over the doll, whose arms and legs he had dismembered. But now and then muffled noises of springs being unwound could be heard, and childish squeaks which his thick fingers extracted as softly as he could from the broken mechanism. And when the doll squeaked too loudly, he stopped short, worried and annoyed, looking to make sure he had not woken Jeanne. Then he started mending again carefully, with only a pair of scissors and a bradawl for tools.

'Why are you crying, my child?' asked the abbé. 'Can I not bring you any consolation?'

'Let me be,' murmured Hélène. 'These tears do me good... In a little while...'

She was too choked to answer. Once before a crisis of weeping had broken her; but then she was on her own, she had been able to weep in the darkness until she was exhausted, waiting for the source of the emotion that was swelling in her to dry up. And yet she was not aware of any great trouble. Her daughter was saved, she herself had gone back again to her monotonous and pleasant routine, her life. Suddenly in her it was like the intense feeling of an immense sadness, an unfathomable emptiness that she would never fill, a boundless despair where she was drowning along with all those people she cared about. She would not have been able to say what misfortune was threatening her in that way, but she was without hope, and she was weeping.

She'd felt like that already in the church perfumed with the flowers of the Month of Mary. The vast horizon of Paris in the twilight affected her like a deep religious experience. The plain seemed to widen, a melancholy rose up out of these two million lives which were being extinguished. Then when the blackness fell and the noise of the city had died away, her heart burst, her tears overflowed as she was confronted by this sovereign peace. She might have put her hands together and stammered out her prayers. A need for faith, love, divine annihilation made her shudder. And it was then that the rising stars overwhelmed her with a holy joy and terror.

After a long silence Abbé Jouve persisted:

'My child, you must confide in me. Why do you hesitate?'

She was still weeping, but softly, like a child who is tired and without any strength left.

'You are afraid of the Church,' he continued. 'For a moment I thought you were conquered for God. But it was not to be. Heaven has its purpose... Well, since you don't trust the priest, why would you still refuse to confide in a friend?'

'You are right,' she stammered. 'Yes, I am afflicted and I need you. I must confess these things to you. When I was young I hardly ever went into churches. Nowadays I can't go to a service without being deeply troubled. And what made me sob just now, you see, was this voice of Paris that is like the thundering of organs, it's this immensity of night, this beautiful sky. Oh, I should like to believe. Help me, teach me.'

Abbé Jouve calmed her by placing his hand lightly on hers.

'Tell me everything,' he said to her simply.

She struggled with herself for a moment, full of anguish.

'It's nothing, I swear. I am crying for no reason, because I can't breathe, because my tears just flow of their own accord. You know what my life is like. At present I could not find in it anything sad or wrong, or anything to regret. But I don't know... I don't know...'

Her voice tailed off. Then the priest slowly uttered these words:

'You are in love, my dear.'

She shivered, not daring to gainsay him. They fell silent again. In the dormant sea of blackness before them, there was a glimmer of light. It was below them, somewhere in the abyss, in a place they could not precisely identify. And one after the other different lights started winking. They came to life at night with a sudden start, all at once, and remained there glittering like stars. It seemed as though there was a new rising of heavenly bodies on the surface of a dark lake. Soon there was a double row of them making a pattern which led from the Trocadéro towards Paris in little leaps of light. Then other lines of luminous dots cut into that line, you could make out curves, a whole constellation that was getting larger, strange and magnificent. Hélène, watching them sparkle, still did not speak; the sky below the horizon flamed and lengthened into infinity, as if the earth had disappeared and the celestial round could be seen from every side. And she experienced again the emotion which had broken her a few minutes before, when the Plough had begun to revolve around the axis of the Pole, its shafts in the air. Paris, which was coming alight, stretched out in all its deep melancholy, bringing with it terrifying thoughts of a whole firmament teeming with worlds.

Meanwhile the priest, in the unctuous monotone acquired from being constantly in the confessional, kept up a ceaseless murmuring in her ear. He had warned her one evening, had he not, that solitude was no good for her? One could not distance oneself from everyday matters without paying a price. She had shut herself away, opened the door to dangerous dreams.

'I am very old, my child,' he said. 'I have often seen women come to us with tears, prayers, a need to believe, and to kneel... So I can hardly be wrong now. These women who seek God so ardently are only poor hearts troubled by passion. It's a man that they adore in our churches.'

She was not listening. In a deep agitation, she was struggling to understand finally what was going on inside herself. She admitted it in a low, choked voice.

'Well then, yes, I am in love. And that's that. What will happen I don't know, I don't know...'

He avoided interrupting her now. She was talking feverishly in short halting phrases. And she took a bittersweet delight in confessing her love, sharing with this old man a secret that had been suffocating her for so long.

'I swear I can't tell... It happened before I knew anything about it. All of a sudden, I suppose. But I wasn't happy at first... Anyway, why pretend to be stronger than I am? I didn't try to escape, I was too happy. Today I am not so brave. You see my daughter was poorly, I almost lost her. Well, my love has been as powerful as my grief, it came back, it was as powerful as ever after those terrible days, it possesses me, I feel carried away by it...'

She stopped for breath, trembling.

'So I am at the end of my strength. You were right, my friend, it is a comfort to me to confide these things in you. But, I beg you to tell me what is going on in the depths of my heart. I was so calm, so happy. It is a thunderbolt in my life. Why me? Why not someone else? I didn't do anything to bring it about, I thought I was safe. And if you only knew! I don't know myself any more. Oh, help me, save me.'

Seeing she had fallen silent, the priest in his usual manner, that of confessor, mechanically asked a question.

'Tell me, what is his name?'

She hesitated when a certain sound made her turn her head. It was the doll that between Monsieur Rambaud's fingers was coming gradually back to life. It had just taken two steps on the side table with the squeaks of the mechanism that was still not working smoothly. Then it had toppled backwards and, but for the worthy fellow, would have bumped back on to the floor. He was following it, with outstretched arms, full of fatherly anxiety, ready to catch it. When he saw Hélène turn her head, he smiled reassuringly at her as though to say she need not worry, the doll would walk again. And he began to fiddle around with the toy with his scissors and his bradawl. Jeanne was asleep.

Then Hélène, in this peaceful atmosphere, relaxed and murmured a name into the priest's ear. He did not move. In the shadow you could not see his face. He spoke, after a silence.

'I knew, but I wished to hear you say it. My daughter, you must be suffering dreadfully.'

And he did not utter one single banality on the subject of her duties. Hélène, exhausted, unutterably sad at the serene pity of the priest, again contemplated the golden sparkling lights in the dark cloak that was Paris. They were multiplying into infinity. It was like those flames that leap across the black ash of burnt paper. First those luminous dots had started from the Trocadéro going towards the heart of the city. Soon another cluster appeared on the left towards Montmartre. Then another on the right behind the Invalides and still another, more to the rear, in the direction of the Panthéon. From all these clusters darted little flames at one and the same time.

'You remember our previous conversation,' went on the priest slowly. 'I have not changed my opinion. You must marry, my child.'

'Me!' she said, completely crushed. 'But I've just told you, you know I can't...'

'You must get married,' repeated the priest, more forcefully. 'You must marry a worthy man.'

He seemed to have gained in stature in his old soutane. His large comical head which usually leaned to one side, his eyes half-closed, was raised, and his eyes were so wide and clear that she saw them gleaming in the dark.

'You must marry a good man who will be a father for your Jeanne and who will give you back your faithfulness.

'But I don't love him... Oh God, I don't love him...'

'You will love him, my child. He loves you and he is a good man.'

Hélène struggled with herself, lowered her voice when she heard the little sounds that Monsieur Rambaud was making behind them. He was so patient and strong in his hope that for the last six months he had not importuned her once on the subject of his love. He waited with a trusting calm, naturally ready to be as heroically unselfish as possible. The abbé made as though to turn round.

'Do you want me to tell him everything? He will take your hand and save you. And you will give him immense joy.'

She stopped him, wildly. Her heart revolted. They both frightened her, these two men who were so quiet and affectionate, who were so cool and reasonable in the face of her own feverish passion. What world did they live in then, to deny like that what made her suffer so much? The priest waved his hand towards the vastness of space.

'My child, see this beautiful night, this supreme peace in the face of your agitation. Why refuse happiness?'

The whole of Paris was lit up. The little dancing flames had pierced the dark sea from one end of the horizon to the other, and now their millions of stars were burning with a steady brightness in the serenity of the summer's night. Not a breath of wind, not a quiver alarmed those lights that seemed suspended in space. Paris, which was invisible, had distanced itself from them in the depths of an infinity as vast as the firmament. Meanwhile below the hills of the Trocadéro a rapid flash from the lamps on a cab or an omnibus cut through the darkness like the long tail of a shooting star. And there in the light of the gas lamps which were giving off a sort of yellow fog, you could make out blurry façades, clumps of trees of a bright green colour, like on a stage set. On the Pont des Invalides stars constantly crossed, while below, along a black, thicker band, was a miraculous thing, a group of comets, whose golden tails stretched out into a rain of sparks. These were the reflections of the lamps on the bridge in the waters of the Seine. But beyond that, began the unknown. The long curve of the river was etched out in a double string of gaslights attached to other strings of lights, from place to place, square to square. You would have thought that a ladder of light had been thrown across Paris, resting at the two ends on the edge of the sky, in the stars. To the left, another gap appeared, the Champs-Élysées led a regular procession of stars from the Arc de Triomphe to the Place de la Concorde, where there was a glittering constellation; then the Tuileries, the Louvre, the blocks of houses next to the river, the Hôtel de Ville right at the back formed a dark shape, separated here and there by a large brightly-lit square. And further back, amongst the jumble of roofs, the lights were more scattered and you couldn't see anything except where a street disappeared, where the corner of a boulevard curved, or a crossroads made a wider space, lit up as though on fire. On the other bank, on the right, only the Esplanade was clearly visible with its rectangle of flames like some Orion of the winter nights who had lost his belt. The long streets in the Quartier Saint-Germain were lit rather despondently at intervals. Beyond them, the populous *quartiers* scintillated, lit up with little flames packed closely together, glowing in a misty nebula. There was, as far as the faubourgs and all round the horizon, a veritable anthill of gas lamps and lighted windows like a cloud which filled the far reaches of the city with myriads of suns, with planetary atoms undiscoverable by mankind. The buildings were submerged with no lanterns tied to their masts. At times you might have thought it was some gigantic celebration, a cyclopean monument lit up, with its staircases, ramps, windows, pediments, terraces, its world of stone, whose rows of lanterns were tracing the strange, enormous architecture in streaks of phosphorescence. But the abiding sensation was that of a birth of constellations, of a continual spreading of the sky.

As she followed the priest's expansive gesture, Hélène had cast a long look at Paris all lit up. She did not know the names of those stars either. She wanted to ask what that bright light was over there on the left that she looked at every evening. Others interested her. Some she liked, while hundreds left her troubled and frustrated.

'Father,' she said, using this appellation of tenderness and respect for the first time, 'let me live my life. It's the beauty of this night that is troubling me. You are wrong, you would not be able at present to offer me any comfort, for you cannot understand.'

The priest opened his arms then let them fall again slowly, in resignation. And after a silence he spoke in a low voice.

'No doubt it was bound to be thus. You cry for help but you do not accept salvation. How many desperate admissions have I heard and how many tears have I been powerless to prevent! Listen, my child, promise me one thing: if ever life becomes too heavy to bear, remember that a good man loves you and is waiting for you. You will only have to put your hand in his to find peace again.'

'I promise,' said Hélène gravely.

And as she made that solemn promise, there was a little laugh in the room. Jeanne had just woken up and was looking at her doll walking on the table. Monsieur Rambaud, who was delighted with his repairs, was still moving his hands forward in case it had some accident. But the doll was solid. It tapped its little heels, turned its head uttering the same words at each step like a parrot.

'Oh, you're a magician!' said Jeanne still half asleep. 'What have you done to her? She was broken and now she's alive again. Give her to me, let me see... You are so kind...'

Meanwhile, over a lighted Paris, a luminous cloud had risen. You would have thought it was the red exhalations from a brazier. First it was nothing but a paleness in the night, a scarcely perceptible reflection. Then gradually as the evening wore on, it became bloodied; and suspended in the air, immobile over the city, created from all the flames and all the rumbling life which the city exhaled, it resembled one of those clouds of thunder and fire which crown the summits of volcanoes.

PART FOUR

CHAPTER 1

THE *rinces-bouches** had been served and the ladies were delicately wiping their fingers. There was a moment's silence around the table. Madame Deberle looked to see if everyone had finished, then rose without a word, while the guests did likewise, amidst a loud scraping of chairs. An old gentleman who was on her right hastened to offer her his arm.

'No no,' she murmured, steering him towards a door. 'We shall take coffee in the drawing room.'

Couples followed her. Two ladies and two gentlemen, oblivious to what was happening, deep in conversation, finally joined the procession. But in the little drawing room people did not stand on ceremony and their gaiety at dessert resumed. The coffee was already served on a huge lacquer tray set on a small table. Madame Deberle went around with the graciousness of a hostess who is concerned about the different tastes of her guests. In fact it was Pauline who bestirred herself the most, and made it her business to serve the gentlemen. There were a dozen people, roughly the regular number invited by the Deberles each Wednesday from December onwards. A crowd arrived at about ten o'clock in the evening.

'Monsieur de Giraud, a cup of coffee?' enquired Pauline, stopping by a bald-headed little man. 'Oh no, I forgot, you don't drink it. So, a glass of chartreuse?'

But she got into a muddle and brought him a glass of cognac. And smilingly, confidently, she did the rounds looking the guests in the eye, circulating at ease with her long train. She wore a splendid white dress of Indian cashmere, trimmed with swansdown, with a square opening at the front. When all the men were standing, cup in hand, averting their chins as they sipped, she pounced on a tall young man, the Tissot boy, whom she thought very handsome.

Hélène did not want coffee. She sat to one side, looking somewhat weary, dressed in a rather austere black velvet dress without any jewellery. They were smoking in the salon, the boxes of cigars were next to her on a console. The doctor approached, selected a cigar and asked:

'Is Jeanne well?'

'Very well,' she replied. 'We went to the Bois today, she played and played... Oh, she must be asleep by now.'

They chatted amicably, with the happy familiarity of people who see each other every day. But Madame Deberle had raised her voice:

'Well, Madame Grandjean will tell you... I came back from Trouville about the tenth of September, didn't I? It was raining, the beach was awful.' Three or four ladies were around her while she was recounting her holiday at the seaside. Hélène had to stand up and join the group.

'We spent a month at Dinard,' Madame de Chermette said. 'Oh, a delightful part of the country, and such lovely people!'

'There was a garden behind the chalet and a balcony facing the sea,' Madame Deberle went on. 'You know I had decided to take my landau and my driver—it's much more convenient for trips. But Madame Levasseur came to visit...'

'Yes, one Sunday,' said the latter. 'We were staying in Cabourg. Oh, you had a very nice place there, though a bit expensive perhaps.'

'By the way,' interrupted Madame Berthier, addressing Juliette, 'didn't Monsieur Malignon teach you to swim?'

Hélène noticed an expression of embarrassment, a sudden irritation, flicker over Madame Deberle's face. She had already several times thought she could detect that Malignon's name suddenly uttered in front of her caused her some discomfiture. But the young woman had recovered her poise.

'Such a good swimmer!' she cried. 'If someone like him gives you a lesson... Do you know I'm scared of cold water! I shiver at the very sight of people bathing.' And she gave a charming little shudder, raising her dimpled shoulders, like a damp bird shaking its feathers.

'So is that story made up?' Madame de Guiraud asked.

'Of course. I bet he invented it. Ever since he spent a month with us there he has had it in for me.'

People began to arrive. The ladies with sprigs of flowers in their hair and arms extended, smiled and inclined their heads slightly. The men in suits, hats in hands, bowed and tried to think of something to say. Madame Deberle, chatting the while, held out her fingers to close friends, and many did not speak, but bowed before passing on. Meanwhile Mademoiselle Aurélie had just come in. She immediately went into raptures over Juliette's dress, a crushed velvet navy gown with a crosswise rib trim. At that point the ladies present appeared to notice only the gown. Oh, charming, really charming! It was from the Worms collection.* They discussed it for five minutes. The coffee had been drunk, the guests put back their empty cups anywhere, on the tray, on the small tables. Only the elderly gentleman, stopping at every mouthful to chat to a lady, had not finished his. There rose a warm smell of coffee mingled with the delicate fragrances of the women's toilettes.

'I did not get anything, you know,' said the Tissot boy to Pauline, who was telling him about a painter whose pictures she had been taken to see by her father.

'What? You didn't have anything?... I brought you a cup of coffee.'

'No, Mademoiselle, you didn't, I assure you.'

'But you simply must have something. Wait, here's some chartreuse!'

Madame Deberle had discreetly nodded to her husband. The doctor understood, opened the door of the big salon himself, and they went through, while a servant took away the tray. It was almost chilly in the large room, which was lit with the bright white light of six lamps and a chandelier with ten candles. Some ladies were already there, sitting in a semicircle round the hearth. Amongst their spreading skirts stood two or three men. And through the half-open door of the pale yellow drawing room you could hear the shrill voice of Pauline left alone with the Tissot boy.

'Now I've poured it out, you'll surely drink it... What can I do? Pierre has taken the tray away.'

Then she came into view, all in white, in her dress trimmed with swansdown.

With a smile that showed her teeth between her young lips she announced:

'Our handsome friend Malignon.'

The handshakes and greetings continued. Monsieur Deberle had taken up a position next to the door. Madame Deberle, who was sitting in the middle of the ladies on a very low pouffe, kept getting up. When Malignon arrived she pretended not to see him. He was dressed very correctly, his tonged hair parted down to the nape. On the threshold he had fixed a monocle in his right eye, with a slight grimace, 'as chic as anything', as Pauline kept saying. And he looked around the salon. He casually shook the doctor's hand without a word, then went over to Madame Deberle, cutting a tall figure in his tight black costume, and made her a deep bow.

'Oh, it's you,' she remarked, aloud so that everyone could hear. 'So it seems you are swimming these days.'

He did not understand what she meant, but nevertheless answered, in order to show how witty he was:

'That's right... One day I saved a Newfoundland dog from drowning.'

The ladies found that delightful. Even Madame Deberle seemed to have dropped her defences.

'I allow you to save dogs,' she said. 'But as you are well aware, I didn't bathe once at Trouville.'

'Oh, that lesson I gave you!' he cried. 'Well now, one evening in your dining room did I not tell you that you had to move your hands and feet?'

All the ladies started to laugh. He was so charming. Juliette shrugged. One could not have a serious conversation with him. And she rose to go and talk to a lady who could play the piano very well and was visiting her house for the first time. Sitting by the fire, quietly composed, Hélène looked and listened. She seemed to find Malignon especially interesting. She had seen him making a sly move to get closer to Madame Deberle and she could hear them chatting behind her armchair. Suddenly the voices changed. She leaned back, to hear more clearly what they were saying. She could hear Malignon's voice:

'Why didn't you come yesterday? I waited for you till six.'

'Leave me alone, you're mad,' whispered Juliette.

At that point Malignon's voice was raised, and rolling his 'r's he said:

'Oh, so you don't believe my story about the Newfoundland dog. But I got a medal, I'll show you.'

And he added very softly:

'You promised, remember...'

An entire family arrived, Madame Deberle gushed compliments while Malignon appeared again in the midst of the women, monocle to his eye. Hearing these rapidly spoken words, Hélène had grown pale. It was like a thunderbolt, something unexpected and monstrous. How could this fortunate woman with the lily-white complexion, so calm and unperturbed, how could she be unfaithful to her husband? She had always taken her as something of a birdbrain, an engagingly egotistical person, who was thereby prevented from doing anything stupid that would cause her trouble. And with a man like Malignon, at that! Suddenly she saw those afternoons in the garden again, Juliette smiling and affectionate beneath the kiss planted so lightly on her hair by the doctor. Yet they loved one another.

Then, with a feeling that she could not explain to herself, she was full of anger at Juliette, as though she had been personally betrayed. She was humiliated on Henri's behalf, a jealous fury came over her, and her discomfort was so evident on her face that Mademoiselle Aurélie asked:

'Whatever's the matter?... Are you unwell?'

The old maid had sat down by her when she saw she was on her own. She felt most warmly towards Hélène, this serious and beautiful woman who was kind enough to listen for hours to her gossiping.

But now Hélène did not answer. She needed to see Henri, to know there and then what he was doing, what his face was like. She got up and looked around in the salon and in the end found him. He was standing there, completely unruffled, chatting to a stout man with a pasty complexion and he looked at ease and wore his habitual distinguished smile. She studied him for a moment. She felt pity for him, and it diminished him a little in her eyes, but at the same time she loved him more, with a fondness in which there was something protective. She felt in some still very muddled way that she should compensate him for his lost happiness.

'Ah, good,' whispered Mademoiselle Aurélie. 'It will be fun if Madame de Guiraud's sister sings. It's the tenth time I've heard her sing "Les Tourterelles". That's her only song this winter. She's separated from her husband, you know. See that dark man over there, near the door. They are intimate. Juliette is obliged to invite him otherwise she wouldn't come.'

'Oh!' said Hélène.

Madame Deberle was moving from one group to the next, asking them to be quiet and listen to Madame Guiraud's sister. The salon was full, about thirty ladies were sitting in the middle, whispering and laughing; but two remained standing chatting loudly, shrugging prettily, while five or six men seemed very much at home there, as though they were lost amongst the skirts of the women. A few discreet 'shushes' could be heard, the talking stopped, faces took on a fixed, bored expression; and the only sound you could hear was the beating of the women's fans in the warm air.

Madame Guiraud's sister sang, but Hélène was not listening. Now she was staring at Malignon, who seemed to be savouring 'Les Tourterelles', affecting a great passion for music. Was it possible! That fellow! No doubt it was at Trouville that they had been playing with fire. The words that Hélène had overheard seemed to point to Juliette not yet having surrendered to him, but it seemed as though she very soon would succumb. In front of her, Malignon was tapping out the rhythm in a delighted fashion; Madame Deberle seemed warm in her admiration, while the doctor remained silent, patient and pleasant, waiting for the piece to come to an end before resuming his conversation with the pale stout man.

When the song was over, a ripple of applause broke out.

And voices gushed:

'Delightful, superb!'

But the handsome Malignon, arms stretched out over the ladies' coiffures, was clapping his gloved hands silently, repeating 'Bravo! Bravo!' in a sing-song voice louder than all the others.

Abruptly then, this enthusiasm ceased, faces relaxed and smiled, a few ladies rose, and conversations began again, in the midst of the general relief. It grew hotter, the scent of musk wafted from the ladies under the beating fans. From time to time in the murmurings of conversation a pearly laugh rang out, a witty remark made in a loud voice made heads turn. Three times already Juliette had gone into the small drawing room to beg the men who had taken refuge there not to abandon the ladies like that. They followed her. But ten minutes later they had vanished again.

'They are too bad,' she said crossly, 'we can't keep a single one here.'

Meanwhile Mademoiselle Aurélie was telling Hélène who the ladies were, for it was only the second time she had attended one of the doctor's parties. All the high society of Passy was there, very rich people. Then, leaning over:

'Goodness me, it's happened... Madame de Chermette is marrying off her daughter to that tall fair-haired young man she has been seeing for the last eighteen months. Well, at least that's one mother-in-law who will get on well with her son-in-law.'

But she broke off in great surprise.

'Look, there's Madame Levasseur's husband chatting to his wife's lover!...'

Yet Juliette had sworn she would stop inviting them both together.

Hélène cast her eyes slowly round the drawing room. In this worthy company, amongst this bourgeoisie which seemed so respectable, were there then only guilty women? Her strict provincial morality was shocked by the promiscuous behaviour tolerated in Parisian society. And she was bitterly chiding herself for having put herself through so much self-inflicted suffering, when Juliette took her hand. Truly she was stupid to be so scrupulous in her behaviour! Adultery was becoming part of bourgeois society—quite smugly, with just a little edge of coquettish refinement. Madame Deberle now seemed to have made it up with Malignon, and the soft, pretty brunette was cosily and curvaceously ensconced and laughing at his jokes. Monsieur Deberle happened to come by.

'So you are not quarrelling this evening?' he asked.

'No,' Juliette replied very gaily. 'He says too many silly things... If you could hear all the silly things he's saying...'

The singing started again. But now it was harder to get people to be quiet. The Tissot boy sang a duet from *La Favorite** alongside a very mature lady with a youthful hairdo. Pauline, standing at one of the doors, surrounded by dark suits, was gazing at the singer in open admiration, just as she had seen people do when looking at paintings.

'Oh, how handsome he is,' she murmured during a quiet passage in the accompaniment, and so loudly that the whole drawing room could hear. The evening wore on, people's faces were suffused with tiredness. Ladies who had been sitting in the same armchairs for three hours, wore an unconsciously bored expression, though they were not unhappy to be bored there. Between two numbers listened to with half an ear, the chatting began again and it was as if the piano itself continued its empty noise. Monsieur Letellier was saying how he had gone to supervise a silk order in Lyons; the waters of the Saône did not mix with the waters of the Rhône, that had struck him forcibly. Monsieur de Guiraud, a magistrate, uttered a few sententious words about the need to contain vice in the streets of Paris. A man who knew a Chinaman, and was telling everyone about him, was surrounded by guests. Two ladies in a corner exchanged confidences about their servants. Meanwhile, in the group of women where Malignon held court, they were discussing literature: Madame Tissot was declaring Balzac to be unreadable; he did not dispute it but simply remarked that Balzac did have the odd page that was well written.

'Quiet!' Pauline cried. 'She is about to play.'

It was the pianist, the lady who had such a fine talent. All heads politely turned. But in the middle of the calm you could hear loud male voices talking in the small drawing room. Madame Deberle looked desperate. She was having a very bad time.

'They are a nuisance,' she said under her breath. 'Let them stay there since they don't want to join us. But at least let them be quiet!' And she sent Pauline, who was delighted to go and fulfil the mission.

'Gentlemen,' said the young girl, brash, unperturbed and virginal in her queenly gown. 'Someone is going to play the piano. You are requested to be quiet.'

She spoke loudly and in a shrill voice. And as she stayed there with the men laughing and joking, the noise grew ever louder.

The discussion continued and she gave her opinion. In the salon Madame Deberle was in torment. Anyway, they had had enough music and were indifferent to it. The pianist sat down again, with pursed lips, in spite of the exaggerated compliments the mistress of the house felt she ought to bestow on her.

Hélène was suffering. Henri seemed not to notice her. He had not come over. From time to time he smiled at her from across the room. At the beginning of the evening she had felt relieved that he was being so sensible. But ever since realizing what the other two were doing she wanted something, she didn't know quite what, some sign of affection, and she was even prepared to be compromised. She was stirred with a vague desire mixed up with all sorts of bad feelings. Did he not love her any more then, since he remained so cold towards her? He must be biding his time. Oh, if only she had been able to tell him everything, make him aware of the unworthiness of the woman who bore his name! So while the piano was tinkling out a series of little notes she was lulled into a dream: Henri had rid himself of Juliette and she, Hélène, was with him as his wife in far-off countries with unknown tongues.

A voice made her start.

'Won't you have anything to drink then?' Pauline asked.

The salon was empty. People had just moved into the dining room for tea. Hélène got up with difficulty. Her head was spinning. She thought she must have dreamed it all, the words overheard, Juliette's impending downfall, the cheerful, insouciant adultery of the bourgeoisie. If those things were true, Henri would be near her and both of them would already have left the house.

'Will you have a cup of tea?'

She smiled and thanked Madame Deberle, who had kept her a place at table. Plates of cakes and sweetmeats covered the tablecloth, and a large brioche and two cakes stood on symmetrical cake stands. Since there was very little room, the teacups were almost touching, separated every two cups by narrow grey napkins with long fringes. Only the ladies were seated. They had removed their gloves and were eating petits fours and glacé fruits with their fingers, passing the cream dish along, pouring with elegant gestures. However, three or four of them had unselfishly taken it upon themselves to see to the gentlemen. The men standing against the walls were drinking, taking the greatest possible care to protect themselves from unintended elbowing. Others remaining in the two drawing rooms were waiting for the cakes to be brought to them. This was Pauline's hour of triumph. People talked more loudly, laughter and the tinkling of silver could be heard, the scent of musk was enhanced by the pungent scent of tea.

'Pass me a piece of brioche please,' said Mademoiselle Aurélie, who sat by Hélène. 'All these sweetmeats do not satisfy one.'

She had already emptied two platefuls. Then, her mouth full:

'Ah, everyone is going... All the more room for us.' Some women were indeed leaving, after shaking hands with Madame Deberle. Many men had discreetly vanished. The rooms were emptying. Then some men took their turn to sit at the table. But Mademoiselle Aurélie did not relinquish her place. She wanted a glass of punch.

'I'll go and fetch you one,' said Hélène.

'Oh no, thank you... Please don't trouble yourself.'

Hélène had been observing Malignon for some little while. He had gone to shake hands with the doctor, and was now saying goodbye to Juliette in the doorway. Her face was pale, her eyes limpid, and from her happy smile you would have thought he was complimenting her on her party. As Pierre was pouring out the punch on the dresser, near the door, Hélène went forward and manoeuvred herself into a position where she was hidden behind the other side of the portière. She listened.

'Please, please,' Malignon was saying, 'come the day after tomorrow... I shall be waiting at three...'

'Can't you be serious for once?' Madame Deberle answered with a laugh. 'You say such silly things!'

But he insisted, repeating:

'I shall be waiting for you... Come the day after tomorrow... You know where?'

Then she whispered hurriedly:

'Yes, all right, the day after tomorrow.'

Malignon bowed and left.

Madame de Charmette was leaving with Madame Tissot. Gaily, Juliette went into the hall with them, saying to the former in her most amiable manner:

'I'll come and see you the day after tomorrow. I've got so many visits that day.'

Hélène had remained motionless, very pale. Meanwhile Pierre had poured out the punch and held it out to her. She took it automatically and carried it to Mademoiselle Aurélie who was attacking the glacé fruits.

'Oh, how kind!' the spinster exclaimed. 'I could have waved to Pierre. They should really offer punch to ladies as well... When you are as old as I am...'

But she broke off when she saw how pale Hélène was.

'But you really don't look well... Why not have a glass of punch?'

'No, thank you, I'm fine... It's very hot in here...'

Unsteadily she returned to the deserted drawing room and collapsed into an armchair. The lamps had a reddish glow; the candles on the chandelier burning very low, threatened to crack their rings. From the dining room you could hear the farewells of the last guests. Hélène had forgotten all about leaving, she wanted to stay there and think. So it was not her imagination, Juliette would go and visit this man. The day after tomorrow. She knew what day. Oh, she would no longer be so afraid of letting herself go, that was what her inward voice was telling her all the time. Then she decided she ought to talk to Juliette, to prevent her committing that sin. But this charitable but unwelcome thought made her freeze and she pushed it to the back of her mind. She stared into the hearth and a dead log crackled. The close, drowsy air retained the perfume of the ladies' coiffures.

'Oh, there you are!' cried Juliette as she came in. 'Oh, how nice of you not to go home straight away! We can breathe at last!'

And as Hélène, taken by surprise, made as though to get up, she said:

'Oh, do stay, there's no hurry! Henri, pass me my smelling salts.'

Three or four people, close friends, were in no hurry to leave. They sat down in front of the fire which had gone out, chatted in a delightfully relaxed way in the already sleepy, exhausted atmosphere of the large room. The doors were open, you could see the small empty salon, the empty dining room, the whole apartment still lit and fallen into a deep silence. Henri was full of gallant tenderness for his wife; he had just been up to their bedroom to get her smelling salts which she breathed in as she slowly shut her eyes; and he asked if she had not overtired herself. Yes, she was rather tired; but she was thrilled, everything had gone really well. Then she said that on the evenings after her parties she was unable to sleep, she tossed and turned in her bed until six in the morning. Henri smiled and they joked. Hélène looked at them and shivered, in this somnolence which gradually seemed to be taking over the whole house.

Meanwhile there were only two people still there. Pierre had gone to fetch a cab. Hélène stayed till last. One o'clock chimed. Henri, completely relaxed, got up from his chair and blew out two candles from the chandelier which were heating the rings. It looked like a sunset with the lights going out one by one, the room gradually sinking into an intimate darkness.

'I'm stopping you from going to bed,' faltered Hélène, getting up abruptly. 'Tell me to go home!'

She was flushed and her colour had risen. They saw her into the hall. But as it was chilly out there, the doctor was concerned for his wife, in her low-cut bodice.

'Go in, you'll take cold... You have been too warm.'

'Well then, farewell,' said Juliette, hugging Hélène, as she often did when she was feeling particularly fond of her. 'Come and see me more often.'

Henri had taken the fur coat and was holding it open to help Hélène into it. When she had slipped into the two sleeves, he raised her collar himself, and smilingly put it on her, in front of an immense mirror which was covering one whole wall of the hall. They were alone, they saw their reflections in the mirror. Then suddenly, without turning round and wrapped up in her fur, she leaned back into his arms. For the last three months they had exchanged nothing but friendly handshakes, trying to subdue their love. He stopped smiling; his face changed, suffused and passionate. Madly he pressed her to him, kissed her neck. And she bent her head back, to return his kiss.

CHAPTER 2

HÉLÈNE did not sleep a wink that night. She tossed and turned in
a fever and whenever she sank into a slumber the same anguish always
woke her with a start. In the nightmare of this half-sleep she was tormented by one thought and could not get it out of her head: she
wanted to know where they would meet. It seemed to her that it would
be some relief to know that. It could not be in Malignon's little flat in
the Rue Taitbout that was often mentioned at the Deberles. Where
then, where then?... And in spite of herself it was going round and
round in her head and she had forgotten all about the affair itself in
order to engage in an enervating research so full of unspoken desires.
When it was light she dressed and caught herself saying out loud:

'It's going to be tomorrow.'

With one shoe on, her hands idle, she now mused that it might take
place in some furnished rooms somewhere. A secret little room rented
by the month. Then she was disgusted by this thought. She imagined
a delightful apartment with thick hangings, flowers, huge bright fires
burning in every hearth. And it was not Juliette and Malignon there,
but herself and Henri in the depths of this cosy hideaway where the
sounds of the world outside could not reach them. She shivered in
her unfastened dressing gown. Wherever was it then, where?

'Good morning, Maman!' cried Jeanne who was the next to wake.

She was sleeping in the adjoining room again since she had recovered
her health. She came in barefoot and in her nightdress, as she did
every day, and threw her arms around Hélène's neck. Then she ran
off and snuggled up for a moment in her warm bed. She liked to do
that, she laughed as she crept under the blanket. She said again:

'Good morning, Maman!'

And again off she went. This time she burst out laughing, she had
thrown the sheet right over her head, and underneath it, a deep
muffled voice cried:

'I'm not here, I'm not here!'

But Hélène was not playing like she did on other mornings. Then
Jeanne grew bored and drifted off to sleep again. It was scarcely light.
Towards eight Rosalie appeared and started to tell them what had
happened to her that morning. Oh, it was a fine mess outside, she had
almost lost her shoes in the mud when she went to fetch her milk. The
thaw had really set in. The air was close because of it. You couldn't

breathe. Then suddenly she remembered: an old woman had called on Madame the day before.

'Goodness!' she cried, hearing a ring at the doorbell. 'I'll wager that's her!'

It was Mother Fétu, but she was extremely clean and resplendent in a white bonnet, a new dress, and a tartan scarf folded over her chest. But her wheedling voice had not changed.

'It's me, dear lady, I hope you don't mind... Come about something I've got to ask you...'

Hélène looked at her, rather surprised to see her so well-turned-out.

'Are you feeling better, Mother Fétu?'

'Yes, yes, I'm better, more or less. I still have something funny in my belly, you know; it rattles around inside, but still it's a lot better. Well, I had some good luck. I was surprised, because you see, good luck and me... A gentleman has asked me to clean for him. Oh, it's quite a story.'

She faltered and her small beady eyes darted around in her wrinkled face with its countless lines and folds. She seemed to be waiting for Hélène to ask her something. But the latter, sitting near the fire that Rosalie had just lit, was only half listening, and wore an absorbed, distressed expression on her face.

'What do you wish to ask me, Mother Fétu?' she enquired.

The old woman did not answer immediately. She had a good look round the room, at the rosewood furniture, the blue velvet curtains. And with the fawning voice of the humble poor, she murmured:

'You've got a really lovely home here, Madame. Forgive me. My gentleman has a room like that but his room is pink. Oh, what a story! Imagine, a high-class gentleman's come to rent an apartment in our house. What I'm saying is that on the first and second floor the apartments in our house are very nice. And so quiet! Not a cab to be heard, you'd think you were in the country... Well, the workmen were there for more than a fortnight; they have made it into a little gem...'

She stopped, seeing that Hélène had become very attentive.

'It's for his work,' she went on, with an even more pronounced drawl. 'He says it's for his work. We haven't got a concierge, you see. That's what he likes about it. He doesn't like concierges, that man, and he's quite right.'

But she stopped talking again as though another idea had struck her.

'But wait a moment! You must know him... He is seeing one of your friends.'

'Oh!' said Hélène, her face pale.

'Yes of course. The lady next door, the one you used to go to church with... She came over the other day.'

Mother Fétu's eyes narrowed, surreptitiously trying to gauge Hélène's reaction.

'Did she go up and see him?'

'No, she changed her mind, she'd mebbe forgotten something... I was at the door. She asked for Monsieur Vincent, then she got back into her cab and shouted to the coachman: "It's too late, go home!" Oh, a very lively lady she is, very respectable. The good Lord doesn't put many like her on this earth. Apart from you, she's the only one. May God bless you all!'

And she went on threading her vacuous words together, as effortlessly as a nun who has been interrupted in her telling of the rosary. And her wrinkled face continued to pucker mysteriously. She was beaming now, very satisfied.

'So,' she went on without transition, 'I'd really like a pair of good shoes. My gentleman has been really kind, but I can't ask him that. I've got some good clothes, as you see, but I need a pair of good shoes. Mine have got holes in, look, and these muddy days you catch the colic. I had colic yesterday, and that's a fact, I was jiggling around all afternoon. With a good pair of shoes...'

'I'll bring you a pair, Mother Fétu,' said Hélène, waving her away.

Then as the old woman was backing out with curtseys and thank-yous, she asked her:

'What time will you be alone?'

'My gentleman's never there after six,' she answered. 'But don't trouble yourself, I'll come and get the shoes from your concierge. Well, whatever you say. You are an angel from paradise. The good Lord will reward you.'

You could hear her exclaiming as she got to the landing. Hélène, still seated, remained dumbstruck by what the woman had just told her, with her oddly pertinent remarks. She knew where it was now. A rose-coloured room in that tumbledown house! She could see the stairs oozing with damp, the yellow doors on each landing blackened by sticky hands, all that poverty which had touched her heart last winter, when she went up to visit Mother Fétu. She tried to visualize the rose-coloured room in the middle of all that ugliness and poverty. But as she was sunk in a deep reverie, two warm little hands were placed on her sleepless red eyes and a laughing voice asked:

'Who is it? Who is it?'

It was Jeanne, who had just got dressed by herself. The voice of Mother Fétu had woken her. And seeing that the door of the adjoining room was shut she had hurried to play a trick on her mother. 'Who is it? Who is it?' she demanded again, more and more overcome with laughter.

Then as Rosalie came in with breakfast:

'Don't say anything, will you? It's not you I'm asking.'

'Stop it, silly!' said Hélène. 'I know it's you.'

The little girl slid on to her mother's lap, and there, leaning back, swinging to and fro, pleased with the idea she'd had, she insisted:

'Well, it could have been another little girl, couldn't it? A little girl who might have been bringing you a letter from her mother to invite you to dinner. Then she would have made you shut your eyes.'

'Don't be a donkey!' Hélène replied, setting her on her feet. 'What are you talking about? Serve us, Rosalie.'

But the maid was studying the little girl, and saying that Mademoiselle was dressed in an odd fashion. In fact, Jeanne in her hurry had not put her shoes on. She was in her underwear, a short flannel petticoat, with a corner of the bodice protruding over the gap. Her unhooked flannelette camisole revealed her naked young body, a flat exquisitely slim chest, and the faint wavy outline of breasts that were scarcely pink. And with her dishevelled hair, walking in her stockinged feet, all put on back to front, she was adorable, all white in her higgledy-piggledy underwear.

She leaned over, looked at herself and burst out giggling.

'Look at me, Maman, how nice I look! Don't you think so? I'm going to stay like that... I look so nice!'

Hélène suppressed a gesture of impatience and asked the question she did every morning:

'Have you washed your face?'

'Oh, Maman,' the child muttered, suddenly in a bad mood, 'oh, Maman... It's raining, it's awful weather...'

'Well, you won't get any breakfast. Wash her face, Rosalie.'

Normally she performed this task herself. But she was feeling really ill. She hugged the fire, shivering, although the weather was very mild. Rosalie had just pulled up the little table on which she had placed a cloth and two white china bowls. In front of the fire the coffee steamed in a silver coffee pot, a present from Monsieur Rambaud. At this time of the morning, the untidy room, still full of sleep and the night's disarray, had a pleasing cosiness.

'Maman, Maman!' Jeanne shouted from the back of the bedroom, 'she's rubbing too hard, it's burning me! Oh, how cold it is!'

Her eyes fixed on the coffee pot, Hélène was in a deep reverie. She wanted to know. She would go. It annoyed and worried her when she thought about the hidden rendezvous in that squalid corner of Paris. She found its mysterious nature in execrable taste. She recognized the signature of Malignon all over it, his romantic imagination, his craze for reviving the *maisons de passe* of the Regency* with little cost to himself. And yet, in spite of her disgust, she was excited, fascinated, her senses full of the silence and the dim light which would prevail in the rose-coloured bedroom.

'Mademoiselle,' Rosalie kept saying, 'if you don't let me wash you I'm going to call Madame.'

'Watch out, you are getting soap in my eyes!' replied Jeanne. Her voice was choked with tears.

'That's enough, let me go! You can do my ears tomorrow.'

But the water kept running, you could hear the sponge dripping in the basin. There was the noise of a struggle. The child cried. Then almost immediately she emerged, very cheery, shouting:

'It's all over, it's all over!'

And, with her hair still damp, and clean-smelling and pink from the rubbing, she gave herself a shake. In the struggle her camisole had slipped; her petticoat was coming undone; her stockings were falling down and revealing her little legs. She really did, as Rosalie said, look like the infant Jesus. But Jeanne was very proud of being clean; she didn't want to be dressed again.

'Look at me, Maman, look at my hands, my neck, and my ears. What do you think? Perfect! You won't believe it, I've certainly deserved my breakfast today.'

She had curled up in a ball in front of the fire, in her little armchair. Rosalie poured the coffee. Jeanne took her bowl on her lap, gravely dunking her toasted bread with a grown-up expression on her face. Normally Hélène did not let her eat like that. But she was still preoccupied. She left her bread and just drank the coffee. When she had got to the last mouthful, Jeanne was remorseful. She was overcome with sadness and threw her arms round her mother's neck when she saw she was so pale.

'Maman, are you poorly now? Did I make you sad?'

'No, darling, you are a lovely girl,' murmured Hélène, giving her a kiss. 'But I'm a bit tired, I didn't sleep very well... Go and play, and don't worry.'

She thought that the day was going to be dreadfully long. Whatever was she going to do until night came? For some time now she had not touched a needle, the work seemed to weigh heavily on her. She sat for hours, her hands idle, finding it stuffy in her room and needing to go out for fresh air, but not moving. It was that room that was making her ill. She loathed it now, cross at having spent two years in it. She hated it, its blue velvet, its panoramic view of the city, and dreamed of a small apartment in a noisy street which would have numbed her feelings. Oh heavens, how slowly the time passed! She took up a book, but the thought which she couldn't get out of her head continually evoked the same images between her eyes and the page she had begun. Meanwhile Rosalie had tidied the room, Jeanne was dressed and had done her hair. Then the little girl, who was having one of her noisy, jolly days, began a great game amongst the furniture which was back in its place, while her mother, at the window, was trying to read. She was alone; but that didn't bother her, she played the part of three or four people with a conviction and a seriousness that was very funny. First she played the part of a lady making visits. She disappeared into the dining room, then came back with a greeting, a smile, and a coquettish turn of the head.

'Bonjour, Madame. How are you, Madame? We haven't seen you for *such* a long time. It really is a wonder... Oh, I've been *so* poorly. Yes, I had cholera, it was very disagreeable. Oh, you can't see it at all. You look younger than ever, I do declare! And how are your children, Madame? I have had three since last summer.'

She went on curtseying in front of the little table, which no doubt represented the lady she was visiting. Then she moved over to the sofa and carried on a general conversation lasting an hour, with a really extraordinary wealth of phrases.

'Don't be so silly, Jeanne,' said her mother from time to time, impatient with her chattering.

'But Maman, I am at my friend's house. She's speaking to me so I have to answer. Isn't it true that when you have tea, you don't put the cakes in your pocket?'

And off she went again:

'Goodbye, Madame. Your tea was delicious... Say hello to your good husband.'

Suddenly it was completely different. She was going out in her carriage, she was going shopping, sitting astride the chair like a boy.

'Jean, not so fast, I'm scared. Now stop! We are outside the hat shop... How much is that hat, Mademoiselle? Three hundred francs, that's not dear. But it's not very nice. I'd like one with a bird on top, as big as this... Come, Jean, drive me to the grocer's. You haven't any honey? Yes, we have, Madame, here it is. It's very good! I don't want any, give me twopence worth of sugar... Oh, do be careful, Jean! The coach has turned over! Monsieur le Sergent, the cart crashed into us. You are not hurt, Madame? No, Monsieur, not in the slightest. Jean, Jean. We're going home. Giddy up, giddy up! Wait, I am going to order some chemises. Three dozen chemises for Madame. I also need some little boots and a bodice. Get along now! Get along, for goodness' sake, we shall never get home!'

And she fanned herself, she acted the part of the lady going home and telling her servants off. She was never short of things to say. It was an excited and constant stream of fantastic imaginings, a condensation of the life that was simmering away in her little head and coming out in stray bits and pieces. In the morning, or afternoon, she ran round, danced, chatted. When she was tired, a stool, a sunshade she saw in a corner, a rag she'd picked up from the floor was enough to get her started on another game, with new spurts of inventiveness. She created everything, the characters, the places, the scenes; and she enjoyed herself as much as if she had a dozen children with her of her own age.

Finally night came. It was about to strike six. Hélène, waking out of her uneasy afternoon somnolence, threw a shawl quickly around her shoulders.

'Are you going out, Maman?' asked Jeanne in surprise.

'Yes, darling, an errand in the neighbourhood. I shan't be long... Be a good girl.'

Outside the thaw continued. A river of mud was flowing along the pavement. Hélène went into a shoe shop in the Rue de Passy where she had already been with Mother Fétu. Then she made her way back along the Rue Raynouard. The sky was grey and a mist was rising from the cobbles. The street was vanishing before her eyes, deserted and frightening, in spite of it not being very late, with occasional gas lamps staining the damp mist yellow. She hurried along, keeping close to the houses, hiding as though she were going to a rendezvous. But when she suddenly turned into the Passage des Eaux, she halted under the arch in real fear. The passage opened up below her like a black chasm. She couldn't see the bottom, she could just see the flicker of the only street lamp lighting the middle of this narrow, dark passage. Finally she made up her mind and caught hold of the iron ramp to stop herself falling. She felt along the wide steps with her toes. To right and left the walls closed round, elongated out of all proportion by the darkness, while the bare branches of the trees above looked like vague outlines of gigantic arms, clutching at her with their gnarled hands. She shivered at the thought that the gate of one of these gardens might well open and a man attack her. Nobody passed her and she went down as rapidly as possible. Suddenly a shadow loomed out of the darkness; when the shadow coughed, her blood ran cold, but it was only an old woman struggling to walk up. Then she felt reassured, and was more careful to pick up the hem of her dress, which had been trailing in the mud. The mud was so thick that her boots stuck to the steps. At the bottom she turned her head as if by instinct. The wet branches were dripping into the passage, the street light shone like a lamp fixed to the wall of a mineshaft that flooding has made dangerous.

Hélène went straight up to the small attic room she had so often visited, at the top of the big house in the passage. But she knocked in vain, there was no answer. She went down again, very uneasy. Mother Fétu was no doubt in the apartment on the first floor. But Hélène did not dare be seen there. She stayed five minutes in the alley, which was lit by a petrol lamp. She went up again, hesitated, and looked at the doors. And was just leaving when the old woman leaned over the balustrade.

'What, is it you on the steps, dear lady!' she cried. 'Come in, come in! Don't stay there to take cold... Oh! What a dreadful day, you can't feel your fingers and toes.'

'No thank you,' said Hélène, 'here is your pair of shoes, Mother Fétu...'

And she looked at the door that Mother Fétu had left open behind her. You could see the corner of a stove.

'I'm all alone, I swear,' repeated the old woman. 'Come in. This is the kitchen. Oh, you're not too proud to mix with the likes of us poor people. That's a fact.'

So despite her disgust, and ashamed of what she was doing there, Hélène followed her in.

'Here's your pair of shoes, Mother Fétu.'

'Dear Lord, how can I thank you? Oh, what nice shoes! Wait a minute, I'll put them on. They are a treat, they fit like a glove... What luck! At least I'll be able to walk in them and not be afraid of the rain. You've saved me, you've given me ten years lease of life, my dear lady. I'm not flattering you, that's what I think, it's as true as that lamp over there lighting the way. No, I'm not one to flatter.'

She had grown more affectionate as she was speaking, taking Hélène's hands and kissing them. There was some wine warming in a pan; on the table near the lamp, you could see the slim neck of a half-empty bottle of Bordeaux. Moreover there were only four plates, one glass, two skillets, and a cooking pot. You could see that Mother Fétu was camping out in this bachelor pad, and had heated the stove for herself alone. Seeing Hélène's eyes move towards the saucepan, she coughed and then began whining.

'I've got a pain in my belly again,' she groaned. 'The doctor can say what he likes, I must have a worm. So a drop of wine sets me up again. I've got lots of troubles, good lady. I don't wish my ills on anybody, it's too bad. So I look after myself a little bit now; when a body has been through what I have you are allowed to look after yourself a little bit, aren't you? I was lucky enough to come across a really nice gentleman. God bless him!'

And she put two big sugar lumps in her wine. She was getting fatter than ever, her small eyes were disappearing into her puffy face. A beatific happiness was slowing her down. Her life's ambition seemed to be satisfied. This was what she was born for. As she was stirring her sugar, Hélène caught sight of some treats at the back of the cupboard, a pot of jam, a packet of biscuits, even some cigars stolen from the gentleman.

'Well, goodbye, Mother Fétu, I'm going,' she said.

But the old woman pushed the saucepan to the corner of the stove and muttered:

'Wait a minute. It's too hot, I'll drink it in a while. No, don't go. I'm sorry I asked you into the kitchen. I'll show you round.' She took the lamp and went into a narrow passage. Hélène followed her with beating heart. The smoky corridor with cracks on the walls oozed damp. A door opened and now she was walking on a thick carpet.

Mother Fétu had gone a few steps into the middle of an enclosed, silent room.

'What do you think?' she said, raising the lamp. 'Nice, isn't it?'

Two square rooms were connected by a double door, both wings of which had been removed and replaced by a portière. Both rooms were decorated in the same pink cretonne pattern with little Louis XV medallions, cherubs with fat cheeks frolicking among garlands of flowers. In the first, there was a little table, two settees, armchairs; in the second, smaller room, a huge bed took up the whole space. Mother Fétu pointed out a crystal night light on the ceiling, hanging on golden chains. This lamp represented for her the height of luxury. And she started to explain:

'You can't imagine how funny he is. He turns all the lights on in the middle of the day and stays there smoking a cigar and staring into space. Apparently he enjoys that, this gentleman... Never mind, he must have spent a fortune!'

Hélène was silent as she visited the apartment. She found it in bad taste. The rooms were too pink, the bed too big, the furniture too new. You felt it was an attempt at seduction, offensive in its crassness. A little milliner would have succumbed straight away. And yet a sense of unease crept over Hélène, while the old woman continued, with a wink:

'He calls himself Monsieur Vincent. I don't mind, as long as the man pays me.'

'Goodbye, Mother Fétu,' replied Hélène, in a strangled voice.

She tried to leave, opened a door, and found herself in a succession of three bare little rooms in a state of disgusting filth. The paper was falling off the walls, the ceilings were black, plaster covered the broken tiles. The place oozed generations of poverty.

'Not that way, not that way!' cried Mother Fétu. 'Normally that door's closed. Those are the other bedrooms, the ones he hasn't decorated. Heavens! It already cost him a pretty penny. Oh yes, it's not so nice of course. This way, dear lady, this way.'

And when Hélène went back through the boudoir with the pink furnishings, she stopped her and kissed her hands yet again.

'Come now, I'm not ungrateful. I'll always remember those shoes. They fit me and they are warm and I could walk three leagues in them! So what can I ask of the good Lord for you? O Lord, hear my prayer, let her be the happiest of women! You who know what is in my heart, know what I wish for her. In the name of the Father, Son, and Holy Ghost, Amen!'

A religious exultation had suddenly come over her, she made several signs of the Cross, genuflected to the big bed and the crystal night light. Then, opening the door to the landing, she whispered in Hélène's ear in an altered voice:

'Knock on the kitchen door whenever you like. I'm always there.'

Hélène, her head in a whirl, with a backward glance as though she was emerging from a bawdy house, went downstairs, climbed the Passage des Eaux again and found herself once more in the Rue Vineuse, without being conscious of having made her way there. It was only out in the street that she found the old woman's last sentence surprising. Of course she would not go back to that house. She had no more alms to give her. Why on earth would she knock at the kitchen door? Now she was satisfied, she had seen what she had seen. And she felt contempt for herself and the others as well. What vileness it was to have gone there! She couldn't rid herself of the vision of the two rooms with their cretonne. With one glance she had absorbed the tiniest details, even where the seats were and how the curtains hung in folds around the bed. But always after that the three other little rooms, the dirty, empty, deserted rooms, flashed before her eyes. And that vision, those leprous walls hidden beneath the fat-faced cherubs occasioned in her as much anger as disgust.

'Well, Madame,' cried Rosalie, who was watching out on the stairs, 'the dinner won't be fit to eat! It's been burning for half an hour!'

Seated at the table, Jeanne deluged her mother with questions. Where had she gone? What had she been doing? Then, as she received nothing but brief replies, she amused herself by playing dinner parties. She had sat her doll beside her on a chair. In a sisterly fashion she gave her half her dessert.

'And, Mademoiselle, you must be sure to eat nicely. Wipe your mouth. Oh, the dirty little girl, she can't even use her serviette properly. There, you look nice again. Here, have a biscuit. What do you say? You want some jam on it? Is that all right? It's better like that. Let me peel you a quarter of the apple...'

And she put the doll's portion on the chair. But when her plate was empty she took the morsels back again, and ate them, speaking in the doll's voice:

'Oh, it's delicious! I've never eaten such tasty jam. Wherever do you buy that jam, Madame? I'll tell my husband to bring me a pot. Did you pick these beautiful apples in your garden?'

She fell asleep as she was playing, staggering into her bedroom with her doll in her hands. She had not stopped since morning. Her little legs could go no longer, the game had completely worn her out; and even asleep she was still smiling, apparently dreaming she was still playing a game. Her mother put her to bed, limp, unprotesting, and in the middle of a great game with the angels.

Now Hélène was alone in the room. She shut herself in, and spent a terrible evening by the fire that had gone out. Her will failed, unspeakable thoughts were doing their secret work in her. It was as if there was an unknown, wicked, sensual woman talking to her in a commanding voice and she could not disobey. When midnight struck, she struggled into bed. But once there her torment grew unbearable. She half-slept, tossing and turning as though on hot coals. Images, magnified by her insomnia, would not leave her. Then an idea planted itself in her brain. She tried to banish it but it was in vain, the idea took root, choked her, took hold of her whole being. At about two o'clock she got up, with the stiff gait of a sleepwalker, lit the lamp again and wrote a letter, disguising her writing. It was an imprecise denunciation, an unsigned note three lines long, asking Doctor Deberle to go to such and such a place that very day, at such and such a time, but not giving any explanation. She sealed the envelope, put the letter into the pocket of her dress, which was thrown over the armchair. And when she had lain down again she went to sleep straight away, lying there apparently not breathing, weighed down by a leaden sleep.

CHAPTER 3

THE next day Rosalie was unable to serve coffee until nearly nine o'clock. Hélène had got up late, stiff and very pale because of the nightmare. She rummaged in the pocket of her dress, felt for the note, shoved it back, and came to sit at the table without a word. Jeanne too had a heavy head, and a grey, worried expression. She was reluctant to get out of her little bed, did not feel like playing that morning. The sky was the colour of soot, the room looked dark and murky, and sudden showers intermittently battered at the panes.

'Mademoiselle is having one of her black days,' said Rosalie to herself. 'She can't have two good days together. That's what you get for jumping around so much yesterday.'

'Don't you feel well, Jeanne?' Hélène asked.

'No, Maman,' said the little girl. 'It's that horrible sky.'

Hélène was silent again. She finished her coffee and sat there absorbed, staring at the flame. When she rose she had just made up her mind that it was her duty to talk to Juliette, to make her cancel her afternoon rendezvous. But how? She did not know. But the need to try had suddenly struck her, and this, the only thought in her head, was obsessing her. Ten o'clock struck, she got dressed. Jeanne was observing her. When she saw her reach for her hat, she clasped her little hands together as though she felt cold, and a black look of pain spread over her face. Usually she was very jealous of her mother going out and leaving her, and insisted on accompanying her everywhere.

'Rosalie,' said Hélène, 'hurry up and finish the room... Don't go out. I'm coming back straight away.' And she bent down and gave Jeanne a quick kiss without noticing her troubled countenance. As soon as she had left, the child, too proud to complain, gave a sob.

'Oh, don't spoil your pretty eyes, Mademoiselle!' repeated the maid, to console her. 'My sakes, they are not going to steal your Maman. You must let her do what she's got to do. You can't always be clinging to her skirts.' In the meantime Hélène had turned the corner of the Rue Vineuse, making her way along the walls to shelter from the shower. It was Pierre who opened the door; but he seemed embarrassed.

'Madame Deberle is at home?'

'Yes, Madame; but I don't know...'

And as Hélène, being a close friend, was going in the direction of the salon, he saw fit to intervene.

'Wait, Madame, I'll go and see.'

He glided into the room, opening the door just a fraction, and Juliette's cross voice could be heard.

'What? You allowed someone in? I strictly forbade you... It's incredible, one can't be undisturbed for a minute.'

Hélène pushed open the door, resolved to fulfil what she perceived as her duty.

'Ah, so it's you!' said Juliette, as she saw who it was. 'I didn't hear.' But she was still cross. It was obvious that the visit was unwelcome.

'Am I disturbing you?' asked the latter.

'No, no. You'll understand. We are working on a surprise. We are rehearsing "Le Caprice"* so we can perform it at one of my Wednesday soirées. Frankly, we chose the morning so that nobody could guess. Oh, stay now you're here. You'll have to keep it secret, that's all.'

And, clapping her hands and addressing Madame Berthier who was standing in the middle of the salon, she went on, without taking any further notice of Hélène:

'Come on. To work! You are not putting enough subtlety into the sentence: "Secretly knitting your husband a purse would be thought by many, a little more than what the heroine of a romantic novel might do." Do that again.'

Hélène, most astonished to find her at this activity, had sat down at the back. They had pushed back the seats against the walls and tables, there was nothing on the carpet. Madame Berthier, a delicate blonde, spoke her monologue, raising her eyes to the ceiling, searching for her words, while in an armchair the sturdy Madame Guiraud, a fine-looking woman with black hair, who had taken on the role of Madame de Léry, was waiting for the right moment to make her entrance. These ladies, in their morning attire, had not removed either their coats or hats. And in front of them, holding the volume of Musset in her hand, Juliette, dishevelled, enveloped in a long white cashmere dressing gown, had adopted the confident attitude of a director indicating to the actors how they should say the words and how they should comport themselves on stage. The light was very dim, but through the little curtains of embroidered tulle, drawn up and held back over the catches, you could see the garden disppearing into the damp night.

'You are not showing enough emotion,' declared Juliette. 'You have to mean it more when you speak, each word must count. "And now, my dear little purse, we'll put the finishing touches to..." Start again.'

'I shall be hopeless,' said Madame Berthier, languidly. 'Why don't you play my part? You would make a charming Mathilde.'

'Me? No, in the first place it has to be a blonde. And then, I'm a very good teacher, but not an actress... Let's get back to work.'

Hélène stayed in her corner. Madame Berthier, concentrating on her part, had not even turned her head. Madame de Guiraud had acknowledged her presence by a slight nod. But she felt she was intruding and ought not to have sat down. What kept her there was not so much the thought that she had a duty to fulfil, as the peculiar feeling, muddled but deep-seated, that she'd had sometimes in that house. She found the indifferent manner in which Juliette had received her hard to bear. She was constantly on and off with her friendships; she would be all over someone for three months, throw herself at them, seemed to exist only for them; then one morning without a word of explanation she acted as if she didn't know them any more. No doubt she was following the dictates of fashion, in that as elsewhere, the need to like people that others in her circle liked. These abrupt changes in her affections cut Hélène to the quick, her calm, open nature always dreamed things would last for ever. She had often come back depressed from the Deberles, truly despairing about how little you could rely on the affections of the heart. But that day, because of the crisis she was going through, the pain was even keener.

'We are leaving out the Chavigny scene,' said Juliette. 'He's not coming this morning. Let's go to Madame de Léry's entrance. You now, Madame de Guiraud... Your speech.'

And she read:

'"Just imagine I show him that purse..."'

Madame de Guiraud had risen. Speaking in a high-pitched voice and adopting a very extravagant pose, she began:

'"Look, it's rather nice. Let's see."'

When the servant had opened the door to her, Hélène had imagined a completely different scene. She thought she would find a nervous Juliette, extremely pale, in a panic at the thought of the rendezvous, hesitant and yet drawn to it. And she imagined herself begging Juliette to reconsider, until the young woman, choked with sobs, threw herself into her arms. Then they would have wept together, Hélène would have gone away with the thought that henceforth Henri was lost to her but that she had ensured his happiness. And it was nothing of the sort. She had arrived right in the middle of a rehearsal, and couldn't for the life of her understand what was going on. She found Juliette, looking relaxed, having obviously slept well, and with a clear enough mind to give her opinion about Madame Berthier's gestures, not in the least bit troubled about what she might be doing that afternoon. This indifference, this superficiality, made Hélène, who had arrived fervent with passion, go cold.

She tried to speak.

'Who is playing this Chavigny?' she asked abruptly.

'Malignon,' said Juliette, turning round, in surprise. 'The annoying thing is that he can't come to rehearsals. Listen, ladies, I'm going to play the part of Chavigny. Unless we do that, we'll never get through it.'

And from then on, she acted too, playing the man's part, with an involuntary deepening of the voice and a gallant mien, as the situation demanded. Madame Berthier cooed, the stout Madame de Guiraud took infinite pains to be vivacious and witty. Pierre came in to put wood on the fire, and covertly looked at the ladies, whom he found amusing.

Meanwhile Hélène who was still resolved to do what she had come for, despite the tightening of her heart, tried to take Juliette on one side.

'Can you spare me one minute? I've got something to tell you.'

'Impossible, my dear... as you see I'm busy. Tomorrow, if you have time.'

Hélène said no more. The distant tone of the young woman annoyed her. She felt angry at seeing her so unconcerned, when she herself had endured such terrible agonies since the previous day. At one point she was about to get up and let things take their course. It was stupid to try and save this woman. The whole nightmare began again. Her hand, which had just tightened over the letter in her pocket, was hot and damp. Why should she love other people since others did not love her and did not suffer in the way she did?

'Oh! Excellent!' Juliette cried suddenly.

Madame Berthier rested her head on Madame de Guiraud's shoulder, sobbing, repeating:

' "I'm sure he loves her. I'm sure of it." '

'You will be a runaway success,' said Juliette. 'Take your time, won't you? "I'm sure he loves her, I'm sure of it..." And leave your head in that position. That's charming... Now you, Madame Guiraud.'

' "No, child, it's not possible. It's a caprice, a fantasy..." ' declaimed the stout lady.

'Perfect! But it's a long scene. What do you say, shall we have a short break? We must get this sequence right.'

Then all three discussed how to arrange the salon. The door of the dining room, on the left, would do for the entrances and exits; they would place an armchair on the right, a sofa at the back, and push the table up against the hearth. Hélène, who had got up, followed them as if she was interested in this arrangement. She had renounced her plan of provoking an explanation, she simply wanted to make one last effort and prevent Juliette from going to the rendezvous.

'I came to ask you, is it not today that you are going to visit Madame de Chermette?'

'Yes, this afternoon.'

'Well, if you allow, I'll come and call for you. I've been promising for a long time I will go and visit her.'

Juliette had a moment's embarrassment, but recovered herself immediately.

'I should like nothing more... except that I've got a lot of errands to do. I am going to the shops first, so I really don't know what time I shall arrive at Madame de Chermette's.'

'Never mind,' Hélène replied. 'That will be a nice walk for me.'

'Listen, may I be absolutely honest? Please don't insist, as I should prefer to be on my own... We'll do that the Monday after.'

That was said without any emotion, so clearly and with such a quiet smile that Hélène, confused, made no reply. She had to give Juliette a hand carrying the table to the fireside. Then she retreated while the rehearsal continued. At the end of the scene, Madame de Guiraud in her monologue declaimed these two sentences with great passion:

' "But what an abyss is the heart of a man! Oh, truly, we are worth more than them!" '

What should she do now? And in the turmoil which this question occasioned in her, Hélène had only vague thoughts of violent action. She felt an irresistible urge to take revenge on Juliette's utter unconcern, as if this serenity was in some way insulting to the fever that possessed her. She dreamed of her downfall, wondering whether she would still retain her indifferent sangfroid. Then she despised herself for having been so fastidious and principled. She should have told Henri a score of times: 'I love you, take me, let us go', and not be afraid, just like this woman with the pale, untroubled expression, who, three hours before her first rendezvous, was performing a play in her house. Even now, this very minute, she was trembling more than her. That was what made her mad, being conscious of her own violent feelings amidst the cheerful tranquillity of this salon, the fear of bursting out suddenly with passionate words. Was she being a coward, then?

A door opened, she suddenly heard Henri's voice saying:

'Don't mind me... I'm not staying.'

The rehearsal was nearly over. Juliette, still in the role of Chavigny, had just grasped Madame de Guiraud's hand.

'"Ernestine, I adore you!"' she cried in a surge of great conviction.

'"So you don't love Madame de Blainville any more?"' recited Madame de Guiraud.

But Juliette refused to continue as long as her husband stayed. The men weren't to know. Then the doctor was very amiable to the women. He complimented them, promised it would be a great success. Wearing his black gloves, very correct with his clean-shaven chin, he was coming back from his visits. On arrival he had simply greeted Hélène with a little nod. He had seen an illustrious actress in the Comédie-Française playing Madame de Léry; and he indicated some moves to Madame de Guiraud.

'At the moment when Chavigny falls at your feet, you walk over to the fireside and throw the purse into the fire. In a detached way, you know, without any anger, like a woman playing at love...'

'Yes yes, let's get on with it,' said Juliette again. 'We know all that.'

And as he was finally pushing open the door to his study, she took up the sequence again.

'"Ernestine, I adore you!"'

Before leaving the room, Henri had acknowledged Hélène with the same nod of his head. She remained silent, expecting some catastrophe. This abrupt appearance of Juliette's husband seemed to pose a real threat... But when he had gone, he seemed ridiculous to her with his courteousness and his blindness. So he too cared about this ridiculous play! And he had shown no emotion in his eyes when he saw her there. Then the whole house seemed to her hostile and ice-cold. It was a collapse, nothing held her back, for she hated Henri as much as she did Juliette. She grasped the letter at the bottom of her pocket again with clenched fingers. She stammered out an 'Au revoir'. She left, feeling giddy, the chairs and tables seemed to be whizzing round, and her ears were burning with the words uttered by Madame de Guiraud.

'"Farewell. You may bear me a grudge today, but tomorrow you will still be my friend and, believe me, that is worth more than a passing caprice."'

Out on the pavement, when Hélène closed the door behind her, she pulled the letter from her pocket in one violent, involuntary movement and slipped it through the letter box. Then she remained for a second or two, dazedly looking at the narrow brass blade which had closed again.

'It's done,' she said under her breath.

She could once again visualize the two rooms with their pink cretonne hangings, the sofas, the enormous bed. Malignon and Juliette were in it. Suddenly the curtain opened and her husband came in. And that was all. She was very calm. Instinctively she looked to see if anyone had seen her putting it through the letter box. The street was empty. She turned the corner and walked back up the road.

'Have you been a good girl, darling?' she said, giving Jeanne a kiss.

The little girl, sitting in the same armchair, raised her sulky face. Without a word she flung her arms around her mother's neck, kissed her, uttering a great sigh. She was really unhappy. At lunch, Rosalie expressed surprise.

'Did Madame have a lot of errands?'

'Why do you ask?' said Hélène.

'Because Madame has such a good appetite. Madame hasn't eaten so well for a long time...'

It was true, she was ravenous, the sudden relief had made her stomach feel empty. She felt at peace, an inexpressible sense of well-being. After the shocks of these last two days a sort of silence had just come over her, her limbs were relaxed and supple, as when she'd taken a bath; she felt only that there was something heavy somewhere, a vague worry weighing on her mind.

When she got back to her room, her eyes went straight to the clock, the hands showed twenty-five past twelve. Juliette's rendezvous was for three o'clock. Mechanically she made the calculation—another two and a half hours. There was no hurry in any case, the hands were moving round, nobody in the world now had the power to stop them, and she let things take their course. A child's bonnet had for some time been lying on the table. She took it up and began sewing by the window. Deep silence fell over the room. Jeanne was sitting in her usual place, but she sat there with her hands empty and idle.

'Maman,' she said, 'I can't do my work. I'm not enjoying it.'

'Well, darling, don't... Here you are, you can thread my needles.'

Then, silently, laboriously, the child did so. She took great pains to cut the ends of cotton equal, spent an eternity looking for the hole in the needle; and she only managed it in the nick of time; her mother used the threaded needles she had prepared one by one.

'You see,' she murmured, 'it's quicker like that... Tonight my six little bonnets will be finished.'

And she turned her head to look at the clock. Ten past one. Still almost two hours to go. Now Juliette must be beginning to dress. Henri would have received the letter. Oh, he was bound to go. The instructions were clear enough, he would find it without any trouble. But all this seemed to her still a very long way off and she was unconcerned. She sewed with regular stitches applying herself to the task like a sempstress. The minutes ticked by one by one. Two o'clock struck.

A ring on the doorbell took her by surprise.

'Who can it be, Maman?' Jeanne asked. She had started in her chair.

And, when Monsieur Rambaud came in:

'So it's you! Why did you ring so loud? You scared me.'

The good fellow looked dismayed. It was true, he had tugged the bell rather hard.

'I'm not well today, I'm poorly,' said the child. 'You mustn't scare me.'

Monsieur Rambaud was worried. What was the matter with the poor darling? And he only sat down, reassured, after a quick glance from Hélène told him that the child was having a black day, as Rosalie called it. It was usually very rare for him to call in the daytime, so he wanted to explain the reason for his visit straight away. It was for a compatriot of his, an old workman who could get no more work because he was so old, and whose wife was paralysed, living in a little room as big as your hand. You wouldn't believe such poverty existed. That very morning he'd gone up to their room to see what it was like. It was nothing more than a hole under the roof with a skylight, its cracked panes let the rain in. Inside there was a mattress, a woman wrapped in an old curtain and her dazed husband crouching on the floor with not even the strength to sweep up a little.

'Oh, the poor things, poor things!' said Hélène, moved to tears.

It wasn't so much the old workman Monsieur Rambaud was concerned about. He would take him to his house and find things for him to do. But his wife, this paralysed woman whom her husband did not dare to leave for a minute and had to turn over, just as if she were a parcel; where could one put her, what could be done with her?

'I thought of you,' he went on. 'You must get her into a hospice straight away. I would have gone to Monsieur Deberle directly but I thought since you know him better than I do, you would have more influence. If he would be so good as to see her it could all be sorted out by tomorrow.' Jeanne had listened all pale, visibly trembling with pity. She clasped her hands together and whispered:

'Oh, Maman, be kind to them, get the poor woman into...'

'Yes of course,' said Hélène, who was becoming more agitated. 'I'll contact the doctor as soon as I am able and he will see to the arrangements himself... Give me their names and the address, Monsieur Rambaud.'

The latter wrote a note on the little table. Then he rose.

'It's two thirty-five,' he said. 'Perhaps you'd find the doctor at home.'

She had got up too, looked at the clock, with a jump that shook her whole body. It was indeed two thirty-five, and the hands were going round. She stammered that the doctor must have left to do his rounds. However, Monsieur Rambaud, hat in hand, kept her standing there and began once more to tell her about them. The poor couple had sold everything, even their frying pan; since the beginning of winter they had been spending the days and nights without any heating. At the end of December they had not eaten for four days. Hélène made an exclamation of distress. The hands pointed to twenty to three. Monsieur Rambaud was a full two minutes taking his leave.

'Well, I'm counting on you,' he said.

And, leaning over to give Jeanne a kiss:

'Goodbye, darling.'

'Goodbye... Don't worry, Maman won't forget, I'll remind her.'

When Hélène came back from the landing after seeing Monsieur Rambaud out, the hand of the clock was three-quarters of the way round. In another quarter of an hour it would all be over. Standing stock-still in front of the mantelpiece, she had a sudden vision of the scene which was going to take place: Juliette was already there, Henri had come in and found her. She knew the room, she could see the minutest details with a frightening clarity. So, still shaken by Monsieur Rambaud's pathetic tale, a great shudder went through her, from top to toe. And she cried out inwardly. What she had done was an infamy, that letter she'd written, that cowardly denunciation. It suddenly appeared thus to her in a blinding light. Had she really committed such a shameful act! And she recalled that gesture when she had pushed the letter in the box, dazed, like somebody watching another person do something wrong, without it occurring to her that she should intervene. She seemed to be emerging from a dream. What had happened then? Why was she there still looking at the hands of this clock? Two more minutes had ticked by.

'Maman,' said Jeanne, 'if you like, we'll go and visit the doctor together this evening. That will be an outing for me. I can't breathe today.'

Hélène did not hear her. Thirteen minutes more. But she couldn't let such an outrage take place. In this new turmoil in her heart there was only a furious desire to stop it happening. She had to, or die in the attempt. And she rushed wildly into the bedroom.

'Oh, so you are taking me!' cried Jeanne, in delight. 'We're going to see the doctor straight away, are we, Maman?'

'No, no!' she replied, searching for her boots and bending down to look under the bed.

She couldn't find them; she made a gesture of utter unconcern, with the thought that she might as well go out in the indoor shoes she was wearing. Now she had turned the large wardrobe upside down to look for her shawl. Jeanne had come over, very coaxingly:

'So are you not going to the doctor's, Maman?'

'No.'

'Oh, take me with you anyway... Oh, please take me, I want to so much!'

But she had found her shawl at last and thrown it around her shoulders. Oh goodness! Only twelve minutes more, just time if she ran. She would go there, do something, no matter what. On the way she would think.

'Please—take me too, Maman,' pleaded Jeanne again in a voice that was more and more urgent and winsome.

'I can't take you,' said Hélène. 'I'm going somewhere where children can't go... Give me my hat.'

Jeanne's face grew pale. Her eyes grew dark, her voice more clipped. She asked:

'Where are you going?'

Her mother, busy tying the ribbons on her bonnet, did not answer. The little girl asked:

'You're always going out without me these days... Yesterday you went out, and now you're going out again. I'm too unhappy and I'm scared all alone. Oh, I'll die if you leave me. Do you hear, Maman, I'll die...'

Then, sobbing, seized by a crisis of pain and anger, she clutched at Hélène's skirt.

'For goodness' sake let me go, be sensible, I'm coming back soon,' said the latter again.

'No, I don't want you to... I don't want you to...' stammered the child. 'Oh, you don't love me anymore, or else you'd take me. Oh, I know very well you love other people more than me. Take me, take me, or I'm going to stay here on the floor and that's where you'll find me, on the floor.'

And she locked her little arms round her mother's legs, she wept into the folds of her dress, clutching at her, dragging on her to prevent her from leaving. The hands were going round, it was ten to three. Then Hélène thought that she would never get there in time. She lost her head and pushed Jeanne violently away, crying:

'What an unbearable child! It's a real tyranny! If you cry, you will make me very angry indeed!'

And she went out, slamming the door. Jeanne had stumbled backwards to the window, stiff and white as a sheet, her tears checked at this brutal behaviour. She stretched her arms out to the door, and shouted 'Maman, Maman!' twice, and remained there, having fallen back on to her chair, with a distraught expression at the jealous thought that her mother was deceiving her.

Hélène was hurrying down the street. The rain had stopped, although the huge splashes running off the gutters wetted her shoulders. She had promised herself she would think when she got outside, and make a plan. But now all that mattered was to get there. When she started down the Passage des Eaux, she hesitated a moment. The steps had become a river, the gutters in the Rue Raynouard had overflowed and were gushing down. Between the narrow walls the steps were splashed with foam, and the surface of each cobblestone glistened, washed by the rain. A pale shaft of light falling from the grey sky was lightening the passage through the black branches of the trees. She hitched up her skirt a little and started to climb down. The water came up to her ankles, she almost lost her little shoes in the puddles, and all the way down she could hear a distinct whispering noise all around her, like the murmur of little streams flowing under the grass deep in the woods.

Suddenly there she was, on the doorstep. She stood there breathless and distressed. Then she remembered and decided to knock on the kitchen door.

'What? Is it you?' said Mother Fétu.

Her voice was no longer whining. The old bawd's small eyes twinkled and her multitude of wrinkles quivered as she broke into a little laugh. Without more ado, she patted Hélène's hands and listened to her incoherent words. Hélène gave her twenty francs.

'May God be good to you!' Mother Fétu brought out, as was her habit. 'May He give you everything you wish for!'

CHAPTER 4

LEANING back in his armchair, Malignon stretched out his legs before the roaring fire and waited patiently. He'd gone to the lengths of closing the curtains and lighting the candles. The first room where he was sitting was brightly illuminated with a little chandelier and two candelabra. In the bedroom, on the other hand, darkness reigned. Only the crystal lamp hanging there gleamed in the half-light. Malignon pulled out his pocket watch.

'Damn!' he muttered. 'Surely she won't stand me up again today?'

And he gave a little yawn. He'd been waiting for an hour and was not enjoying himself. However, he rose, glanced at his preparations. He did not care for the arrangement of the chairs, he moved a *causeuse** across in front of the fireside. The lighted candles cast rose-coloured reflections in the cretonne hangings, the room was getting warmer, silent, stuffy, while outside there were sudden gusts of wind. He went into the bedroom one last time, and felt satisfied with what he had laid on: it seemed very good to him, extremely 'chic', a real love nest, the bed deep in voluptuous shadow. Just as he was tweaking the lace on the pillows, there were three rapid knocks at the door. It was the signal.

'Finally!' he said aloud, in triumph.

And he hurried to open the door. Juliette, veil drawn over her face, all wrapped up in furs, came in. While Malignon was quietly closing the door, she stood still for a moment, concealing the emotion that prevented her from speaking. Then, before the young man could take her hand, she lifted her veil, showing him her smiling face, rather pale but very composed.

'Oh, you've lit the candles,' she cried. 'I thought you hated them lit in daylight.'

Malignon, who was getting ready to take her in his arms, in the passionate gesture that he had planned, was taken aback and explained that it was such a dull day and his windows looked out on to waste ground. Anyway he loved the night-time.

'I never know with you,' she went on, teasing him. 'Last spring, at my children's party, you made a terrible fuss: we were in a cave, you said, it was like going into a morgue. Well, let's just say that your tastes have changed.'

She acted as though she was on one of her visits, and affected a confidence which made her voice huskier. That was the only indication she was uneasy. Now and then her chin contracted a little, as if she had something in her throat. But her eyes were bright, she was taking a keen delight in her bold action. It was a change for her, she was thinking of Madame de Chermette, who had a lover. Goodness, this was fun, anyway!

'Show me round,' she said.

And she visited the apartment. He followed, thinking he should have kissed her straight away. Now he couldn't, he had to wait. But she was looking at the furniture, examining the walls, raising her head, drawing back, chatting all the while.

'I hate your cretonne, it's extremely vulgar. Where on earth did you find that horrible pink? Oh, look, here's a chair that would be nice if there weren't so much gilding on the wood... And there are no pictures or ornaments, nothing but your chandelier and candelabra, they're not very stylish. Oh, my dear Malignon, now see if you dare make fun of my Japanese conservatory!'

She laughed, avenging herself for his former cutting remarks which she had always resented.

'Your taste is execrable, indeed it is! You don't realize that my *magot* is worth all your furnishings put together! Even a shop assistant would not have chosen that pink you have there. Have you been dreaming of seducing your laundry girl?'

Malignon, extremely vexed, did not answer. He tried to guide her into the bedroom. She stayed in the doorway, saying she would not go into such dark places and in any case, she could see quite enough as it was. The bedroom was just like the salon. Everything came from the Faubourg Saint-Antoine. The hanging lamp was especially the object of her mockery. She was pitiless. She kept harping on about the tawdry night-light, the kind of thing aspired to by working-class girls who don't have homes of their own. You could get lamps like that in any bazaar for seven francs fifty.

'I paid ninety francs for it,' Malignon finally shouted in exasperation.

She seemed delighted to have made him angry. He calmed down and asked her slyly:

'Are you not going to take off your coat?'

'Yes, I am,' she answered. 'It's so hot in your place!'

She even removed her hat, which he took from her and put on the bed. When he came back she was sitting by the fire, still gazing around her. She had grown serious again, and allowed herself to make peace with him.

'It's very ugly, but all the same you are quite well-off here. The two rooms could be made very nice.'

'Oh, nice enough for what I want,' he remarked, with a shrug.

He immediately regretted that stupid remark. He could not have been more coarse or inept. She had bowed her head, feeling choked again, as though there was a lump in her throat. For one moment she had just forgotten the reason she was there. But he wanted at least to press his advantage after the embarrassment he had caused her.

'Juliette,' he murmured, leaning over towards her.

She motioned to him to sit down. It was at Trouville when they were bathing that Malignon, bored by the sight of the ocean, had had the excellent notion of falling in love. They had now been living in a sort of quarrelsome familiarity for the last three years. One evening he had taken her hand. She did not get cross, and at first made light of it. Then, her head empty and her heart free, she decided she was in love with him. Until that time she had done more or less what all her women friends were doing. But the passion was missing, she was impelled by curiosity and the need to be like everyone else. In the beginning, if the young man had gone about it forcefully enough, there's no doubt she would have given in. He was foolish enough to want to win her over through his wit, he allowed her to get into the habit of playing the coquette. So when he made his first determined approach one night as they were gazing at the sea together, like lovers in a comic opera, she had rejected him, surprised and annoyed by his spoiling this romance she was relishing. Back in Paris, Malignon swore to himself he would be smarter. He had just taken up with her again in a period of boredom at the end of a tiring winter, when she was starting to find the familiar pleasures, the dinners, the dances, the first theatre premieres, monotonous. The thought of an apartment fitted out for this purpose in a secret location, the mystery of such a rendezvous with its whiff of immorality, had attracted her. It seemed to her exciting—you had to experience everything in life! And her nature was so calm that she was no more troubled in Malignon's apartment than she was at the studios of the painters she visited to ask them for canvases for her charity fairs.

'Juliette, Juliette,' the young man repeated, trying to make his tone of voice caressing.

'Come now, let's be sensible,' she said simply.

And taking a Chinese screen from the mantelpiece, she continued unabashed, as though she was in her own drawing room:

'We rehearsed this morning you know... I'm very afraid I didn't make a very good choice with Madame Berthier. Her Mathilde is whining, unbearable. That pretty monologue when she addresses her purse: "Poor little thing, I kissed you one moment past..." Well, she recites it like a schoolgirl who's prepared her little speech. I'm very worried about her.'

'And what about Madame de Guiraud?' he enquired, pulling up his chair and taking her hand.

'Oh, she's perfect. I've discovered an excellent Madame de Léry there, she'll be sharp and lively.'

She let him carry on holding her hand, which he was kissing while she was talking, without her appearing to notice.

'But you see, the worst thing is that you are not there. For one thing, you could say what you thought to Madame Berthier; and for another, it's not possible for us to work together properly if you are never there.'

He had got as far as putting his arm around her waist.

'As soon as I've learned my part,' he murmured.

'Yes, fine, but we all need to know our movements on stage. It's naughty of you not to give up three or four mornings for us.'

She could not go on, his kisses rained down on her neck. Then she was obliged to recognize that he had taken her in his arms, she pushed him away, tapping him with the Chinese screen still in her hand. Obviously she had sworn not to let him go any further. Her pale face was reddening in the glowing reflection of the fire. She was pursing her lips, pouting like a woman surprised by her feelings. Really, was that all it was! She should have seen where it would all end! She was overcome with panic.

'Leave me alone,' she stammered, smiling awkwardly. 'I shall get cross again.'

But he thought he'd had some effect. He was thinking very dispassionately: 'If I allow her to leave in the same condition she arrived, I've lost her.' Words were useless, he took hold of her hands again, tried to feel for her shoulders. For one moment it seemed as if she would surrender. All she had to do was close her eyes, and that would be that... The desire entered her head and she struggled with it, her mind crystal clear. But it seemed to her that someone was crying 'No.' It was she who had cried out, before she had even answered herself.

'No, no,' she said again. 'Let me go, you are hurting me... I don't want to, I don't want to.'

As he was still silent, pushing her towards the bedroom, she tore herself away. She was obeying a strange impulse, that had nothing to do with what she really wanted. She was annoyed with him and with herself. Upset, she uttered disjointed phrases. Oh, this was a fine reward for her trust in him. What was he hoping for in behaving like a brute? She even called him a coward. She would never see him again. But he let her tie herself in knots, he followed her with his nasty, stupid laugh. She started stammering in the end, having taken refuge behind an armchair, suddenly defeated, realizing she belonged to him though he had not yet taken her in his arms. It was one of the most unpleasant moments she had lived through.

And there they were, looking at each other, crestfallen, ashamed and angry, when they heard a loud noise. At first they did not realize what was going on. The door had opened, footsteps crossed the bedroom and a voice was shouting:

'Go, go! You are going to be found out.'

It was Hélène. Both of them, in a state of shock, looked at her. Their surprise was so great they forgot how compromising their situation was; Juliette did not look in the least embarrassed.

'Go!' Hélène repeated. 'Your husband will be here in two minutes.'

'My husband, my husband...?' stuttered the young woman. 'Why? What does he want?'

She was starting to behave like an imbecile. Everything was getting muddled in her brain. It seemed to her extraordinary that Hélène should be standing there talking about her husband. But Hélène made an angry gesture.

'Oh, if you think I have time to explain... He's on his way. So you've been warned. Leave now, both of you.'

Then Juliette became dreadfully agitated, She rushed around the rooms in complete panic, uttering disconnected words:

'Oh God, oh God, thank you. Where's my coat? How stupidly dark this room is! Give me my coat, bring me a candle so that I can find my coat... Please don't mind me if I don't thank you, my dear... I can't find my sleeves, no, I can't find them, I can't do it...' She was paralysed with fear, Hélène had to help her with her coat. She put her hat on awry, did not even do up the ribbons. But the worst thing was that she lost a whole minute or so looking for her veil which had fallen under the bed... She was stammering, her hands were shaky and uncontrolled, and she was feeling herself all over to ascertain if she had forgotten something that would give her away.

'What a lesson! Oh, what a lesson! Oh, it's definitely over now!' Malignon, who had gone very pale, wore a stupid expression. He was pacing up and down feeling hated and ridiculous. The one clear thought he could muster was that he was definitely not a lucky man. The only question he could formulate was:

'So do you think I should leave as well?'

And as he received no answer, he picked up his cane, and carried on talking, pretending total unconcern. They had all the time in the world, for in fact there was another staircase, a small, forgotten, servants' staircase, that was usable. Madame Deberle's cab was still waiting outside; the two of them could drive along the banks of the Seine. And he repeated:

'Calm yourselves, ladies. All will be well. Come along, it's over here.'

He had opened a door and you could see the succession of dark and dingy little rooms unused and in a filthy state. There was a draught of damp air. Before she stepped through all this grime, another wave of disgust came over Juliette and she exclaimed:

'How on earth could I have come here! How revolting! I can never forgive myself.'

'Hurry,' said Hélène, in her anxiety.

She gave her a little push. Then the young woman threw her arms round her neck and wept. It was a nervous reaction. She was overcome with shame. She wanted to defend herself, say why she had been found in this man's apartment. Then in an instinctive gesture she pulled up her skirts as though about to cross a stream. Malignon, who had gone ahead, was clearing away the pieces of plaster on the servants' staircase with the toe of his boot. The doors closed again.

Meanwhile, Hélène had remained standing in the centre of the small drawing room. She was listening. A silence reigned around her, a deep silence, warm and airless, punctuated only by the sparks from the embers. Her ears were buzzing, she couldn't hear a thing. But after what seemed an eternity, there was the sudden sound of a vehicle. It was Juliette's cab leaving. Then she gave a sigh, and, alone in that room, made a sign of thanks. The thought that she would not have to be everlastingly remorseful for having acted in such a base manner filled her with a feeling that was very sweet and with a vague grati-tude. She was comforted, very thankful, but suddenly so weak after the dreadful crisis she had come through, that she did not feel strong enough to leave either. Deep down she was thinking that Henri was about to arrive and that someone should be there for him. There was a knock and she opened the door immediately. His initial reaction was astonishment. Henri came in, preoccupied with the anonymous letter he'd received, his face white and worried. But when he saw her, he uttered a cry.

'You! My God, it was you!'

And he sounded more flabbergasted than pleased. He was not in the least expecting this rendezvous that had been so boldly arranged. Then at this unforeseen opportunity in that voluptuous and secret hiding place, all his male desires flared up.

'You love me, you love me!' he stammered. 'So here you are, and I didn't realize!'

He opened his arms, wanting to hold her. Hélène had smiled at him as he came in. Now she drew back, white-faced. Obviously she had been waiting for him, had told herself they would have a little chat, she would invent some story. And suddenly she saw the situation clearly. Henri was thinking it was a rendezvous. She had never intended that. A feeling of revulsion swept over her.

'Henri, I beg you, leave me alone!'

But he had taken hold of her wrists and was drawing her slowly towards him as though to conquer her with a kiss. The love which had been growing in him for months, and quelled later by the rupture in their intimacy, broke forth all the more violently now that he was beginning to forget Hélène. His heart's fire rose to his cheeks and she struggled against him when she saw in his face a passion that she recognized and that frightened her. He had already looked at her twice before with those maddened eyes.

'Leave me alone, you are frightening me. I swear to you that you are mistaken.'

Then he looked surprised once more.

'You are the one who wrote to me?' he said. She hesitated a second. What could she say, what could she reply?

'Yes,' she finally admitted.

But she could not give Juliette away after she had saved her. It was like an abyss into which she herself was sliding. At present Henri was studying the two rooms, astonished by the lighting and decoration. He dared to question her.

'Is this your apartment?'

And as she was silent:

'I was greatly upset by your letter. Hélène, you are hiding something from me. I beg you to put me out of my agony.'

She wasn't listening. She was thinking that he had every reason to think it was a rendezvous. What would she have been doing there, why would she have been waiting for him? She couldn't think of a plausible story. She was now not even certain she had not arranged this rendezvous with him herself. She was enveloped in his embrace, she was slowly vanishing.

He pressed her further. He was questioning her closely, his lips on her lips, to get at the truth.

'You were waiting, you were waiting for me?'

Then, surrendering, sinking into a passivity and a tenderness which she could no longer struggle against, she agreed to say what he would say, to want what he wanted.

'I was waiting for you, Henri...'

Again their lips met.

'But why write this letter? And to find you here! Where is this anyway?'

'Do not ask, never try and find out... You have to swear to me... I am here, I am near you, you can see that. What more do you want?'

'Do you love me?'

'Yes, I love you.'

'Are you mine, Hélène, all mine?'

'Yes, I am all yours.'

They kissed full on the lips. She forgot everything, she yielded to a superior force. It seemed to her natural and inevitable. Peace had descended upon her, all that came to her now were memories and the feeling of being young again. On such a winter's day when she was a girl in the Rue des Petites-Maries she had nearly suffocated in an airless room before a great coal fire that had been lit for the ironing. Another day in summer the windows were open and a chaffinch lost in the dark street had flown suddenly round her room. Then why was she thinking of death, why did she see that bird fly off? She felt wholly sad and like a child again in the delicious annihilation of her whole being.

'But you are wet through,' murmured Henri. 'Did you walk here?'

He lowered his voice and called her 'tu'. He whispered in her ear, as though someone might hear. And now that she could not resist him, trembling with desire there in front of her, he enclosed her in his arms with a passionate, shy caress, not daring to do more, putting off the moment. He felt a brotherly concern for her, he must look after her in intimate and small ways.

'Your feet are soaked, you'll catch cold,' he repeated. 'Oh heavens, is it sensible to go out on the streets with shoes like that!'

He made her sit down in front of the fire. She smiled, did not draw back, gave him her feet to take off her shoes. Her little slippers which had split in the puddles going down the Passage des Eaux were sodden as sponges. He pulled them off and put them on each side of the fireplace. The stockings, too, were still damp, and spattered with mud up to her ankles. Leaving her no time for embarrassment, with a gesture that was at once brusque, cross, and full of tenderness, he took them off, saying:

'That's how you catch cold. Warm yourself.' He had pushed up a stool.

Her two snow-white feet glowed pink in front of the flames. It was rather stuffy in the room. At the back of the apartment the room with its big bed was sunk in slumber. The night lamp had gone out, one of the curtains on the portière, come off its loop, was half concealing the door. In the small salon the flames of the candles gave off the warm smell that betokens the end of an evening. From time to time you could hear the rain streaming down, a dull pounding in the deep silence.

'Yes, it's true, I'm cold,' she whispered, shivering in spite of the great heat.

Her white feet were ice-cold. Then he insisted on taking them in his hands. His hands were hot, he'd warm her up immediately.

'Can you feel them?' he demanded. 'Your feet are so small they fit perfectly into my hands.'

He squeezed them between his burning hot fingers. Only her little pink toes protruded. She raised her heels and they heard the slight friction of her ankles. He opened his hands, looked at her feet for a few seconds, so fine, so delicate, with the big toes a little separate. The temptation was too much for him, he kissed them. Then, as she shuddered:

'No, no, get warm. When you've warmed up...'

Both had lost all consciousness of time and place. They had the vague feeling they were far advanced into a long winter's night. These candles, nearly extinguished in the drowsy dank room, made them imagine they must have been awake for hours. But they no longer knew where. A desert stretched out around them. No sound, no human voice, it felt like a dark sea with a storm blowing. They were far from the world, a thousand leagues away from the earth. And this forgetfulness of the bonds that attached them to beings and things was so absolute they seemed to have been born there at that moment and would die there in a little while when they took each other into their arms.

They could not even speak. Words no longer expressed the way they felt. Perhaps they had known each other in another place, but that former life was of no significance. Only the moment existed, and they dwelt in it for a long time, not speaking of their love, quite used to each other as if they had been already married for ten years.

'Are you warm?'

'Oh yes, thank you.'

A troubling thought made her lean over. She murmured:

'My slippers will never dry.'

He reassured her, picked up the little slippers and propped them up against the andirons, saying in a very low voice:

'They'll be bound to dry like that.'

He turned round, kissed her feet again and went on kissing her all the way up her leg. The coals which filled the hearth were burning them both. She was not upset by these hands, straying again with his desire, feeling their way. In the blotting out of everything surrounding her, and that included her own self, all she could think of was her young days, spent in a room as hot as this, a large stove with irons over which she had crouched; and she remembered that she had experienced a similar feeling of annihilation then, and the sensual delight, the sensation of slowly dying was no more voluptuous now under the rain of Henri's kisses. But when suddenly he seized her in his arms to carry her into the bedroom, one last worry beset her. She thought that someone had cried out, she thought she could hear someone sobbing in the darkness. But it was nothing but a little frisson; she looked around the room but there was no one there. This room was unknown to her, the objects in it meant nothing to her. The rain lashed down ever more violently, making a continuous racket. Then, as though overwhelmed by the need for sleep, she collapsed on to Henri's shoulder, allowed herself to be carried off. Behind them, the other curtain on the portière slipped from its loop.

When Hélène came back in her bare feet to fetch her slippers from in front of the dying embers, it occurred to her that never had they loved one another less than they had that day.

CHAPTER 5

JEANNE, her eyes on the door, was still very upset by the abrupt departure of her mother. She looked round. The bedroom was empty and silent, but she could still hear the sounds of her leaving, the hurried steps retreating, the rustle of her skirts, the landing door banging shut. Then, nothing. She was alone.

All alone. All alone. On the bed was her mother's dressing gown hastily jettisoned, undone, and with one sleeve lying across the pillow in a strange crumpled position, like someone who has fallen sobbing there, as if collapsed under the weight of her own pain. Underclothes lay around all over the place. A black scarf made a funereal mark on the floor. In the disorder of overturned chairs and the little table, which had been shoved against the large wardrobe, she was alone. She felt the sobs rise in her throat, when she saw this dressing gown without her mother in it, laid out and looking for all the world like an emaciated dead woman. She wrung her hands and called one last time: 'Maman, Maman!' But the blue velvet hangings muffled the sound in the room. It could not be helped, she was all alone.

Time passed. The clock struck three. The light through the window was a murky grey. Clouds the colour of soot floated past, darkening the sky even more. Through the window panes covered in a light film,

Paris was a blur, blotted out by the mist, the distances lost in great swirls. Even the city was not there to keep the child company, as it did in the bright afternoons when she thought that if she leaned out a little she would be able to touch the neighbouring houses with her hand.

What could she do? Her small, desperate arms clutched one another against her chest. Her abandoned state seemed black, limitless, the injustice and wickedness of it all made her furious. She had never encountered anything so mean, and imagined that everybody and everything would leave her and never come back. Then she saw her doll near her in an armchair, sitting propped up by a cushion, its legs stuck out and staring at her like a real person. It wasn't her wind-up doll, this was a large doll with a paste head, curly hair, and enamel eyes, and a stare that she sometimes found uncomfortable. In the last two years as she dressed and undressed her, the head had become scuffed on her chin and cheeks, the pink limbs stuffed with bran had started to look lanky and gangling like flabby old underclothes. At the moment the doll was in her nightwear, wearing only a vest, her arms dislocated, one pointing up and one down. Then Jeanne, feeling there was someone with her, was briefly less miserable. She caught hold of her, squeezed her very hard, so that her head swung back and her neck hung loose. And she chatted to her, she was a very well-behaved doll, she was kind, she never went out and left her all on her own. She was her treasure, her darling, her sweetest dolly. Shaking and still holding back her tears, she covered her with kisses.

This fury of kisses assuaged her feelings a little, the doll fell back in her arms like a rag. She stood up and looked out, her forehead pressed against the glass. The rain had stopped, the clouds from the last downpour had been carried off by gusts of wind and were moving across the horizon to the heights of Père-Lachaise that were hatched in grey lines. And against this stormy background and illuminated in an unvarying bright light, Paris assumed a solitary, gloomy grandeur. It seemed empty of people, like those cities in nightmares you see in the reflected light of some dead planet. Of course it wasn't a pretty sight. In an abstracted way she thought about the people she had loved in her life. Her oldest best friend in Marseilles was a large and very heavy marmalade cat. She would catch hold of him under his tummy, squeezing him in her little arms. She would carry him like that from one chair to the next without him getting angry. Then he had disappeared. That was the first bad thing she could remember.

After that she'd had a sparrow. It had died, she'd picked it up one morning from the bottom of its cage. That made two. That was not counting the toys that broke just to annoy her. She suffered a great deal because of the unfairness of it all, though it was silly of her. Especially one, a miniature doll, drove her to despair when it let its head get crushed. She had been so fond of it, she had even buried it secretly in a corner of the yard. And later, with a pressing need to see her again, she had dug her up and made herself sick with fear, when she found she was so blackened and ugly. It was always others who stopped loving her first. They broke, or they left you. Well anyway, it was their fault. But why? *She* did not change. When *she* loved someone it was for life. She could not understand why they went away. It was a terrible thing, monstrous, her little heart broke when she thought of it. She shuddered at the muddled thoughts which were slowly dawning on her. So one day they left you, you went your separate ways, you did not see them any more, you did not love them any more. And as she contemplated the immensity and melancholy that was Paris, the passionate twelve-year-old felt chilled by what she divined about the cruelty of life.

Meanwhile her breath had misted over the glass again. She rubbed away the film that prevented her from seeing anything. There were brown reflections of distant landmarks, washed by the rain, in the glass. Rows of houses, clean and distinct, with their pale fronts, looked like underclothes hung out on a line, like some colossal washing drying on fields of rust-coloured grass. It was getting lighter, the last piece of cloud which cloaked the city in mist let the milky rays of the sun through. And you could sense a hesitant gaiety above the different neighbourhoods, certain spots where the sky was going to smile. Jeanne looked down, on the bank and on the slopes of the Trocadéro at the life in the streets beginning again after the harsh rain which fell with sudden violence. The cabs started slowly bumping along again while in the silence of the still deserted streets the omnibuses rolled along twice as noisily. Umbrellas were folded, pedestrians sheltering under the trees ventured from one side of the street to the other, crossing the puddles running down into the gutters. Her attention was particularly taken by a very well-dressed lady and a little girl she saw standing under the awning of a toyshop near the bridge. They had probably taken shelter there, caught in the rain. The little girl was looking longingly at the shop, pestering her mother to buy her a hoop.

And both were leaving now, the child ran laughing and free, bowling the hoop along the pavement. Then Jeanne became very gloomy again, her doll seemed ugly to her. It was a hoop she wanted, and to be down there, running along while her mother walked slowly behind her shouting to her not to run on too far. Everything misted up again. She wiped the pane constantly. She had been forbidden to open the window, but she felt full of rebellious indignation; well, at least she could *look* out, even if she hadn't been taken out. She opened it and leaned on the sill like a grown-up, like her mother when she stood there in silence.

The air was mild and damp, it smelled good to her. A shadow, gradually creeping over the horizon, made her look up. Above her she felt as if there were a gigantic bird with spreading wings. At first she saw nothing, the sky was clear. But a black stain appeared on the corner of the roofs, spilled over and invaded the sky. It was a new squall propelled there by a blustery wind from the west. The light had faded rapidly, the town was black in a livid-coloured light which imparted the hue of old rust to the fronts of houses. Almost immediately the rain came down. The streets were swept clean. Umbrellas blew inside out, walkers fled for cover everywhere and disappeared like straws. An old lady clutched at her skirts with both hands while the rain beat down on her hat with the force of a downpour. And the rain cloud was moving across, you could follow it in its full-on rush towards Paris. The bore of heavy drops careered down the avenues by the river like a runaway horse raising a dust, that in a small white cloud rolled over the surface with prodigious speed. It went down the Champs-Élysées, surged into the long straight streets of the Quartier Saint-Germain, with a leap enveloping the wide spaces, the empty squares, the deserted junctions. In a few seconds, behind this cloth that was getting ever more opaque, the city grew paler and seemed to melt away. It was as if a curtain were being drawn from one side of the vast sky down to the earth. Vapours rose, the immense lapping noise made a din like the clatter of old iron.

Jeanne drew back, her head spinning with the noise. It seemed to her that a pale wall had risen in front of her. But she loved the rain, she came back to lean on the windowsill, and stretched out her arms to feel the big cold drops splash on to her hands. She liked that, she was soaked up to her sleeves. Her doll probably had a headache, like her. So she had just put her astride the sill and leaning against the wall. And when she saw the drops splashing on to her, she thought it was doing her good. The stiff doll with her little teeth and everlasting smile had one soaking shoulder as the wind blew, lifting her chemise. Her poor body, devoid of sawdust, was shivering.

So why had her mother not taken her with her? Because of the rain beating steadily on her hands, Jeanne was again tempted to go outside. How nice it would be out in the street! And again she could see, through the veil of rain, the little girl bowling her hoop along the pavement. You couldn't deny it, that little girl was out with her mother. And indeed they looked as though they were both very happy to be there. That proved that little girls went out, even when it was raining. But people had to want to do that. Why hadn't they wanted to? Then she thought once more of her marmalade cat who had gone away with its tail in the air up on to the houses opposite, and of that little sparrow creature which she had tried to feed when it was dead and which had pretended not to understand. Things like that were always happening to her, nobody loved her enough. Oh, she could have been ready in two minutes; some days when she wanted to she dressed herself quickly, her boots buttoned up by Rosalie, then the woollen jacket, the hat, and she was ready. Her mother might have waited for her for two minutes. When she was going down to visit friends, she did not throw her things all over the place like that. When she was going to the Bois de Boulogne, she walked along with her, holding her hand nicely, she stopped with her at all the shops on the Rue de Passy. And Jeanne could not understand; her black eyebrows furrowed, her fine features assumed the jealous, hard look and the pallor of a malevolent old maid. She had a vague feeling that her mother was somewhere where children are not allowed to go. She had not taken her, they were hiding something from her. At these thoughts her heart tightened in inexpressible sadness and pain.

The rain eased off. There were openings through the curtain which hung like a veil over Paris. The Dôme des Invalides was the first to reappear, light and trembling in the shining vibrations of the rain. Then some of the *quartiers* emerged from the water, which was receding, the city seemed to be rising out of a flood with its streaming roofs while rivers were still filling the streets with steam. But suddenly a flame burst forth and a ray of light struck into the midst of the showers. For an instant it was a smile through tears. It was not raining any more on the *quartier* of the Champs-Élysées, the rain cut its way along the Left

Bank, the Cité, the distant faubourgs. And you could see the drops like strokes of steel, coming thick and fast in the sun. To the right a rainbow lit up the sky. As the ray of light gradually broadened, pink and blue hatched stripes were daubed on the horizon in splatters of childish watercolours. There was a flaming, a falling of golden snow on a city of crystal. And the ray of light faded, a cloud had rolled across, the smile was drowning in tears, Paris was draining away in one long sound of sobbing beneath the leaden sky.

Jeanne, her sleeves soaked, had a fit of coughing. But, so preoccupied with the thought that her mother had gone down into Paris, she did not feel the cold penetrating her body. She managed to recognize three monuments, Les Invalides, the Panthéon, the Tour Saint-Jacques. She repeated their names, she could pick them out with her finger without being able to imagine how they would look close to. Probably her mother would be over there, and she thought likely she was in the Panthéon, because that was the building she found most astonishing, enormous as it was and sticking up in the air like the city's plume. She pondered the matter. For her, Paris was still the place where children did not go. Nobody ever took her there. She would have liked to know, to be able to tell herself quietly: 'Maman is there, she is doing such and such a thing', but it seemed too vast and you could not see anyone. Her eyes skipped to the other end of the plain. Was she not rather among that pile of houses on the left, on a hill? Or really close by under the tall trees, whose bare branches resembled logs of dead wood? Oh, to be able to lift off their roofs! And what was that very black monument? And that street in which there was something big running? And all that district she was afraid of, because for certain there were fights going on there. She could not make it out clearly. But truth to tell, there was something moving there, it was very ugly, little girls ought not to look. All sorts of vague suppositions which made her want to cry were troubling her in her childish ignorance. At this time of melt and thaw, Paris the unknown, with its smoke, its constant rumbling, its powerful life, was breathing out an odour of poverty, putrefaction, and crime which made her young head spin, as if she was leaning over one of those pestilential wells, which exhale their invisible mud and suffocate you. Les Invalides, the Panthéon, the Tour Saint-Jacques, she named them all, she counted them. Then, at a loss, she remained there, afraid and ashamed, and she couldn't rid herself of the idea that her mother was there among these sordid things, exactly where, she couldn't tell, over there in the distance.

Abruptly Jeanne turned. She could have sworn that there was a footstep in the bedroom, and even that there had been a light touch on her shoulder. But the room was empty, and still in the very untidy state Hélène had left it. The dressing gown was still lying prostrate and crumpled, apparently weeping into the bolster. Then Jeanne, pale as a ghost, looked quickly round the room, and her heart broke. She was alone, all alone. Oh God! Her mother, leaving, had pushed her, and so very violently she had fallen to the floor. That came back to her with anguish, she could feel once more the pain of that brutal action in her wrists and shoulders. Why had she struck her? She was a good little girl, she wasn't to blame for anything. Usually people spoke kindly to her, she was disgusted by this punishment. She felt as she had when she was scared as a little girl, when they threatened her with the wolf and she looked for it but couldn't see it; it was as if in the shadows there were things coming to crush her. However, she was suspicious and her face grew deathly pale with jealous rage. Suddenly the thought that her mother must love the people she had rushed to see more than her, throwing her so roughly out of the way, caused her to clutch her chest with both hands. Now she knew. Her mother was betraying her.

A great anxiety hung over Paris, in expectation of another squall. The darkened sky muttered, thick clouds were amassing. Jeanne at the window coughed violently. But she felt that by being cold she was getting her revenge, she wanted to be ill. Her hands held against her chest, she felt her discomfort increase. She was suffering and her body was delivering itself up to it. She shook with fear and dared not turn her head, the thought of looking at the bedroom again made her blood run cold. We do not have much strength when we are small. So what was the nature of this new pain, whose crisis filled her with both shame and a bitter satisfaction? When they teased her, tickled her, in spite of her laughter, she had felt this shudder of exasperation. She waited, her innocent, virgin limbs stiff and tense in revolt. And deep in her heart, from her loins where her womanhood was stirring, a sharp pain pierced her as if it were a blow she had received from somewhere far off. Then, half-fainting, she uttered a stifled cry: 'Maman, Maman!' without it being possible to detect if she was crying to her mother for help or if she was accusing her of sending her those ills which were causing her such agony.

At that moment the storm broke. The wind howled through the heavy, anxious silence hanging over the blackened city. And a prolonged noise of fracturing could be heard across Paris; shutters were rattling, slates were flying, chimney pots and gutters were bouncing down on to the cobbled streets. A few seconds' calm. Then came a new blast and filled the horizon with such almighty gusts that the ocean of roofs quaked and seemed to rise in waves and disappear in a whirlwind. For an instant all was chaos. Enormous clouds, spreading like ink-stains, ran into the midst of the smaller ones and broke them up, tearing them to bits like rags ripped apart by the wind, and carrying them off strand by strand. For one moment two clouds did battle with one another, broke up noisily, and scattered debris into the copper-coloured space; and every time the hurricane rose like that, blowing from every direction in the sky there was a violent colliding of airborne armies, an immense collapsing whose wreckage, suspended there, would come down and crush Paris. It was not yet raining. But suddenly a cloud burst on the centre of the city, torrents of rain flowed back up the Seine. The green ribbon of river, riddled and soiled by the pounding rain, turned into a stream of mud. And one by one behind the downpour the bridges reappeared, thinner, lighter in the vapour, while to right and left the deserted banks shook their trees in fury along the grey line of paths. In the distance above Notre-Dame, the cloud split and such cataracts poured down, the Cité was drowned. Alone above the submerged *quartier* the towers floated like wreckage in a pool of light. But the sky opened up in all directions, the Right Bank seemed to be submerged three times over. A first wave from the distant faubourgs, increasing in size, beat against the spires of Saint-Vincent-de-Paul and the Tour Saint-Jacques which whitened under the flood. Two more such torrents, one after the other, streamed down on Montmartre and the Champs-Élysées. At times you could see the glass in the Palais de l'Industrie steaming as the rain bounced off it; Saint-Augustin whose cupola rolled round in the depths of a fog like an extinguished moon, the Madeleine with its flat elongated roof like the thoroughly washed flagstones on some ruined forecourt. Behind these, the enormous, dark mass of the Opéra put you in mind of a dismasted ship, its hull caught between two rocks, resisting the assaults of the storm. On the Left Bank, through a haze of water, you could see the Dôme des Invalides, the towers of Sainte-Clotilde, the towers of Saint-Sulpice blurring at the edges and melting in the damp, soaking air. The cloud got bigger, the colonnade of the Panthéon loosed sheets of water which threatened to inundate the lower *quartiers*. And from that moment the rain beat down in every part of the city. You would have thought the sky was throwing itself at the earth. Streets foundered, went under entirely and resurfaced again, in great shuddering gusts whose violence seemed to presage the end of the city. A continuous grumbling noise could be heard, the voice of the swollen gutters, the thundering water emptying into the sewers. Meanwhile above the murky city, coloured a uniform dirty yellow by the downpours, the clouds were fraying, turning a pale livid hue, spreading evenly across the sky without fissure or stain. The rain became thinner, straighter, sharper. And when another gust came, great waves made the grey hatching shimmer, you could hear the oblique, almost horizontal rain lashing with a whistling noise against the walls until the wind dropped and it became vertical again, stabbing and stabbing at the ground until it quietened down from the heights of Passy to the flat land in Charenton. Then, as though it had been destroyed and had died in the wake of one final convulsion, the city lay effaced under the sky like a field of toppled stones.

Jeanne, slumped at the window, stammered 'Maman, Maman' again and in an immense fatigue, very weak, saw Paris under water. In this annihilation, her hair hanging down and her face wetted by the rain-drops, she still felt the bittersweet sensation which had just made her tremble, while inside she lamented for something that could never be mended. Everything seemed to be over, she thought she was growing very old. The hours might go by, she would not even look into the bedroom. It was all one to her to be alone and forgotten. Such despair filled her childish heart, everything went dark around her. It would be very unfair of them to scold her like they used to when she was ill. It was burning her, it hurt like a headache. Just now, something in her had been broken, that was certain. She could do nothing about it. She had to put up with whatever they decreed. When all was said and done, she was too tired. She had folded her two little arms on the windowsill and was growing sleepy; her head was propped up and from time to time she opened her eyes very wide to look at the rain.

And still it fell, the pale sky was melting into water. The last gust had passed and a monotonous rumbling could be heard. The sovereign rain was beating down ceaselessly into the solemn stillness, the silence and abandon of the subdued city. And a ghostly Paris in trembling shapes seemed to be dissolving into the crystalline streaks of this deluge. All it had to offer Jeanne now was the need to sleep, and have horrible dreams, as if all the mystery, the unknown evil, had breathed out its fog and was entering her body and making her cough. Every time she opened her eyes she had a coughing fit and she remained there, looking out for a few seconds; then, letting her head fall again, she carried that image in her, it seemed to her that it was spreading and crushing her.

It was still raining. Whatever time was it now? Jeanne could not have said. Perhaps the clock had stopped. It seemed to her she was too weary to turn round and look. Her mother had been gone at least a week. She had stopped waiting for her, she was resigned to not seeing her again. Then she forgot everything, the misery they had caused her, the strange pain she had just endured, even being left, abandoned by everyone. It was like a stone-cold weight upon her. But she was very unhappy, oh, she was as unhappy as those poor little lost children in doorways to whom she gave money. It would never end, she would be like that for years, it was too big and too heavy to bear for a little girl. Oh heavens, you coughed so much, you felt so cold when nobody loved you any more! She closed her heavy eyes, dizzy with fever and fatigue, and her last thought was a vague memory of her early childhood, visiting a windmill with yellow corn, very small grains which fell under millstones as big as houses.

Hours and hours went by. Every minute lasted a hundred years. The rain fell without stopping, at the same unhurried pace as though it had all the time in the world, an eternity, to flood the plain. Jeanne slept. Near her, the doll hanging over the windowsill, with her legs in the room and her head outside, looked as if she were drowned, with her chemise sticking to her pink skin, her eyes staring, her hair streaming wet. And she was pitifully thin, in her comical, desolating posture looking like a little dead thing. Jeanne coughed in her sleep. But she did not open her eyes. Her head dropped on to her folded arms, the cough tailed off in a whistle as she slept. And that was all, she was asleep in the dark, she did not even withdraw her hand; clear drops fell from her reddened fingers, one by one, into the vast spaces opening up under the window. It lasted for hours and hours. On the horizon Paris had vanished like a shadow city, the sky was lost in the bewildering chaos extending everywhere. The grey rain continued to fall, obstinately.

PART FIVE

CHAPTER 1

WHEN Hélène returned, night had long fallen.

As she struggled up the stairs holding on to the banisters, her umbrella dripped on to the steps. Outside her door she stayed there for a second or two to catch her breath, being still rather light-headed from the rain pouring down around her, the jostling elbows of people running, the reflection of the lamps dancing in the puddles. She walked in a dream, stunned by the kisses she had just received and given. And while she was looking for her key she was thinking that she felt neither remorse nor joy. It had happened and there was nothing she could do to change it. But she could not find her key. Probably she had left it in the pocket of her other dress. Then she was very put out, it seemed to her she had been shut out of her own house. She had to ring.

'Oh, it's Madame,' said Rosalie as she went to open it. 'I was beginning to get worried.' And taking the umbrella into the kitchen, she put it on the stone sink:

'What rain, eh? Zéphyrin has just arrived and is soaked as a sponge... I asked him to stay for supper, Madame, I hope that's all right? He's got ten hours' leave.'

Mechanically, Hélène followed her. She seemed to need to go into all the rooms in her apartment before taking her hat off.

'That was quite right, my dear,' she replied.

She stayed in the kitchen doorway one moment, looking at the lighted stove. Instinctively she opened a cupboard door and shut it again. All the furniture was in its place; she was glad to see it again. Meanwhile Zéphyrin had got up out of respect. She smiled and gave him a slight nod.

'I didn't know if I should put in the roast,' said the maid.

'Why, what time is it?' Hélène asked.

'It will soon be seven, Madame.'

'What? Seven o'clock!'

And she was very surprised. She had lost all track of time. This woke her.

'And what about Jeanne?' she said.

'Oh, she's been very good, Madame. I think she might even have fallen asleep because I haven't heard her.'

'So did you not take her a light?'

Rosalie was embarrassed, unwilling to admit that Zéphyrin had brought pictures. Mademoiselle had not made a sound, therefore Mademoiselle did not need anything. But Hélène was not listening. She went into the bedroom and went very cold all over.

'Jeanne, Jeanne!' she called.

There was no answering voice. She bumped into an armchair. The dining-room door which she had left half-open threw some light on a corner of the rug. She shivered, the rain seemed to be pouring in, blowing continuously right into the room. Turning, she saw the pale square of the window etched against the grey sky.

'Whoever opened that window!' she cried. 'Jeanne! Jeanne!'

Still no answer. She was worried to death. She tried to look out of the window, but as she groped towards it she felt someone's hair. Jeanne was there. And as Rosalie arrived with a lamp she could see the child, all white and sleeping with her cheek on her folded arms, the raindrops falling off the roof and wetting her. She was stricken with fatigue and despair, but she was no longer wheezing. Her large bluish eyelids still held two great tears on the lashes.

'Oh, my poor child!' Hélène stammered. 'What on earth! Oh God, she is so cold! Going to sleep there in such weather when she's forbidden to go near the window! Jeanne, Jeanne, answer me, wake up!' Rosalie had prudently kept out of the way. The little girl, whom her mother had taken in her arms, let her head flop as though she couldn't shake off the leaden sleep which had taken possession of her. But finally she opened her eyelids and remained there rigid, dazed, her eyes hurting in the light from the lamp.

'Jeanne, it's me. What's the matter? Look, I've just come in.'

But she did not understand, muttering stupidly:

'Oh... oh!'

She gazed at her mother as though she did not know her. Then suddenly she shivered as though she could feel how cold it was in the room. Her head cleared, the tears on her lashes rolled down her cheeks. She struggled, not wanting her mother to touch her.

'It's you, you! Oh, let me go, you are squeezing me. I was all right before.'

And, as if afraid of her, she slipped out of her arms. With an anxious look, she put her arms up to her mother's shoulders. One of her hands did not have a glove on and she shrank back from the bare wrist, the damp palm, the warm fingers, as wildly as she would flee from the caress of a stranger's hand. It wasn't the same verbena scent, the fingers had grown longer, her palm was softer. And she was unnerved by the contact of that skin, which seemed to have altered.

'Look, I'm not scolding you,' Hélène went on. 'But really, are you being a sensible girl? Give me a kiss.'

Jeanne still shrank from her. She could not recall seeing that dress, nor that coat her mother was wearing. The belt was loose, the folds fell in a way that she found irritating. Why then had she come back in such disarray, with something so very ugly and dowdy about her person? She had mud on her skirt, her slippers were bursting at the seams, *nothing was right*, as she was wont to say herself when she got angry with little girls who couldn't dress themselves properly.

'Give me a kiss, Jeanne.'

But this voice, which seemed louder to her, wasn't recognizable either. She looked up at her face and was surprised at how small and tired her eyes were, how feverishly red her lips, how strange the shadow which bathed the whole of her face. She did not like what she saw, she was starting to have a pain in her chest again, like when they hurt her. So, unhappy at all these things—subtle or crass—that she sensed, and realizing that she was breathing in the odour of treachery, she burst out sobbing.

'No no, please don't! Oh, you left me all alone, oh, I've been so unhappy!'

'But I've come back, darling... Don't cry, I'm here.'

'No, I can't any more... I don't want you... Oh, I've been waiting so long, I'm so poorly.'

Hélène had caught hold of her again and was drawing her gently towards her, but the little girl was obstinate:

'No, it's not the same any more, you are not the same.'

'What? What in the world are you saying, child?'

'I don't know, you are not the same.'

'Do you mean I don't love you any more?'

'I don't know, you are not the same. Don't say you are. You don't smell the same. It's over, it's over. I want to die.'

Hélène went very pale and held her in her arms again. So did it show on her face? She kissed her but the little girl shuddered with a look of such discomfort that she did not kiss her again on her forehead. She kept her arms around her, however. Neither spoke. Jeanne was weeping quietly in the nervous state of revolt which was making her rigid. Hélène was thinking that one must not take much account of the capricious behaviour of children. The fact was she was secretly ashamed, the weight of her daughter on her shoulder made her blush. Then she put Jeanne down. Both were relieved.

'Now be sensible, dry your eyes,' said Hélène again. 'It will be all right.'

The child obeyed, was very amenable, a little fearful, looking at her from under her lashes. But suddenly an attack of coughing shook her body.

'Oh God, now you are poorly! I can't leave you for a second. Were you cold?'

'Yes, Maman, my back.'

'Here, put this shawl round you. The stove in the dining room is lit. You'll warm up. Are you hungry?'

Jeanne hesitated. She was going to tell the truth and say no. But she gave her another sideways glance and drew back whispering:

'Yes, Maman.'

'Come along now, you'll soon be better,' declared Hélène, who needed to reassure herself. 'But please, you naughty girl, don't scare me like that again.'

When Rosalie came back to tell her that Madame was served, she gave her a good telling-off. The little maid bowed her head, and mumbled that it was quite true, she should have kept an eye on Mademoiselle. Then, to calm Madame, she helped her change her clothes. My word! Madame *was* in a dreadful state! Jeanne watched her clothes fall off her one by one, as though she wanted to interrogate them, as though she expected to see the things she was not to know slither out from those mud-bespattered underclothes. The tie of her petticoat was especially unyielding. Rosalie had to work hard for a moment to loosen the knot. And the child drew nearer, sharing the maid's impatience, getting cross with the knot, overcome with curiosity to know how it was tied. But she couldn't stay there, she took refuge behind an armchair, a long way from the warmth of the clothes that bothered her. She turned her head away. Never had she been so embarrassed by her mother changing her dress.

'Madame'll feel the benefit,' said Rosalie. 'It feels so good to have dry clothes when you have been wet.'

Hélène in her blue flannelette dressing gown uttered a little sigh, as if she were indeed now in a state of well-being. She was back at home, and felt lighter since she did not have to drag around the weight of the clothes any more. It was no good the maid reminding her that the soup was on the table, she insisted on a thorough wash of her face and hands. When she was completely clean, still damp, her dressing gown buttoned up to her chin, Jeanne came back to her side, took her hand, and kissed her.

However, at table neither mother nor daughter spoke. The stove roared, the little dining room was cheerful with its shining mahogany and its bright china. But Hélène seemed sunk once more in a torpor that prevented her thinking. She ate mechanically, as though she was hungry. Opposite her, Jeanne eyed her covertly over her glass, not missing a single move her mother made. She coughed. Her mother, forgetting her, was suddenly concerned.

'What! Are you still coughing? So are you not warming up?'

'Oh yes, Maman, I'm lovely and warm.'

She wanted to feel her hand, to find out if she were lying. Then she saw that her plate was still full.

'You said you were hungry... So don't you like it?'

'Yes, I do, Maman, I am eating.'

Jeanne was making an effort, swallowing a mouthful. Hélène watched her for a moment, then her mind went back to that room, and the darkness. And the child saw that her mind was no longer on her. Towards the end of the meal, her poor exhausted limbs had sunk on to the chair and she looked like a little old woman, with the pale eyes of those aged spinsters that no one will love any more.

'Mademoiselle doesn't want any stewed fruit?' Rosalie asked. 'So shall I clear away?'

Hélène still looked vague.

'Maman, I'm tired,' said Jeanne, in an altered voice. 'May I go to bed? I shall feel better there.'

Again her mother seemed to come back to her surroundings with a start.

'You are poorly, darling! Where is the pain? Tell me!'

'No, I told you! I'm sleepy. It's time to go to bed.'

She got down from her chair and stood up, to make her believe she was not ill. Her small stiff feet stumbled on the wooden floor. In the bedroom she leaned on the furniture, she was brave enough not to cry in spite of the fever that was burning her all over. Her mother came to put her to bed, and was only in time to tie back her hair, she was in such haste to take her clothes off herself. She slipped under the sheets and shut her eyes quickly.

'Are you all right?' asked Hélène, pulling the blankets over her and tucking her up.

'Yes, I am. Leave me alone, don't disturb me. Take the light away.'

She only wanted one thing, to be in the dark where she could open her eyes and feel her pain without anyone's eyes on her. When the lamp had been taken away, she opened her eyes wide. Meanwhile Hélène was walking back and forth in the bedroom next door. A strange urge to move around kept her on her feet, the thought of going to bed was unbearable. She looked at the clock. Twenty to nine. What was she going to do? She rummaged in a drawer, and then couldn't remember what she was looking for. Then she went over to the bookcase, glanced at the books, without taking down any. Just to read the titles bored her. The silence in the room was throbbing in her ears; the solitude, the heavy atmosphere, were becoming difficult for her to bear. She wanted noise, people, anything that would take her out of herself. Twice she listened at the door of the little bedroom, where Jeanne was breathing too softly to hear. Asleep. She walked round, picking up trinkets she came across and putting them down again. But then a sudden thought struck her: Zéphyrin must be with Rosalie still. Relieved and glad at the thought of no longer being on her own, she padded into the kitchen in her slippers.

As she pushed open the glass door in the little passage she heard the smack of a hefty slap. Rosalie's voice cried:

'Don't do that again! Get your paws off me!'

But Zéphyrin gave an answering growl:

'Don't mind me, my darling, I love you, that's all!'

But the door had creaked. When Hélène came in, the little soldier and the cook were seated serenely at the table with their eyes fixed on their plates. They were all innocence, it wasn't them making a noise, but their faces were very red. Their eyes glowed like candles, they were shifting around uneasily on their straw chairs. Rosalie made haste to get up.

'Does Madame need anything?'

Hélène had not thought of an excuse. She had come to see them, to chat, to be with someone. But she was embarrassed, she did not dare say she did not want anything.

'Have you any hot water?' she asked finally.

'No, Madame, and my fire is going out. Oh, I can do it, I'll give you some hot in five minutes. It'll boil straight away.'

She topped up with coal, put the kettle on. Then, seeing her mistress was still in the doorway:

'I'll bring it in five minutes, Madame.' Hélène made a vague gesture. 'I'm not in a hurry. I'll wait... Don't disturb yourself, my dear. You eat. This man will have to go back to the barracks soon.'

Rosalie consented to sit down. Zéphyrin, still standing, gave a military-style salute and attacked his meat again, spreading his elbows to show that he had manners.

When they ate together like that after Madame's dinner, they didn't even pull the table out into the middle of the kitchen, they preferred to sit side by side facing the wall. In that way they could rub knees, pinch and slap one another without missing a mouthful. And if they looked up, the splendid sight of the saucepans met their eyes. A bunch of laurel and thyme was hanging there, there was a peppery aroma from the spice box. Bits and pieces of the dessert lay around them in the kitchen which had not yet been cleared, but it was very pleasant there nevertheless for lovers with hearty appetites to treat themselves to dishes which were never served in the barracks. It smelled of roast meat, with a touch of vinegar, the vinegar of the salad dressing. The reflections from the gas danced in the copper and beaten iron pans. As the stove was ferociously hot, they had partly opened the window and the fresh air blew in from the garden and made the blue cotton curtain billow out.

'Do you have to be back at exactly ten?' asked Hélène.

'Yes, Madame, thank you kindly, I do,' Zéphyrin replied.

'It's a fair step! Do you take the omnibus?'

'Oh yes, Madame, sometimes... But sometimes I get there quicker by Shanks's pony.'

She had stepped down into the kitchen, and was leaning against the sideboard, with her hands clasped to her dressing gown. She was still chatting about the dreadful weather, about what they had to eat in the regiment, of how dear eggs were. But every time she asked a question and received an answer the conversation dried up. They were embarrassed by her being there behind them like that. They did not turn round any more, but talked while they ate, bending their shoulders under her gaze and swallowing small mouthfuls to eat politely. She, calmer now, felt comforted.

'You'll have to be patient, Madame,' said Rosalie. 'The water's bubbling now... If the flame was stronger...'

Hélène stopped her getting up. There was no hurry. But her legs were feeling extremely tired. Mechanically she crossed the kitchen, went over to the window where she saw the third chair, a very high wooden one which became a ladder when you turned it upside down. But she didn't immediately sit on it. She noticed a pile of pictures on a corner of the table.

'Oh, look at these!' she said, picking them up, wishing to be nice to Zéphyrin.

The little soldier laughed silently. He glowed with pleasure, looking at the pictures, nodding when Madame lit upon a particularly good one.

'I found that one in the Rue du Temple,' he said. 'It's a beautiful woman with flowers in her basket.'

Hélène sat down. She studied the beautiful woman, the cover of a glossy gold sweet tin that Zéphyrin had carefully wiped. A tea towel on the back of the chair was preventing her from leaning there. She pushed it out of the way and became absorbed in the picture once more. Then the two lovers, seeing Madame was being so friendly, were no longer embarrassed. They even forgot she was there. Hélène had dropped the pictures on her lap one by one. Smiling vaguely, she watched, she listened.

'Tell me, my love, don't you want some more lamb?'

He answered neither yes nor no, swung back on his chair as though someone was tickling him, and then stretched out luxuriously when she placed a thick slice on his plate. His red epaulettes rose and fell while his round head with the sticking-out ears was shaking in his yellow collar like a monkey's. You could see from his back he was laughing—fit to burst his tunic, which he never unbuttoned in the kitchen out of respect for Madame.

'This tastes better than old Rouvet's turnips!' he said finally, his mouth full.

That was a memory from home. They both split their sides laughing, and Rosalie held on to the table so as not to fall over. One day, before their first communion, Zéphyrin had stolen three turnips from old Rouvet. They were hard, oh, hard enough to break your teeth. But all the same Rosalie had eaten her share behind the school. Then, each time they had eaten together, Zéphyrin always said:

'That tastes better than old Rouvet's turnips!'

And every time he said it, Rosalie burst out laughing, so much that the strings on her petticoat snapped. You could hear the string going.

'Hey, have you broken it?' asked the little soldier in triumph.

His hands reached out to find the answer. But all he got was a slap.

'Keep your hands off! I don't s'pose you'll be the one mending it... It's stupid of you to snap the string. I have to sew another one on every week.'

Then as his hands were still all over her, she pinched up the skin between his fat fingers and twisted it. This affectionate gesture was exciting him even more, when she eyed him furiously, motioning in the direction of Madame who was watching. Without being too put out, and taking another mouthful, so big it swelled out his cheeks, he gave a knowing soldierly wink as though to say that women, and even ladies, didn't dislike that sort of thing. Of course, it's always nice to see when people love one another.

'Have you still got five years in the army?' asked Hélène, who had relaxed into the high wooden chair, forgetting herself in her present sense of well-being.

'Yes, Madame, or perhaps only four if they don't need me.'

Rosalie realized Madame had her marriage in mind. Pretending to be angry, she cried:

'Oh, Madame, he can stay another ten years, for all I care, I shan't be after depriving the government of him... He can't keep his hands to himself. I think that lot are bad for him. Oh, you may laugh. With me that doesn't wash. When Monsieur le Maire is here, that will be the time to have a joke.'

And as he chuckled louder, pretending to be a seducer in Madame's presence, the cook really lost her temper.

'Be off, is my advice to you! You know, Madame, he's such an oaf. Once they're in uniform they get like that. When they're with their comrades they give themselves airs. If I was to put him out, you'd hear him snivelling in the passage... and see if I'd care, my lad! And whenever I like, you'd still be there trying to find out what sort of stockings I'm wearing, wouldn't you?'

She eyed him closely. But when she saw him looking like that with an anxious expression creeping over his good-natured freckled face, she suddenly took pity on him. And without any noticeable transition, said:

'Oh, I forgot to say, I had a letter from my aunt. The Guignards are looking to sell their house. Yes, it costs almost nothing. Perhaps later we could...'

'I'll be damned!' said Zéphyrin, his face one big smile. 'We'd have our own little place. We could have a couple of cows.'

Then they were silent. They were on to their dessert. The little soldier was licking the grape jam off his bread, like a greedy child, while the cook was peeling an apple, carefully, with a motherly air. He had shoved his free hand under the table and was stroking her knees, but so very gently that she pretended not to feel it. While he kept within the bounds of decency, she did not get cross. She must even have enjoyed it without admitting as much, for she kept jigging up and down on her chair in little starts of pleasure. Truly that day it was all a great treat.

'Your water's boiling, Madame,' said Rosalie after a pause in the conversation.

Hélène did not move. She felt cocooned in their warmth for one another. And she elaborated on their dreams, she pictured them there in the Guignards' house with their two cows. It made her smile to see him so serious, his hand under the table while the little maid was holding herself very straight to avoid suspicion. The distance between them all seemed not so great, she no longer knew which was herself and which the others, where she was or what she was doing there. The copper pans shone bright on the walls, and she was kept there by a sort of inertia, lost to the world, not offended by the state of the kitchen. This self-abasement satisfied a need in her and she was relishing it mightily. She was, however, very hot, the heat from the stove produced drops of sweat on her pale forehead. But behind her, the half-open window blew delicious puffs of breeze down the back of her neck.

'Madame, your water's boiling,' Rosalie said again. 'There won't be anything left in that kettle.'

She put the kettle down in front of her. Taken momentarily by surprise, Hélène had to get up from her chair.

'Oh yes, thank you.'

She no longer had a pretext, and slowly, regretfully, she withdrew. In her room the kettle was an encumbrance. But her heart was bursting with passion. That torpor in which, like an imbecile, she had been confined, was dissolving now in a flood of excitement, that coursed through her, burning her. She shivered with the voluptuousness that she had not felt before. Memories revived in her, her senses awoke with a huge unquenched desire, too late. Right there in the middle of the room she stretched out her body, she raised and twisted her hands, feeling the tension cracking in her fingers. Oh, she loved him, she wanted him, she would give herself to him like that next time.

And the moment she took off her dressing gown and looked at her bare arms, a noise disturbed her, she thought she could hear Jeanne cough. Then she picked up the lamp. The child's eyes were shut, she seemed to be asleep. But when her mother, reassured, turned her back, she opened her eyes, her big black eyes and followed her as she left the room. She was not yet asleep, she did not want to be made to go to sleep. A new fit of coughing racked her throat, and she burrowed under the blanket, stifling it. Her mother would no longer notice now if she left. She kept her eyes open in the darkness, knowing all, as though she had just been reflecting, and was dying because of it, without a whimper.

CHAPTER 2

NEXT day Hélène was full of practical ideas. She woke with a compelling need to protect her own happiness, trembling with the fear she might lose Henri by doing something wrong. Getting up in the chill of the morning while the bedroom was still steadfastly slumbering, she adored him, she desired him, her whole being burst into life. Never before had she felt this need to be cunning. Her first thought was that she should see Juliette that very morning. In that way she could avoid embarrassing explanations, and enquiries that might compromise everything.

When she arrived at Madame Deberle's towards nine, she found her already up, pale and with reddened eyes like a tragedy queen. And as soon as she saw her, the poor woman threw herself into her arms, weeping, calling her her good angel. She swore she did not care in the slightest for that Malignon. Oh God, what a stupid affair! It would have been the death of her, for certain. She couldn't be doing with such things any more, the lies, the pain, the tyranny, feelings that were always the same. How good it was to find yourself free! She laughed in relief, then started sobbing again, begging her friend not to despise her. At bottom, this feverish cry was a cry of fear, she thought her husband must have found out everything. The day before, he had come back in a state of agitation. She bombarded Hélène with questions. Then, with an audacious facility which surprised even herself, the latter told her a story, inventing details liberally one after the other. She swore that her husband did not suspect anything. It was she who had found out about it all and in the desire to save her, had thought of breaking up the rendezvous. Juliette listened, went along with this tale, her face shining with a joy in the midst of her tears. Again she threw herself round her neck. And Hélène was not in the least embarrassed by her embraces, she did not have any of the scruples of loyalty that she had suffered before. When she left, after making her promise to remain calm, she laughed inwardly at how clever she had been, and went away, delighted with herself.

A few days passed. Hélène's entire life was disrupted. She no longer lived at home, in her every thought she lived at Henri's. Nothing existed except the house over the way, where her heart was. As soon as she had a pretext she ran round there, forgetting herself, happy to be breathing the same air as him. In the first ecstasy of possession, seeing Juliette made her feel happy since she was Henri's dependant. However, Henri had not managed to see her on her own even for a moment. She seemed to be making an art of delaying the time of their second rendezvous. But one evening in the hall when he was seeing her out, she had made him swear not to go back to the house in the Passage des Eaux, adding that that would compromise her. But both thrilled in expectation of the passion they would enjoy, they knew not where, somewhere, some night. And Hélène, haunted by that desire, lived only for that minute, indifferent to the rest, spending her days in hope, very happy except for the nagging feeling that Jeanne was coughing just nearby.

Jeanne coughed, an obstinate little dry cough, that worsened towards evening. Then she had a slight temperature. Sweating in her sleep weakened her. When her mother questioned her, she said she wasn't poorly, was not in pain. It was probably her cold dragging on. And Hélène, reassured by this explanation, and in her rapturous state not having a clear view of what was happening around her, dimly felt the weight of sorrow bruising and wounding her in some place she could not determine. Sometimes, in the middle of one of those inexplicable moments of joy which bathed her in love, she was overcome by anxiety and it seemed to her that something maleficent was behind her. She turned round and smiled. When one's happiness is too great, one is always fearful. No one was there. Jeanne had just coughed but she was drinking herb tea, so it was nothing.

Meanwhile one afternoon old Doctor Bodin, who was coming to pay a friendly call, had prolonged his visit, thinking hard and studying Jeanne surreptitiously with his little blue eyes. He questioned her, pretending to be having a game. That day he said nothing. But two days later he came again, and this time did not examine Jeanne, but with the benign air of an old man who has seen many things in his time, began to talk about travel. He used to be a surgeon in the army. He knew Italy well. It was a splendid country you needed to see in the spring. Why didn't Madame Grandjean take her daughter there? And so he skilfully brought the conversation round to advising a holiday there in the land of sun, as he called it. Hélène stared at him. Then he asserted that of course neither one of them was ill! But the change of air would do them good. She had gone a deathly white, ice-cold at the thought of leaving Paris. Oh God! To go so far away! To lose Henri so suddenly, leaving their love in limbo! It was such torture for her that she bent over Jeanne to hide her emotion. Did Jeanne want to go? The child had locked her little fingers together as if she were cold. Oh yes, she would love to! Oh, she would love to go to the sun, all on their own, just her mother and her. And on her poor little thin face, with the fever burning her cheeks, the hope of a new life beamed forth. But Hélène, sickened and suspicious, was not listening, now persuaded that everybody was against her, the abbé, Doctor Bodin, and Jeanne herself, on purpose to keep her away from Henri. When he saw that she was so pale the old doctor felt he had spoken out of turn. He hastened to say that there was no hurry, and resolved to bring up the subject at a later date.

Madame Deberle, in the event, must be at home that day. As soon as the doctor had left, Hélène hurriedly put on her hat. Jeanne refused to go out. She felt better by the fire. She would be good and not open the window. For some time now she had not pestered her mother to take her with her, she just stared at her as she left. Then when she was alone she curled up in her chair and remained there for hours without moving.

'Maman, is Italy a long way away?' she asked when Hélène came to kiss her.

'Oh, a very long way, darling.'

But Jeanne clung to her neck. She did not let her stand up again straight away, but murmured:

'Why can't we go? Rosalie could look after your things. We shouldn't need her... With a small trunk, you know... Oh, it would be lovely, Maman! Only us two! I would be really plump by the time I came back, look, like this!'

She puffed out her cheeks and her arms described a curve. Hélène said she would see. Then she slipped away, telling Rosalie to keep a close eye on Mademoiselle. So the child curled up in a ball by the fireside, looking at the fire burning, sunk in a reverie. From time to time she put her hands to the fire, mechanically, to warm them. The reflection from the fire tired her big eyes. She was so lost to the world that she did not hear Monsieur Rambaud come in. He was making lots of visits. He had come, he said, on account of the disabled woman that Doctor Deberle had not yet managed to get into the hospice. When he saw that Jeanne was all alone he sat down on the other side of the fire and chatted to her as if she were a grown-up. It was very worrying, this poor woman had been waiting for a week. But he'd go down in a while and see the doctor, who would perhaps be able to give him an answer. Still he did not move.

'So didn't your mother take you with her?' he asked.

Jeanne gave a slight shrug in a tired sort of way. She couldn't be bothered to go out. Nothing pleased her now.

She added:

'I'm growing up, I can't go on playing for ever. Maman likes going out and I like staying in. So we are not good company for one another.'

There was a silence. The child shivered and held up her hands to the fire that was burning with a bright rosy flame. And she did indeed resemble a little old lady wrapped up in a huge shawl, with a scarf round her neck and another round her head. You could well imagine that underneath all those clothes she was no bigger than a frail little bird, dishevelled and blowing into its feathers. Monsieur Rambaud, hands clasped on his lap, was gazing into the fire. Turning to Jeanne, he asked her if her mother had gone out the previous day. She nodded.

And the day before, and the day before that? She kept nodding her head in assent. Her mother went out every day. Then Monsieur Rambaud and the little girl looked at each other for a long time with faces that were pale and solemn, as though they had a deep sorrow to share. They did not speak of it, because a little girl and an old man cannot speak of things like that to each other. But they knew why they were so sad and why they liked staying there on the right and left of the fireside in the empty house. That gave them some consolation. They drew closer to each other so that they wouldn't feel quite so abandoned. They felt moved by a great tenderness and pity, they wanted to hug each other and cry.

'You are cold, I am sure you are. Come nearer the fire.'

'No no, darling, I'm not cold.'

'Oh, you fibber! Your hands are like ice. Come a bit nearer or I'll be cross.'

Then he was the one to get worried.

'I'll bet nobody has left you any herb tea... I'll make some for you, shall I? Oh, I know how to make it. If I were looking after you, you'd see, you would have everything you needed.'

He did not allow himself to make any further innuendoes. Jeanne protested that she found herb tea disgusting, they made her drink too much of it. But on occasions she let Monsieur Rambaud fuss around her like a mother. He propped her up with a pillow, gave her the medicine she would have forgotten, offered her his arm to hang on to in her room. They were both very attached to these little attentions. As Jeanne explained with the intense look the good fellow found so upsetting, they were playing at being father and daughter while the mother was out. Suddenly they were overcome with sadness, said no more, but studied one another covertly, pityingly.

That day after a lengthy silence, the child repeated the question she had already put to her mother:

'Italy, is it a long way away?'

'Oh yes, I think so,' said Monsieur Rambaud. 'It's over there beyond Marseilles, somewhere. Why do you ask?'

'No reason,' she declared solemnly.

Then she complained of her ignorance. She had always been ill and hadn't gone to school. Both were silent, the very hot fire was sending them to sleep.

Meanwhile Hélène had found Madame Deberle and her sister

Pauline in the Japanese conservatory where they often spent the afternoon. It was very warm in there, a gas heater gave off a suffocating heat. The large windows were shut. You could see the narrow garden in its winter garb, like a big sepia photograph, perfectly finished, with the little black branches of the trees standing out against the brown earth. The two sisters were having an acrimonious discussion.

'Oh, don't be silly!' cried Juliette. 'It's in our interest to support Turkey, obviously.'

'I've been speaking to a Russian,' Pauline replied, just as animated. 'People in St Petersburg like us. Our true allies are in that part of the world.'

But Juliette adopted a grave attitude and folded her arms: 'So what do you do about the balance of Europe?'

The Eastern question* was the talk of Paris, it was on everyone's lips, any half-enlightened woman could not decently discuss anything else. So for the last two days Madame Deberle had been deep into foreign politics, and spoke with some conviction. She held very fixed opinions about the different impending outcomes. Her sister Pauline annoyed her a great deal because she was of the bizarre view that they should support Russia, which was quite obviously contrary to the interests of France. She tried persuasion at first, and then got cross with her.

'Oh, be quiet, such foolish things you say. If only you had studied the question as I have...'

She broke off to greet Hélène who had come in.

'Good morning, my dear. So nice of you to come. You haven't heard the news: they're talking about delivering an ultimatum. The Chambre des Communes has had a very turbulent session.'

'No, I haven't heard anything,' Hélène replied, taken aback by the question. 'I get out so rarely.'

Juliette had not waited for her reply in any case. She was explaining to Pauline why they had to make the Black Sea a neutral zone, dropping first names of the English and Russian generals into the conversation from time to time, in a very careful accent. But Henri had just appeared, holding a pile of newspapers in his hand. Hélène realized he'd come down to see her. Their eyes had met, and they had let them dwell on one another; then their entire selves were enfolded in a long, silent handshake.

'What's in the papers?' Juliette asked feverishly.

'In the newspapers, my dear?' asked the doctor. 'There's never anything.'

The Eastern question was forgotten for the time being. Several times they spoke of someone they were expecting who had not arrived. Pauline remarked that it was nearly three o'clock. Oh, he would come, affirmed Madame Deberle. He had promised faithfully. But she didn't say who. Hélène was listening, but did not take it in. Anything which did not have to do with Henri was of no interest to her. She no longer brought her needlework, she stayed two hours, took no part in the conversation, her head often full of the same childish fancies, imagining that by some miracle everyone else had disappeared and that she was left alone with him. However, she did answer Juliette when she asked something, at the same time painfully and deliciously aware of Henri's eyes for ever on hers. He went over behind her chair as though to raise one of the shutters and she could tell, by the slight brushing against her hair, that he was demanding a rendezvous. She was willing, she could not resist him any longer.

'There's the bell, it must be him,' said Pauline suddenly. The two sisters feigned indifference. It was Malignon who appeared, even more smartly turned out than usual, with a touch of the formal about him. He shook the proffered hands, but avoided his normal pleasantries, he was coming back formally into the house he had not frequented for some time. While the doctor and Pauline complained of the rarity of his visits, Juliette leaned over to whisper to Hélène, who, although she was really indifferent, was taken by surprise.

'Are you surprised then? Oh my goodness, I don't bear him a grudge. Basically he is such a nice boy, you can't be cross with him for long. Just think, he has unearthed a husband for Pauline. That's nice of him, don't you think?'

'Of course,' Hélène replied, to be agreeable.

'Yes, one of his friends, a very rich man, with marriage the last thing on his mind, and whom he swore to bring along... We were expecting him today, to have a definite answer... So, as you can imagine I had to shut my eyes to a lot of things. Oh, there's no problem, we are good friends now.'

She laughed prettily, blushing a little at the memory. Then she quickly commandeered Malignon's attention. Hélène smiled back. This easy-going attitude meant her conduct was also excused. It was quite wrong of her to imagine dire tragedies, everything was resolved in such a delightful, good-natured fashion. But just while she was experiencing the pusillanimous happiness of telling herself that nothing was out of bounds, Juliette and Pauline opened the door of the conservatory and were conducting Malignon into the garden. All at once behind her head she heard Henri's voice, low and urgent:

'Please, Hélène, I beg you.'

She shivered and looked about her, worried once more. They were definitely on their own, she caught sight of the other three walking slowly along a path. Henri went so far as to catch hold of her by the shoulders; she trembled, but her terror was full of rapture.

'Whenever you like,' she faltered, realizing that he was asking for a rendezvous.

And they exchanged a few swift words.

'Wait for me tonight in that house in the Passage des Eaux.'

'No, I can't. I told you, you swore...'

'Somewhere else then, where you like, as long as I can see you. At your house, tonight?'

She was repelled, but could only show it by a gesture, seized as she was with terror again at seeing the two women and Malignon coming back. Madame Deberle had pretended to take the young man to see something marvellous, clumps of violets in full flower in spite of the cold weather. She hurried back and was first to come in, smiling happily.

'It's done!' she said.

'What is?' asked Hélène, still shaken and unable to remember what she meant.

'This marriage, of course! Oh, that's a good thing done. Pauline was starting to make difficulties. The young man has seen her and thinks she's charming. Tomorrow we'll all have dinner at Papa's. I could have hugged Malignon for bringing us such good news.'

Henri, perfectly cool, had managed to manoeuvre himself away from Hélène. He too thought Malignon charming. He seemed fully to share his wife's delight at seeing their younger sister set up.

Then he told Hélène that she was about to lose one of her gloves. She thanked him. In the garden you could hear Pauline's voice joking. She was leaning over to Malignon, whispering one or two words to him and bursting into laughter when he whispered back in her ear. No doubt he was telling her things about her intended. Through the door of the conservatory which had been left open Hélène was drinking in the fresh air.

Back in her house, at that very moment, Jeanne and Monsieur Rambaud had fallen silent, lulled into torpor by the heat of the fire. The child emerged from the long silence and suddenly asked, as though this question was the conclusion of her reverie:

'Shall we go into the kitchen? We'll see if we can see Maman.'

'Yes, all right,' answered Monsieur Rambaud.

She was rather stronger that day. She walked without help and flattened her face against the window. Monsieur Rambaud also looked out into the garden. There were no leaves, through the large clear glass you could easily see inside the Japanese conservatory. Rosalie, who was tending a stew, told Mademoiselle she was being nosey. But the little girl had recognized her mother's dress, and she pointed it out, pressing her face to the glass for a better view. Meanwhile Pauline had looked up and waved. Hélène appeared and beckoned to her.

'They have seen you, Mademoiselle,' said the cook. 'They are telling you to go down.'

Monsieur Rambaud had to open the window. They asked him to bring Jeanne down, everybody wanted her to come. Jeanne ran into her bedroom again, in a passionate refusal, accusing her friend of tapping deliberately on the window. She liked to watch her mother but she didn't want to go to that house again. And to all the pleadings of Monsieur Rambaud she replied with her dreadful word 'because', as though that explained everything.

'You are not the one who should be making me go,' she said finally in dark tones.

But he told her again that she would make her mother very sad, that you couldn't behave in that silly way with people. He would put a warm coat on her, she wouldn't be cold. And as he spoke he tied the shawl around her waist, took off the scarf she had over her head and replaced it with a little woollen hat. When she was ready, she still protested. Finally she allowed herself to be taken out on condition he would bring her back straight away if she felt too ill. The concierge opened the communicating door and in the garden there were joyous greetings and exclamations. Madame Deberle especially showed a great deal of affection towards Jeanne. She settled her into a chair near the heating vent, wanted them to shut the windows immediately, remarking that the air was a little fresh for the poor child. Malignon had left. And as Hélène tidied the little girl's dishevelled hair, a little ashamed to see her like that in society, wrapped up in a shawl and with a woollen hat, Juliette exclaimed:

'Leave her alone! We are all family here! Poor Jeanne! We have missed her so.'

She rang to ask if Mademoiselle Smithson and Lucien had returned from their daily walk. They had not. In any case Lucien was getting out of hand, he had made the five Levasseur girls cry the day before.

'Shall we play "I Spy"?' asked Pauline, light-headed at the idea of her approaching marriage. 'It's not too tiring.'

But Jeanne shook her head. Slowly, from under her lashes she observed the people around her. The doctor had just informed Monsieur Rambaud that his protégée had at long last been taken into the hospice and the latter, very touched, took hold of his hands as though he had received from him a personal kindness. Everyone relaxed in an armchair and the conversation became charmingly informal. The talking tailed off and there were occasional silences. Since Madame Deberle and her sister were chatting together, Hélène said to the two men:

'Doctor Bodin has recommended a trip to Italy.'

'Oh, so that's why Jeanne was asking me!' cried Monsieur Rambaud. 'Would you like to go there?'

The child did not answer but put her two little hands on her chest, and her grey face lit up. Her eyes had slid fearfully over to the doctor, for she realized that her mother was consulting him. There was a slight tremor but he remained very cool. Then suddenly Juliette intervened, wanting, as usual, to be in on every conversation.

'What? Were you talking about Italy? Were you saying you are going to Italy? What a coincidence! This very morning I was pestering Henri to take me to Naples... Just think, I've been wanting to go to Naples for the last ten years. Every spring he promises me and then doesn't keep his word.'

'I didn't say I didn't want to,' murmured the doctor.

'What? You didn't say that? You refused point-blank, you said you couldn't leave your patients.'

Jeanne was listening. A long line creased her innocent face, and she fidgeted with her fingers, mechanically, one after the other.

'Oh, as far my patients are concerned,' went on the doctor, 'I could entrust them to a colleague... If I thought you would enjoy it so much...'

'Doctor,' Hélène interrupted, 'are you also of the opinion that such a trip would be all right for Jeanne?'

'It would be excellent, it would get her completely back on her feet. A trip always does a child good.'

'So let's take Lucien,' cried Juliette, 'and we'll all go together. Would you like that?'

'Of course, whatever you like,' he replied with a smile.

Jeanne hung her head and wiped away two large tears of anger and despondency that stung her eyes. And she slumped down into the armchair, as if she did not wish to hear or see any more, while there was a rush of loud exclamations from Madame Deberle, delighted by this unexpected offer of entertainment. Oh, it was so kind of her husband! She kissed him for taking the trouble. She immediately started talking about preparations. They would go next week. Oh my goodness, she would never have time to get everything ready! Then she wanted to work out an itinerary; they had to go via such and such a town; they would stay a week in Rome, then stop in a charming little place that Madame Guiraud had told her about. And she ended up quarrelling with Pauline who asked if they could put off the trip so that her husband could come as well.

'Oh, good gracious no!' she said. 'We'll have the wedding when we get back.'

Jeanne was quite forgotten. She was studying her mother and the doctor closely. Hélène was definitely in favour of this trip now, which would surely bring Henri and her closer. It would be a great delight to go away together to sunny climes, live side by side all day, take advantage of any hours that might be free. A relieved smile spread across her lips; she had been so afraid of losing him, she was so happy to be able to go away, with all her love intact! And while Juliette was listing all the places they would go through, both of them were already imagining walking into an ideal springtime, saying with a look that they would love one other in this or that place, everywhere they visited together.

Meanwhile Monsieur Rambaud, who had grown somewhat quiet and gloomy, noticed Jeanne's distress.

'Are you not feeling well, darling?' he whispered to her.

'No, I am really poorly... Take me back up, please.'

'But we have to tell your mother.'

'No, no, Maman is busy, she hasn't time. Take me back up, take me back up.'

He picked her up in his arms, saying to Hélène that the little girl was rather tired. Then she asked him to wait for her upstairs, she would follow. Although Jeanne did not weigh much, she slipped out of his hands and he had to rest on the second floor. She had leaned her head against his shoulder and the two of them looked mournfully at one another. Not a sound came to disturb the icy silence of the staircase. He whispered:

'You are pleased about going to Italy, aren't you?'

But she burst out sobbing, stammering that she didn't want to any more, she'd rather die in her bedroom. Oh, she would not go, she would be ill, she could sense it. Nowhere, she wouldn't be going anywhere. They could give her little shoes to the poor. Then through her tears she whispered to him.

'Do you remember what you asked me one evening?'

'What was that, darling?'

'If you should live with Maman for good. Well, if you still want to, I'd like that too.'

Monsieur Rambaud's eyes filled with tears again. He kissed her gently, while she added, still more quietly:

'Perhaps you are cross because I got angry. I didn't know then, you see. But you are the one I want. Oh, tell me right now, now... I love you more than the other one.'

Downstairs in the conservatory Hélène was forgetting herself again. They were still talking about the trip. She felt an overwhelming desire to open her bursting heart and spill out to Henri all the feelings of happiness which were suffocating her. So while Juliette and Pauline were discussing which dresses to take with them she leaned towards him and agreed to the rendezvous she had refused an hour earlier.

'Come tonight, I'll expect you.'

But when she finally came up, she met a distraught Rosalie, who was running down the stairs. As soon as she saw her mistress, the maidservant cried out:

'Madame, Madame! Hurry! Mademoiselle is unwell. She is spitting blood.'

CHAPTER 3

WHEN they left the table the doctor told his wife there was a lady about to give birth, whom he would doubtless have to spend the night attending. He left at nine, went down to the waterside and walked along the deserted banks, in the black night. A little damp breeze was blowing, the swollen Seine was flowing in ink-black waves. When it struck eleven he went back up the slope by the Trocadéro and started prowling around the house, whose dark square shape just looked like a darker shadow in the night. But there was still light from the windows of the dining room. He walked once round the house, there was also a bright light from the kitchen window. Then he waited in surprise, growing more and more anxious. Shadows passed behind the curtains, people seemed to be moving around the apartment. Perhaps Monsieur Rambaud had stayed for dinner? And yet this good man never allowed himself to stay beyond ten o'clock. And he did not dare go up. What would he say if Rosalie opened the door to him? Finally, towards midnight, mad with frustration, casting all precautions aside, he rang the bell, and passed Madame Bergeret's lodge without a word. At the top of the stairs it was Rosalie who greeted him.

'Oh, it's you, Doctor. Come in. You've arrived. Madame must be expecting you, I'll tell her.'

She showed no surprise at seeing him there at that time of night. While he entered the dining room without a word, she went on, very upset:

'Oh, Mademoiselle is very poorly, sir, very poorly. What a night! And my legs are killing me.'

She left. The doctor instinctively sat down. He had forgotten he was a doctor. Along the banks he'd been dreaming of that room where Hélène would receive him, finger to her lips, that he shouldn't wake Jeanne asleep in the adjoining room. The night light would be burning, the room shrouded in darkness, they would kiss silently. And here he was apparently making a formal call, waiting, with his hat on his knees. Behind the door nothing broke the silence but a hacking cough.

Rosalie reappeared, crossed the dining room rapidly, a bowl in her hand, and said curtly:

'Madame says not to come in.'

He remained there, unable to leave. So was the rendezvous then to be another day? It stopped him in his tracks like an impossibility. Then he thought: poor Jeanne was really not a healthy child. Children gave you nothing but trouble and strife. But the door opened again and Doctor Bodin came out, apologizing the while. He strung together a few brief words: they had come to get him, but he would always be very happy to consult his illustrious colleague.

'Of course, of course,' Doctor Deberle repeated, his ears buzzing.

Reassured, the old doctor said he was perplexed, couldn't make up his mind about a diagnosis. Lowering his voice, he discussed the symptoms, using technical words in sentences that were interspersed and concluded with a blink of his eyes. There was a cough without expectoration, total exhaustion, and a high temperature. Could it be typhoid fever? However, he could not reach a conclusion, the chloranaemic neurosis which the patient had been treated for over such a long period, made him fear unforeseen complications.

'What do you think?' he asked after each phrase.

Doctor Deberle replied with evasive gestures. While his colleague was speaking he became more and more ashamed of being there. Why had he come up?

'I've placed two vesicants on her,' the old doctor continued. 'We shall see how she is, shan't we? But you go and look at her. Then you'll be able to make up your own mind.'

He took him into the room. Henri trembled as he went in. The room was dimly lit by a lamp. He remembered other nights like that, the same warm smell, the same close, peaceful atmosphere and deep shadows of the furniture and curtains which seemed to be asleep. But no one came over to him as they had before, with hands held out. Monsieur Rambaud, collapsed in an armchair, seemed to be dozing. Hélène in a white dressing gown was standing by the bed and did not turn her head. And her white face seemed very large. So for a minute he examined Jeanne. She was so weak and she could not open her eyes without it fatiguing her. She was heavy and bathed in sweat, her cheeks flushed red in her pale face.

'It's acute consumption,' he muttered finally, speaking out loud without meaning to, and not showing any surprise, as though he had seen it coming for a long time.

Hélène heard and looked at him. She was completely cold, dry-eyed, and terribly calm.

'Do you think so?' said Doctor Bodin nodding, in the approving manner of a man who would not have wanted to be the first to pronounce.

He listened to the child's breathing again. Jeanne, limbs inert, lent herself to the examination without appearing to understand why they were torturing her like that. A few words were exchanged between the two doctors. The old doctor muttered something about amphoric respiration and the 'cracked pot sound', yet he still seemed to waver, talking now of a capillary bronchitis. Doctor Deberle explained that there must have been an accidental reason for the illness, catching cold probably, but that he had already several times observed the chloro-anaemia that gave rise to chest infections. Hélène was standing behind them, waiting.

'You listen to her now,' said Doctor Bodin, making way for Henri.

Henri leaned over to lift Jeanne up. She had not opened her eyes, but abandoned herself to the fever that was burning her. Her nightdress was undone and you could see her childish chest, and the scarcely visible naissant swelling of her breasts. And nothing was more chaste or heartbreaking than this puberty already touched by Death. She had not resisted the hands of the old doctor at all. But as soon as Henri's fingers touched her, a sort of jolt went through her body. A fierce modesty roused her from the unconscious state into which she had sunk. She made a movement like a woman taken by surprise, violated, she clutched at her breast with her two poor thin little arms, and stammered in a trembling voice:

'Maman... Maman...'

And she opened her eyes. When she recognized the man standing over her, she was terrified. She saw her nakedness, she sobbed in shame, rapidly drawing the sheet up round her. In her agony she seemed to have aged by ten years all at once, and, near to death, her twelve years were enough to understand that this man should not touch either her, or her mother through her. She cried again, in a desperate call for help:

'Maman, Maman, please...'

Silently, Hélène came and stood by Henri. She stared at him, stonyfaced. Touching him, she uttered just one word in a strangled voice:

'Go!'

Doctor Bodin tried to quieten Jeanne, who was shaken by a fit of coughing in the bed. He swore they would not disturb her any more and that everyone would go away and leave her in peace.

'Go!' repeated Hélène, in her low, deep voice, in her lover's ear. 'You can see we've killed her.'

Speechless, Henri left. He stayed a moment in the dining room, waiting for something to happen, he knew not what. Then seeing that Doctor Bodin did not come out of the room, he groped his way downstairs without Rosalie even lighting his way. He was thinking of the alarming rate at which acute consumption advanced. He had studied cases in depth. The miliary tubercles would multiply, there would be an increase in fits of choking, Jeanne would not live more than three weeks.

A week went by. The sun rose and set in the great Paris sky which stretched away outside the window, without Hélène being exactly aware of the rhythm of the days inexorably passing. She knew her daughter was going to die, she was like a woman stunned, horrified by the laceration within her. She waited without hope, only certain that death would not bring any forgiveness. She could not shed tears, she walked softly around the room, was always on her feet tending to the sick girl with slow, measured movements. Sometimes, overcome with tiredness, she collapsed into a chair and looked at her for hours on end. Jeanne was getting weaker. She was assailed and exhausted by bouts of vomiting and the fever did not abate. When Doctor Bodin arrived, he examined her briefly and left a prescription. And as he withdrew, his bent back conveyed such impotence that her mother did not even bother to go out and question him. The very next day after the crisis, Abbé Jouve had hurried along. He and his brother called every evening and exchanged a silent handshake with Hélène, not daring to ask for news. They had offered to take it in turns to sit with her, but she sent them away before ten, not wanting anyone in the room during the night. One day the abbé, who had seemed very preoccupied for a couple of days, took her to one side.

'I've been thinking,' he said quietly. 'The dear child has been held back on account of her poor health. She could make her First Communion here.'

At first Hélène seemed not to understand. The thought that, in spite of his open-mindedness, the priest in him, with his concerns about heaven, had wholly resurfaced, surprised her and even offended her a little. She shrugged and said:

'No, no, I don't want her disturbed. If there is a paradise, she will go straight there.'

But that evening Jeanne had one of those illusory revivals that deceive the dying. Her hearing, made more acute by her illness, had picked up the abbé's words.

'Oh, it's you, my dear friend,' she said. 'You said something about communion. We can do it soon, can't we?'

'Of course, darling,' he replied.

Then she wanted him to come closer to have a talk. Her mother had raised her on her pillow, she was sitting up, and looked very small. Her chapped lips were smiling, while in her bright eyes, death was already passing.

'Oh, I'm very well,' she said. 'I'd get up if I wanted to. Tell me, would I have a white dress with a bouquet? Will the church be as beautiful as it is for the Month of Mary?'

'More beautiful, sweetheart.'

'Truly? Will there be that many flowers? And will they sing such lovely hymns?'

She was suffused with joy. She looked at the curtains around her bed, in a sort of ecstasy saying that she loved God and had seen Him when they were singing the canticles. She could hear the organ music, and see moving lights, while the flowers in the great vases floated down like butterflies. She was racked by a violent fit of coughing and was thrown back on to the bed. But she went on smiling, not apparently realizing she was coughing, but saying over and over:

'I'm getting up tomorrow, I'll learn my catechism by heart and we shall all be very happy.'

At the foot of the bed Hélène uttered a sob. She, who could not weep, felt floods of tears rising in her throat as she listened to Jeanne's laughter. She was choking, she escaped into the dining room to hide her despair. The priest followed her. Monsieur Rambaud had quickly got up to distract the little girl.

'Oh, Maman cried out, has she hurt herself?' she asked.

'Your Maman?' he replied. 'She didn't shout, no, no, she was laughing because you are well.'

In the dining room, Hélène, at the table with her head in her hands, was making an effort to suppress her sobs. The priest bent down, begging her to stop. But lifting up her streaming face, she blamed herself, saying she had killed her daughter. And an entire confession in broken phrases issued from her mouth. She would never have given in to that man if Jeanne had been with her. She had been obliged to go and meet him in that secret room. Oh God, why didn't Heaven take her at the same time as her daughter? She could not go on living. The priest in alarm calmed her down and promised her forgiveness.

There was a ring on the doorbell and the sound of voices on the landing. Hélène was wiping her tears away when Rosalie came in.

'It's Doctor Deberle, Madame.'

'I don't want to see him.'

'He's asking for news of Mademoiselle.'

'Tell him she's dying.'

The door had remained open and Henri heard.

Then, without waiting for the maidservant, he went downstairs. Every day he went up to the apartment, received the same answer, and went away again.

But it was the visits that broke Hélène's heart. The few ladies she had got to know at the Deberles felt they should come to express their sympathy. Madame de Chermette, Madame Levasseur, Madame de Guiraud, among others, arrived. They did not insist on coming in, but questioned Rosalie so loudly that the sound of their voices came through the thin walls of the little apartment. Then, her impatience getting the upper hand, Hélène received them standing in the dining room, without saying much. She wore her dressing gown all day, forgetting to change her linen, her lovely hair simply twisted up at the back. Her eyes in her flushed face kept closing through tiredness, her sour breath, furred mouth could no longer find any words. When Juliette came up, she could not very well forbid her to come into the bedroom, but let her sit briefly next to the bed.

'My dear,' said Juliette one day in a friendly fashion. 'You are letting yourself go. You must be brave.'

And Hélène was forced to answer, while Juliette tried to take her mind off it by discussing the things people were talking about in Paris.

'We are definitely going to war, you know. I am very worried. I've got two cousins who will go and fight.'

She came up like that when she returned from her shopping trips across Paris, animated from a whole afternoon's chatting, brushing into this quiet sickroom with a whirl of her long skirts; and it was no use her keeping her voice down and putting on a sympathetic expression, her radiant indifference shone through, you could see that she was happy and triumphant that she herself was in good health. Hélène, worn-out and dejected, suffered jealous torments when Juliette was there.

'Madame,' whispered Jeanne one evening, 'why doesn't Lucien come and play with me?'

After a moment's embarrassment, Juliette made do with a smile.

'Is he ill as well?' asked the little girl.

'No, darling, he's not ill. He's at school.'

And as Hélène went out on to the landing with her, she tried to explain her lie.

'Oh, I would certainly bring him, I know it's not contagious. But children get scared so quickly and Lucien is so silly! He might well burst into tears when he saw your poor little angel.'

'Yes, yes, you are quite right,' Hélène interrupted, heartbroken at the thought that this happy woman had her healthy child at home.

A second week went by. The illness ran its course, every hour it carried away a little of Jeanne's life. At a terrifying speed, but without hurry, moving through all its predictable phases, sparing her none, it was destroying her frail and adorable body. The spitting of blood had disappeared; occasionally the coughing stopped. The child was crushed under the weight of the illness and you could keep track of the damage it was doing in that little chest by her difficulty breathing. It was too hard for such weakness; the eyes of both the priest and Monsieur Rambaud filled with tears when they heard her. Day and night the sound of her breathing could be heard from behind the curtain; the poor little creature who, it seemed, might have been extinguished by the merest touch, sweated and laboured and could not finish dying. Her exhausted mother, unable to bear the noise of her rattling breath any more, went into the room next door and leaned her head against a wall.

Jeanne was becoming more and more remote from the world. She could no longer recognize anyone, she wore the expression of a person drowned, lost, as if she was already living in some place apart. When the people around her wanted to attract her attention and said who they were so that she would recognize them, she gazed at them unsmilingly, then turned to face the wall with an air of weariness. A shadow had descended on her, and she was leaving the world in a state of anxious brooding like that of the bad days of her jealousy. Yet in her sickness she might still be made alert by some whim. One morning she asked her mother:

'Is it Sunday today?'

'No, my love,' Hélène replied. 'It's only Friday. Why do you ask?'

She no longer seemed to know what question she had asked. But two days later when Rosalie was in the bedroom, she said in a little voice:

'It's Sunday. Zéphyrin is here—ask him to come.'

The maid hesitated, but Hélène, who had overheard, made a sign to her that it was all right. The child repeated:

'Bring him here, both of you come, it would make me happy.'

When Rosalie came in with Zéphyrin, she raised herself on her pillow. The little soldier, bareheaded, spreading his hands, shuffled uneasily back and forth to hide his emotion. He was fond of Mademoiselle and was truly upset to see her 'with her back to the wall', as he said in the kitchen. So in spite of Rosalie's injunctions—she had told him to be cheery—he stood there foolishly and his face fell when he saw she was so pale and nothing but skin and bones. For all his swagger, his was a sensitive soul. He could not bring to mind a single one of the fine phrases he had acquired of late. The maid, standing behind him, pinched him to make him laugh. But he only managed to stammer out:

'I am sorry... Mademoiselle, friends...'

Jeanne was still raised on her thin arms. She opened her big vacant eyes, she seemed to be searching for something. Her head trembled, no doubt the bright light blinded her in the shadows into which she was already sinking.

'Come over here, my dear,' said Hélène to the soldier. 'Mademoiselle wants to see you.'

The sun was coming through the window, creating a wide patch of yellow in which the dust from the rug was dancing. March had arrived, outside the spring was coming into life. Zéphyrin took a step forward into the sunshine. His little round freckled face had the golden hue of ripe corn, while the buttons on his tunic glinted and his red trousers looked like a blood-red field of poppies. Then Jeanne saw him. But her eyes again grew worried, uncertain, moving from one to the other.

'What do you want, my love?' asked her mother. 'Everybody's here.'

Then she realized.

'Rosalie, come over here... Mademoiselle wants to see you.'

Rosalie in her turn moved forward into the sunlight. She was wearing a bonnet with the ribbons thrown back over her shoulders, flying out like the wings of a butterfly. A golden dust fell on to her coarse black hair and honest face with its squashed nose and thick lips. And they had become the only ones in that room, the little soldier and the cook, standing side by side in the rays of the sun. Jeanne looked at them.

'Well, darling,' Hélène said, 'aren't you going to speak to them? They are both here.'

Jeanne looked at them, her head shaking with the slight tremor of a very old woman. There they were, like husband and wife, ready to return arm in arm to their village. The mild air of springtime warmed them and, wanting to cheer up Mademoiselle, they ended up laughing together in a simple, loving way. Around their strong shoulders was an aura of rude health. Had they been on their own, it was certain that Zéphyrin would have seized hold of Rosalie and would have received a good slap from her. You could tell from the way they looked at each other.

'Well, darling, have you nothing to say to them?'

Jeanne looked at them, more choked than ever. She said nothing. Suddenly she burst into tears. Zéphyrin and Rosalie had to leave the room forthwith.

'I am sorry..., Mademoiselle... friends...', repeated the little soldier, aghast, on his way out.

And that was one of Jeanne's last caprices. She fell into a sombre mood and nothing could draw her out of it. She detached herself from everything, including her mother. When the latter leaned over her bed to look closely at her, the child's face was blank as if only the shadow of the curtains passed before her eyes. She was silent, in the black resignation of someone who has been totally abandoned and who feels death is near. At times she remained with her eyelids half-closed and from her half-shut lids nobody could guess at the unrelenting thought that absorbed her. Nothing existed for her any more, with the exception of her big doll lying beside her. They had given it to her one night to distract her from her unbearable suffering, and she refused to give it back, she protected it fiercely as soon as they tried to take it from her. The doll, its cardboard head on the bolster, was lying there like a sick person with the blanket up around her shoulders. No doubt the little girl looked after her, for from time to time she touched the pink limbs, torn away and emptied of their bran stuffing, with her feverish hands. For hours on end her eyes did not leave the doll's constant fixed enamel stare, the white teeth which did not stop smiling. Then she would be overcome with love for her, and feel the need to clutch her to her breast and lean her cheek against the little mop of hair, which seemed to comfort her when she touched it. And so she took refuge in the love of her big doll, making sure when she emerged from her sleepy state that she was still there, seeing nothing but her, chatting to her, sometimes with the shadow of a smile on her face as though the doll had whispered words in her ear.

It was nearing the end of the third week. The old doctor came and sat down by her one morning. Hélène understood it meant that her daughter would not last the day. Since the day before, she had been in a stupor, not even conscious of what she did. Now they were not fighting for the child's life, they were counting the hours. As the sick girl was suffering from a burning thirst, the doctor had recommended just giving her a drink laced with opiates to make her dying easier. And this abandoning of any remedy unbalanced Hélène's mind. As long as there were potions lying on the bedside table, she still hoped for a miracle cure. Now that the vials and tins were no longer there, her last shred of faith vanished. All she felt was the instinct to be near to Jeanne, not to leave her, to watch over her. The doctor, who wanted to take her away from this terrible vigil, tried to induce her to leave her daughter, tasking her with little jobs. But she came back, drawn to her, with the physical need to see her. Straight-backed, with her arms to her sides, in a despair which made her face puff up, she waited.

Towards one o'clock Abbé Jouve and Monsieur Rambaud arrived. The doctor went to meet them and whispered to them. Both turned pale. They stood there, horror-stricken. And their hands trembled. Hélène had not turned her head.

The day was splendid, one of those sunny afternoons in the first few days of April. Jeanne was tossing and turning in her bed. The thirst which devoured her now and then caused painful little movements of her lips. She put her poor little translucent hands outside the blanket and was waving them gently to and fro in the air. The unseen work of the malady was over, she did not cough, her faint voice was nothing but a breath. She turned her head a moment, searching for the light. Doctor Bodin opened the window wide. Then Jeanne was quiet and rested her cheek on the pillow, her eyes towards Paris, her laboured breathing growing slower and slower.

During those three weeks of pain, her face had often turned towards the city spread out along the far horizon. Her expression became grave and thoughtful. At this last hour, Paris smiled in the pale April sun. From outside came the warm breeze, children's laughter, the chirping of sparrows. And the dying girl made a last supreme effort to still see, to follow the spirals of smoke which rose from the distant faubourgs. She could make out the three monuments she knew, the Invalides, the Panthéon, the Tour Saint-Jacques; then the unknown began, her lids half closed before this vast sea of roofs. Perhaps she dreamed that she was gradually becoming very light and flying away like a bird. Well, she would soon know, she would land on the domes and the spires, after seven or eight beats of her wings she would see the forbidden things they don't let children know about. But again she became agitated, her hands reached out once more, and she was only quiet again when she held her big doll in her little arms against her breast. She wanted to take her with her. Her gaze vanished into the distance, amongst the chimney-tops that glowed pink in the sun.

It had just struck four, the blue shadows of evening were already falling. The end had come, a slow, still, suffocating death. The little angel had no more strength for the fight. Monsieur Rambaud, defeated, collapsed on to his knees, shaken by silent sobs, crouched behind a curtain to hide his grief. The abbé knelt down at the bedside, his hands together, gabbling the prayers for the dying.

'Jeanne, Jeanne,' whispered Hélène, ice-cold with a terror that blew a cold draught through her hair.

She had pushed the doctor aside, thrown herself on the floor, leant over the bed to look closely at her daughter. Jeanne opened her eyes but did not look at her mother. Her eyes still went over to vanishing Paris. She squeezed her doll tighter, her last love. A huge sigh swelled her chest, then came two lighter sighs. Her eyes paled, and briefly her face expressed a terrible anguish. But soon she seemed relieved as she breathed her last, her mouth open.

'It's over,' said the doctor, taking her hand.

Jeanne was looking at Paris with her big, unseeing eyes. Her fawn-like face grew longer still, and sterner, a grey shadow spread down under the frowning eyebrows. And so too in death her face was the pallid face of a jealous woman. The doll with her head hanging back, her hair falling down, seemed, like her, to be dead.

'It's over,' said the doctor, relinquishing the cold little hand.

Hélène, her features strained, pressed her fists against her forehead as if she feared her head might burst open. She did not weep, she looked wildly about her. Then a sob caught in her throat. She had just spied a small pair of shoes, forgotten at the foot of the bed. It was over, Jeanne would never put them on again, they could give the little shoes to the poor. And her tears flowed, she remained there on the floor, rubbing her face over her dead daughter's hand, which had slipped down. Monsieur Rambaud was sobbing. The abbé had raised his voice, while Rosalie, at the half-open door of the dining room, was biting her handkerchief so that she wouldn't make too much noise.

Just at that moment Doctor Deberle rang the doorbell. He could not refrain from going up to enquire.

'How is she?' he asked.

'Oh, Monsieur,' stammered Rosalie. 'She is dead.'

He stood stock-still, devastated at this ending that he had been daily expecting. Then he whispered:

'My God! The poor child! What a terrible thing!'

And this desperate banality was all he could think of to say. The door had closed. He went downstairs again.

CHAPTER 4

WHEN Madame Deberle learned of Jeanne's death, she wept, she had one of those passionate outbursts that sent her into a frenzy for forty-eight hours. A noisy despair, out of all proportion. She went up and threw herself into the arms of Hélène. Then, at something that was said, she became obsessed with the idea of arranging a touching burial for the little girl and it soon occupied every waking minute. She offered her help, took responsibility for every last detail. The mother, exhausted by crying, sat defeated upon a chair. Monsieur Rambaud, acting on her behalf, was losing his wits. He accepted with effusive and grateful thanks. Hélène roused herself for a moment to say that she wanted flowers, lots of flowers.

So Madame Deberle promptly went to immense trouble. She spent the next day running round to all her lady friends to tell them the dreadful news. She dreamed of having a procession of little girls in white dresses. She must have at least thirty, and she did not go home until that quota was reached. She had herself visited the Funeral Directors, discussing what class it should be and choosing the drapes. The hangings would cover the garden railings, the corpse would be on display in the middle of the lilac which was already covered with little green shoots. It would be charming.

'Oh my goodness, let's hope it's fine tomorrow,' she pronounced, when all her errands were done.

The morning was radiant, blue sky, golden sun, with the pure, living breath of spring. The funeral procession was at ten o'clock. At nine, the drapes were hung. Juliette came to advise the workmen. She wanted them not to cover the trees completely. The white cloths with silver fringes made a porchway between the two iron gates which had been pushed back into the lilac. But she returned to the salon quickly to greet the ladies. They were meeting at her house, so as not to encumber Madame Grandjean's apartment. But she was very annoyed that her husband had had to leave that morning for Versailles: a consultation that could not be postponed, he said. She was on her own. She would never be able to manage.

Madame Berthier arrived first with her two daughters.

'Would you believe it!' cried Madame Deberle. 'Henri has abandoned me! Well, Lucien, aren't you going to say hello?'

Lucien was there, all ready for the burial, wearing black gloves. He seemed surprised when he saw Sophie and Blanche dressed up as if for a procession. A silk ribbon was bound round their muslin dresses and their veils which reached down to the ground hid their little caps of *tulle illusion*.* While the two mothers were chatting, the three children looked at each other rather stiffly in their costumes. Then Lucien said:

'Jeanne is dead.'

He was upset, but he was smiling in an astonished sort of way. Since yesterday, the idea that Jeanne was dead had made him well behaved. As his mother did not answer him, being too busy, he had questioned the servants. So did you not move any more when you were dead?

'She's dead, she's dead,' echoed the two sisters, all pink in their white veils. 'Are we going to see her?'

He reflected for a moment and looking into the distance with his mouth open as though trying to guess what was over there, beyond his own little world, he said in hushed tones:

'We shan't see her again.'

Meanwhile more little girls came in. At a signal from his mother, Lucien went to meet them. Marguerite Tissot, in a cloud of muslin with her big eyes, looked like a child Virgin. Her blonde hair, which was escaping from the little cap, looked like a gold braided pelerine under the whiteness of the veil. A discreet smile went round at the arrival of the five Levasseur girls. They all looked alike. You would have thought they were from a boarding school, the oldest first, the youngest at the end of the line. And their skirts were so voluminous they took up a whole corner of the room. But when the little Guiraud girl appeared the whispers grew louder. They laughed and passed her around to look at her and kiss her. She looked like a white turtle dove in her ruffled feathers, no bigger than a bird, in the rustling layers of gauze which made her look enormous and round. Even her mother couldn't find her hands. The salon gradually filled up with this snow-fall. A few boys in coat-tails stained the purity with black. Lucien, because his little wife was dead, was looking for another. He wasn't sure, he would have liked one bigger than him, like Jeanne. However, he seemed to settle on Marguerite, whose hair astonished him. He did not leave her side.

'The corpse has not been brought down yet,' Pauline came to inform Juliette.

Pauline was busy, as though she had to make preparations for a ball. Only with difficulty had her sister been able to persuade her not to come in white.

'What!' cried Juliette. 'Whatever are they thinking of? I'll go up. Stay with the ladies.'

She left the salon swiftly, where the mothers in dark clothes were chatting in low tones, while the children did not dare risk moving for fear of creasing their clothes. Upstairs when she entered the dead girl's room, she was petrified. Jeanne was still lying on the bed with her hands together; and like Marguerite, like the Levasseur girls, she was wearing a white dress, a white bonnet, white shoes. A crown of white roses placed on her bonnet made her queen of all her little friends, celebrated by everyone waiting below. In front of the window the satin-lined oak coffin lay across two chairs and looked like an open jewellery box. The furniture was in its place, a candle burned. The room, enclosed and dark, smelled like a damp, silent vault that had been walled up for some time. And Juliette, coming in out of the sun-shine, out of the joyous outdoors, was speechless, stopped in her tracks, and did not dare tell them to make haste.

'There are a lot of people here already,' she finally whispered.

Then, not having received an answer, she added, in order to say something:

'Henri has had to go to a consultation in Versailles, and sends his apologies.'

Hélène, seated in front of the bed, raised her vacant eyes. It was impossible to drag her away from that room. She had been there for thirty-six hours, in spite of the entreaties of Monsieur Rambaud and Abbé Jouve, who were keeping vigil with her. She had found the two nights especially agonizing. Then there had been the torment of dressing her for the last time, the white silk slippers which she had insisted on putting on the little dead child's feet herself. She could not move, she was quite exhausted, as though the excess of sorrow had sent her to sleep.

'Have you got flowers?' she stammered with an effort, her eyes still on Madame Deberle.

'Yes, yes, my dear, don't fret,' the latter replied.

Since her daughter had breathed her last, Hélène had only been concerned with that one thing: flowers, armfuls of flowers. She anxiously asked every new person about that, seeming to be afraid that they would never find enough flowers.

'Have you some roses?' she went on, after a moment's silence.

'Yes, you will be pleased, I assure you.'

She nodded and sank into a torpor again. But the undertakers were waiting on the landing. They needed to get on with their task. Monsieur Rambaud, stumbling around like a man who was drunk, made a pleading gesture to Juliette to help him take the poor woman downstairs. Both of them took her gently by the arm. They got her to her feet and led her towards the dining room. But when she realized what they were doing she pushed them away in one last despairing outburst. It was a heartbreaking scene. She threw herself on her knees in front of the bed, clutching at the sheets, filling the room with the tumult of her revolt. But Jeanne's face, as she lay in her eternal silence, cold and rigid, still looked like stone. It had hardened a little, her mouth had taken on the expression of a vindictive childish pout. And it was this dark, unforgiving mask of jealousy that drove Hélène into a frenzy. She had clearly seen her in the last thirty-six hours becoming more and more frozen in her resentment, and fiercer as she drew nearer to the earth. What comfort it would have been if Jeanne had been able to smile at her one last time!

'No no!' she cried. 'Leave her there a moment, I beg you. You can't take her away from me. I want to kiss her. Oh, one moment, just one moment...'

And she held her in her trembling arms, defying the men who were out of sight on the landing, with their backs turned, looking bored. But her lips could not warm the cold face, and she sensed Jeanne's obstinate refusal. Then she gave herself up to the hands that were leading her, and collapsed on a chair in the dining room, repeating her dull moan a score of times:

'Oh God, oh God...'

The outpouring of emotion had exhausted Monsieur Rambaud and Madame Deberle. After a short silence, when Madame Deberle half-opened the door, it was all over. There had not been the least noise, scarcely a rustle. The screws, which had been previously oiled, closed the lid for ever. And the bedroom was empty, the coffin hidden under a white sheet.

Then the door remained open and Hélène was left alone. When she went back in she looked distractedly at the furniture, and round the walls. They had just carried off the corpse. Rosalie had pulled up the coverlet to obliterate the very slight imprint of the girl who had gone. And opening her arms in a wild gesture, her hands outstretched, Hélène rushed out on to the stairs. She tried to go down. Monsieur Rambaud held her back, while Madame Deberle explained to her that it wasn't done. But she swore she would be sensible and not follow the cortège. Surely they would let her watch, she would sit quietly in the conservatory. Both of them were crying as they heard her words. They must get her dressed. Juliette concealed her indoor dress beneath a black shawl. But she could not find a hat. Eventually she found one and tore a sprig of red verbena off it. Monsieur Rambaud, who was chief mourner, took Hélène on his arm. When they were in the garden Madame Deberle whispered:

'You stay with her. I've got a lot to do.'

And she escaped. Hélène walked with a struggle, searching ahead of her. As she went out into the daylight she uttered a sigh. Oh God! What a lovely day! But her eyes had gone straight to the gate, she had just caught sight of the little coffin under the white sheets. Monsieur Rambaud only let her walk another two or three steps.

'Come now, be brave,' he said, trembling all over.

They looked. The narrow coffin was bathed in a ray of light. A silver crucifix was placed on a lace cushion at the foot. On the left an aspergillum was soaking in a stoup. The large candles were burning without a flame, staining the sunshine with their little dancing spirits darting off into the air. Beneath the draperies branches of trees formed a cradle with their violet buds. It was a corner of springtime, where, through a gap in the drapes, the golden dust fell from the wide shaft of sun and opened the cut flowers strewn over the coffin. There was a profusion of flowers. Sheaves of white roses were piled high, white camellias, white lilac, white carnations, a whole snowdrift of white petals. The corpse was vanishing, white sprays slid off the sheet, on the ground white periwinkles, white hyacinths had slipped off and were losing their petals. The occasional passers-by in the Rue Vineuse stopped with a sympathetic smile outside this sunny garden where the little dead girl slept beneath the flowers. All this whiteness sang, a dazzling purity blazed in the light, the sun warmed the drapery, the bouquets of flowers, the wreaths with a shiver of life. Above the roses a bee buzzed.

'The flowers... the flowers...', Hélène whispered, unable to say anything else.

She pressed her handkerchief to her lips, her eyes filled with tears. It seemed to her that Jeanne must be too hot and that thought was even more painful, in an access of love where there was also gratitude to those who had just covered the child with all these flowers. She made to move forward, Monsieur Rambaud no longer thought to hold her back. How pleasant it was under the draperies! The warm air was perfumed and there was no breeze. So she leaned over and chose just one rose. It was a rose she wanted, to place in her corsage. But she started to shake and Monsieur Rambaud was afraid.

'Don't stay,' he said, leading her away. 'You promised not to make yourself ill.'

He was trying to usher her into the conservatory, when the door of the salon opened wide. Pauline was the first to appear. She had taken charge of organizing the funeral procession. One by one the little girls came down. They seemed like a sudden flowering, may trees miraculously in flower. Their white dresses billowed out in the sunshine, creating against the light a watery effect, through which all the delicate tones of white passed, as though on swans' wings. An apple tree shed its petals, gossamer threads floated round, the dresses were the very essence of spring. They came on and on, surrounding the lawn and still they were coming lightly down the steps, taking flight like thistledown, blossoming suddenly in the fresh air.

So when the garden was completely white, looking at that mass of little girls who had issued forth, Hélène suddenly remembered something. She recalled the ball from that other spring with the joyous dancing of little feet. And she once more pictured Marguerite as a milkmaid, with her milk-can hanging from her belt, Sophie as a soubrette, turning on the arm of her sister Blanche, whose Folly costume jangled like a ring of bells. Then she thought of the five Levasseur young ladies, the multitude of Red Riding Hoods with their bright red satin caps edged in black velvet, while the little Guiraud girl with the Alsatian butterfly clip in her hair jumped around like a mad thing opposite a Harlequin who was twice as big as her. Today they were all in white. Jeanne was also in white on a pillow of white satin, among the flowers. The exquisite Japanese girl, her chignon fastened with long pins, with the tunic of purple embroidered with birds, was leaving dressed all in white.

'How they have grown!' murmured Hélène, bursting into tears.

Everyone was there, except her daughter. Monsieur Rambaud made her go into the conservatory, but she stayed in the doorway, wanting to see the start of the cortège. Some ladies came over and discreetly shook hands. The children looked at her with blue bewildered eyes.

Meanwhile Pauline was going round giving orders. She kept her voice down, in the circumstances, but she forgot from time to time.

'Come on now, behave yourselves. Look, you little pig, you've already dirtied yourself... I'll come and fetch you, don't move.'

The hearse arrived, they could leave. Madame Deberle appeared and cried:

'They've forgotten the bouquets! Quick, Pauline, the bouquets!'

Then there was some confusion. A bouquet of white roses had been prepared for each little girl. They had to give them out. The children, delighted, held the large bunches in front of them, like candles. Lucien, who still stood close to Marguerite, was sniffing them ecstatically while she pushed them under his nose. All these little girls, their hands full of flowers, were laughing in the sunshine, then all at once grew serious as they watched the men loading the coffin on to the hearse.

'Is she in there?' Sophie enquired in a whisper. Her sister Blanche nodded. Then she said to her:

'For a man, it's as big as this.'

She was talking about the coffin, and opened her arms as wide as she could. But little Marguerite laughed with her nose buried in the roses, saying that it tickled. Then the others buried their noses in them as well to see. Someone called them, and they were well behaved again.

Outside the procession started off. At the end of the Rue Vineuse, a woman in slippers with her hair loose was crying and wiping her cheeks with the corner of her apron. Some people had gone to their windows, exclamations of sympathy rose into the silent street. The hearse rolled along quietly, draped in white with silver fringes. All you could hear was the rhythmic clip-clop of the two white horses, muffled by the earth surface of the road. It was a real harvest of flowers, bouquets and wreaths borne along by the funeral cart; the coffin was invisible, little bumps shook the sheaves of blossoms, the cart strewed branches of lilac in its wake. Long streamers of white watered silk were held at the four corners by four little girls, Sophie and Marguerite, one of the Levasseur girls and the little Guiraud girl, the last so sweet, tottering along, that her mother walked along beside her. The others crowded around the hearse, holding their bouquets of roses. They walked quietly, their veils rose and fell, the wheels turned amid the chiffon as though borne along on a cloud, through the delicate heads of smiling cherubins. Then, behind, after Monsieur Rambaud, his face pale and bowed, came some ladies, a few little boys, Rosalie, Zéphyrin, the Deberles' servants. Five empty funeral carriages followed. In the sunny street, white pigeons flew off as the spring procession passed by.

'Oh my goodness, how annoying!' Madame Deberle said again, when she saw the cortège move off. 'If only Henri had postponed his consultation! I told him to.'

She did not know what to do with Hélène, who had sunk on to a seat in the conservatory. Henri could have stayed with her. He would have comforted her a little. It was very disagreeable him not being there. Luckily Mademoiselle Aurélie was happy to help. She did not care for sad events, and at the same time she would look after the food the children were to find there on their return. Madame Deberle hastened to join the procession that was heading for the church along the Rue de Passy. Now the garden was empty, workmen were clearing away the hangings. All that remained on the sandy path, where Jeanne had been, were the petals of a camellia. And Hélène, suddenly sunk into this solitude and deep silence, felt once more the anguish, the agony of the eternal separation. One more time, to be near her only one more time! The idea which she could not get out of her head, that Jeanne had left the world discontented, with her mute face dark with resentment, went through her like the sudden burning of a hot iron.

So when she saw that Mademoiselle Aurélie was keeping watch on her, she looked for a chance to escape and run to the cemetery.

'Yes, it's a great loss,' repeated the old maid, settling comfortably back into an armchair. 'I would have loved children, especially a little girl. Oh well, when I weigh it up, I am pleased I didn't get married. It saves you a lot of worries.'

She thought she was taking Hélène's mind off it. She talked about one of her friends who'd had six children. They were all dead. Another lady was left on her own with a grown-up son who hit her. He should have died himself, his mother would have had no trouble getting over that. Hélène was apparently listening. She did not move, but shook with impatience.

'You've calmed down a little now,' Mademoiselle Aurélie said finally. 'Heaven knows you have to come to terms with it eventually.'

The door of the dining room led into the Japanese conservatory. She got up, pushed open the door, and stretched. Plates of cakes covered the table. Hélène quickly fled into the garden. The gate was open, the workmen from the funeral parlour were taking away their ladders.

The Rue Vineuse turns left into the Rue des Réservoirs. That's where the cemetery of Passy lies. A colossal retaining wall rises from the Boulevard de la Muette, the cemetery is like an immense terrace towering over the hill, the Trocadéro and the avenues, and over the whole of Paris. In twenty strides Hélène was outside the wide-open gate, revealing the deserted field of white tombs and black crosses. She went in. Two large lilac trees were in bud at the end of the first avenue. They did not use that place for burial very much, weeds grew there, some cypresses pierced the greenery with their dark shapes. Hélène hurried straight ahead. A band of sparrows took fright, a gravedigger shovelling out earth looked up. The procession had very likely not arrived yet, the cemetery looked empty. She cut across to her right, and pushed on as far as the parapet of the terrace. And as she was walking round it, she caught sight of the little girls in white behind some acacias kneeling down in front of the temporary vault into which they had just lowered Jeanne's body. Abbé Jouve, his hand held up, was pronouncing a last blessing. All she heard was the dull thud of the stone falling shut. It was over.

Meanwhile Pauline had caught sight of her and pointed her out to Madame Deberle. The latter was almost annoyed, murmuring:

'What! She's come! But it's not done! It's in very bad taste.'

She went over and showed her disapproval by her expression. Other ladies drew near as well out of curiosity. Monsieur Rambaud had joined her, and stood silently next to her. She had leant against one of the acacias, feeling faint and tired with all the crowd of people. While she answered the expressions of sympathy with nods, one thought, and one only, was choking her. She had arrived too late, she had heard the sound of the stone falling shut. And her eyes constantly returned to the vault, whose step was being swept by a graveyard attendant.

'Pauline, look after the children,' instructed Madame Deberle.

The little girls, who had been kneeling, rose like white sparrows taking flight. Some who were too tiny, with legs hidden in their skirts, sat down on the ground and had to be picked up. While Jeanne was being lowered, the older ones strained to see the bottom of the hole. It was extremely black, they shivered and turned pale. Sophie assured everyone in a whisper that you stayed there for years and years. 'Night-time too?' enquired one of the Levasseur girls. Of course night-time too... For ever. Oh, Blanche would die if she had to be there at night! They all looked at one another with very wide eyes as though they had just heard a story about robbers. But once on their feet and let loose from around the vault the colour came back in their faces; it wasn't for real. People told you such silly stories. It was lovely weather, this garden was pretty with its tall grasses. They could have had such good games of hide-and-seek behind all those stones! Their little feet were already dancing, the white dresses beating like wings. In the silence of the tombs, the warm, steady falling of the sunshine made these children blossom. Eventually Lucien had shoved his hand under Marguerite's veil. He touched her hair, wanting to find out if she put anything on it to make it so yellow. The little girl puffed up with pride. Then he told her they would get married. Marguerite wanted to, but was afraid he would pull her hair. He touched it again, and discovered it was as soft as tissue paper.

'Don't go so far off!' cried Pauline.

'Well, let's go,' said Madame Deberle. 'We are not doing anything here and the children must be hungry.'

They had to round up the little girls who had scattered like a boarding-school at recreation. They counted them. The little Guiraud girl was missing. At last they spied her in a distant avenue solemnly toddling along holding her mother's sunshade. Then the ladies headed for the gate, pushing the stream of white dresses in front of them. Madame Berthier congratulated Pauline on her marriage which was to take place the following month. Madame Deberle said she was leaving in three days' time for Naples with her husband and Lucien. The crowd dissolved. Zéphyrin and Rosalie were last to leave, but finally moved away. They took each other's arm, pleased to be out walking despite their great sorrow. They slowed down and the backs of the lovers moved in rhythm together for a moment more in the light at the end of the avenue.

'Come,' said Monsieur Rambaud.

But Hélène, with a gesture, begged him to wait. She remained there alone, it seemed to her that a page of her life had been torn out. When she saw the last people vanish, she knelt, suffering, in front of the vault. Abbé Jouve in his surplice had not yet risen. Both prayed for some time. Then saying nothing, his eyes showing a lovely charity and forgiveness, the priest helped her to her feet.

'Give her your arm,' he said simply to Monsieur Rambaud.

On the horizon Paris leaped up in the radiant spring morning. In the cemetery a chaffinch sang.

CHAPTER 5

TWO years had gone by. One December morning the little cemetery was sleeping in the bitter cold. It had been snowing since the day before, a fine snow whipped up by the north wind. The snowflakes, rarer now, were falling soft and light as feathers from the pale sky. The snow was getting thicker, there was a deep ledge of swansdown along the parapet of the terrace. Beyond that pure line, Paris spread out towards a blurred pale horizon.

Madame Rambaud was still on her knees in the snow in front of Jeanne's tomb. Her husband had just silently got to his feet. They had married in November in Marseilles. Monsieur Rambaud had sold his house in Les Halles, and was in Paris for three days to conclude this business. And the carriage awaiting them in the Rue des Réservoirs was to call at the hotel, pick up their trunks, and take them thence to the railway. Hélène's one thought in making the journey was to pray in that spot. She remained motionless with her head bowed, as though in another world, not feeling the cold earth turn her knees to ice.

Meanwhile the wind was dying down. Monsieur Rambaud had gone to stand on the terrace in order to leave her to the silent grief of her memories. A mist was rising over the furthest parts of the city, its immensity was vanishing in that pale blur of cloud. At the foot of the Trocadéro, Paris was the colour of lead, and looked dead beneath the slow falling of the last shreds of snow. In the air, which had grown very still, they were pale flecks on a murky background, steadily, imperceptibly, incessantly falling. Beyond the chimneys of the Military Depot, whose brick towers took on the tones of old copper, the endless gliding whiteness grew thicker, you would have said it was gauze floating, unravelling thread by thread. Not a sound rose from this dreamlike precipitation, miraculously transformed in the air and sinking as though it had been lulled asleep. The flying snowflakes seemed to slow down when they met the roofs. They dropped, one by one, never ceasing, millions of them, so silently that flowers dropping their petals make more noise than did they. And a sovereign peace, a forgetting of life and of the world, descended in that moving multitude silently falling through space. The sky grew steadily and uniformly bright, all at once, a milky hue, still troubled at times by wisps of snow. Gradually the sparkling islets of houses appeared, in a bird's-eye view of the city, crisscrossed by its streets and squares with their lines and gaps of shadow throwing the gigantic skeleton of the *quartiers* into relief.

Slowly Hélène stood up. On the ground her two knees had left marks in the snow. Wrapped in a capacious dark cloak edged with fur, she looked tall and stately against all the white. The barrette through her hat, of black velvet braid, shaded her forehead like a diadem. Her face had recovered its refined, peaceful expression, her grey eyes and white teeth, her round, somewhat determined chin, gave her a confident, sensible air. When she turned her head, her profile again took on the grave purity of a statue. Her lifeblood lay somewhere beneath the quiet pallor of her cheeks, you felt she had returned to a dignified respectability. Two tears had rolled down her cheeks, her calm reflected her former grief. And she remained standing in front of the tomb, a simple column where Jeanne's name was followed by two dates, that measured the brief existence of the little twelve-year-old girl.

Around her, the whiteness spread like a sheet over the cemetery, pierced by the edge of a rusty tomb, or an iron cross, raised like the arms of a mourner. Only the footsteps of Hélène and Monsieur Rambaud had made a path in this deserted place. It was an unsullied solitude in which the dead were sleeping. The avenues vanished among the frail ghosts of the trees. The occasional parcel of snow fell noiselessly off an overloaded branch. Nothing stirred. At the far end were the black footsteps of people who had passed that way. They were burying someone under that shroud. A second cortège was approaching from the left. The biers and the carriages drove silently along like silhouettes cut out of white linen.

Hélène was just emerging from her reverie when she caught sight of a beggarwoman hovering nearby. It was Mother Fétu, the sound of her men's boots muffled by the snow, split and mended with string. Never had she seen her in such a miserable state of poverty, wearing such filthy rags, even more gross and half-witted. The old woman, in bad weather, icy-cold, drenching rain, followed the funeral processions nowadays to try her luck with charitable folk who might take pity on her. And she was well aware that in a cemetery the fear of death makes people give money. She visited each tomb, approaching people on their knees at exactly the moment they burst into tears, since at that point they could scarcely refuse. She had gone in with the last cortège, and had been observing Hélène for a while from a distance. But she did not recognize her, and told her, snivelling, and with her palm held out, that she had two children at home dying of starvation. Hélène listened, dumbfounded by this apparition. The children didn't have any fire, the eldest was dying of consumption. Suddenly Mother Fétu stopped. Amid her myriad wrinkles her face started to change, her narrow eyes blinked. What! Was it the good lady? God had answered her prayers then! And without amending the story of the children, she began to groan and a ceaseless babble came pouring out. She had lost even more teeth, you could scarcely make out what she said. God had sent all His misfortunes upon her. Her gentleman had fired her, she had been in bed for three months. Yes, she was still poorly, she was itching all over, a neighbour had said that she must have swallowed a spider while she was asleep. If she only had a little fire she would be able to keep her belly warm. That was the only thing that would bring her any relief. But she had nothing—not a scrap of wood to burn. Perhaps Madame had been travelling? Well, that was her business. Anyway, she thought she was looking very well and very pretty. God would reward her for everything. As Hélène was getting out her purse, Mother Fétu leaned against Jeanne's tomb, breathing heavily.

The cortèges had left. Somewhere in a nearby pit you could hear the regular blows of a pickaxe, wielded by an invisible gravedigger. By now the old woman, with her eyes fixed on the purse, got her breath again. Then, to increase the amount, she grew very ingratiating and talked about the other lady. You couldn't deny she was a kind lady. But she didn't give her enough to make a difference. She looked warily at Hélène as she said that. Then she went so far as to mention the doctor. Oh, he was good as gold. Last summer he had gone travelling with his wife. Their little son was growing. But Hélène's fingers shook as she opened the purse, and suddenly Mother Fétu changed her tune. Stupid, shocked, she had only just realized that the good lady was there next to her daughter's grave. She faltered, sighed, tried to bring her to tears. A little sweetheart with such lovely little hands, she could see them now giving her silver coins. And what lovely long hair she had, and her eyes brimful of tears when she looked at poor people! Oh, you couldn't replace an angel like that. They didn't exist, you couldn't find one in the whole of Passy. On fine days she would always pick a bunch of daisies in the ditch by the ramparts and bring along for her. She stopped speaking, anxious at the gesture Hélène made to cut her short. So didn't she have the right words any more? The good lady wasn't in tears and she only gave her a twenty-sou coin.

Monsieur Rambaud meanwhile had approached the terrace parapet. Hélène went to meet him. Then, seeing this man, Mother Fétu's eyes lit up. The gentleman was unfamiliar. He must be somebody new. She shuffled along behind Hélène, calling down all the blessings of paradise upon her head. And when she was near Monsieur Rambaud, she again mentioned the doctor. That would be one man who'd have a fine funeral when he died, if the poor folk he'd tended for nothing were following his body! He was a bit of a ladies' man, nobody could deny that. The ladies of Passy knew all about that. But that didn't stop him adoring his wife, such a nice woman, she might have misbehaved herself if she'd wanted, but didn't dream of it now. A pair of turtle doves they were. Had Madame gone to call on them? They were certainly at home, she had just seen the shutters open in the Rue Vineuse. They had been so fond of Madame at one time, they would be so pleased to see her! As she mumbled these disjointed words, the old woman had her eye on Monsieur Rambaud. He was listening to her calmly, good man that he was. The memories she had brought back in his presence cast no shadow on his tranquil face. But he sensed that this insistent beggarwoman was importuning Hélène and he rummaged in his pocket and gave her something too, gesturing her to go away. When she saw a second silver coin Mother Fétu burst into exclamations of gratitude. She would buy a bit of wood, she'd warm her body where it hurt. That was the only thing that would give her belly any comfort. Yes, a real pair of turtle doves, and the proof was that the lady had had a second child the winter before last, a beautiful little girl, pink and bonny, who must be nearly fourteen months by now. The day of the baptism the doctor had put a hundred sous in her hand at the church door. Oh, good people seek each other out, Madame brought her luck. God grant she be spared sorrow, and every good fortune be showered upon her! In the name of the Father, Son, and Holy Ghost, Amen!

Hélène stood looking across at Paris while Mother Fétu shuffled off between the tombstones, mumbling three Paters and three Aves. It had stopped snowing, the last flakes had landed, slowly, languidly, on the roofs. And in the vast sky of pearly-grey, beyond the melting mist, a rosy brightness glowed in the golden sun. One single band of blue over Montmartre edged the horizon, of such a light, soft blue that you would have thought it was a shadow on white satin. Paris was rising out of the mist, growing larger among its snowfields, breaking out of the ice which had been freezing it in the immobility of death. Now the feathery flakes no longer sent a great shiver, rippling palely over the city's rust-coloured façades. The houses emerged, black from the white mass where they had been sleeping, as though mouldy from centuries of damp. Entire streets looked ruined, eaten away by saltpetre, the roofs about to collapse, the windows already broken. You saw a square, its chalky surface seeming to be piled with rubble. But as the blue strip expanded in the direction of Montmartre, light flowed out, as cold and limpid as the waters of a spring so that Paris lay as though under ice and even the distant parts had the clarity of a Japanese print.

In her fur-lined cloak, with her hands lost in her sleeves, Hélène was thinking. One single thought kept coming back to her, like an echo. They'd had a child, a bonny little rosy girl. And she could imagine her at the age when Jeanne was beginning to talk. Little girls of fourteen months are so sweet! She counted the months; fourteen, so that was almost two years, if you counted the rest. It was just *that* time, near enough to a fortnight. Then she had a vision of sunny Italy, a dream country with golden fruit, where lovers walked in perfumed nights, their arms around each other. Henri and Juliette were walking in front of her in the moonlight. They loved one another like married couples who have become lovers again. A bonny little rosy, naked girl-child laughing in the sunshine and babbling her muddle of words that her mother stifled with kisses! And she thought about those things without anger, her heart silent, increasing her serenity in her sadness. The land of sunshine disappeared, she contemplated Paris, with its great body hardened by the winter. Colossal marble figures seemed to be lying in the sovereign peace of their frigidity, their limbs weary with an age-old pain they were no longer able to feel. A blue gap had opened up over the Panthéon.

Yet memory fetched back her days. She had lived in a trance in Marseilles. One morning, as she went along the Rue des Petites-Maries, she had started sobbing outside her childhood home. That was the last time she had wept. Monsieur Rambaud came to visit frequently; she felt him at her side protecting her. He demanded nothing, never declared himself to her. Then towards autumn she saw him arrive one evening, his eyes red, crushed by a great sorrow. His brother, Abbé Jouve, had died. It was her turn to console him. From then on she couldn't remember exactly what happened. The abbé seemed to be always behind them, pressing her to resign herself, and she gave in. Since that was still what he wanted, she found no reason to refuse him. That seemed to her very sensible. As she was coming to the end of her period of mourning she had calmly sorted out the details with Monsieur Rambaud. The hands of her old friend shook with uncontrollable delight. It was as she wished, he had been waiting for her for months, all she had to do was give him some sign. They had married in black. The night of the wedding he too had kissed her bare feet, her beautiful feet, like those of a statue turning into marble again. And so life went on.

While the blue sky widened on the horizon, this awakening of her memories was a surprise to Hélène. Had she been out of her mind, then, for a whole year? Today when she remembered that woman who had lived for three years in the room in the Rue Vineuse, she seemed to be passing judgement on a stranger, whose conduct she despised and found shocking. What a time of peculiar folly, what an abominable evil act, like a blinding thunderclap! And yet she had not asked for it. She had been living quietly, hidden away in her little corner of the world, absorbed in the adoration of her daughter. The path before her had stretched out without curiosity or desire. But a puff of wind had knocked her over and she had fallen. She could not find a reason for it even now. Her being had ceased to belong to her, the other person was acting inside her. Was it possible? She had actually done those things! Then she went ice-cold, Jeanne was vanishing beneath the roses. In the rigidity of grief, she became calm again, without desire, without curiosity, continuing slowly forward on the dead straight path. Her life was taken up again where it had left off, in stern tranquillity and proud respectability.

Monsieur Rambaud stepped forward, to lead her away from this place of sorrow. But with a gesture Hélène indicated she wanted to stay there a little longer. She had gone over to the parapet and was looking down on to the Avenue de la Muette, where the carriages, a line of them, old and ramshackled, were pulled up beside the pavement. The whitened hoods and wheels, the horses bathed in lather, seemed to have been rotting away there for centuries. Coachmen stiff in their frozen coats sat unmoving. One by one, more coaches were trundling with difficulty over the snow. The animals were slipping and sliding, stretching out their necks, while the men had got down from their seats and were leading them by the reins, swearing at them. And you could see behind the glass the faces of the patient travellers, leaning back on the cushions, resigned to spending three-quarters of an hour on a ten-minute journey. The cotton-wool snow muffled the sounds. Only the sound of voices rose from the streets, shrill and distinctive, each with a particular resonance: shouting, the laughter of people slipping down on the ice, the bad temper of the carters cracking their whips, the snorting and puffing of a frightened horse. Further off on the right the tall trees on the banks were a sight to behold. You would have thought they were made of spun glass, enormous Venetian chandeliers on which artists had whimsically twisted branches studded with flowers. The north wind had transformed the tree trunks into the shafts of columns. Above them was a tangle of downy branches, plumes of feathers, an exquisite cut-out of black twigs, edged with white net. It was freezing, and there was not a breath in the limpid air.

And Hélène told herself that she didn't really know Henri. For a year she had seen him almost every day. He had stayed for hours and hours close to her, chatting, and looking into her eyes. Yet she did not know him. One evening she had given herself and he had taken her. But she didn't know him, she was trying her utmost, but she couldn't understand. Where had he come from? How did he come to be near her? What kind of man was he to make her give herself, she who would have died rather than yield to another? She did not know, she felt giddy, her mind reeled. To the last, as on that first day, he had remained a stranger to her. Vainly she mustered the sparse details, his words, his actions, everything she could remember about the way he looked. He loved his wife and child, he had a distinguished smile, he always behaved properly, like a gentleman. Then she saw his passionate face again, his hands all over her body, desiring her. Weeks had gone by, he had vanished, he was gone. At this moment she wouldn't be able to say where she had spoken to him for the last time. He passed on, his ghost went with him. And their story had no other ending. She did not know him.

Over the city the sky was turning a spotless blue. Hélène raised her head, weary of her memories, glad of this purity. It was very pale and limpid, nothing more than a reflection of blue in the white sun, low on the horizon, which looked bright as a silver lamp. It burned without warmth, in the glare of the snow, in the icy air. Down below, vast stretches of roof, the tiles of the Military Depot, the slates of the houses on the banks, spread out their white sheets edged in black. On the other side of the river in the square of the Champ de Mars a steppe was opening up, where dark spots, cabs that had got lost, put you in mind of Russian sledges sliding along with the sound of little bells, while on the Quai d'Orsay, smaller in the distance, rows of elms blossomed in fine crystal, with bristling spines. In the stillness of that sea of ice flowed the Seine, its muddy water between its banks bordered with ermine. It had been washing along for two days and you could clearly see the blocks of ice being crushed against the pillars of the Pont des Invalides and vanishing beneath the arches. Then came the bridges, strung out like white lace, more and more delicate until they reached the spectacular rock that is the Île de la Cité, dominated by the towers of Notre-Dame with their snowy peaks. Other points to the left punctured the uniformity of the *quartiers*. Saint-Augustin, the Opéra, the Tour Saint-Jacques, were like mountains with everlasting snow on top. Closer, the pavilions of the Tuileries and the Louvre, connected by the new buildings, made the ridge of a chain of immaculate summits. And further to the right were the snowy crests of the

Invalides, Saint-Sulpice, the Panthéon, this last in the far distance, looking like a fairy palace, faced with bluish marble, against the azure sky. No voice could be heard. You could guess where the streets were from the grey slits, the crossroads in the hollows looked as if they had been split open. Whole rows of houses had disappeared. Only the neighbouring façades were recognizable because of the myriad reflections in their windows. The snowfields became indistinct then, and vanished into the glittering distance in a lake whose blue shadows seemed like an extension of the blue sky. Paris, vast and clear in the intensity of this freeze, glowed in the silver sun.

Then Hélène, gazing out at it one last time, took in the impassive city which, like Henri, remained a mystery. It was peaceful as ever and as if immortal under the snow, just as she had left it, just as she had seen it for three years. Paris for her was full of her past. It had been with her when she had fallen in love, and when Jeanne died. But that companion of all her days was still serene, indifferent, its gigantic face dispassionate, the silent witness of the laughter and tears which seemed to float down the Seine. At one time or another she had thought it possessed the ferocity of a monster, or the bounty of a Colossus. Today she sensed that she would never fathom its indifference, its vastness. It unfolded. It was Life.

Meanwhile Monsieur Rambaud touched her lightly, to make her come away. His kind face was beginning to look worried. He murmured: 'Don't torment yourself.'

He knew everything she was feeling, but that was all he could think of to say. Madame Rambaud looked at him and was calmed. Her face was rosy with the cold, her eyes clear. She had already begun to move away. Life was beginning again.

'I am not sure if I've shut the large trunk properly,' she said.

Monsieur Rambaud promised to check. The train was not leaving till midday, they had plenty of time. The streets were being sanded. Their cab would take less than an hour. But suddenly he raised his voice.

'I'll wager you have forgotten the fishing rods?'

'Oh yes, you are quite right!' she cried, surprised and cross at forgetting. 'We should have got them yesterday.'

They were very handy rods, of a make you couldn't buy in Marseilles. They owned a little cottage by the sea where they were to spend the summer. Monsieur Rambaud consulted his watch. They could still buy the rods on their way to the station. They would tie them on, along with the umbrellas. Then he bore her off, cutting across the graves as they went. The cemetery was empty, there was nothing except their footsteps in the snow. Jeanne lay dead and alone, facing Paris for all eternity.

EXPLANATORY NOTES

5 *February night*: February 1853, according to Zola's manuscript notes.

Rue Vineuse: today this street is situated between the Rue Franklin and the Avenue Paul-Doumer in the 16th *arrondissement*, near the Place du Trocadéro, in Passy. In 1853 Passy was still an independent commune of Paris, until its incorporation into the city in 1859. It was a quiet, well-to-do locality, not unlike a small provincial town, looking down on the Seine. It was full of town houses with gardens, and little parks.

7 *asylum*: a reference to Adélaïde Fouque (Aunt Dide), who features prominently in the first novel of the Rougon-Macquart cycle, *The Fortune of the Rougons*. She is the common ancestor of both the Rougon and Macquart families, and the origin of the 'hereditary lesion' that afflicts them. Hélène Grandjean (née Mouret) is the daughter of Ursule Mouret (née Macquart), the illegitimate daughter of Aunt Dide; and so she is the sister of Silvère (*The Fortune of the Rougons*) and François Mouret (*The Conquest of Plassans*). Aunt Dide slides into alcoholism and eventually into insanity. Her death at the age of 105, in the asylum at Les Tulettes, near Plassans, will be described in the final novel of the cycle, *Dr Pascal*. Jeanne is thus placed in the lineage of mental disorder that marks the family heredity (while her mother remains unaffected).

14 *Vaudeville*: the Théâtre du Vaudeville, on the Place de la Bourse, was one of the most prominent theatres in Paris during the Second Empire. In 1852, *La Dame aux camélias* by Alexandre Dumas fils was premiered there. The discussion here reflects Zola's writings as a drama critic, in particular his championing of 'realistic' theatre, as opposed to the kind of theatre, prevalent at the time, that indulged in meretricious staging and artificial 'effects': see Zola's *Naturalism in the Theatre* (*Le Naturalisme au théâtre*, 1881).

15 *hatmaker*: Mouret appears in *The Fortune of the Rougons*, where his dramatic death by suicide is described (cf. here p. 46). His wife, Hélène's mother, Ursule, dies, like her daughter-in-law Marthe (*The Conquest of Plassans*) and Jeanne in *A Love Story*, of a nervous condition that turns into consumption.

35 *Japanese pavilion*: a fashion for all things Japanese took hold in Paris during the 1860s. It had a marked influence on painting (a Japanese print is clearly visible in Manet's famous 1868 portrait of Zola), but also captured the imagination of the general public. Jeanne wears a Japanese costume for the children's ball (see p. 85), while the view of Paris in the novel's final chapter is compared to 'a Japanese print' (p. 262).

Variétés: the Théâtre des Variétés opened on the Boulevard Montmartre in 1807. It plays a prominent role in Zola's *Nana*, as the theatre in which

Nana achieves celebrity in the opening chapters, in a production that clearly echoes Jacques Offenbach's operetta, *La Belle Hélène*, which had its premiere at the Variétés on 17 December 1864.

36 *Bignon's*: a well-known restaurant situated on the corner of the Boulevard des Italiens and the Chaussée d'Antin.

37 *Folies-Dramatiques*: a small theatre specializing in comedy and operetta. In the 1850s it was situated on the Boulevard du Temple.

La Dame blanche: a comic opera by Adrien Boieldieu (1775–1834), first produced in 1825. It was based on episodes from the novels of Walter Scott and remained popular throughout the nineteeth century.

40 *She wore a grey dress… golden halo rising into paradise*: this description of Hélène's dress and of the light in the garden is clearly a transposition of Renoir's painting *The Swing*, which was shown at the Impressionist exhibition of 1877, precisely when Zola was writing *A Love Story*.

43 *Ivanhoe*: a highly sentimental historical novel by Walter Scott (1771–1832), published in 1820. It was immensely popular throughout Europe.

48 *Military Depot*: this depot was situated on the Quai Debilly (today the Avenue de Tokyo).

Opéra: a deliberate anachronism: the Opéra was not inaugurated until 1875. Similarly, the Palais de l'Industrie was built between 1853 and 1855, the new Louvre was completed in 1857, and the church of Saint-Augustin (see p. 151) built between 1860 and 1871. Zola justified these anachronisms in terms of his desire to use these buildings as reference points in his panoramic descriptions of Paris: see Zola, *Les Rougon-Macquart* (Paris: Gallimard, Bibliothèque de la Pléiade, 1960–7), ii. 1607–8.

85 *Yeddo*: an old name for Tokyo.

86 *réveils*: a painterly expression designating the use of contrasting colour.

89 *compotier*: fruit bowl.

croquignoles: small crisp cakes.

99 *glory*: an expanding circle of light.

146 *Trouville*: Trouville, on the Normandy coast, was the favourite seaside resort of fashionable Parisian society.

161 *rinces-bouches*: small bowls containing water for rinsing the mouth or fingers after a meal.

163 *Worms collection*: the 1850s saw the emergence of haute couture, which was dominated by an Englishman, Charles Frederick Worth (1826–95). Worth brought a new level of tailoring to women's fashion, turned visits to his salons into special social events, and introduced the now celebrated live mannequin to the Paris fashion world. Dictator of style, Worth attained a social standing unheard of by any tailor before him. He became internationally famous after being taken up by the Empress Eugénie, who was considered the epitome of fashion in her day. Cf. Zola's *The Kill* (Oxford World's Classics edn.), 85.

167 *La Favorite*: an opera by Gaetano Donizetti (1797–1848), first performed in Paris in 1840.

185 *"Le Caprice"*: one-act play written in 1837 by Alfred de Musset (1810–57) and first performed in France at the Comédie-Française in 1847.

176 *maisons de passe of the Regency*: *maisons de passe* are low-class hotels, where rooms are rented out by the hour, especially to prostitutes and their clients. The Regency in France is the period between 1715 and 1723 when King Louis XV was a minor and the country was governed by a regent, Philippe d'Orléans, nephew of Louis XIV.

195 *causeuse*: small sofa for two people.

230 *Eastern question*: the allusion is to tensions with Russia in relation to the latter's designs on Constantinople. In 1854, Napoleon III joined England in declaring war on Russia: France's involvement in the Crimean War lasted from March 1854 to September 1855.

249 *tulle illusion*: fabric made of very fine, transparent silk (hence the term 'illusion').

The Oxford World's Classics Website

www.worldsclassics.co.uk

- Browse the full range of Oxford World's Classics online

- Sign up for our monthly e-alert to receive information on new titles

- Read extracts from the Introductions

- Listen to our editors and translators talk about the world's greatest literature with our Oxford World's Classics audio guides

- Join the conversation, follow us on Twitter at OWC_Oxford

- Teachers and lecturers can order inspection copies quickly and simply via our website

www.worldsclassics.co.uk

American Literature

British and Irish Literature

Children's Literature

Classics and Ancient Literature

Colonial Literature

Eastern Literature

European Literature

Gothic Literature

History

Medieval Literature

Oxford English Drama

Philosophy

Poetry

Politics

Religion

The Oxford Shakespeare

A complete list of Oxford World's Classics, including Authors in Context, Oxford English Drama, and the Oxford Shakespeare, is available in the UK from the Marketing Services Department, Oxford University Press, Great Clarendon Street, Oxford OX2 6DP, or visit the website at www.oup.com/uk/worldsclassics.

In the USA, visit www.oup.com/us/owc for a complete title list.

Oxford World's Classics are available from all good bookshops. In case of difficulty, customers in the UK should contact Oxford University Press Bookshop, 116 High Street, Oxford OX1 4BR.

A SELECTION OF   OXFORD WORLD'S CLASSICS

HONORÉ DE BALZAC	**Cousin Bette** **Eugénie Grandet** **Père Goriot**
CHARLES BAUDELAIRE	**The Flowers of Evil**
DENIS DIDEROT	**Jacques the Fatalist** **The Nun**
ALEXANDRE DUMAS (PÈRE)	**The Count of Monte Cristo** **The Three Musketeers**
GUSTAVE FLAUBERT	**Madame Bovary**
VICTOR HUGO	**Notre-Dame de Paris**
J.-K. HUYSMANS	**Against Nature**
PIERRE CHODERLOS DE LACLOS	**Les Liaisons dangereuses**
GUY DE MAUPASSANT	**Bel-Ami**
MOLIÈRE	**Don Juan and Other Plays** **The Misanthrope, Tartuffe, and Other** **Plays**
ABBÉ PRÉVOST	**Manon Lescaut**
ARTHUR RIMBAUD	**Collected Poems**
JEAN-JACQUES ROUSSEAU	**Confessions**
MARQUIS DE SADE	**The Crimes of Love**
STENDHAL	**The Red and the Black** **The Charterhouse of Parma**
PAUL VERLAINE	**Selected Poems**
VOLTAIRE	**Candide and Other Stories**
ÉMILE ZOLA	**L'Assommoir** **Germinal**